REVIEWS OF OTHER BOOKS BY SEAN GABB

D1354374

C333661214

Also by Sean Gabb

Novels

The Column of Phocas
The Churchill Memorandum
The York Deviation

Writing as Richard Blake

Novels

Conspiracies of Rome
Terror of Constantinople
Blood of Alexandria
Sword of Damascus
Ghosts of Athens
Curse of Babylon

Non-Fiction by Sean Gabb

Dispatches from a Dying Country
Cultural Revolution, Culture War
Smoking, Class and the Legitimation of Power
Literary Essays
Selected Essays
Freedom of Speech in England
War and the National Interest

Sean Gabb is a writer and broadcaster whose previous novels have been
translated into Italian, Spanish, Greek, Hungarian, Slovak and Chinese.
He lives in Kent with his wife and daughter.

THE BREAK

SEAN GABB

....a broad and beat'n way
Over the dark Abyss, whose boiling Gulf
Tamely endur'd a Bridge of wondrous length
From Hell continu'd reaching th' utmost Orbe
Of this frail World; by which the Spirits perverse
With easie intercourse pass to and fro....
(Paradise Lost, Book Two)

LONDON
THE HAMPDEN PRESS
MMXIV

The Break, by Sean Gabb

First edition published in June 2014

© Sean Gabb, 2014

Published by
The Hampden Press
Suite 35
2 Lansdowne Row
London W1J 6HL
England

Telephone: 07956 472 199
E-mail: *sean@libertarian.co.uk*
Web: *www.seangabb.co.uk*

Paperback ISBN: 978-1-291-88468-5

British Library Cataloguing in Publication Data: A catalogue record for this
book is available from the British Library

Printed and bound by Lulu Books

*I dedicate this book
to my dear wife Andrea
and to my little daughter Philippa*

ACKNOWLEDGEMENTS

This book was read in beta version by:

David Davis
James Oliver Deckard
Robert Grözinger
Mario Huet

I thank them for proofing and for their general comments. The faults of this novel, of course, are entirely my own.

I also thank Christopher Bevis for his improvements to my product description.

The cover image is my own work.

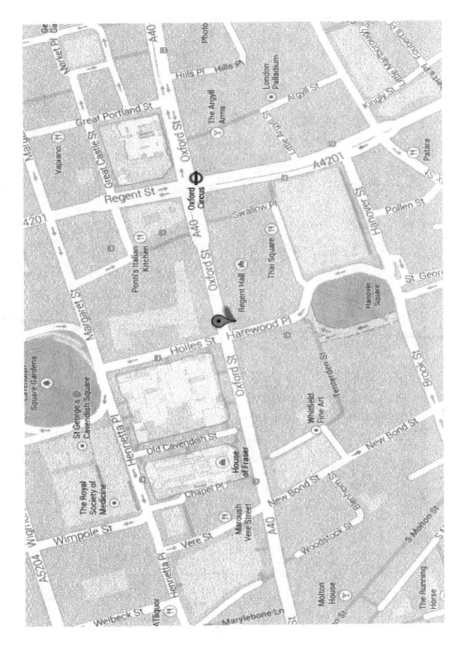

Oxford Street

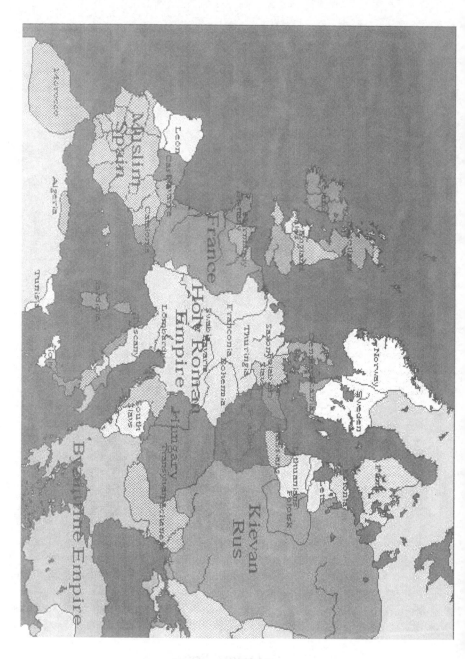

Europe in 1065

CHAPTER ONE

Though it could hold a dozen oarsmen, the longboat had a draft shallow enough to get it within a few yards of the shore. Jennifer had to clutch hard to steady herself as a sudden ebbing of the waves made it scrape on the shingle. With an easy motion, Count Robert was straight over the side. For a moment, the sea came up to his waist. Then it dropped below his knees.

"Come on, my Little Bear!" he cried in Latin. He laughed and said more, but the massive roar of the waves on shingle swamped all other sound. He stepped back for a better position and held his arms out. Jennifer looked for a moment at his teeth, bared in a smile that, with his neat beard, made him look like the predatory barbarian that he really was. But it was either those strong arms or the certainty of ruining a pair of trainers that she'd have great trouble replacing—great trouble, that is, unless the Government was telling the truth about an eventual reversion to normality. She stretched forward and let him take her in a massive embrace. He swung straight round and dumped her on the dark and glistening stones of St Margaret's Bay. "Your father did well to trust you in my hands!" he added, now speaking above the roar. Jennifer scrambled farther up to the dry stones just in time to avoid another wave.

She waited for Robert to finish squeezing seawater out of his cloak and to take her hand and lead her towards the concrete wall separating the beach from what had once been the car park. She told herself to forget the little grope he'd just given her and sat beside him on the wall. He lit a cigarette and looked up at the sky. Fifty yards away, the boat was rising and falling with every movement of the waves. A hundred yards or so beyond that, the English Channel faded into mist. She looked up to her right. Here, where the cliff separated the bay from Dover, was the most likely point of surveillance. As usual, no one was watching.

With an ostentatious wave he'd developed for showing off to his own people, Robert looked at his wrist watch. "Another forty minutes, I think, before the flying machine floats into view." He showed her the two inch display. Nine months earlier, her father had offered him something more elegant. What he'd chosen, though, was large and plastic, with a picture of Peppa Pig within its ring of numbers. He'd still done nothing about the alarm. Twice a day, it would play the theme tune and end with a double grunt. It had pleased him at once. His only change since then had been to replace the plastic strap with gold.

"But where *is* your father?" He looked again at his watch and then along the abandoned shore. Jennifer had already wondered that. Ever since the boat had started its swift crossing, she'd been worrying about the degree of the embarrassment that might be waiting—not just her father on the beach, hopping up and down with rage, but her mother too. A clip round the ear for going off alone like this might have been the least she could expect. The one thing she hadn't considered was that the beach would be deserted. She looked briefly over to where the road to the village was hidden by trees. Robert was right about the timings. The boat had come in on schedule. The little box it carried would jam the radar defences. Another forty minutes, though, and the darkness of the airship against the sky would expose them all to visual inspection by the Border Protection Service and the certainty of an air to sea missile. Robert gave her another of his thoughtful stares. Even without her father there to set him off, he might start picking away at the lies she'd told him five days before.

Out in the boat, the oarsmen were straining to keep it steady with the shore. The monk who'd come over with them was on his feet and praying with outstretched arms towards the accursed shore of England. Robert flicked his cigarette end onto the beach, and, with a sudden scrape of leather on concrete that spoke of his growing impatience, swung over the wall and began walking across the expanse of asphalt towards a heap of canvas. After another look up the hill to see if her father were hurrying towards them, Jennifer followed.

Robert lifted the stiff canvas with one hand and pulled out her bicycle with the other. It was just as she'd left it. Doubtless, the saddlebag still contained the letter of apologies her father had sent her out to deliver. Jennifer looked round again. Still nothing. Robert held up the bicycle and spun the front wheel, admiring how smooth and silently it moved. He put it onto the asphalt and squeezed the brakes. Watching him lean onto the handlebars, she thought he'd get on and try a slow and wobbly circuit of the car park. If he fell off, it would be a loss of face in front of his men. But he smiled grimly and let her take it and prop it upright against a fence. He reached inside his padded tunic and took out a sealed bag about the size and appearance of a deflated football. "Do you wish to count it?" he asked. She shook her head. There was no need for that. Besides, it would only complete the souring of his temper. She took its heavy weight into both hands and put it into her large saddlebag. Yes, if now rather limp from five days in the open, there was the letter she'd been supposed to deliver. She made sure the bag of silver covered it entirely. Robert stood back and watched as she pulled off the woollen robe she'd worn in France. He clicked his tongue appreciatively as she stood before him in her jeans and sweatshirt. In a silence broken only by the crash of another big wave on the shore, she screwed her robe into a ball and pushed it into the saddlebag on top of the purse.

Robert still hadn't turned back. Much longer, though, and he'd need to be off again. He glanced over at the boat and again at his watch. "I feel a strong obligation to come with you," he muttered. He turned and stared at the tree-covered road that led up to St Margaret's. "After all, my Lord *is* the rightful King of England, and I am to have lands here." He stopped and reached again inside his tunic, now quickly. But it was only an unhunted rabbit that had broken cover and was hopping across the road. He took aim with his revolver and made a shooting noise with his lips. He blew imaginary smoke from the barrel and put the gun away. He was all easy smiles again. "Your company has been most enjoyable, Jennifer, and I look forward to our next little trip—a trip that should be in somewhat difference circumstances. At the same time, I was hoping to see your father." He looked searchingly into her face, and seemed about to start asking all those difficult questions again. This time, her answers might not come out so glibly as they had first time round. Instead, he reached higher inside his tunic and took out a stained and folded sheet of A4 paper. "Do give him this." She looked at the small but elaborate script on the outer side of the letter. Though she spoke Latin well enough, Jennifer still had trouble with the radical contractions of anything written by the Outsiders. But the name and titles were clear. She swallowed and gave Robert a scared look. He shrugged and looked away. "It is for Master Richard alone," he said quietly. "Our need to speak with him is becoming urgent."

She heard a stray noise from the boat. The oarsmen had joined the monk in a long and worried prayer. They had no watches of their own, but knew the movements of the Border Protection Service as well as didn't matter. Robert went into his businesslike tone. "I am informed by His Excellency of Flanders that his wife is much pleased by the contraptions that were sent over. So were her ladies." He blushed slightly and looked away. "They prefer the ones that are called Tampax. Those called Tesco are, I am told, of much lower quality." He cleared his throat. "Since all the officials in Dover were replaced, the illegal trade out of that port has had problems." His face blackened and he pushed his chest out. "They may think we are nothing but savages. But we do know when medicines don't work, or cause rather than cure sickness. I need to sit over wine with your father and discuss many things—many, many things. A much enlarged order is just one of them."

He might have said more, but the monk was now leaning over the side of the boat and calling in a loud voice. Robert stepped back and bowed. Then, with a bound, he was over the wall and onto the beach and hurrying towards where his men were visibly impatient as well as scared.

Jennifer stood watching till the boat vanished into the dawn mist. Alone, she looked up into the sky. By all appearances, it would be another glorious March morning. Across the water, it would be a morning in June, plus nearly two hours ahead and a different day of the week. But, just as there was no need any more to reset the time after a crossing, it was best not to think about the larger question of the date. It was enough to know that the boat would be half way across the Channel before the mist burned away—and that would be enough, now that Border Protection had given up on sinking anything outside the Exclusion Zone.

Even with no additional weight to carry, the road up to the village was too steep for cycling. Still, she mounted up and pedalled to where, under cover of the trees, she'd have to get off and start pushing.

► ▼ ◄

Once through the village and on to Station Road, Jennifer went into top gear. It was a road of steep descents and rises. But, if she could build up enough momentum going down, she could usually coast all the way to the top again. The main obstacle to this was knowing when to begin swerving to avoid the hole in the road, where, shortly after The Break, someone had filled his car with a petrol substitute, and it had gone up in a ball of flame visible from Ramsgate.

Mostly, she had to keep her eyes on the road for broken glass and other obstacles. Every so often, though, as she sped downhill, she allowed her self to look over the trees and luxuriant hedges that lined the road. It was still barely six in the morning—English time, that is. But she could already see the long lines of people in the fields as they went about the work that had to be done, of guaranteeing the first proper harvest since The Break.

Another ten minutes, and she was at the junction with London Road. Turning left here would take her uphill to the Dover Roundabout where the A2 began. Right would lead down, through Walmer, to Deal. It was at this junction that the local Hill of the Dead had been created. There had been perhaps only five thousand bodies from Deal to be buried. The great majority of those who'd starved to death, or been killed in The Pacification, were from Dover. But it was here that the bodies had been heaped up and covered with earth. Jennifer stopped and looked again at the mound. It was only ten months since the army of diggers had finished their job. Since then, however, three seasons of the year had done their work. Smoothed over and covered in grass, the mound was already becoming as fixed and as natural a part of the landscape as the memorials set up to the lesser catastrophes of war.

It wasn't even a year—but it might have been a decade, or a whole age, for all that had passed. Jennifer could remember the day, when, after endless assurances in the media, that everything was under control, the shops had run out of food. Or, if there was still food, no one had been allowed the fuel to transport it. The looting of homes had begun within hours. It was now that those who'd previously broken the law, and accumulated weapons against a chance of breakdown that few really believed would come, could think themselves lucky. But they were the minority. The begging—by those who hadn't stocked up, or had lost their stocks at gunpoint, or those who had neither contacts nor things that others wanted to buy—had been pitiable. The frantic pleas of the starving had been terrible to behold—terrible and, once the police began raiding anyone who, by giving charity, showed he had a surplus, quite unavoidable. It had toughened those who had. It had prepared those who had not, but who still managed to survive, for their place in the new order of things. And, once the gulf of The Hunger had been crossed, this new order had emerged as quickly and as logically as the movement of iron filings in a magnetic field.

Jennifer let her eyes rest on the Hill of the Dead. So many times she'd seen it. So many times, she'd passed it by with a shudder, or with indifference. Now, she watched as perhaps fifty labourers were allowed their time for the morning remembrance. There was Mrs Hardman, the lawyer, digging tool in both hands, her lean and toughened body still wrapped in the rags that had been her business suit. There was Jennifer's Science teacher. His face was in shadow under his hat, and she couldn't see the branding mark left there after he'd been denounced for cutting down a tree to keep warm. There was the little man who'd used to sell expensive chinaware from a shop in Deal. They were the lucky ones—those who had once gambled on, and appeared to do well from, a division of labour that no longer made sense, and who had survived the collapse of the old world. They stood together in memory of those they had lost, their right hands clenched into fists and beating out on their chests the now customary pattern of despair. But the ruddy man on horseback now rang his bell, and it was back to the endless work of hoeing and trenching and weeding.

Once everyone was back to work, Jennifer looked over the miles of farming land that stretched before here. There was a time when she'd have needed to wait for a gap in traffic that raced in both directions. Though she looked from habit up and down the road, all was peaceful here. The only sound was of twittering birds too small to be hunted, and of trees that sighed gently in the breeze. She turned right, and, squeezing gently on the brakes, was carried downhill again. There was a minute of pedalling as she crept uphill towards the old service station where Slovak immigrants had once earned a few pounds by washing cars. After this, it would be an easy ride back to the coast.

As she reached the edge of the built-up area, she had to give more attention again to the road. The cars themselves had long since been requisitioned for scrap. But quite a few of the owners had made sure to vandalise their property first. Even before then, cars had often been ripped open by armed men to get at the petrol. The road hereabout still had the occasional cube of glass to be avoided. Braking, she lost most of her speed, and was now coasting forward at little more than a brisk walking pace.

CHAPTER TWO

She was still a quarter of a mile away when she saw the trouble. It was by the Sacred Heart Church—the one where the huge brick porch looked directly over the road. If she couldn't yet smell it, she could see the cloud of organic diesel smoke from the black van, and the two uniformed figures standing above someone who crouched in the road beside the porch. She could see the glint of sunlight on the plastic visors, and the dark shapes of the rifles that were levelled at the crouching figure.

"Don't let them see that you're looking," she muttered grimly as she covered the last fifty yards. These were her first words in English since she'd lied her way on to Count Robert's boat, and her voice grated slightly from the unfamiliarity of the words. She tried to look straight ahead. But nothing could keep her from seeing the graffito that someone had scrawled in white characters a foot high on the outside wall of the church.

+1065+

It said nothing more. But that was enough. For letting this go up, the priest would be lucky if all he got was a clubbing. She'd slowed still more, and had to choose between coasting past, and risking that one of the officers would try to grab her, and speeding up—though that would raise obvious suspicions.

The choice was made for her. "Stop!" The officer stepped in front of her and lifted his rifle. Jennifer squeezed the brakes and stopped six feet short of the uniformed man. She resisted the urge to reach back and pat the bulging saddlebag. She forced a smile onto her face, and tried to look like any other teenage girl who'd been out early to gather food. "Get in there," he ordered with a nod at the church. "Get buckets and a broom." He turned back to the priest, who was now on his knees.

"What year is it?"

"2018, Sir!" The priest reached up and wiped away the blood where it had run into his eyes. As the rifle was cocked, he put his arms up again. "It's Wednesday the 7th March."

"Who's the Pope?"

"John Paul III—and God bless His Holiness, wherever he may be," he added, before going into an ever more irrelevant babble. The officer turned back to Jennifer and raised his visor. She looked into the sweaty face and eyes that reminded her of a rattlesnake, and hurried to prop her bicycle inside the porch. She passed through a cloud of exhaust and had to hold her breath to avoid going into a coughing fit that might get her more attention than she already had. She found a bucket and broom in a cupboard and managed to use the tap in a toilet. By the time she was back outside, the priest was already at work on the graffito with his jacket. She nudged him and got the wet broom into his hand. The problem with graffiti is that it takes longer to remove than to put up. Also, it usually doesn't come off entirely. But, by much scrubbing and refilling of buckets, they did eventually turn an act bordering on Hate Crime into a smudge that only a close inspection would be able to make out.

"Where's your ticket, love?" The officer's voice was half friendly and half domineering. Jennifer tried for another smile and took out her identity card. His lips moved as he read the details of her name and address and age. He looked closely at the blurred picture of a fifteen year old girl that dated from the first emergency tagging of the population after The Pacification, and then at the young woman before him. There was little obvious correspondence. Ten months had been long enough for Jennifer to grow up. The officer squinted harder, but didn't look as if he'd go to the trouble of arresting her. Even so, Jennifer made a bigger effort with her smile. You didn't cross the officers of the Citizen Protection Service. One word out of place—one wrong look—and half-friendly tone would fade like the warmth of the sun as it passed into shadow. He'd then demand a look in her saddlebag, and she'd be in trouble. If it was followed by a search of her clothing, she'd be lost for sure.

She was saved by a crackle of static from the radio inside the van. This was followed by a burst of demented shouting that she couldn't make out. But—"Sarge, Sarge!" the other officer cried. "There's a Code Red in Dover Docks." The officer swore and spat and swaggered back to the van. Before getting in, he turned to her. "Mind how you go, love," he snarled.

The priest waited till the van was fifty yards back up the hill. "*My Pope*," he said in a surprisingly clear voice, "is Alexander II. And no tyranny of armed thugs shall forever keep his Apostolic Vicar out of England." Jennifer froze and looked quickly round. "*Deus vult! Deus vult!*" he cried with quiet intensity. He crossed himself. They were alone. But, if those whitewashed numbers had bordered on Hate Crime, this was the real thing. Saying these words in front of an informer, and it would be Ireland if you were lucky. Unlucky, and you'd just vanish on the forced march to Liverpool. She turned away from the priest and pretended not to have heard him. After all, he might be an informer. She got on her bicycle and began pedalling as fast as shaking legs could carry her towards The Strand.

The traffic directions still said to turn right by Deal Castle and continue along Beach Street. But Jennifer was on a bicycle, and even motorised traffic didn't bother nowadays with one way systems. She carried on into Victoria Road, and then into Deal High Street. "MAKE DO AND MEND!" said the banner that was stretched overhead from one boarded up shop to another. "WE'RE ALL IN THIS TOGETHER!" said a poster stuck on a disused bus shelter. There was a smell of fresh bread from the bakery, and a low chatter of conversation from the shabby queue that stretched along the pavement. The telescreen that covered the upper part of the Town Hall was still blank, but there was enough noise from the scraping of old supermarket trolleys as the shops that had survived The Break took delivery of fresh goods.

As she reached the junction with Oak Street, Jennifer wobbled slightly from the weight in her saddlebag and came to a stop. A cart drawn by dust-covered women was turning into the High Street to deliver wet fish. She nodded at the fishmonger, who was waiting expectantly in the middle of the road. He looked back at her and waved a greeting. But now the side street was clear, and Jennifer got off her bicycle and walked the last few yards of the journey home.

Leave aside the heap of uncollected rubbish against a wall, and the scurrying of a few rats, the Deal Conservation Area looked as she'd always known it. A few centuries before, it had teemed with drunken sailors from the Channel Fleet, and been one of the nastiest dens in England of whores and cut-throat smugglers. But, following its long decline, and an abortive plan to knock it all down and build again from scratch, it had gone through a long process of gentrification. Anyone who'd known these streets at any time before about 1980 would have scratched his head and stared at the rows of neatly-painted houses. For Jennifer, it was as it always had been. With every step towards the green door that fronted the biggest of the Georgian houses, she could feel her mood rising and falling. If scared of a reception she could easily imagine, she was glad to be home.

She leaned her bicycle against the front wall of the house and pulled out her keys. "I'm back, Mummy and Daddy," she called softly as she pushed the door open. No answer. Jennifer bit her lip and fought against the slight tremor in her knees. Perhaps they were still in bed, she told herself. Or perhaps she'd passed them in the bread queue without noticing. She waited for her eyes to adjust to the gloom, then, taking care not to scrape against the banisters— why give her parents additional grounds for going ballistic?— carried her bicycle into the little entrance hall. She now heard someone downstairs in the basement kitchen, and could smell fresh coffee. "Count Robert took me all the way to his castle," she said with forced brightness. "He was ever so funny on the journey." She carried the bicycle down a couple of stairs and unlocked the door to the courtyard garden. She carried it out and leaned it against the side wall. She was back inside the house when she remembered the big purse she'd brought. Daddy usually brought back more, but she thought how nice it would be to dump it with a flourish onto the breakfast table. It might serve as mitigation. A seabird called mournfully overhead as she unlaced the straps and rummaged about for the purse.

"I've got a letter for you," she said, hurrying down the stairs to the kitchen, "and there's news all about...."

Her voice trailed off as she looked across the kitchen. "What are you doing here?" she asked coldly.

Mrs Maggs leered back at her. "Well, who's been a well-brung up little Miss? She lifted her coffee cup in an ironic toast.

Jennifer felt a sudden chill run down her back, and she had to pause to keep her voice from shaking. "Where are my parents?"

"Now, those got tooken off early this morning," the old woman cackled. "I heard the men roll up for them just after three. Soft-spoken man what was in charge—though your poor mother shouted your name most tearfully, I might add." She took out a cigarette and held it carefully level to stop the tobacco substitute from running out. She struck a match and took a deep drag. "So, aren't you going to thank me for coming in and locking up after them?" She breathed out a cloud of dark smoke.

Jennifer sat down on the other side of the table. She'd already seen the opened wine jar and the half-empty glasses. Mummy would never have gone to bed with these left out. She could feel the blood draining from her face. She wanted to get up and run through every room in the house, checking that this wasn't some bizarre home-coming joke. But Mrs Maggs had now put her cigarette onto the table, where it would soon leave a burn mark. Her job, every Monday and Thursday, was to come in and clean. That she was now careless about creating a mess left nothing to be said.

"It's a funny old world," she said after a long cough. "You know, my boy studied hard on his Financial Services degree. He done his MBA and all. Now, instead of a cushy job up in London, what's he doing? He's out in them fields, digging fourteen hours a day to keep body and soul together. Found us a dead rabbit on Sunday, and we was glad of it. And what's it all with them that wasted their time on old things and dead languages? Why, aren't they just living the life of Riley from dealings with them nasty Outsiders?" She looked down at her cup. "Do you know when it was," she asked menacingly, "when I last even saw real coffee? Your mother wasn't never a generous woman in that respect." She cleared her throat and spat onto the brick-tiled floor.

It was time for the siren above the Town hall to sound. In a moment, the morning electricity would come on. The interruption gave Jennifer time to pull herself together. Had the old woman grassed her parents? She got up and went to the cutlery drawer. She took out the biggest carving knife. "Get out of here!" she said with quiet passion. "Get out before I kill you."

If Robert had seen how she flourished the knife, he'd have taken it as an invitation to foreplay. But Mrs Maggs scraped her chair back as she got quickly to her feet. "Now, don't you go threatening me, little lady," she said defensively. "Unlike where you've just come from, there's laws in this country. Even in kitchens, steel knives ain't allowed no more."

"Get out of my house!" Jennifer shouted. She picked up one of the glasses and threw it across the kitchen. It missed, but smashed loudly on the wall. She stepped forward and shoved the old woman in the chest. Still holding the knife, she got her out of the kitchen and up the stairs. All that kept her from bloody murder was the competing urge to sit down and cry.

Mrs Maggs looked back from the street. "Don't think you'll be left alone in this place," she sneered. "The police will be back here later to seal it up. Then they'll take you as well." She laughed and brushed ash off the front of her dress. "You'll see your mum and dad again if you're lucky. But, if I'm told right, it'll be in Ireland— where there's work a plenty for them that's set to it."

Jennifer slammed the door shut and locked it and slipped the chain into place. Then she ran upstairs. Her parents' bedroom was as neat and clean as ever. The bed hadn't been slept in. The indoor clothes were carefully folded and put on their usual racks. She pulled open a drawer in the dressing table. Her mother's jewellery was untouched. So too the purse of gold coins they had been filtering from the normal takings of their business. Jennifer pulled open one of the walk-in cupboards. The leather bag that Daddy always used for his French trips was still there. If she looked in any of the drawers, she'd surely see where socks and sweaters and other clothes hadn't been removed for packing. She bent to look under the bed. Probably still loaded, the illegal shotgun was in its usual place.

There was no denying her parents were gone, nor any point in doubting the assurance that they'd been taken away. All that was missing was any sign that the police had been in the house—no smashed in front door, no scattered and trampled chaos of a search, no blood from the sadistic beatings that accompanied an arrest. Whoever had come had scooped them off as if for drinks round the corner, though giving no time to pack, nor to clean things away.

And Mrs Maggs—why hadn't she gone through the house? Jennifer bit her lip again, this time so hard it nearly bled.

Suddenly, all the lights came on, and there was an expectant whirring of the electric typewriter in the upstairs office. Down in the kitchen, the wireless played the closing bars of Elgar's *Symphony in A flat*, before giving way to the staccato voice of the presenter. She crept back downstairs and sat in the kitchen. The Radio 3 presenter was reading the authorised news bulletin. This carried an announcement from the National Government about another try at getting the Heart of Oak platform into the North Sea. "British ingenuity" might at last have found a way round the shortage of things from an abroad that no longer existed. But Jennifer seldom bothered with the news. Daddy only paid attention when he wanted to poke fun at the lies. Instead, she pulled the leather bag towards her. Using the knife she still had in her hand, she cut the knotted cords that had closed it and let the stream of coins fall onto the table. Seven pounds of silver, at a street price of £800 to the ounce. Daddy usually brought more than this. But he always took more than the tampons and paracetamol she'd gathered up when her parents were fussing over a piano key that had stopped working. Still, this would have been enough to pay for electricity and water and Community Levy and food, and all the appearance of a normal life.

She noticed an oddity in the dull and misshapen heap. She picked up the bright disc and looked at it. Daddy had brought a couple of these back from his own last trip. "It's a gold *solidus* of Isaac I Comnenus," he'd said learnedly. "He was Emperor between 1057 and 1059. Quite unusual, you know, to see anything Byzantine this far away." He'd then set them aside for adding to the purse upstairs.

Remembering his voice, Jennifer felt a lump come into her throat. But the BBC was playing something by Eric Coates, and she was aware again of the smell of coffee. She got up and turned off the bottled gas stove that Mrs Maggs had left burning. She cleared away the fragments of broken glass and dabbed at the patches of red on the wall. She took out her own special cup and filled it to the brim with coffee. Sitting in her usual place at the table, she reached inside her sweatshirt for the letter that Count Robert had given her. It was easier to read than she'd supposed. Most children pass into adulthood as insensibly as the outside scenery changes on a long railway journey. For all she'd thought herself so very grown up in France, Jennifer now realised that this had been no more than the descending rhythm that closed a sentence in Latin. Here was the real full stop in the story of her life so far—here the paragraph break.

When Jennifer finally got up from the table, it would be as a woman. For the moment, she leaned forward and cried and cried. She cried like a child who knew she'd suffered an inconsolable loss. She felt as if she'd cry forever.

She knew, however, that she wouldn't.

CHAPTER THREE

Like any cautious diplomat, his uncle had been sceptical right up to the last moment. But Michael had believed everything the Flemish barbarians told him. And why not? It only confirmed what had had been drifting for months into Constantinople. He got up from the bench for a better look at the large boats that were coming out at incredible speed from the shore.

"Sit down, you stupid boy!" the pilot croaked in a semblance of Latin. "Those long tubes poking at us can take your head off before you'd even draw breath. Just sit down and let me do the talking."

"Do as he says," Uncle Simeon added in Greek. "We are envoys of the Great Augustus. These people will surely respect that." Michael sat down with a bump and looked into the reflection cast by the now reasonably still waters. Boys don't have beards, he told himself. He resisted the urge to put up a hand to feel the glossy brown growth that would, in due course, be full answer to his prayers. But he looked down only for a moment. He was straight back to looking over the prow of the open boat at the unimaginably vast and magnificent docks that seemed to have been built out from the shore of Britain. Behind these, all the way to the high, foliage-covered cliffs, there was a mass of buildings hardly less astonishing in their size and design.

Though distorted, there was a voice from across the water so loud, its owner might have been shouting in his ear. He couldn't understand the words, but he did know they were repeated once and then again. The pilot stood up, and standing as only sailors can without falling overboard, stretched out both arms. With a roar that reminded him of a water mill running at full speed, one of the smaller boats sped alongside. A beardless official in a peaked hat looked down at everyone, and shouted angrily in an unknown

16

language. The pilot called back haltingly in the same language. He turned and pointed at Michael and his uncle and shrugged. The official's mouth fell open as if with surprise, and he looked hard at the two ambassadors. Then he stepped back into the glass cabin of his boat and started what looked like a shouted conversation with himself.

While the officer shouted and pulled faces, Michael turned his attention to the cold and sparkling sea and the great birds that fluttered and called loudly overhead. He was about to try again for a look across the mile of water separating the boat from those docks. But the official now finished his conversation and came out again. No longer angry, he called detailed instructions down at them. The pilot bowed respectfully at every phrase, breaking in now and again with what were obviously questions prompted by a defective understanding of the language.

At last, the official's boat turned back to the shore, and the pilot sat down again. Looking troubled, he glared at the Greeks. Then he shouted something at the oarsmen in his own language, and the boat continued towards the artificial harbour.

The boat was too low for any of the docks, and Michael had to help his uncle up the rusted iron ladder where the boat was eventually able to put in. The pilot had gone up first, and was already in conversation with several more officials as Michael stepped onto the impossibly wide expanse of the dock.

"On behalf of His Imperial Majesty," Simeon cried in Latin, "I bring greetings and felicitations to your king." It could be doubted whether anyone heard him above the sound of the wind and the endless flocks of white seabirds. Certainly, no one took notice of his rank. Even as he spoke, several men stepped forward and pointed blunt but threatening weapons at him.

"For Christ's sake," the pilot called sharply. "Keep still, and put your hands over your heads. Haven't I said these people can kill you on the spot?" He turned back to his conversation with perhaps the most senior of the officials. After much waving of hands and shouting, he pointed at the Greeks. Now he produced and handed over the purple-edged sheet of parchment they had carried with so much care by sea from Constantinople to Bari, and then all through

Italy and France to the grey and surging waters of the Outermost Ocean. Excepting in Benevento, the Normans themselves had respected the Emperor's letter. This official, though, couldn't even tell which way up it should be read. Still holding it, he let his arms drop down, so it unravelled and trailed in the dockside puddles.

"Let it be, uncle," Michael said as softly as he could. He looked at the old man's face. Anyone else would have seen total impassivity behind the grey beard. Not Michael. They'd been warned repeatedly on the French shore not to try for a crossing. Even after Simeon had talked the pilot into carrying them, they'd had to leave all their attendants and baggage behind. Michael's own sword had been taken away as he boarded. Now, they were in the total power of a people whose very existence had, till lately, been unknown to the world. The pilot was still deep in his broken, gesticulating conversation. Michael looked about. What he guessed were the civilian officials were dressed in dark trousers and high coats. The armed guards wore a kind of padded armour and helmets with smoked glass visors to cover their faces. Several dozen of these were being lined up behind the officials. All carried what looked like glass shields and long clubs. The shields carried words in Roman letters that might have indicated they were part of a city guard.

With a final bow, the pilot finished his conversation and stood back. He stared at Michael and shook his head. There was no time to wonder what this could mean. At almost the same moment, he felt something press on his back, and someone barked instructions that had only one meaning. Keeping his hands over his head, he stumbled forward.

After a strange and almost joyous smile, the old man put a stack of papers onto his side of the table and fiddled with a metal stylus. "My name is Gordon Jessup," he said in a rather fussy Latin. He stopped and repeated the unfamiliar sound of his family name, spelling it a letter at a time. "I have been appointed as your interpreter. Whatever anyone else may say or do, please accept my own heartiest welcome to England, and please do count on me for any help that I can give you." He looked up at the ceiling and smiled again. He took off the framework of glass discs that covered the upper part of his face, and closed his eyes for a long moment. Then he leaned forward across the table and repeated himself in a slow Greek that would have sounded barbarous if it hadn't been for the careful attention to grammar. This done, he took out a handkerchief and polished one of his discs.

"How long are we to regard ourselves as prisoners?" Michael asked coldly in Latin. He tipped his head gently backwards, acknowledging the two silent guards behind him. So far as he could tell without turning, their faces were still hidden by smoked glass.

"I regret, Your Excellency," the interpreter replied, "that you are prisoners for the moment. There is nothing I can do yet. But I do promise to make a full report to London that will surely bring about a change of circumstances. For the moment, be assured that none of the animals set to watch over you understands a word of any civilised language."

He stopped and gave a long and now openly joyous look at the two men before him. "You are from Constantinople?" he asked with a catch of his voice. Simeon nodded gravely, and asked if Jessup had been there. "No, not to the real City," came the enigmatic reply. "But, all my life, I've longed that I could have seen it in all its glory—the civil and religious buildings, the markets, the museums, the—the—*libraries* filled with ancient learning...." He trailed off in a decidedly odd reverie.

Simeon leaned forward. "Master Jessup, if I cannot ask for our release, I might at the least observe that my nephew and I have eaten nothing since we set out early this morning. A meal of some kind would be much appreciated." Jessup started slightly in his chair and apologised. He spoke to the guards. One of them answered with an insolent laugh. Jessup scowled and banged on the table. It was to no effect. He apologised again and got up and bowed. Once he was out of the room, the two guards began a conversation in their own language. Keeping his hands on the table, Michael stared across at the metal stylus. About six inches long, it had a solid look about it. He wondered if he could get to it before the guards could jump into action. Neither was armed with a

19

sword. He was reasonably sure he could take them both on.

Simeon noticed what he was looking at. "Don't even think about it, boy. You wouldn't get a dozen yards." One of the guards bent forward and screamed something into the old man's ear. Trying to look as dignified as their bedraggled robes allowed, they sat in silence.

After a long wait, the door opened again. Jessup came back in. He had no food with him. Instead, there were two other men in white coats. "I must apologise for the indignity, My Lords," he explained, a ghastly look on his face. "But our laws require that you should be tested for any sickness. These men must take a sample of your blood."

Not worried about the threatening presence behind him, Simeon got to his feet. "This is outrageous! Have we found ourselves among a race of blood-drinkers?" One of the men in white coats smiled nervously and held up a small glass tube with a steel needle at its far end. Michael did now make a lunge for the stylus. He'd barely got his hand across the table, though, when four strong arms pulled him back into his seat and held him fast as the man in white came towards him.

CHAPTER FOUR

Once he'd talked his way out of school, two years earlier, Michael's first diplomatic mission with his uncle had been to the Turkish Sultan in Baghdad. The Arab capital had only recently fallen, and no one was certain whether and how long the Turkish leader could maintain himself on the ancient throne of the Caliphs. The whole city, when they'd arrived, was a riotous mosaic of Moslems and Christians and Jews and Arabs and Turks and all their many divisions and sub-divisions, each group struggling against the others for position. It had been impossible to say who had influence, and for what, with Tughrul, the new Commander of the Faithful. At least, however, the background of life in Baghdad had made sense. If hardly anyone knew Greek, and his own knowledge of Arabic was at first taxed to the limit, at least there was the same order of dining and bathing and sleeping arrangements. Making the obvious allowance for changes of religion and language and even of weather, he'd been among civilised men whose ways he could understand.

This new land of Britain was different. Leave aside every report until recently of a country filled with yellow-headed, cider-drinking barbarians, there was nothing familiar—nothing he could seize hold of to try and understand what has happening. Whether it was bizarre sanitary fittings, or lights without fire, or food that smelled bad and tasted of nothing, or machines in every place, all doing things and working on principles he couldn't begin to follow, everything was alien. Had he been in this dockside prison two days, or four, or six? He'd soon lost track of time. It didn't help that he was shut up with his uncle in a room without windows, where the lights came on and went off apparently at random.

At the moment, the two ambassadors were back in the interview room where they'd first been taken. "Since you have no passports,"

Jessup apologised, "the authorities have decided to treat you as asylum seekers." Not bothering to explain the odd collection of words, he paused again, and listened to another of the questions from the sweaty, jabbering official who sat beside him on the other side of the table. He tried to reply for Simeon and Michael. All this got him was a burst of angry shouting from the official. "The man wants to know which countries you passed through on your way here," he asked in a tone of resignation.

Simeon pursed his lips and sat back in the metal chair. "Master Jessup," he said firmly, "I have already told these men our route. We took ship from Constantinople, stopping at Corinth, and then at other places within the Empire on our way to Bari in Italy. From here, we passed through sundry territories of the Normans, and of the Latin Patriarch, and of the German Emperor. We passed through the Kingdom of France, and at some point we cannot closely describe through the lands of the Duke of Normandy, coming at last into the County of Flanders, which lies directly opposite this shore. We bring greetings from what Westerners call the Greek Emperor—though I am sure you know him by his correct title of the *Roman* Emperor. Apart from this, I will only repeat that the law of nations requires full respect for our persons. Our mission is diplomatic in nature, and we came unarmed."

Michael listened closely as Jessup put this into the language of the Britons. It is one of the main duties of a diplomat to observe everything and to recall everything. If he was far from any general understanding of these British, he could pay attention to their language, many words in which bore a debased relationship to Latin and even Greek. He listened for the names of places and peoples as Jessup interpreted. It was interesting that all reference to the Pope seemed to be left out. Were these people actually Christians?

Jessup had left off interpreting, and was putting another case of his own. This only sent the official into more angry shouting. The door opened and another official looked in. With him came more of those guards in their glass helmets. The door still open, both officials began shouting at Jessup, and then at each other. One of them snatched at Jessup's notes and tore them across and then across again. He threw them onto the floor and went into an aggressive laugh. He blurted out a sentence of atrociously bad Latin that contained an accusation of spying. Simeon stared calmly back. This only set the man off into more shouting in his own language. The other official shouted back louder. A third official now came in and closed the door, and the conversation settled into a quieter discussion, in which the native word for London came up with possibly hopeful frequency.

Michael looked at Jessup. Ignored by everyone else, he'd taken the glass discs from his face and was again polishing the lenses. Michael had soon guessed that the main function of these wasn't decorative. They allowed a man who may have been in his sixties to read the very small lettering of various forms and other documents. When the lights were on in their room, and he wasn't sleeping or in anxious conversation with his uncle, Michael had spent time looking at a big notice stuck to the wall. These people used a Latin script, and it was from the notice that he'd confirmed the derivation of perhaps half their words from the civilised languages. So far, he'd gathered that the verbs were inflected, though not, it seemed, the nouns. As it was written, the language looked simple compared with Arabic and the dialects of Turkish. The main problem was an apparent divergence between spelling and pronunciation. Because his study would have to be in secret, he'd make little further progress. He could follow nothing more of these official conversations than he could get from their context.

He glanced left as Simeon began coughing again. Almost at once, their fine diplomatic clothes had been taken from them. They had since been given single, close-fitting garments of bright orange. As Simeon put up a hand to cover his mouth, his left sleeve fell back, showing the bruise that had come up after the extraction of blood. The puncture in Michael's own arm had soon disappeared. Was this bruise on Simeon's arm growing? Hard to say—but it was a sight that added to his worries.

The conversation ended. Though no one appeared to have spoken directly to him, Jessup cleared his throat and turned to Michael. "You must go back to your place of confinement," he said wearily. "Tomorrow, or the next day, these idiots will have meaningful instructions. These may be to your advantage—but please don't take this as any kind of promise." He ignored the suspicious looks of three officials and five guards, and smiled brightly. "It's often hard to say, since the combined agency was set up, who is in charge here for any specific purpose. But there must eventually be a reply from London."

►▼◄

Jessup had put on a clean shirt, and fastened the collar with a strip of dark cloth that reached to his waist. "I shan't be coming with you," he said, leaning forward to be heard above the noise of the seabirds. "My normal clients have insisted that I should be with them tonight." He pulled his jacket closer about his meagre body. Though the sun shone brightly overhead, the wind from the sea was decidedly chilly. Even June by this northern sea was colder than late autumn at home.

This was the following day—or the day after that—and the two ambassadors had been allowed to wash themselves under a jet of water and given clean orange clothes. They now stood beside a vehicle of black and shiny metal that had arrived beside them with no apparent human or animal force to move it. The director of this vehicle was a young black man, who stood before them in clothes similar to, though less creased than, the ones that Jessup had put on. He grinned at them and chewed endlessly on something that he neither swallowed nor added to.

Simeon gave a little speech of thanks. Jessup said, when he'd finished interpreting, that it was a model of grace and clarity, though it had obviously gone on too long for the officials who stood away from the group and kept staring at the bracelets on their left wrists. Jessup ignored every hint to hurry things along. "Your driver has no Latin, let alone Greek," he said with a nod at the young man. "But you will be met in London by men of greater learning than I. They will be able to speak fluently with you in your own language." He paused and looked through his lenses before polishing them again. "They will ask you many questions that you may find unusual. Take my advice and answer truthfully. They know many things about your world that will surprise you." He stood forward and shook hands with Simeon and then with

Michael. "God go with you," he said with a final tone. "If I can ever be of genuine service to you, I promise that I will do whatever I must." With that, he nodded to the young man, who opened one of the back doors in the vehicle.

▶ ▼ ◀

Michael leaned closer to the darkened window of the vehicle and looked out again at scenery that was flashing past at inconceivable speed. In Constantinople, Simeon had got an ancient map of Britain dug out of the archives. It was copied from an original that had been made when Britain was still a province of the Empire. This had told them that Dover was about eighty Roman miles from London. Assuming two, or possibly three, days on the road, Simeon had tried to ask about warmer clothing for the nights. At this speed, however, they would surely be in London before dark. Michael could see that the width of this long and straight road wasn't far off that of the great Hippodrome in Constantinople. Despite this, he'd so far seen no more than a few dozen vehicles of the same kind as the one in which he was travelling. On each edge of the road, there was a long stream of much slower traffic— people walking about their business, and carts pulled mostly by people or sometimes by horses or other beasts of burden. For all it made a thin stream on this immensely wide road, it was a stream that would easily have blocked any road in the Empire.

Further evidence for the great wealth of this country could be seen in the fields. Every piece of England appeared to be under cultivation. Every piece that he saw was filled with gangs of men—and possibly also of women—hard at work. Once, when the car was slowed by a spilling of foot travellers across this lane of the road, he'd caught sight of a man trussed up in a field for flogging. Other men had been dancing round the unfortunate, throwing their arms in the air. A useful thing to have seen. That, plus the size of the fields, suggested this was a slave society on the ancient pattern. The free peasantry of the Empire tended much smaller and narrower fields.

"What do you suppose the population is of this country?" he asked. Simeon opened his eyes and looked past Michael out of the left window. Together, they watched as the vehicle caught up with a group of what looked like the Norman poor. A large wooden cross carried before them, they were trudging slowly in the direction of London. They were no sooner seen than the vehicle was past them, and was approaching a bridge across the road that was suspended in ways that would have excited any engineer.

"You know of the report, made three years ago," Simeon answered, his voice carefully neutral, "that described this whole island as a desolation of ruins and barbarian settlements. Yet many of these structures have a solidity that suggests decades or even centuries of endurance. How long do you think it took to build even this road? A hundred years? Two hundred?" He sat back and closed his eyes again. Though sealed, this vehicle was noticeably cooler than the air outside. Yet Simeon's clothing was wet through. It must be the start of a fever. But he made an effort and sat up. "Your mind has always been fertile of hypotheses," he said with a little smile. "Would you care to explain what we are seeing in terms of human reason? Or will you join me in supposing it is all one Act of God for a purpose that is yet to be revealed?"

Michael's attention was drawn by a renewal of the driver's rhythmical grunting. Once out of Dover, the young man had put on a pair of ear plugs joined by a thin cord. They conveyed a buzzing sound of drums and what may have been stringed instruments. Since he appeared to know only his own language, there was nothing lost by the absence of any ability to communicate with him. But Michael was interested by the motions of his feet and hands. However it was that the vehicle was propelled, the workings of its guiding wheel were comprehensible. The pedals spoke of some braking and gearing system. Assuming it might one day be required, could Michael direct one of these vehicles by himself?

The pilot of their boat had spoken grandly of magic. Until now, apart from the usual prayers that kept him half the night from his bed, Simeon had refrained from comment. From the first encounter, Michael had set aside any thoughts of the supernatural. So far as he could tell, these people ranged between the moderately intelligent and the slow-witted. There was an impenetrable mystery in how they had so far evaded the notice even of visitors to their island. An equal mystery was how a people of such manifestly low grade could have acquired these machines and facility in their use. It was plain that no answer would come from asking. But it was for what the Emperor himself had called "an unusual quickness of the intellect" that the seniority rules had been set aside for Michael's advancement. He'd observe. He'd remember. He'd hypothesise. Sooner or later would come a degree of understanding. It always had so far.

CHAPTER FIVE

"This must be the centre of London," Michael insisted for the third or fourth time since coming off the big road. Each time he had insisted, though, they'd continued through an endless network of streets overshadowed by high buildings and crowded with people and carts drawn in various ways. You could take the whole of Constantinople and Baghdad—and Alexandria and Rome as well—and drop them into the suburbs alone of this megalopolis, and they'd all be lost within it.

Simeon looked out of the window at a river crowded with barges and other shipping. "A big city indeed, if it needs so many bridges," he observed. "But look at the air outside. Either London is covered in brown fog, or these people burn more coal every day than we do in a year." He smiled wearily and turned from the window. He looked at Michael and sat up straight, all weariness gone. "Michael, are you all right?" he asked with urgent concern. Michael wasn't. The blackness that he'd hoped would never return was passing over him in waves of increasing power. He tried to sit up and smile. But his teeth chattered, and he began to shake. He pressed his teeth together and closed his eyes. He tried to relax all the muscles that had gone tight in his upper body.

"Not here—not now!" he told himself with furious intensity. There was no epilepsy in the family, everyone had agreed the year before, when Michael went into his two days of nearly continuous seizures. Whatever his other merits, you can't have an Imperial envoy subject to epileptic fits, and the family had conspired to cover things up with a story about a chill brought on by swimming in an unheated pool. Then, as quickly and inexplicably as they'd come on, the seizures had gone away. "It happens," was the best explanation anyone had found. This was from the old servant whose job it had been to sponge cold water over Michael while he'd raved in a dozen unknown languages. "It happens," was all the man had been willing to say when Michael asked about the dreams he'd reported in the intervals between his raving—dreams that had passed out of his memory even as the force of the seizures relaxed. If the driver stopped listening to his drum music, and looked round, he'd see a Michael unfit for any of the trust reposed in him by the Emperor. It wouldn't do! he screamed inside his head. Simeon squeezing his hand, and helping to keep his body from rocking out of control, Michael held his breath and tried to focus his mind on the beat of the driver's music.

At once, he was better. The blackness didn't so much retreat as vanish, and he was looking calmly into his uncle's face. "How is your arm?" he asked in a voice that, if still dreamy, wouldn't disgrace him. Simeon shook his head and reached down for a glass bottle of water.

"Drink this very slowly," he whispered with a look at the driver. "I fear this is the end of our journey. But I'll get you to bed as soon as we can finish with whatever reception is waiting here." Michael took the bottle and drank as he was told. He was feeling better by the moment, though relief at having avoided another seizure was evenly balanced by shame. The driver had seen nothing. Simeon would never say anything. But Simeon had passed over any number of possible secretaries for this mission. Nepotism is all very well—but not when it comes to promoting the unfit. He waited till his uncle was looking again out of the window, then reached up and wiped away the tears that trembled on his eyelids.

"On behalf of His Majesty's Government, I am pleased to welcome you to London," the bald man said in the smooth and perfect Greek of someone who could only have spent years among the best people in Constantinople. Jessup's efforts at Greek had been marked by a sounding of vowels and diphthongs that the educated might know but never voiced, and by a placing of accents according to the rules of Latin. What this man spoke might almost have been an imitation of the speech patterns of his two guests. "My name is Tarquin," he added. "What else might be said about

29

me is not currently important." He paused and spoke rapidly to the driver, who stood to attention and opened a rear compartment in the vehicle to take out a couple of bags.

They'd stopped outside a building that imitated in its size and style the grand buildings that had survived from the earliest days of Constantinople as an imperial city. Michael looked round. The air of London was foul beyond belief. Breathing was rather like putting your head into the smoke of a bonfire. He could almost taste the coal that Simeon had guessed was the cause of the surrounding fog. He looked back to see how his uncle was coping on his feet, only to find that he was the one offered support. "Take my arm," Simeon muttered. "Make it look as if you're helping an old man up these steps." But, even as he spoke, the driver got hold of him and pulled him the half dozen steps to the entrance of glass and polished wood. Michael looked along the road. Every other building was imposingly high and decorated in lavish style.

Tarquin cleared his throat and drew Michael's attention from a bronze statue of a man dressed in the clothing of the ancient Romans. "I am aware of your unfortunate experience in Dover. Of course, I do apologise for any offence given to your dignity as ambassadors. I promise that a full enquiry will be made, and that, should it be necessary, lessons will be learned and new procedures put in place to prevent any recurrence of the manner in which you may have been received. Can I take it, then, that you will desist from a formal protest when you meet His Majesty's chief minister?"

Simeon looked down from the entrance to the building. "We are not to be received by His Majesty himself?" he asked sharply. At home, even poor barbarian envoys could expect one meeting with the Emperor. He came back down the steps and pretended to adjust the collar of Michael's orange suit. Then he did give his arm, to make it look as though he was receiving the help.

Tarquin shook his head. "It is the custom of our King to speak mainly with his potted plants. Effective government is left in the hands of ministers responsible to the Senate." He looked closely at Michael, who looked steadily back, hoping his face wasn't as pale as it felt. They were now joined by obsequious men in tall hats and tight-fitting grey coats from inside the building. These took up the bags the driver had dumped on the pavement and carried them through a door that revolved about a central spindle. His eyes showing nothing at all, Tarquin smiled and led the way through those doors into an entrance hall of many-coloured splendour.

Simeon stood back from their long inspection of a city that spread for miles in every direction they had been able to look. Had they been able to see through the brown haze, it might have spread still further. He and Michael were on one of the higher floors of the building, and they had a better view over London than the Emperor, from his summer palace, had over Constantinople. No matter where they looked, nor how far they looked, they saw evidence of long settlement—buildings of the ancient kind, though of huge size, frighteningly tall buildings of an unknown style, parks and broad squares, wide and crowded streets. They could have looked and looked till the coming of darkness. Still, they'd have seen no limit to the forbidding vastness of a London that every report had assured them was a heap of unpeopled and overgrown ruins. But it would only have confirmed their own insignificance.

The old man picked up a sheaf of papers fastened together at the top left and squinted at the unabbreviated words in block capitals. "Do I not see at least one spelling mistake?" he asked with a smile. He sat down in one of the padded chairs and leafed through the papers. "To call for attention," he summarised from what he read, "you must pick up that instrument on the table between our beds and press the green button. That, apparently, will bring an attendant, who will wait for us to point on this document to whatever we desire. Shall we try calling for dinner? You can then go to bed." This had been more a command than a question. But Michael was long since recovered. Going to bed had dropped off his list of things to do. He'd already looked through the sheaf of paper. It was a clever, though a demeaning, production. On the left column of each page was a word or a phrase in Greek. On the right was its equivalent in the British language. When Tarquin had left it with them, the idea had obviously been that they would point in silence, and get what they requested. For Michael, it was a key to the whole language.

Simeon might have read his thoughts. "There is a book in that cupboard," he said, nodding towards the beds, "the lettering on which suggests it is a Bible. If so, it may belong to a man called Gideon. I'll not comment on its manner of production. But you will, I know, find it of use." Holding his left arm at an angle that showed continuing discomfort, he pushed himself out of the chair. Michael waved at this uncle to sit back and hurried to the book. He'd not speculate either on how such small but clear writing had been impressed on page after page of thin paper. But this obviously was a Bible, and in the British language. Trying not to tear the delicate pages, the two men leafed through to what anyone could see was The Acts of the Apostles.

"So, I was right—their language is pretty well uninflected," Michael said, feeling pleased with himself. "The nouns have one plural form, and the verbs have a different form only for the third person singular. The tenses appear to be compounds, and may take a while to unravel." He looked again, and brightened still further. If it killed him, he'd never let Uncle Simeon think he'd brought a deadweight invalid with him half way across the world. "And look at this word, and this one, and this one, and this one here—why, these are almost direct transliterations, with little change of meaning, from Latin or Greek. This will be even easier than I thought." He looked up and smiled happily at Simeon, whose watering eyes suggested he might benefit from a set of those lenses. The old man gave up on trying to read the tiny script and nodded, adding, with his first laugh in many days, that the boy would finally see some benefit in the floggings that had inspired him to get Holy Scripture by heart. Michael said nothing, and raised the book into a shaft of late sunlight, and was about to remark on how the copyist's pen had left no impression on the paper.

He was stopped by a loud whining that came from the other side of the glass sheet of the only window in this main room. As it fell silent, he stared again at the book he was still holding. But the lights came on, and there was a loud gurgling and splashing from the bathroom. By the time he was back from closing off the tap that had suddenly started gushing water into the bathtub, Simeon was looking at an illuminated panel on the wall. This was filled with a brightly-coloured picture that moved and very softly spoke. Michael reached forward to touch the panel. He drew his forefinger across a smooth and slightly flexible membrane. On closer inspection, this covered a mass of tiny dots that changed colour to produce the effect of movement.

He stood away. "I suppose we can ask Tarquin about what function this thing serves. I doubt its name would be embossed so prominently. So we can take the word Sony as the name of its original owner." He tipped the panel forward, noting how it was barely a half inch thick, and was attached to the wall by flexible cords. As he turned to speak again, there was a knock on the door and the sound of a key. Two men with brown faces walked in, one of them pushing a metal trolley loaded with food and drink.

Simeon appeared to have trouble with pulling his eyes away from the moving panel. It was for Michael to smile and nod at the attendants as they set out plates and jugs on a small wooden table beside the window. "Eat, drink and be merry," he told himself. Who could tell what the next day might bring?"

CHAPTER SIX

The American insurance agent paused his narrative and joined in the chorus of *Amens* from about the campfire. "It was now that I was sore afflicted," he began again, sounding, though not entirely looking, like one of the more restrained televangelists of old, "and given up for dead by many. But, if, when I awoke, I had lost my business, and if all my loved ones were taken from me, yet had I heard from the Lord God Himself in my visions, that I was reserved to witness the final working of His Heavenly Will. Yea, though I come before you with no possessions but the clothes that I wear, shall I not stand with you, O brethren, and see God?"

There was a ragged chorus of "Praise the Lord!" in a variety of accents. Jennifer took advantage of the movement in the crowd to push herself closer to the heap of wood splinters that had been gathered and set alight. With the coming of darkness, they'd taken shelter under the M25 flyover. The following afternoon, she'd been assured, they'd pass into the outer suburbs on London. She wondered again if she should have got off her bicycle to walk with this group. It had meant losing more time. But her legs had been tired from the endless cycling, and the invitation had been pressing and repeated.

Her rising doubts were quelled by the American. Still on his feet, he'd noticed her. "But tell me, young Sister in Christ," he asked, pointing straight at her, "what brings you to seek the Lord?" He put a pitying smile into his voice. "Did you lose your mummy and daddy in The Break? Or was it in The Hunger?"

She nodded and got up. She could have tried a few tears before dodging back into the shadows. But this was a semi-regular prayer meeting. If these people had willingly shared their bread and soup with her, the least she could do was play along. She waited for the

ritual grunting and carrying of hands between stomach and mouth
that was the approved response when The Hunger was mentioned.
"Not in The Hunger," she said. "They were visiting friends in
Holland." No one there seemed to be Dutch, so she'd not be
questioned about where in Holland. "Before the mobile network
went down, they told me they'd set out home once the Great Storm
was passed." She paused and turned her mouth down. "That was
the last I heard of them." There was a murmur of sympathy from
everyone about the fire. An old woman whose black armband
showed clearly against the grey of her cardigan embraced her. "I
am now travelling to London to take aspirins to a sick friend of my
aunt." A young man who looked Japanese turned round and smiled
sorrowfully.

That was enough of her. It was back to the American, who passed
into a loud sermon about the worthlessness of the possessions he
had lost—and there had, by his account, been many of these—and
then a self-deprecating and almost funny account of how, once
recovered from his sickness during The Break, he'd gone about,
trying to use his credit cards. Of course, he'd been turned out of his
hotel, and there had been a few weeks of begging for charity from
the organisers of the conference he'd been attending in Brighton.
The story would once have passed for something from one of the
more inventive episodes of *The Outer Limits*. But, its personal
touches aside, there must have been millions of similar stories
nowadays to be heard.

Once the American had finished, it was the turn of the young
man, who was indeed Japanese. England hadn't been all that he
had hoped, he ended with a certain reserve. Even so, he had
improved his English, and had found Christ into the bargain. Life
as a *salariman* in Kyoto had never offered this much. As everyone
seemed likely to join in another sad rendition of *O God, Our Help
in Ages Past*, someone else got up and asked the obvious question:
"Before we can see God, we have to get through the barriers. How
shall we be allowed to pass though those to the appointed place?"

Before Jennifer could turn to the woman and ask what was this
"appointed place," another woman was on her feet. "We are many;
they are few!" she cried vehemently in an accent that was
somewhere between French and German. There was a murmur of

35

approval from the crowd, and the American smiled again, raising his arms in a gesture of piety. Jennifer looked at the woman. Where was she from? It would have been useful to see more of her. But her head was covered, and she spoke from just beyond the glow of the fire. "Was not the army of the English mostly out of this land when The Break called England away?" she went on. "Is not the rest of that army fighting the natives of Ireland? Have not the natives taken up English weapons in defence of their land and liberty? I tell you—there will be little food out of Ireland this year," she added in a voice still louder and more dramatic. "Such food as may be wrested from the children of the soil shall be watered in English blood!" There was a cheer from all assembled. "Are there enough armed men in all England to chase away the multitudes that shall now assemble in waiting? I tell you, my brothers and sisters in Christ—we are many; they are few. None shall block our path to the glory that waits in the great city of London."

This got a round of "Praise the Lord!" from several dozen excited mouths. Jennifer looked nervously out into the surrounding darkness. *The woman was an Outsider*. During the first chaotic weeks, before the imposition of iron control, Outsiders had been a common sight in the streets of Deal. They had been welcomed for the food they brought in exchange for those items of modernity that had value across the Channel. Since then, the law had been plain: all contact with the Outside was forbidden, and any Outsider found in England was to be shot on sight. Yet here was one in plain view—one who'd even learned good English. It would have been interesting to take her aside, and ask for her story. It would be more interesting than those of the various foreigners caught out by The Break. But Jennifer moved quietly out of the crowd. If she'd decided in the late afternoon that there might be safety in numbers, she had changed her mind.

Alone, she stood in the shadow of the flyover and looked up at the brownish sky. There was no moon tonight. Even if there had been, it would have had trouble shining through the dense blanket of smog that covered London and the great penumbra stretching far beyond its outer suburbs. Here and there, one of the brighter stars showed through. But there was nothing like the mass of shining points that nowadays turned the sky above Deal into a gentle and almost unified glow. There was no artificial light beyond the fires lit by those camping on the road. The trees and fields were lost in the gloom. It was barely possible to see the long and silent streak of the M2 as it ran between London and the Kent coast.

Perhaps an hour after setting out from the Dover roundabout, a lorry had almost knocked her off her bicycle. Since she'd fallen in with this set of travelling companions, and wheeled her bicycle ever west, perhaps a dozen cars had sped by. But, if motor travel was a luxury that few could gather the coupons to afford, the pilgrims had been one tiny component in the endless and often jolly stream of unmotorised traffic. Sooner or later, they'd have to come off the motorway. They would have to face a barrier thrown across the road, and unblinking officers would check every identity card. Perhaps the Outsider had been right—that the motorway exits would be too crowded for every single card to be checked. It was on this that Jennifer had been counting. But being caught with even one Outsider was a danger she couldn't afford.

There was a voice behind her—deep and rich and a touch mournful. "He went by this afternoon, Honey," it said. Not turning, Jennifer could see the large black woman in her mind's eye. She'd been one of the loudest respondents in the prayer sessions laid on by the American. "You hadn't even joined us yet," she added, now very mournful. "It's only the Devil out there now." Not answering—still not looking round—Jennifer stared harder out into the darkness. The farthest she could see was beyond the central barrier of the motorway, just where the tarmac ended and the darkness of a grass bank began. There might be a party there of travellers out of London—funny, she supposed, how people still kept to the left lane, even when the old traffic rules made no sense. But whoever might be over there was wholly out of her sight. "It's you he's looking for, isn't it, Honey?" the woman asked.

Still not turning round, Jennifer shrugged. She might have argued that two dozen loud pilgrims were a more likely target of satanic interest than one girl with a bicycle. Then there was the family of East European Gypsies slumped in quiet despondency about their own fire. No one could assume they were up to any good. But why bother with the obvious? You don't argue with religious fanatics—

37

not when there's so much to get fanatical about. There was a shift of the night breeze, and a cloud of filthy smoke drifted over from the fire.

"Why you don't take the train?" the woman asked accusingly. "I see the gold and silver in your money belt." Jennifer stiffened slightly and resisted the urge to reach for her knife. The woman laughed. "I see all things," she explained. "The Lord has given me the gift of sight." Jennifer smiled. If she'd somehow got this much right, it was worth asking how she'd managed to lose her man and both her sons when they were caught celebrating Christmas in September. Being overlooked when the police swooped, and so not being packed off to build roads in Ireland, required less than some Divine Revelation. The one oddity was that the police had chosen her men, rather than others, for one of the random acts of barbarity with which they managed to keep everyone terrorised into obedience.

The woman moved closer, and Jennifer was aware of the slightly asthmatic breathing. Time for some kind of response. Though a nuisance, the woman was useful to keep Jennifer's mind from going back over a plan of action that only made sense when she didn't think about it. "Have you tried buying a railway ticket since The Break?" No answer. Possibly, the woman hadn't. Anyone who, in the Olden Days, had thought the old airports were rigidly policed hadn't now tried getting into Charing Cross without a valid permit to travel. Being caught out on the railways was a shooting matter. That much she'd seen for herself on the one trip her father had allowed her to make with him. It really had been two wheels and two legs or nothing.

"You don't belong with us," the woman said, now in a sorrowful croon. "Your man is already waiting for you in London. You must leave us." Jennifer smiled again. She'd already decided it was time to strike out on her own. All considered, it might be safer to creep round the police barriers. This mad creature might believe that God would allow her and her friends through—and with at least one Outsider for company. But, however slight, the risk of being caught, and then detained when her own documents were found out of order, was too great. The black woman was only jogging her arm. If he didn't yet know it, there *was* a man waiting for her in

London; and she knew that he could be found there only at certain fixed times.

The singing behind them both had given way to an exalted chanting, and Jennifer could see the glow from the fire behind her as the American repeated his act of dancing barefoot on hot ashes. She made her mind up. There was no one out there to watch her or anyone else. But, if she turned out to be wrong, the smoke would give enough cover for a quiet getaway.

Or had she really made up her mind? She could simply turn back for the coast. Another three days, and there would be another boat setting into St Margaret's Bay. She thought of Count Robert. But she thought again. Where her parents were concerned, what use would the Outsiders be?

CHAPTER SEVEN

Her watch said 3am as she reached the top of Blackheath Hill. So much wondering about how to squeeze past in the shadows, and she'd found the Kidbrooke exit from the motorway unmanned. Even the bar across the road had been raised. No one had challenged her as she made her way in darkness along the silent main road that led from Shooter's Hill and across the empty Heath. If she hadn't known better, she might have supposed she was still coming through Sidcup. But there could be no doubt she was deep inside London. The dark haze overhead and the increasingly foul air had made this plain.

She stopped where the Heath ended and the inner city began. She looked left, and saw the dark outline of one of the gigantic Hills of the Dead that had risen above every open space in London. In Kent, The Hunger had been a grievous thing. But Kent had its countryside, where food could often be gathered. Her father had likened the suffering in London to a game of musical chairs in which half the chairs were missing from the outset. She looked right. The high towers of Canary Wharf would once have blazed with light. The pyramid that topped the highest tower would then have shown plain ten or twenty miles back along the motorway. But this, and all the other lights that once had shone there, belonged to a world of seven billion people that had looked to London as its undisputed banker. She knew that the towers themselves had survived the quelling of the Food Riots. Unless empty, they must be filled to bursting with those who'd huddled in from the outermost suburbs. Whatever the case, the only lights now to be seen from the top of Blackheath Hill were the dull and flickering reds that glowed from a thousand factory chimneys— that and the incandescent glare of bulbs over one of the street markets in a city that, if much changed and somewhat diminished, could still be said never to sleep. Jennifer kicked her bicycle forward and coasted down to the junction with Greenwich South Street. Here, she had no choice but to get off and push her way into the crush of pedestrians and carts and brightly-lit stalls.

"You mind where you's stepping, Lovey!" a woman shrieked as Jennifer nearly unbalanced the pile of things she was carrying on her head. She tried to apologise, but stood transfixed by the pattern of tribal scars that gleamed on the woman's face. According to her father, more than half the Londoners bulldozed into the Hills of the Dead had been black. Perhaps by accident, perhaps by design, blacks had suffered terribly in The Hunger, and worse in The Pacification. Her one London trip since The Break had been confined to the absolute centre—here, just about everyone had been white. It was a shock, after so long, to see so many black faces. She stepped back, and someone swore loudly behind her. She gripped hard on her handlebars and pushed her way deeper into the crowd. Never mind the incidentals of colour—after so many days, when she'd heard nothing but the twittering of birds and the murmured conversations of slow-moving travellers, the loud babble of voices and the hum of treadmill-powered generators was a shock she had to fight hard to overcome. So too the omnipresent smell of coal smoke and of unwashed humanity. She ignored the reek of close-packed, sweaty bodies. She skirted the crowds of drunks reeling from every pub. She hurried past the piteous beggars and the raucous whores of every age and sex.

The noise and bustle were alarming, and they were reassuring. Half a dozen times, she'd stopped after leaving the M25 flyover, and looked back into the gloom. She'd had no impression of being followed along the road. There had been no sound of a helicopter overhead. Nor, even before the brighter stars vanished into the smog, did she see one of those surveillance balloons that she'd heard kept London sealed off and in an uneasy peace. Unless one of the armed officers who kept order here took it into his mind to stop her, she was probably safer in every way that counted than since she'd cycled out of Deal.

At first, Deptford Broadway seemed impassable. Its wide expanse was crowded with stalls selling everything from fire tongs to used notebook computers. Here, the hum of generators was joined by the throbbing of factory machinery that, like the markets it fed, worked day and night. But, keeping her head down, and mindful of hands that, might at any moment, flutter against her tight backpack and the zipped pockets of her anorak, she pressed slowly forward.

There was a spot patrol where the Broadway narrowed and gave way to the darkness of the New Cross Road. Here, the police were checking identity cards. Jennifer heard the crackle of radios just in time, and was able to dodge without drawing attention to herself into the queue at a food stall. Here, £30 bought what was described as a hamburger. Its inner part might contain traces of something that was once alive and breathing, but seemed mostly to be the grey, industrial protein nowadays fed to the poor.

> *RTProt! RTProt!*
> *Half a kilo in your pot!*
> *Healthy and lean,*
> *Clean and green,*
> *Eat it while it's steaming hot!*

So the speakers beside the stall blared every minute or so, while the cracked video screen flashed random colours and the occasional picture of contented enjoyment. Some kind of grease dribbling off his chin, a man stood opposite her and raised his own circular mass of nourishment in a gesture of friendship. Jennifer looked away and took another bite of her pseudo-hamburger. The bun itself had the dry taste of flour bulked out with chalk dust. This made the grease that leaked from the compressed sausage a useful lubricant. It was food of a sort, and she chewed grimly on the thing as she glanced sideways at the endless checking of documents. The side road that might have led her round was sealed with rubble. She thought of the map she'd inspected at home. If she forced herself back to the main junction, she might get onto the wide road that hugged the Thames. But would this be any easier to get through?

"You t'ieving raasclarth!" the stall holder suddenly yelled at an old woman who was stuffing one of the burgers into her mouth. "You tek dese back and wipe you's ass!" He held up one of the notes she'd given him and ripped it across. Someone behind her in the queue laughed. Someone else called out in anger at the delay. All about, there was a sudden chatter of interest and of disapproval. The chance of a disturbance brought two of the officers over. The crowd parted to let them swagger through. Jennifer pulled herself and her bicycle out of their sight. But the police weren't interested in her. A few words from the stall holder, and the bigger officer got the old woman across the shoulders with his long club. As she went down, still frantically pushing food into her mouth, both officers set properly about her. Concentrating on her own food, poor as it was, took Jennifer's mind off the woman's rapidly animalistic screams and the shouts of encouragement from the crowd that had closed round.

It was as the screams ended, and the police began cocking their rifles to bring the crowd into order, that Jennifer felt a gentle pressure on her backpack. She twisted round, knife in hand. "Don't want no friction!" the spotty boy whined. He raised his hands and stepped back onto the heaps of rubbish that blocked the pavements here. He managed a single step onto the soft debris, before sprawling onto his back. His head splashed inside the foot thickness of wet filth. What may have been animal or human excrement soaked into his matted hair, he grinned, and raised his hands in another gesture of peace. "No friction, mate!"

Jennifer looked at him. Though smaller than her, he had the wiry look of the underclass. A year of reduced nutrition might have done nothing to abolish the difference of speed and strength between them. She set her face like stone and put her knife away. Slowly, she backed into the crowd. One of the officers was laughing into his radio. The other was poking his rifle at anyone who came too close by the unmoving heap that had been human. The officers at the checkpoint had, for the moment, given up on asking for documents, and were straining for their own look at the body. She pushed her way under cover of a wall that was bulging out the higher it rose, and crept past into the dark silence that lay beyond Deptford Broadway.

▶ ▼ ◀

It was half a mile to the top of the next hill. Jennifer was soon used to the comparative silence. She stopped at the double junction with Lewisham Way, and rested on the edge of one of the places that must have been flattened in the Pacification. A year before, when the news reports hadn't yet lost touch with reality, the fires in a dozen cities had flared nightly on every television screen that still worked. Safe in a house stuffed with food, and with shotgun ever loaded, Jennifer had sat with her parents and watched the beginning of the new order of things. Long before genuine footage was dropped in favour of gushing descriptions of "wartime spirit" in the Cotswolds, word of mouth reporting had taken over the function of the news. Then, she'd heard of the mass shootings and the transporting of multitudes to work on the recreation of Ireland as a gigantic penal colony and food plantation.

But that was a year ago. All that marked the last stand of the hungry was the space cleared by the bombing. Even this was now being filled in by workshops to employ the poor and provide England with some of the things it had been thought the rest of the world would always send in exchange for a complex shuffling of paper. Here was a place of manufacture, not of selling, and Jennifer could now set out along a road that was mostly empty and where, from behind every bricked-up shop window, and from every old university building, came the endless hum of machinery. Twice, she passed over railway bridges and was aware of the low, continuous rumble of wagons that fed and were fed by the ceaseless whirr of steam-powered generators and machinery.

CHAPTER EIGHT

Cycling in the dark is inadvisable. But, when it would be madness to put the lights on, and when young eyes have grown used to their surroundings, it is possible. Jennifer was half way along the Old Kent Road, and passing at the speed of a brisk walk through an area that was neither commercial nor industrial. She might once, in the Olden Days, have been driven this way by her father. If so, it would then have been a road jammed with perpetual traffic and illegally parked vehicles. But that would have been then. The road now was clear of traffic. The only evidence that vehicles had once been parked here was the usual litter of smashed windscreens and of metal parts too small or worthless to be swept up for recycling in the workshops. But for the glass, she might have gone faster. But for the need to get through this place of potential danger, she might have got off and walked. Instead, her eyes straining to see the faint glitter of glass cubes on the road, Jennifer made her way towards the Elephant and Castle roundabout.

From habit, she came to a stop at one of the main junctions. On the off chance that hers wasn't the only vehicle on the road, she looked both ways before passing across. It was here that the road was narrowed by mountains of rubbish too organic for recycling and too rancid for scavenging. In London, even the rats were now in short supply. With a splashing of tyres on seepage, Jennifer stopped pedalling and put her main effort into keeping her balance.

Overhead, on her left, there was a sudden noise. It might have been the call of a night bird. She was aware of the low whistle, but paid it no attention. When, after a few seconds, the call was repeated from on her right, she came carefully to a stop and looked about. There was no change in the darkness. But the steady hiss of tyres on unswept asphalt, and the tick of ball bearings tight-packed in grease, had given a comfort she only realised once all about was in silence. She suppressed the urge to cough again in the sulphurous air and listened hard. She was almost relieved when, after a long and comparative silence, she heard the scrape of a sash window directly above, and a sniggering laugh.

She was wearing clothes that had been dark before they were dirty. Her bicycle was black and without reflective parts. If she picked it up and crept slowly forward, she might be able to escape the attention she'd excited. No luck. Three more silent steps, and she was aware of a red flash so faint and so brief, she'd normally have put it down to a trick of her own eyes. But she saw it again— a still faint but now continuous glimmer from an upper window on her right. There was the scrape across the road of another window pushed up, and another glimmering of red. One voice called low and incomprehensibly from an open window, and was answered by another. Even before she heard a high, rhythmical scraping from behind, Jennifer realised what was happening. All her life, she'd heard people at home talk slightingly about the ways of London. In the safety of Deal, those grim and whispered jokes about the Strange Meaters had blended into the general condemnation. Now, she was in London, and at night, and alone.

She twisted her bicycle round and switched on its double turbo-lights. For the two men hurrying towards her on their roller skates, it was too late to pull off their night glasses, or to look away. For them, it must have been the equivalent of coming out of a darkened room to stare straight into the midday sun. She saw two pairs of hands go up to faces and heard the simultaneous cries of pain and of anger.

She'd been seen. Bathed in a glow of light not visible to the naked eye, she could be seen. There was no value in turning the lights off. And she needed them. She got back on her bicycle and pressed hard on the pedals. Shooting forward, she changed into a higher gear. Now she could see everything about her, she was able to go as quickly as if she were coasting downhill. Another half mile or so, and she'd reach the Elephant and Castle. This might be silent and in darkness. Or the expanse of its roundabout might be filled by another street market. Whatever the case, she'd heard that the Strange Meaters mostly kept to their own districts. If she stayed ahead for long enough, these might turn back.

Because she'd passed into what was still a main road, used by the authorities and for the carriage of goods, the way ahead was clear. There was no glass or sharp metal pieces to slow her down. She could hear only the creak of her bicycle and the sound of her own rapid breathing. For a moment, she was able think she'd outrun her pursuers, or that they had given up on her. Again no luck. Before she could slow and look round, she heard a closer scrape of roller skates, and the high, panting squeal of a voice that sounded scarily close. She barely had time to gasp in another breath of the polluted air, when she felt a scrabbling hand lay hold of her saddlebag. She twisted a little to her left, and barely avoided crashing into a high kerbstone. The hand fell away, and she clutched harder on the handlebars and prayed she'd not run over a pothole.

But young men on roller skates can pick up an impressive speed. On a racing bicycle, Jennifer might have had some chance of outrunning them. On a bicycle made for getting safely about her normal business, she had no chance. Even if she'd dared trade an ounce of present speed for a switch into top gear, they were faster. She heard the shrill, anticipatory cry of the one who was almost beside her, and felt herself wobble as the other grabbed hold of her backpack. She could feel the bicycle go increasingly out of control. She could slow down, or she could be pulled over. There was another shrill cry, and then a low joint giggling as of youths high on cannabis. Another moment, and they'd pull her to a stop. Then, she'd be off the bicycle. A hand clamped over her mouth, she'd be dragged into the dark shadows that lined the street. They'd not let her see the dawn, she could be sure. This wasn't the Olden Days. It wasn't robbery they were after, nor rape—though these might be part of the incidental details.

It was too late to be sensible: time instead to try for the big advantage a bicycle has over roller skates. Without warning, Jennifer stopped pedalling and squeezed hard on the brakes. As rubber tyres scraped and she wobbled over, she felt both attackers go down at the same time. Skidding and tumbling and rolling in the pool of light before her, they were carried forward on the road with much the same effect on their bodies as pumice stone has on a pencil rubber. As if in slow motion, she heard the sharp crack as one struck his head on a kerbstone. The other screamed as he fell head over heels and landed on his knees. With another scream, he lurched at her. But both kneecaps must have gone in his fall, and there was no getting up.

Far behind, Jennifer heard shouts of rage, and then the loud movement of metal blinds. She untangled herself from the fallen bicycle. Then, before she could put herself into order and get on again, two hands clamped about her left ankle. The attacker who'd knocked against a kerbstone was twitching away as if at the end of an epileptic fit. The one who'd done his knees was still mobile. Somehow, in the seconds she'd spent panting and shaking and leaning on her bicycle, he'd dragged himself across the five yards that separated them. Now, he had her fast.

"Eatie meatie!" he shrilled through the pain. "Eatie sweety meatie!" She kicked out and tried to dislodge the hands. But, if stricken, the youth was plainly drugged on something more exotic than cannabis. His response was an obscenity that hissed through the gaps in the ski mask covering his face. She kicked again, now at his head. But this was his opportunity to tug suddenly on her ankle. She hit the road with a bump that took her breath away. The youth gave a laugh that turned into a cry of maniacal joy as he took hold of her knees. "Treatie eatie sweety meatie!"

Still far behind her, but growing closer, Jennifer could hear shouts and pattering steps. She tried again to shake free of that iron grip. But the youth now had his arms about her waist. She twisted over on her side and pulled out her knife. She struck at random and almost lost the knife as it got caught in his padded anorak. He let out a cry of pain and relaxed his hold on her waist. Before she could take advantage of this, he'd made a grab at the knife. He missed, but pulled his entire weight onto her body and got both hands about her throat. She felt the plastic mask pressing against her cheek, and was aware of the smell of flesh that might not have been washed since The Break. She heard a low and expectant gibber: "Lunchie munchie—*gooood*!" She struck again with the knife. This time, it went straight through the anorak, but glanced off his ribs. Then, as the youth jerked briefly upward, she hit out with all the strength of despair and buried the knife in his throat.

And that did it. This time, there was no cry of pain or anger—no tighter grip on her own throat. All she felt was the warm, pressurised spray from severed blood vessels, and a convulsion that had the youth over on his back. She heard the kicking of his trainers on the road, as he went into spasms, and a buzzing, choking sound from his throat. He might have been a ghastly thing to see, but the lights on her fallen bicycle were pointing away, and she could see nothing. Jennifer scrambled to her feet. As if in a dream, she pulled the bicycle upright and got on. Her bloody hands slipped on the handlebars, but she wobbled slowly forward. She thought she'd fall off. But she righted herself and thrust harder on the pedals. She thought of changing gear, but found she couldn't loosen her hold on the handlebars. There may have been the sound behind her of a woman screaming. But all she really heard was a pulse beating loud in her ears. Still wobbling, she strained to pick up speed in top gear. The next time she looked up, it was to see the lights of the street market that overspread the Elephant and Castle roundabout.

Beyond the jostling crowd, Jennifer huddled in a doorway and wept. With Count Robert, she'd put on a brave face, not even turning pale when he'd taken a stick to one of his men. Now, she'd just killed someone, and it was as much as she could do not to vomit. The police never bothered nowadays with actual crimes—not unless someone bribed them to take action, and it was an easy matter of sweeping a suspect off to Ireland. Regardless, though, of whether anyone would pay attention, she'd just cut a man's throat and cycled away from the body. Shock struggled with plain astonishment. It was only with a mighty effort that she was able to understand the woman who'd come over to her, and, dressed in the ragged livery of an estate agency chain, was trying to recruit her for one of the strange, apocalyptic cults that had sprung up to compete with both official and underground churches. She was pointing at a line of her co-worshippers, who were starting a slow and penitential wailing that might end in a tearing off of clothes and the usual flagellation. Jennifer got up and showed her bloody hands and face in the light from one of the stalls. That scared the woman away. Alone, she sat down and pulled her bicycle closer, as if for comfort. She discovered that the front tyre was flat. She pushed her forehead onto her knees and wept again.

CHAPTER NINE

While the sun rose behind her, and the smog turned a kind of fluorescent grey, it seemed as if every factory whistle in London went off at once. Jennifer had heard that all the bridges had checkpoints at each end. She'd also heard there were times of the day when all the police could do was enforce a few basic rules for the traffic. On both accounts, she'd heard right. Vauxhall Bridge at dawn was a chaos of mainly human traffic. Most crossings seemed to be from the north, as industrial workers left their warrens in Victoria Street, and, still wearing the increasingly shabby suits of their old lives, hurried off to work in the factories just across the River. It was a comparatively thin stream of traders pushing through that wall of stinking humanity from the north.

Once past the shouting, gesticulating officers, Jennifer hurried across the junction with Millbank, and, propping her bicycle against a lamppost, had her first proper look in over a year at this part of London. Like the suburbs, it was much changed. Here, in particular, the maps she'd studied before setting out were obsolete. It was across Vauxhall Bridge that the crowds had poured on the fourth day of The Hunger. The idea, apparently, had been a peaceful demonstration outside Parliament. Almost a year on, it was useless to ask about activating causes. It was enough that the official response had flattened nearly the whole area between the River and the north side of Victoria Street. Now, from where she stood, Jennifer had an unbroken view across the shanty town that had once been Pimlico, right over to the still intact Westminster Cathedral. Looking right, there was a view, no less unbroken, towards Parliament. She would have heard Big Ben sounding the hour. But the factory whistles were insistent and never-ending—those and the lower but more dense flow of human chatter.

There was a sudden smell of petrol exhaust. In Deal, petrol had run out within days. Since then, it had been organic diesel at best for those with money or connections to get the coupons. This, however, was the great city of London. All things still happened here. All was still for sale. Jennifer straightened up and gawped at the large and shiny car that had purred gently from Grosvenor Road, and was pushing past her into Millbank. The driver sounded his horn several times, and the escort officers were rearing up on their horses to club and trample those workers who didn't get out of the way. But this wasn't the right time for a drive along the Embankments. Stuck in a crowd too solid for pushing aside, the driver came to a stop and turned off his engine. Jennifer pulled her bicycle into the relative openness of Vauxhall Bridge Road and ignored what she'd been telling herself about a dash into the Centre. Thought tired—though in a state of growing moral numbness—this was a sight and smell to remind her of the Olden Days.

She was still straining to see over the heads of the shuffling crowd, when an old man almost crashed his shopping trolley into her. "That's capitalism, that is!" he said approvingly. Ignoring the car, he pointed at a couple of Orientals who, just inside a little park across the road, were selling unplucked pigeons. "More capitalism's what this country needs," he added, with a hungry look that suggested he might do with some of his own. He pulled his eyes off the queue that was forming and reached into the trolley for an old cloth supermarket bag. He looked up and pushed his spectacles further onto his nose. Jennifer smiled vaguely back, and was about to make her excuses, when there was a commotion over by the car. While she was looking away, the police had cleared a passage through the crowd. The car door now opened, and a thin man, dressed with a smartness she'd almost forgotten, was climbing out.

"General Rockville," a young man shouted in a harsh and decidedly common voice—"this isn't part of the schedule. It's, it's...."

"What in God's name has happened here?" the General rasped in an American accent. He stopped about six feet from Jennifer and looked over what had been Pimlico. He took a few more paces, then got out a handkerchief. "And the air—what have you done with it?"

"General, please—get back in the car," the young man whined. "Abigail did specify no personal contact." The young man began hopping from foot to foot in his agitation. He took out a mobile telephone and began pacing about in search of a signal. Jennifer could see the dandruff on the collar of a jacket that was too small for him.

The General swore at him to shut up, and put out a hand to stop one of the hurrying industrial workers. "Who are you?" he demanded into the man's scared face? "No—tell me who you *were*!" He pointed at the darned and greasy pinstripe clothing and laughed at whatever response he was given. He turned back to the young man. "OK," he drawled, "Seeing is believing. Some things are beyond even you Goddamn Limeys to lie about. Yes, Siree," he chuckled, "seeing is believing. Take me back to Hooper!" He got back into the car, which left a thin cloud of petrol exhaust as it started up again and was at last able to move slowly into Millbank.

"If I'm not mistaken," the old man said, "that was Madison Rockville Jr." Jennifer was fighting off another wave of tiredness, and noted without exploring the faint confusion at the back of her mind. "The American Secretary of State," he prompted. Jennifer nodded vaguely. She did know that—or thought she might. "In the last news before the Great Storm," the old man added in a strange tone, "he was at a meeting in Tokyo. How do you suppose he got here in time for The Break?"

She was saved the trouble of answering by the approach of another vehicle. This was just an old lorry that had been pushing forward, an inch at a time, across the Bridge. It was now through the crowds, and the driver was pressing hard on the accelerator. As it rumbled past in a cloud of the usual organic diesel, she looked briefly up. Pipe in mouth, the driver had taken his hands off the wheel, and was rejoicing. The armed guard beside him looked shiftily about. Faces pushed against nine inch slits along the side, she glanced into the terrified eyes of dozens of sheep. There may have been a hundred others who couldn't push through to the light and air. The factory whistles had stopped, and she could hear the bleating of the sheep. As it reached a junction further along the road and turned right, Jennifer was aware that the old man had gone into a rambling speech that involved a lost battery for his camera, before settling into speculations on whether the Americans had ever started their exchange of nuclear missiles.

The old man stopped in mid-flow about flying times from the Far East, and looked closely into her face. The blood was already dry before she'd been able to rub at her face. There had been no getting if off her hair. The best she'd been able to do before trying her luck on the Bridge was to push her head into an ash heap and brush off the excess. She wondered if he'd remark on her appearance. Instead, he turned and waved vaguely at somewhere within the shanty town. She looked over the low huddle of waferboard and cardboard boxes and saw nothing remarkable. But she forced out another smile. "I'm sure you'll find it," she said. She leaned wearily on her bicycle and set out in the direction of Victoria. Before she passed out of hearing, the old man was into a sorrowful lecture about how price controls had lowered the quality of bread. Perhaps he'd found someone else to buttonhole. More likely, he was talking to himself.

£500 a night—up front," the old Indian said without looking up. "£200 for every client you service." He gave one of those high-pitched Asiatic laughs and watched Jennifer count the heap of dirty notes. He pulled one out and held it under his violet lamp. He grunted and repeated his scan with two other notes from the bottom of the pile. He looked up. "£50 for me to put the water on." He giggled. "If you want to look like a street whore, you can do business in the street." Jennifer stood aside as he came out from behind his desk and led the way into a building that smelled of dirt and stale spices. He took her upstairs to the second floor and showed her into a windowless room that might once have housed a photocopier, and that was now largely taken up with a mattress. He waited for her to put her backpack on this and take out a few things, then led her along an unlit corridor to the bathroom.

"Five minutes of hot water." He held up the fingers of one hand for emphasis. "Don't try stealing the soap."

Alone, Jennifer found that the door didn't lock. She pulled off unbelievably dirty clothes and, stepping under the shower, waited for the dribble of cold water to start. As promised, it ceased after five minutes. She looked at the towel that had been provided. Leaving it untouched, she rubbed most of the water from her body with the inside of her sweatshirt and waited for the rest to evaporate. This had been the executive washroom in the little office block. Though it looked as if someone's face had been smashed into it, the bloody smear and pattern of cracks covered only one end of the long mirror opposite the row of toilet cubicles. In the light of the single bulb that flickered overhead, she stared at her reflection. It takes effort to make a teenage body ugly, and Jennifer, most decidedly, wasn't ugly. She had her father's neck, and much of his wide shoulders and big chest. But the hard and endless travelling of the past year had kept her from the Baldwin tendency to stoutness. And she did have her mother's colouring and features. Perhaps she wasn't beautiful in the conventional sense. Perhaps she never would be. But no one could deny that young Jennifer Baldwin was a fine-looking girl. Count Robert had always thought so. Even in the baggy robe she wore among the Outsiders, it wasn't just knowledge of who she was that turned every male head.

Thoughts of her parents, and of what had soon become her normal life, might have set her off on a long moment of the blubbers. But she was suddenly aware of the Indian's loud breathing as he watched her through a hole in the door. She stepped closer to the mirror and unfolded the clothes she'd picked up at a stall in Vauxhall Bridge Road. They were shabbier than they'd looked in the sunshine, and the moth had eaten a few holes in the lower part of the dress. But a coat of paint on her face, and she'd pass for what she was pretending to be. Leave the paint off, and she'd pass for respectable. She couldn't ask more than that.

Back in her room, she lit the candle and propped a chair against the door. Fully clothed, she lay on the stained mattress. The thin partition walls didn't keep out the grunts and squeals of pleasure that came from all about. She squeezed her eyes shut and tried to put the noise out of mind. But her hair was still wet, and she was feeling hungry again. She sat up and took out the yellow loaf she'd earlier stuffed into her backpack. It came apart with a shower of crumbs, and she washed it down with the boiled water the Indian had left in the room. She was about to take out the motion detector she'd also bought and hang this on the door. Instead, she played with the key to the deposit box where she'd put everything of real value. Nothing was totally safe, one of her father's dodgier contacts had often assured her. But there were levels of security, and anywhere might be safer than this ghastly place. Since she was still probably being watched from somewhere, she resisted the impulse take the key from round her neck and fiddle properly with it. She now did unpack the motion detector. She hooked it over the door handle. More than a hard bang on the door, and it would deafen everyone within twenty feet. What she could do if it did go off was another matter. She'd left her knife in someone's throat. But, if she was to be murdered in her bed, she might as well be awake when it happened.

Jennifer lay back again on the mattress. "You're ever such a grown up little girl," her father had been telling her for as long as she could remember. He'd never believed that, she knew—if he ever got to discuss her trip into France with Count Robert, he'd certainly act on different assumptions. Her mother had never said anything so stupid, and had countered every assertion of independence with a mixture of scolding and sound advice. Now, both her parents were gone. It was for her to get them back. And only she could get them back. But how? Yes, how? This was a question she'd repeatedly asked on the way up to London—asked and failed to answer. Here, finally in London, the little games she'd played in her mind to blank out the failure no longer worked. Half riding, half walking, she'd taken days to get here. She'd killed a man. And what next? She might have cried herself to sleep. But there are some horrors so overpowering that tears themselves are stilled.

With a fizzing of cheap wax, the candle began to gutter, and she looked up at the shadows it cast on the ceiling. Then, just as she was beginning to think there'd never be an end to the wave after wave of cold misery sweeping through her mind, she was asleep.

CHAPTER TEN

Basil Radleigh switched off the mobile telephone that had burst once more into life, and turned his attention back to Jennifer. "Of course, my dear," he said with smooth and avuncular charm, "this is a most delightful if unexpected pleasure. I wasn't expecting a visit from your father today in my little home from home. I certainly wasn't expecting to be able to say that a very pretty girl has become a very beautiful young woman." He stopped for the waiters to serve afternoon tea. Any number of times in the Olden Days, Jennifer had sat with her father in the National Liberal Club. "The biggest public urinal the Victorians ever built," he'd called it with a laugh the first time he took her there. It wasn't an original comment. And the glazed tiles that covered every wall and column did give the place a strongly lavatorial appearance. Her father had also once pointed at the stains on the high ceiling in the Lloyd George Room, and suggested that a Roman palace might have looked like this some time between the Vandal sack and the first siege by Belisarius.

The Club's genteel seediness had finally come into its own. Being no shabbier than it had ever been, it seemed, by comparison with almost everywhere else in London, the height of luxury. Jennifer picked up her teacup and sniffed at the sparkling Earl Grey. She put it down and reached for one of the fresh teacakes. She cut it in half and spread it thickly with yellow butter that didn't separate and run from her knife. She caught a momentary glance at herself in the reflection from the teapot. Though distorted, it told her she'd made the right choice of hat in John Lewis. It made her look older than sixteen, and immeasurably more elegant than she'd ever felt before. The dress, she was sure, was exactly right. It would have given both her parents a fit to see her in it. The club doorman had followed her with his eyes all the way up the grand staircase. Every head in the Lloyd George Room had turned in her direction as she walked in and crossed over to the man for whom her mother had never hidden either loathing or contempt. Even today, £8,000 was hardly a worthless sum. She had no doubt it had caused the shop assistants in John Lewis to do her proud.

"Mummy and Daddy were taken into custody last Wednesday," she said when they were alone again. She'd rehearsed the artless and almost childish tone of her statement, and was expecting a panicky reaction. Instead, Radleigh put his teacup carefully into its saucer and looked at her to continue. "It was very early last Wednesday," she said, filling the sudden void in their conversation. "I'd been away—on, on business. When I got back, I was told they'd been taken."

Radleigh glanced about the room and leaned forward. "So, they were arrested, last Wednesday?" he asked in his softest, most silky voice. "I suppose you went to the local police station with a bag of cash?" She shook her head. Was that the tiniest flicker of relief on his baggy face? Before she could think about the question, his expression had changed, and he made a show of thinking. "Well, my dear," he said grimly, "they must be half way to Liverpool by now. Couldn't you have got here a little sooner?" Jennifer took a sip of hot tea and said nothing. If she could have written an epic poem about her journey, it wasn't something she wanted to bring to the front of her mind. Radleigh frowned. Then he smiled, parting his lips to show the expensive dentistry they covered. "I'll do what little I can, though I can't promise a quick result after this delay." Jennifer nodded and took another sip of tea. She crossed her legs, making sure not to notice how it raised her dress another inch and a half. It was to let him see this that she'd sat herself not opposite him, but at a right angle. "I'm having dinner tomorrow night with the Justice Secretary," he sighed. "I can speak to him then about your parents. It will take a few telephone calls, and then a day or so to see if they've reached the holding pens in Liverpool. If they've been shipped off already to Ireland, getting them back will mean calling in some big favours."

Jennifer put her cup down and stared for what seemed a long time into Radleigh's eyes. There was a woman at a table on the far side of the room, talking in a loud, affected voice about the prices she was getting for the antiques she'd picked up during The

Hunger. Two young men at a table closer by were quietly discussing how many convicts it would take to pump water from an old tin mine in Cornwall. They had to be members of the new engineering *élite*. At last, Radleigh let go of her stare and smiled at the tablecloth. "You should have stayed in Deal and waited for the police to come round to see you." He looked up and set his face back into a friendly smile. "It would have saved everyone a lot of time and hardship if you'd stayed around to bribe them on the spot. Wednesday was a long time ago."

Jennifer uncrossed her legs and sat forward in the chair so he could no longer see her thighs—not that he seemed to have been looking at them. She tried again. "I should add that this isn't a police matter. I have reason to believe that my parents were taken by the State Security Bureau."

She'd expected him to jump up and try for the exit. She'd been practising the look of polite implacability with which he'd be fixed in his place. Instead, he looked as if he was covering a smile. "The SSB?" he said eventually in a flat voice. He brushed crumbs from the sleeve of his dark suit. "I won't ask for your evidence. I'll just take your claim as true." He dropped his voice very low. "This being so, I fail to see what more is to be said. Your father was mixed up in an illegal trade with the Outsiders. We all have to make a living, and, since there's no demand for his books any more, I suppose his classical languages made him the perfect middleman. But your father gambled, and has lost. You should be glad that he won for so long. Most people won nothing at all from The Break." He threw his napkin aside and looked about to call for the waiter.

Jennifer swallowed and made a big effort to stop her voice from shaking. "Don't try walking away, Basil," she said quickly. "If Daddy was gambling, you put up the stake money. Let's not pretend that Daddy's business was confined to selling a few bits and pieces to the Outsiders. I was given a letter in France that drops you in everything up to your neck." She sat back in the chair and tried another flash of her legs. She had wondered, in the John Lewis changing room, about a cigarette holder. What had put her off in the end was ignorance of where in London to buy proper cigarettes—oh, and the fact that her one experiment with the cigarette she'd begged off Count Robert hadn't been a success.

But Radleigh was no longer even pretending interest in her legs. He looked into her eyes and brought out a mocking laugh. "So that's your plan, is it?" he sneered. "You come here dressed like a cheap little tart. When that doesn't excite my amorous propensities, you try blackmail." He laughed again and waved aside the photocopied sheet Jennifer had produced from her bag. "Don't push that under my nose. I can't read Latin, and I don't care what it says. But listen to this, my dear." He pushed his face close to hers. "I don't remember whether William of Normandy could—or, rather, *can*—write his own name. But, if the original of that 'document' was in his own hand, and mentioned me a dozen times, I could still brush it aside with an accusation of forgery—and an army of experts wouldn't be able to prove otherwise." He sat back and smiled more easily. "One thing you probably do know about me," he took up again, "is that I'm the sort of man who still gets due process in this country. Don't think you can come here and put the frighteners on me."

Desperately, she tried again. "I want my parents back," she said in a voice that she couldn't keep from shaking. "Do I have to sleep with you to make you act?"

He sat back and laughed. One of the young engineers looked round and stared at them. Radleigh saw this, and fell silent again. Then: "My dear Jennifer, if I were the kind of man you plainly think I am, my answer to that would be that you had to sleep with me to find out!" With a languid move, he refilled both teacups and smiled.

Jennifer felt a tear break free from her eye and roll onto her cheek. Another moment, and she'd have to reach for a handkerchief. If Radleigh did stand up to go, she'd never get out of her own chair. She fought with failing strength to keep control. Even as her vision blurred, she looked into Radleigh's face. Though dreadful, it seemed to keep her from dropping into the void that had opened deep within her. But, when Radleigh did move, it was only to shove his right thumb into one of the teacakes and break it to pieces with savage ill-humour. He looked for a moment into its wreckage, then reached into his jacket for a gold cigarette case. He opened it and offered it across the table. "They're only Lambert & Butler," he said with a return to smooth charm. "But you can't be too fussy nowadays." He smiled at Jennifer's refusal and lit one for himself. "Go away!" he snapped at the waiter who came fussing straight over. He looked up at the ceiling and breathed out a stream of grey smoke. He looked back at Jennifer and went through the motions of relaxing. "Very well, my dear," he said at last. "Since you've been there, you might at least tell me what it's like across the Channel. Is everyone really dying of typhus, as the news reports claim?"

As if hearing someone else, Jennifer found herself speaking of the dense forests, or the clearings planted with crops, of the dirt and universal poverty—and also of the cheerful monasteries dotted along the broken road left by the Romans that led deeper and deeper inland. She spoke of the ceremonious politeness and honesty of even the common people, and of the endless music and dancing on holy days, and of the eager welcome that she and her father had always had since his first contact with Count Robert and his friends. She ran on and on, in no particular order. Then—"So you will help Mummy and Daddy?" she asked, no longer trying to keep her voice from shaking.

"Your father's an idiot," he sniffed. "The worst I can say about him is that he probably knows the full nature of what he's got himself into. If it were him alone, I'd already be across the road with you in Charing Cross, to arrange your return to Deal. You should never have left it." He paused and looked steadily at her spoiled makeup—perhaps this hadn't been quite as elegant as she'd thought it. He sighed and changed tone. "However, your mother is a most remarkable woman—too good for Richard. If I will now do whatever I can to get them back from the SSB, I want you never to forget that it's for your mother alone—oh, and of course for you, my dear," he added with an enthusiasm even she could see was contrived.

Radleigh took a long puff on his cigarette and looked happily about the room. One of the waiters mistook his glance and had to be waved away. "When we walk out of this room," he said, not moving his lips, "you'll hold onto my arm and smile." He frowned and sat upright. "I'll do what I can. There's someone I know who has a contact. It will mean calling in some very big favours. I don't promise anything, mind you—this is the SSB, not the police." He raised his voice back to its normal volume. "You'll have to pardon me for one of those calls that Nature makes with pressing urgency on men of my age," he said, trying for the air of a jolly uncle. "I suppose you know the ladies is also up the iron staircase?" he whispered.

CHAPTER ELEVEN

S tepping out into Whitehall Place, Radleigh made sure to give the doorman a silver penny. "Some people, I'm sure you'll agree, deserve more than rubbishy paper." He looked up and down the wide pavement, before leading Jennifer to the kerb.

Behind them, one of the dozen or so geriatrics who'd been brought out into the sun was talking in broken sobs about a house in Edmonton. Apparently, his wife was waiting there for him to get back from the office. He was silenced by a Catholic nun, who leaned over him with a bowl of soup. Jennifer had sometimes wondered about the fate of the old in modern England. The news reports had alluded to the closure of all the care homes and their replacement by "care in the community." It made sense that those of the incapable old who'd made it through The Hunger were being looked after by the churches.

"Come and see me tonight in my flat," Radleigh said. "I'm sure you can remember the way. For now, I'll have you taken past Trafalgar Square. The beggars who are tolerated there can be most pressing."

He was again looking about, when what may have been the car Jennifer had seen the previous morning purred round the corner and came to a stop. One of the rear doors opened. It *was* the same car. And it was the same young man. "You're late!" he said with haughty impatience. "I've been sent to get you." He pulled himself out of the car and noticed Jennifer. His eyes widened. "Nice one, Basil!" he said with a change of tone. "I didn't know you were into cradle snatching." He laughed and gave her a leering inspection that started at her white high-heeled shoes and finished at her probably beautiful hat. No doubt, he was less interested in what she was wearing than in what she might look like out of it. He took out a creased handkerchief and tried to wipe dandruff from the lapel of his jacket.

"My dear Wapping," Radleigh said, charm competing with a certain stiffness, "I was unexpectedly delayed. But there really was no need for you to come over." He gave up altogether on the charm, and frowned. "I thought we had all agreed on confidentiality. I don't regard official cars outside my club as within the spirit of our agreement."

His frown deepened to an impatient scowl. Wapping shrugged and poked out his tongue at one of the dead CCTV cameras. Radleigh turned back to Jennifer. "I do regret," he said, speaking very soft, "that the joy of your acquaintance had quite abolished all thoughts of other business." He looked at Wapping, who'd been listening. He spoke up, as if wanting to be generally heard. "You must come and see me this evening in my flat." He paused for a stare of theatrical lust into the top of her blouse. "Do come at midnight."

"You're supposed to be in Tenterden tonight," Wapping said, haughty again. He looked at his watch. "So it's just your belly you'll be feeding tonight!" He sniggered and gave Jennifer another long stare of his own. "But I suppose I could stand in for you." He wrapped his handkerchief about his left forefinger and began cleaning black dirt from his nostrils.

A baffled look on his face, Radleigh stared at one of the more decayed geriatrics. She'd put both hands over her face, and was crying inconsolably. Jennifer noticed that her ring finger was missing and her ear lobes were torn to shreds. "Yes, I *am* busy tonight," he sighed. "So come to me tomorrow at midnight." Wapping stepped forward and opened one of the car doors. He motioned Radleigh to get in with him. Radleigh didn't move. He was watching two men with brooms hurry forward from the direction of Northumberland Avenue. "But you can't possibly be thinking to cross that road by yourself," he cried with an enthusiasm he didn't remotely show. He waved at the carpet of steaming filth that lay between both kerbs. London had more motorised traffic than Jennifer had seen since before The Break. But it also contained a growing volume of animal traffic, and this made crossing the road a problem for anyone with shoes to spoil.

With a forced laugh, Radleigh clapped his hands together. The two men broke into a trot. "Ah, my good men! Do help this young lady across the road. Indeed, do take her beyond Trafalgar Square." He fished out a bundle of notes and began counting them for the appropriate fee. The larger of the two men leaned forward to show more of his hump. Judging from his the tatters of his suit, he'd once been fat. His fall from whatever eminence he'd enjoyed before The Break hadn't been kind. Upstairs in the club, Radleigh had said this was a world with many more losers than winners. Here was another of the losers. The humpy man made an obsequious bow.

Radleigh's telephone broke suddenly into the opening bars of Beethoven's *Fifth Symphony*. He peered at the display and gritted his teeth. Wapping went into a smirk of vindication. "I told you the Boss would be angry. You'll be for it now." He looked significantly at the car. He shook his head. The driver would be able to hear any conversation. A few seconds of faint but angry buzzing, and Radleigh was muttering away under cover of the club entrance. The humpy man coughed politely and bowed low to Jennifer. The other man looked steadily at his bare feet.

Wapping ended the stillness with a predatory laugh. He stepped forward and took hold of the humpy man's hair. "Don't I know you?" He pulled the man's face up and looked at it in the orange sunlight. "Of course I know you. I know you both. Fancy seeing you still alive—and here, of all places!" He laughed, and, with a sideways glance at Jennifer, spread his arms wide. Avoiding his face, she noticed what looked like a silver spot on the inside of his lower left forearm. It was about the size of one of the redundant fivepenny coins. Or it might have been a button that had come loose from somewhere in his clothing, and was stuck to his greasy skin. But she looked harder. Wasn't it something *underneath* his skin? What she'd assumed was a reflection of the sunlight seemed instead to be a bright, internal glow. She couldn't tell. It showed only briefly, until he realised it was showing, and pulled his sleeve back into place. The two sweepers looked at each other, before bowing low again.

But Wapping wasn't finished. "Look at this, you little slag." He pushed against the humpy man, forcing him to stand upright. "Look how we've made jobs for everyone. Even lobbyists and general time wasters now get the chance to do honest work." He laughed louder, and, perhaps still worried about his silver spot, pulled the sleeves of his jacket over frayed and dirty shirt cuffs. He jabbed the humpy man in the chest. His colleague drew his lips open in a smile that revealed a line of broken teeth. Both looked at Radleigh, who was absorbed in a quiet though detailed conversation. Wapping put a clammy hand on Jennifer's face and pulled it round for a better view. "Look how grand I am!" his own pale, unshaven face almost screamed at her. He stood back and looked again at her thighs, and then up a few inches. His lips quivered, and he turned again to the sweepers.

"I suppose you've finally shut up about 'market-based solution,'" he jeered at the humpy man. "You can be sure I never believed in them—no, not when Madsen himself paid my salary." He bared his teeth and struck a pose on the kerb. "Free trade, low taxes, civil liberties—how you people wittered on, when you were still let inside that club! Well, it's all in the past now, isn't it? The best you can say is that there *was* a use for the lard you piled up in your freezer against the collapse."

He looked at Jennifer again, to see if she was paying attention. "You know what Abigail tells me? She says everything you people ever believed in boiled down to selfish atomism. Self, self, self— that's all it ever was." There was a cry of pain from one of the geriatrics, and the splash of an emptied chamber pot. A couple of nuns hurried about the business of cleaning, while another led everyone in a rising sound of prayer.

Ignoring this, Wapping leaned towards Jennifer, and painted onto his face a smile greasier than an RTProt sausage. "I'm Abigail Hooper's secretary." He found a card to give her. "Come and see me at the Home Office when you're free." What he might have said next was silenced by the siren that heralded the late afternoon power cut. While he moved back to avoid fouling his shoes in a patch of urine that had spread over the pavement from another overflowing chamber pot, she allowed herself a look at the card. *Frank Wapping*, it said—*Private and Personal Secretary to*

Abigail Hooper. It had a mobile telephone number. Though this was crossed out in pencil, it also had an e-mail address.

Jennifer knew that Radleigh was well-connected. She'd never thought he knew the Home Secretary, the most ferocious and energetic mover in the National Government. She it was who'd restored order after the first few weeks of spreading chaos that had followed The Break. She it was who'd turned what armed forces weren't committed to the Azerbaijani War on the demonstrators, and who remained a nightly and feared presence on the television news. She looked into Wapping's grinning face. "I'm a man who's going places," he said. "Come with me if you want to see them."

"I think that will do, Wapping," Radleigh's telephone call was ended. With an impatient wave, he directed the sweepers about their business. He watched as, with more force than skill, they cleared a path across the road. For some reason, the stump of the nearest sawn-off street lamp had still been clicking softly. It went off with the expiry of the five minute power cut warning. He looked at his watch. "Yes, I know she's waiting!" he snapped at Wapping, whose face was turning nasty with impatience. He smiled again, and took Jennifer by the arm, and escorted her across the glistening asphalt.

"One final word, my dearest young woman," he breathed in her ear as they embraced on the other side of the road. "You're wearing the wrong shade of lipstick for your hat. Oh—and I do suggest that mascara shouldn't be applied with a paintbrush." He nodded at the humpy man, before making for the car.

Jennifer watched it start again and, with hardly a sound, move with slow grace towards the junction with Whitehall. Before she could move, she felt a tight grip on each of her arms. "If you know what's good for you," one of the men whispered, "you won't make any fuss."

CHAPTER TWELVE

Tarquin twisted round from his place beside the driver and arranged his face into one of his deader smiles. "Everything is under control," he said. Sat bolt upright, Simeon might as well not have heard the assurance. Michael nodded vaguely and went back to looking through the tinted rear window. The glass muted the defiant chanting of the crowd that pressed so closely about the vehicle that the driver had stopped. But he looked at the brown, bearded faces, most of them shining with an exaltation he'd seen more often then he wanted. Generally, these people wore the same close-fitting clothes as everyone else in this country. Enough of them, however, wore the loose robes of their own civilisation. He looked up at the banners that fluttered above the crowd. None of them seemed to be in Arabic, though the script was plainly related to Arabic. But, as the crowd thinned for a moment, he caught sight of a larger banner, covered in English. If the long inscription itself made no sense to him, it seemed to contain transliterations of the Arabic words for holy war and Empire of the Faith.

Simeon leaned closer to his nephew. "What is going on?" He nodded at the jostling crowd. "What are these people doing here?" Good question, Michael thought—though less important than the one that still claimed his attention. Tarquin had collected them just after breakfast. After what may have been a random progress through the wide and endless streets of London, he'd stopped looking nervously out of the windows and taken them to a museum that was shocking in more than its size. In silence, he'd led them through gallery after gallery. His long fingers had fluttered over the contours of smashed statuary of naked gods and heroes, and he'd pulled embarrassing faces at Michael. "You watch yourself, my boy," Simeon had whispered as Tarquin stroked the buttocks of a work they both knew from the original set up on the central spine

68

of the Hippodrome. "This man is a slave to the abominable vice of the ancients." But this wasn't what had so troubled them. Tarquin had finally stopped before what had to be the original of the east pediment of the Church of the Virgin in Athens. "How could they have got hold of this?" Simeon had groaned into Michael's ear. "And why is it so damaged?"

Michael hadn't answered this question aloud. Unlike the presence in London of an Islamic mob, it was a question easily answered— so long, that is, as you overlooked all the known laws of nature. "Once you eliminate the impossible," old Psellus had told him many times in class, "whatever remains, no matter how improbable, must be the truth." More than once, Michael had taken himself through every step in the reasoning—and it always directed him to one bizarre and unthinkable conclusion. How to put this to his uncle? Or had he got there too?

"Is that *Khilafah, Khilafah!* These people are shouting?" Simeon asked. Michael pulled himself into the present and nodded. He patted the old man's shoulder and cast about for soothing words. In Baghdad, Simeon had been at his considerable best. He'd cut straight through the wild confusion of the higher classes, and seeded everyone with just the right degree of misinformation to call off the projected attack on the Empire. Here, he was as lost as any of the barbarian envoys who were given the run around in Constantinople. That museum had completed his unnerving. Now, he sat beside Michael, twitching every so often as he fought to control himself. Perhaps Michael should ignore Tarquin's presence, a couple of feet in front of them, and just open the whole matter. What to do?

There was a sudden shift in the crowd, and bodies pressed harder against the vehicle, causing it to shake. Begun by a few men immediately outside, the shouted call was spreading through the crowd. Almost without warning, thousands of voices resolved themselves into the single chant—"*Khilafah! Khilafah!*" they chanted. This was one of those times, Michael knew, when people of sense took to their heels. Instead, they were stuck fast. How secure was this vehicle? As if in answer, the driver opened a cupboard beside his steering wheel and took out what was probably a weapon of some kind. With a loud click, he pulled it into readiness and put in full view of anyone who might be inclined to look through the window. One man did look. The wild stare went immediately from his face, and he pressed himself back into the shouting crowd.

With a loud purring, Tarquin's communication machine lit up. He pulled its leather flap open and began a low and nervous conversation with someone. The vehicle shook again, and his voice rose to a terrified squawk before he looked again at Michael and brought himself under control. "It may be necessary for the pair of you to get onto the floor," he said with a failed effort to seem in control of things. He swallowed and licked dry lips. As he began another of his conversations, there was the clatter overhead of one of the flying machines that Michael had seen at regular intervals. This one was flying very low—barely over the heads of the crowd. There was a deafening and repeated warning that reminded him of what he'd heard in the waters off Dover. The response from the crowd was a unified roar of defiance, and then more chanting of that Arabic word. Just beside the window, a young bearded man with a head dress painted red in the unreadable script threw his arms up and went into an enthusiastic screaming fit. Two other men began whirling round and round as if, high on cannabis, they were about to throw themselves into battle against a Christian army.

Now, the clattering overhead was joined by a rhythmical drumming sound that came in bursts. The car shook again, and the roar of the crowd changed without warning to a great collective wail of terror. "Get down!" Tarquin screamed. He and the driver pressed themselves against the floor of the vehicle and covered their heads. "Get down!" he repeated. "For God's sake, get on the floor!" Helping his uncle down, Michael heard the terror outside turn to panic. The bursts of drumming from overhead came closer, and went on and on, and their sound wasn't covered even by the frantic screaming of the crowd. The vehicle shook from the gathering stampede. A few times, its metal casing rang as if struck by a stone.

And then, as quickly as it had started, the commotion was over. Without waiting for permission, Michael got off the floor and looked through the front window at a carpet of the dead or dying that covered the road all the way to its far junction. The driver was already back in his seat and turning the key that would bring the vehicle back to life. With a continual and sickening bump of wheels over the bodies of the fallen, they crept forward. Another minute, and Michael saw a few dozen men on horseback coming slowly towards them. He could hear the muffled sound of hooves on the soft stone of the road, and the approving shout whenever one of the men leaned over to club one of the blood-covered fallen into stillness. He thought they'd challenge the driver. Instead, they parted at the last moment and let the vehicle pass through. As they approached the junction, the way ahead cleared. With a cry of relief, the driver pressed one of his pedals and the vehicle shot forward.

Tarquin reached into his pocket for a paper box. "I shouldn't think too much about what you've just seen," he said, trying for an easy drawl. "City mobs, I'm sure you'll agree, can be dangerous things." He flicked the box open, biting his lip when he found it was empty. "We should soon have you back to your lodgings." He turned and spoke to the driver, who said nothing. They reached another big junction and turned right. They were back in one of the quieter parts of London. The road itself was clear, though the pavements were filled with crowds that stopped and looked in silence at the vehicle.

They turned into a narrower street lined with the glass windows of the London shops. Tarquin spoke again to the driver, who this time answered, and slowed to a stop. "I need to go outside for some business," Tarquin explained to Simeon. "I shan't be long." The old man nodded blankly. Tarquin opened his door and looked up and down the silent street. With a soft thump, he pushed the door shut behind him. The driver pressed a button on his own door, and there was the usual clicking sound of locks being engaged. Tarquin darted inside one of the few shops that were open. He came out with another small box. From this he took a white tube and put it between his lips. He took something else from inside his jacket and, with shaking hands, set light to the tube. Sucking furiously on the burning tube, and breathing out the smoke, he walked up and down the street, deep in yet another of his maniac conversations.

"These people shouldn't be here," Simeon said, coming out of his virtual trance. "Every notice we could find spoke of Britain as a country of western Christians."

The driver turned round. "Too right, My Lords!" he rasped in a sort of Greek. "The sooner this scum is packed off—every man, woman and child of them—to Ireland, the better it will be for all of us." It was Greek, and it was a more obviously native Greek than Tarquin spoke. Even this short statement, though, had come out in an almost impenetrable accent, and was more radically degraded than the language of the most common people back home.

"Who are you?" Michael asked. The driver looked quickly out at Tarquin. With a gesture half baffled, half vicious, he'd thrown his burning tube onto the pavement and started on another. He ignored everyone inside the vehicle, and was taken up with shouting into his machine. The driver looked forward out of his window, and spoke in the voice of a man who is trying not to move his lips.

"They let me in on this job because I've got an English name," he said. "This may be the only chance I have to speak with you. Listen—we know who you are and what you want. There's not much we can do at the moment. But, when the time is right, there are tens of thousands of us who will do everything possible to get help to the Empire. You must persuade these people to help. It'll take a hundred men with the right weapons to see off the Turks. They've got to be nipped in the bud."

"Where are you from?" Simeon asked, pulling himself together.

The driver laughed softly. "My mother's people are from Cyprus. The Turks came in and took everything. Now, the Government here is doing its best to let it happen all over again."

"But there is no Turkish navy," Simeon blurted out. "They can't raid Cyprus or any other island. And how have they sent ambassadors here?"

Michael put a warning hand on his uncle's knee. "What year is this?" he asked.

"It's 2018 after the birth of Christ," the driver said after a brief pause. "And the Government will murder anyone who tries to say otherwise. But use the right pressure at your end, and there's many of us—not just Greeks—who'll turn things round. If you need help, get yourselves to the Church of All the Saints in Camden. The priest there hasn't been bought like all the others."

That was all he managed to say. Tarquin pulled his door open and climbed back into the vehicle. Smelling of the aromatic drug he'd been smoking, he looked round with another of his smooth smiles. "I've arranged a change of plan. We're going off now for a meeting with His Majesty's chief minister." In the central mirror of the vehicle that was used for looking behind, Michael saw the driver's face tighten. But he waited for Tarquin to give an instruction in English before turning on the throbbing machine that moved them about.

"All things are of God," Simeon whispered uncertainly. He might have continued, but he now sat up and leaned over to Michael. He took the suddenly bloodless and trembling hand in his own. "Again?" he asked with soft concern. Michael was just able to nod when all his muscles went rigid. But, just as he could feel the familiar blackness rising through the lower depths of his mind— rather like the hold of a sinking ship fills with water—it was over. He sat up and managed a scared smile at his uncle. If his last visitation of the sickness hadn't gone into a seizure, this wasn't even that. Except for what they both knew had happened with him the previous year, this could have been put down to a dizzy spell— brought on, perhaps, by the shock of being caught in the riot.

Tarquin turned round to speak. But his voice was cut off by a long roar as of thunder. It came from what may have been far off, and was followed by the sort of vibration that, in Constantinople, heralded an earthquake. Tarquin's response was a long and thoughtful glance at the body shape revealed by Michael's clothing and a comment about the weather. As the vehicle turned back into one of the crowded main streets, there was more clattering overhead of flying machines. Michael wondered if all of this might be related. He rather thought it was, but leaned back in his seat and looked up at the neat two inch hole punched in the ceiling by one of those death-dealing weapons. How it hadn't gone through him before making another hole in the floor might count as a miracle if he were in the mood for supernatural explanations.

CHAPTER THIRTEEN

"Confused? Alarmed?" Michael answered. "I see no reason for either." He stared impassively at Tarquin, who had finally commented on his slight pallor. He turned away and looked into one of the big mirrors in the entrance hall of where they were lodging. He put every thought from his mind and focussed on the two correctly-dressed ambassadors looking out from the mirror. This much reassured him. Even Simeon looked happier now they were both out of the orange clothes they'd been wearing since their arrest in Dover. Needless to say, Tarquin had insisted on helping Michael into his own robes. He'd then started what was intended to be a light conversation about what the youth of the Empire wore when they took exercise.

From here to the office of the man who governed England on behalf of its king was a drive of perhaps half a mile along a wide processional avenue. They stopped at a narrow turning secured by a gate. Behind this lay a row of buildings. The guard outside the black entrance to one of these saluted as they got out of the vehicle. Almost at once, the polished door opened from the inside, and the two ambassadors walked into a hall, from where, lined with pictures along its wall, a staircase led up. They were taken along a broad, windowless corridor decorated, as seemed to be the rule in this country, in the style of an ancient palace. They stopped beside a door covered with elaborate carvings also in the ancient style.

Tarquin leaned forward to Michael. "His Majesty's chief minister speaks with full authority," he whispered. "But don't be worried by anything he says. I'll see to it that everything goes right." He smirked and turned to knock softly on the door, somehow managing to brush one of his thighs against Michael. The door was opened by a blonde girl, who stood aside for them to enter. Inside the magnificent room—also without windows—a man, dressed smartly in black, sat at the head of a long table. He was dictating to a secretary. Falling silent, he got up and twisted his closed and podgy face into a smile.

"On behalf of His Britannic Majesty," the Prime Minister said through Tarquin, "please accept my warmest greetings to our country, and every felicitation to the Great Augustus whom you represent." Simeon presented his stained letter from the Emperor, and nodded graciously as he was led across the office to a seat at right angles to where the Prime Minister sat.

"Please, my dear young boy," Tarquin said, waving Michael to sit beside his uncle. Michael sat down behind the table and unscrewed the metal cap from the bottle of water that had been placed before him. He filled his uncle's glass cup with the sparkling contents and then his own. Keeping his face neutral, he looked across at the Prime Minister. It was hard to tell age among these people. But, in spite of the perfect teeth, this man must have been in early middle age. Though dressed in the same manner as his secretaries, he radiated power. He got up and, with his own hands, took the pen that had been given to Michael and showed how, by depressing a button at one end, it could be made to write on the neat block of paper supplied with it. He straightaway spoiled the effect by not bothering to hide his glance at the clock set into the bracelet on his left wrist. Plainly, he assumed that he was receiving a couple of men who were too intimidated by what they'd seen to have understood any of it. He smiled again and spoke softly to Tarquin. What he said was too rapid for Michael to catch any of the individual words. Sooner or later, though, his furtive though relentless study of that English Bible would bring some tangible benefit.

"You will, My Lords, pardon me," Tarquin said briskly, "if I do not for the moment interpret. It will be faster if I speak for myself, though with full authority." Simeon nodded, his face pale and slightly sweaty. Michael took up his pen and clicked it into working order, and made a preliminary note at the head of the top sheet of paper.

"Let me begin," Tarquin opened in the tone of a man who is used to lecturing, "by saying that we have full knowledge of your Empire's situation." He pointed a small box at the fireplace and pressed one of its buttons. There was an immediate and gentle whine, and the fireplace was obscured by a white screen that glowed all over. Simeon blinked with surprise. Michael contented himself by adding a flourish of blue ink at the end of his first sentence. Unlike his uncle, he'd long since decided to show no surprise at anything he saw. Unlike his uncle, he was losing any sense of surprise at the machines these people had at their control.

Tarquin pointed up at one of the lights that had started flickering again and spoke what sounded like an apology. The Prime Minister answered in a reassuring tone, but looked again at his wrist. Tarquin pressed another button, and the screen was covered all over with an image of many colours that could only be a map. It was a map of a kind Michael never seen before, and it might have been of anywhere if he hadn't already guessed that it was centred on Mediterranean. Without asking permission, he got up and went over to look at the contours and at the small captions. Yes, it was as he'd guessed. He could see a red point that was marked Constantinople in Roman characters. Once he'd made sense of how the land and waters were distinguished, and of the odd distortions that, he had no doubt, showed greater accuracy of drafting than he'd yet seen, it was easy enough to find Rome and Alexandria and Ravenna and all the other places of his own world. It helped that the captions were in Latin rather than English.

Tarquin waited until Michael had gone back to his seat, then continued in his smooth and perfect Greek. "This is a map of the Empire as it was around four hundred years after the birth of Christ. You will see that the Empire contains within itself the whole Mediterranean, and reaches from Gibraltar to the Crimea, from York in this country, all the way to the Euphrates. Observe how the Empire is divided into East and West areas—one ruled from Rome and one from Constantinople. I will not insult your historical knowledge by explaining how the two Emperors were jointly and severally sovereigns over the whole Empire."

He pressed his button again, and the map was replaced by another in which different lines and colours were superimposed over the same area. "Here is the Empire as it was about a century later. You can see that the Western half has disappeared, to be replaced by various barbarian kingdoms. The Eastern half continues without any loss of territory. I will not show a later map that describes the reconquest of Italy and Africa and parts of Spain that was carried out by the generals of the Great Justinian. We know that this was a temporary revival, and that much of the Eastern Empire itself was, within a generation, conquered by the Persians. Nor will I show this, as the Persians were soon utterly destroyed by your Emperor Heraclius, and the Eastern Empire was restored." He smiled sadly and pressed his button again. "But here is a map showing the Empire as it was about eight hundred years after the birth of Christ. You will see that the driving out of the Persians was almost immediately followed by the unexpected flood of Arab conquests that stripped you of Egypt and Syria and Africa and various other territories. You will also see how Greece itself and much of Italy were lost to various tribes of barbarians." Yet again, he pressed his button, now showing the Empire as Michael knew it. "The Arabs, of course, together with the western barbarians, soon fell into a decadence of which your more recent emperors took advantage, and the Empire now includes its core territories of Asia Minor and Greece, together with northern Syria and much of southern Italy. With the conquest of the Bulgarian Kingdom, it has also re-established its northern frontier in Europe at the Danube."

Tarquin paused for a long moment. "I know it is your intention to tell us that the Empire is wealthy and powerful, and that its friendship is eminently to be sought by any Christian ruler. But our knowledge of your circumstances is greater in many respects than your own. The Turkish victory over the Arabs has raised up a new and aggressive power on your southern and eastern frontiers in Asia. To this must be added the emergence on your Italian frontier of large and powerful states ruled by the Normans.

"Either of these new threats would be a problem for you. Together, they have put you into a strategic vice that is tightening by the year. It doesn't help that that your internal affairs are falling rapidly into disorder. The victory in Constantinople of an aristocratic faction has led to the scrapping of most of your navy and the virtual abolition of your armies in favour of an unwise reliance on mercenaries." Though Simeon's face had remained as grave and still throughout this lecture as that of an ancient statue, Michael could feel the confused tension in the old man's body. Doubtless, Tarquin knew as much of the Empire's general situation as of its language. But it was almost as if he had somehow been listening to the anxious discussions and rehearsals that had filled the hours when they were alone in their lodgings. Michael tried to think of a question or comment that would let them recover their poise. But Tarquin was smiling again, ready to continue implacably to an end that was only whispered about in the Imperial Council.

"Within a dozen years at most," he went on, "we know that the Turks will move properly against you. The diplomatic settlement that we understand the pair of you made in Baghdad will not hold. The Turks will move against you with their undivided weight. Such as they are, your own armies will crumple, and you will lose virtually the whole of Asia Minor, leaving you with a strip of territory ten or twenty miles inland from the coast. The Empire will then comprise this strip of Asia, Constantinople itself, a large part of Greece, and some islands of greater or lesser significance. Your remaining Italian territories you will lose to the Normans. You will then think it a good idea to come west, asking the so far despised barbarians for help. This will be given—but you will find that the Latins are no longer stupid barbarians. Even without taking us into account, the westerners are organised into warlike kingdoms that will help you only so far as it promotes their own interest. You will then find yourself inescapably forced to choose between making the Empire a satellite of Latin states that will protect you so long as you accept their schismatic version of the Christian Faith, and letting the Empire be absorbed by an Islamic Turkish empire that will leave you untouched in the profession of your Orthodox Faith."

He grinned. "It doesn't look very good, does it? I suppose, when you heard of us and our miraculous powers, you thought the Almighty had answered your prayers and saved you from the need to make this choice. So your Great Augustus called for his most senior and trusted envoy and sent him straight off to 'invite' our assistance."

Tarquin's mouth was still open, and his next words were forming, when there was a peremptory knock, and the door flew open.

CHAPTER FOURTEEN

P en still in hand, Michael turned and looked at a woman dressed, according to the British custom, in mannish clothes. She walked confidently into the room and stared at the two envoys. She frowned and asked a question of the Prime Minister, whose answer was a laugh and a shifty look. She snorted and turned back to the envoys. At first, what took Michael's attention was the oddly shaped pendant that showed briefly within her buttoned jacket when she turned. Deep within its jewelled centre, it was glowing with a pattern of colours he didn't recall having seen before. With a start, he feared it was bringing back the nausea he'd fought off in the vehicle, and he made himself look at her face. But she'd now given up on her brief and contemptuous inspection, and was looking at the Prime Minister. They began an argument of great bitterness.

Michael forced his mind into order and tried to make sense of the rapid conversation. At first, the Prime Minister spoke back in an emollient tone that made it possible to suspect he wasn't the main power in the country. Indeed, this must surely be the woman he'd often seen on the illuminated panel in their lodgings. She always came on in the evening, and spoke with stern authority, surrounded by deferential men in uniform. As their voices rose, however, and they shouted back at each other, continually using the English word for "agreement," it became clearer that the Prime Minister was the senior party. Was the woman the King's wife, perhaps? Michael put this out of mind. He'd already seen enough women in positions of authority. His main impression was that she was another minister, and that there was some lack of agreement at the top. Her name seemed to be Abigail. He might have misheard a word in English that meant something else. But its tone and repetition indicated that he was up to determining the names of these people.

The woman rested her hands on the table and leaned close to the Prime Minister, as she repeated the same phrase twice. *"Too soon to look outside—not yet,"* she said with slow and helpful clarity. They stopped, and a look of understanding flashed suddenly between them. The woman glanced over at Simeon and Michael. The Prime Minister shook his head. They both looked at Tarquin. Together, they shouted a two syllable command that required no skill with languages to understand. He was followed from the room by the blonde woman and the other secretaries.

Once the door was closed, they started arguing again. The woman spoke angrily about something that got increasingly sceptical and even dismissive answers from the Prime Minister. They were soon shouting at each other. The woman finally leaned menacingly over the Prime Minister, and, though speaking slow again, used words he still couldn't make out. The Prime Minister's response was an evasive look at one of the pictures on the wall behind her. Then, he leaned back in his chair and laughed at her. He used what must have been the word Constantinople, and then Baghdad. He got half out of his chair and leaned across the table to get at Tarquin's satchel. Various sheets of paper fell out. Sorting through them, the Prime Minister took one of the sheets and pushed it at the woman. She picked it up and skimmed the opening paragraph. With a disgusted snort, she screwed it into a ball and threw it at the Prime Minister. He watched it land on his desk, and laughed again, flicking the ball back at her. It struck her on the chest and fell inside her jacket. As she reached to pull it out, she looked at her pendant. It was still flashing urgently. She stopped in mid-movement, her face taking on a look of shock and of wonder. No longer interested in the Prime Minister, she held her pendant up, and Michael saw its riot of inner colours shine on her painted face.

The Prime Minister asked a question. She paid no attention, but glanced about the room. Still ignoring the Prime Minister, she walked across to Simeon. With a soft motion of his chair on the carpet, he was up and bowing his respects. She touched him with her pendant and waited. She put a smile onto her face and motioned him to be seated. The woman stood behind Michael. He felt something touch the back of his head, and could smell her perfume and hear breathing that came in astonished gasps. She rapped a question at the Prime Minister, whose answer contained the word Tarquin. Michael might have tried to understand what was said. But, if still deep within him, he could feel waves of nausea that stopped him from doing more than writing the probable name of the Prime Minister in Greek transliteration—James Duffy, it might have been. Forcing himself to dwell on the name, he wondered if that was the pronunciation of the Apostle's name he'd seen in English. If so, it would be another step to understanding the loose relationship in this language between words and their spelling. There was the same lack of correspondence in Greek, he told himself. Similar facts often have similar causes. If so, English would be an old language, in which the rules of spelling had emerged when the pronunciation was different. This carried him to his earlier speculations, and the continuing but faint nausea went from his mind.

They brought Tarquin back into the room. He sat on the chair they'd readied for him, looking nervously from face to face, as he went into detail about Michael, with much mentioning of Constantinople. He fawned and simpered, before trailing off in a stammer that indicated more was expected of him, but that he couldn't think what or why. There was no pretence of dignity this time when he was sent again from the room.

Now in calmer tones, the woman and the Prime Minister began another conversation. She looked several times at Michael. She even smiled at him. He got up and bowed politely. But she was talking again with the Prime Minister. No longer arguing at all, they laughed at something, and said something more about the person called American. The Prime Minister nodded eagerly, and used her own name several times. There could be no doubt that her name was Abigail. With every smooth use of it, she answered back in a tone of rising excitement. At last, she gave Michael another thoughtful look, before tucking her pendant out of sight. Then she walked quietly from the room. Another few moments, and Tarquin was back.

He pulled his face into his usual expression as he listened to a low mumble from the Prime Minister. "The King's chief minister apologises for this interruption," he said smoothly, "and wishes to reiterate his Majesty's fullest and most unambiguous welcome to our shores. He also impresses on you that whatever is agreed in this room is the settled will of our government." Simeon coughed and sipped at his water. Michael looked at his head note, focussing briefly on the date he'd given it. He heard a slow comment from the Prime Minister, and Tarquin went back to the fireplace and played again with his black box.

Simeon wiped sweat from his forehead and steadied his shaking left hand by pressing it onto the dark wood of the table. Michael kept his head down and continued playing with his minute of the lecture. Simeon cleared his throat. "How you know these things is of no present importance," he began with surprising firmness. "Your assurances about our future are, equally, of interest, but for later discussion. Perhaps we should come to the main business, and ask what material assistance you may feel able and inclined to make to keep the forces of Islam from overwhelming the one bastion that has, for many ages, preserved the whole of Christendom. All else aside, if the Empire falls, the Caliph will surely make his way into France."

"An argument that has no terrors for us, My Lord Simeon," Tarquin replied with a cold smile. Bullying an old man was clearly the least he'd have done to restore his own loss of face. He waved at the glowing map and sat down beside the Prime Minister. "The Lord Minister whom I serve has only to sign one sheet of paper," he gloated, "and Baghdad itself will, within a few hours, be made a heap of smoking ruins. I believe you have seen a little of our naval power. I know you have seen how easily we can disperse riotous assemblies with our flying machines. You will believe me if I say that we have other machines able to fly at an unimaginable speed to any point on the Earth and pour fire and destruction as they will. The Caliph does not frighten us."

Michael put down his pen. He managed an easy smile. "I will not deny, Master Tarquin, that your kingdom is possessed of great power. But it would interest me to know why this has not so far been announced to the whole world. I might also speak of what I heard in France—of how a Norman raid on your southern coast last year was not repelled for many days, and of how, whatever your capacity for attack, your people are not organised for their own defence. I am told that a city called Hastings preserved itself from total massacre only by acknowledging the Duke of Normandy as King of England. The Duke seems to have acquired some of your weapons, and enough understanding of their use to stand his ground." He paused and waited for Tarquin to put this into English. The Prime Minister's face set like stone, and there was a long silence. Michael ignored the urgent jabbing of his uncle's knee and continued: "More importantly, however, since no meeting at this high level can be without an object, I will ask what you would have of us in return for your help." Tarquin nodded and put this into English. The Prime Minister relaxed and allowed a greasy smile to spread over his face. He turned to a secretary, who gave him two sheets of paper. He looked at these, as if to compare them and passed one over to Tarquin, who pressed another button and called up a new map—this one again of the modern Empire, but with a pattern of blue dots drawn within it and within the territories of some of its neighbours.

Tarquin got up again and went over to the new map. "We offer to guarantee the present frontiers of the Empire against all its enemies," he said briskly. "If you want help in securing the Holy Places of Bethlehem for Christian missionaries, do not expect us even to consider such a request." He jabbed at the blue dots with a pointing stick. "In return for the strictly limited help we offer, you will give us control of Larnaca in Cyprus as a base for our navy. You will also give us control of these places along the southern shore of the Black Sea. These will all be recognised as territories under the sovereignty of our King, and you will give the administrators that we send out your full and unquestioning co-operation in all that they ask." He pressed his button, and what looked like a city as it might appear to a bird came onto the screen. With a shock that drained his face of colour, Michael recognised the dome of the Great Church and the long oval of the Hippodrome. "These dockside areas of Constantinople," Tarquin said, pointing here and there with his stick, "will be remodelled by our own engineers to accommodate our trading ships. Several quarters of the City will need to be evacuated and demolished for the expansion of your docks. You will provide labour and building materials as we direct, and you will manage the gangs of workers with all necessary discipline."

Simeon got unsteadily to his feet and walked across to the picture. He looked at the Prime Minister, whose face carried an expression of cheerful triumph, and then at Tarquin. "What you are demanding," he grated, "amounts to a protectorate over the Empire. Do you suppose any Emperor would consent to this kind of arrangement?"

Tarquin opened his mouth to answer, but smiled instead and began a rapid explanation to the Prime Minister, who made some effort to straighten his face. "My Lord tells me," Tarquin eventually answered, "that you have no choice in the matter. What you will not give us we will simply take. The deal we offer at least preserves the territory of the Empire from conquest by the Turks. And, if the force available to us is absolutely unlimited, it really suits our interests better to take what we want by agreement rather than force."

Michael caught the look on his uncle's face, and stood up. They'd heard enough. It was now a question of arranging for their return to Constantinople. But the Prime Minister waved them back into their places. He spoke at some length in English, not bothering to pause for Tarquin to interpret. Tarquin's response was a narrowing of his eyes and then a sharp reply that bordered on argument. The Prime Minister spoke sharply back. Tarquin tried again—now with great urgency of tone. It was to no effect. The Prime Minister scowled and tapped his fingers impatiently on the table.

"There are further conditions," Tarquin said, not looking into either face. He paused to gather the necessary words. He looked at the Prime Minister's expectant face, then pursed his lips and began again in a low and nervous tone. "We require that you should take swift and effective action to enable that half of all the children in every school supported by the Emperor should be girls. We further require that all barriers to the entry of women into all areas of the Imperial service should be removed, and that those women who may be suitably qualified should be speedily promoted to senior positions." He paused and looked once more at the Prime Minister, who smiled eagerly and nodded. Tarquin sighed and looked up at the ceiling. "You must abolish all laws that constrain the freedom of men to lie with men, and you must allow them to enter into marriages before the appropriate civil authorities. You must emancipate your Jews and other religious and national minorities. Furthermore, you must take effective action to ensure that all domestic and commercial waste within the Empire is gathered, where possible for re-use. And you must sign a treaty with us in which you undertake to limit your production of any kind of air that may cause a change in the weather."

Tarquin gave an embarrassed sniff and sat down. Simeon stared at Michael. Michael looked at his shorthand note, wondering how he could make even grammatical sense of some of these final demands. But it still wasn't finished. The Prime Minister grinned and appeared to mention the names Sappho and Theopompus. Tarquin relaxed and nodded. He looked at Michael. "Our further condition," he said more easily, "is that you should welcome a team of scholars under my personal direction into Constantinople, and that you should there give unconditional access to any library that I name. No book—no matter how old or precious—shall be withheld from our inspection." He stopped and seemed likely to drift into a quiet reverie over what he might find in Constantinople. He didn't bother interpreting the soft and smiling final words of the Prime Minister. Michael helped Simeon to his feet and bowed curtly. "Tell your master that we will make our report to the Emperor as soon as we can," he said. "In the meantime, we shall go back to our lodgings to await our departure from this country."

Tarquin answered for the Prime Minister. "Oh," he said with an airy wave, "I think we can get you home in next to no time." He'd spoken too soon. As he began packing his things away, the Prime Minister spoke in a low tone that sounded shifty even by his standards. Tarquin stiffened, then sighed. He looked at Michael. "You and I will be collected tomorrow morning," he said, "and taken for a meeting with the Minister in charge of internal security. Don't ask me why," he added as they got up to leave.

CHAPTER FIFTEEN

"Are you watching this?" Michael asked. It was an irrelevant question. Since getting back to their lodgings, Simeon had done nothing but watch the moving picture machine. It was currently showing scenes of battle in several shades of grey. It might have counted as useful research to see this people's mode of fighting wars—all explosions and firing of invisible projectiles—if Simeon hadn't now become as addicted to watching the thing whenever it was on as an opium eater to his poppy cake. Michael picked up the little box and pressed the button that controlled the sound. This he turned up, until the room was filled with the sounds of machine-assisted bloodshed.

"I've been thinking," he whispered into his uncle's good ear. "Tarquin's Greek, when we first met, was very good. Since then, it's become almost a copy of your own. This afternoon, he even brought out your deliberate misquote to me of Polybius." He stopped as the screen went silent. Then, as music began to swell louder: "Since these people are able to capture and reproduce sounds, I suspect we are being overheard in all we say."

"What manner of people are these?" the old man groaned.

Michael decided that now was the time to come out with his theory. "Do you remember that sermon before we set out—about how heaven and hell exist in separate universes, and how we can only reach them by miraculous intervention?" That was as far as he got. The noise about them had blotted out the siren call. But it was time for the lights to go out across London, and for every machine to lose its moving force. Michael got up and fiddled with the switch on the portable lamp that had been provided. Before he could speak again, there was a polite knock on the door, and the usual sound of a key in its lock.

He waited for the attendants to clear away the remains of the dinner they'd earlier served, and tore at the wrapping that enclosed a stack of paper. "It's stuff sent over by Tarquin," he said impatiently once they were alone again. He pushed the note in Tarquin's own Greek script under the lamp. "There's been another change of plan. We've been told to get our things ready for a midnight departure from London. Tarquin regrets that a further meeting with the Prime Minister keeps him from assisting us with packing. But he'll be here shortly before we are due to leave." Simeon's lips moved in a prayer of silent thanks. Suddenly, he winced and pulled himself heavily to his feet. Michael got first to the bathroom and turned on the portable lamp in there. Once his uncle had shuffled inside, he shut the door and turned his attention to the transcript of their meeting with the Prime Minister. It was superfluous to wonder how what amounted to a *verbatim* transcript had been made when he was the only person there taking notes. He stared at the neat and flawless Greek that covered half a dozen sheets of paper. The first time he'd seen this machine-written script, it had taken him a while to read it. But the oddities were consistent.

He was comparing this transcript with his own memorandum, when he heard a ragged cry from the bathroom. This was followed by the crash as of many things swept off the washbasin surround.

It was time for Michael to try a few words of English. "*He fell down while emptying his bowels*," he shouted as he ran beside the trolley that carried Simeon from one chaotic and brightly-lit room to another. The men pushing the trolley stopped in the middle of the corridor and one of them shouted something back that he couldn't understand. "*Blood and vomit there was over him*," he added. The man who'd shouted said something more. He took down the glass bottle of liquid that was connected by a flexible tube to Simeon's arm, and shook it violently. He pointed at the dark blotches that had overspread the whole arm and asked what sounded like a question. Michael shook his head and looked up and down the corridor.

Finding his uncle slumped forward on the lavatory had shown

just how thin was the veneer of normality Michael had imposed on his surroundings. He'd called for help. At once, everything had jumbled as incomprehensibly as when they'd been intercepted off Dover. Now, as the trolley began hurrying back in the direction from which it had come, Simeon's eyes opened, and he moved his lips. It was impossible to know what he was saying. Michael found English words to call everyone to stop.

"God and the all-holy Virgin, the Mother of God," Simeon croaked softly in the comparative silence that had fallen, "protect the City and the Christian Empire." Michael bent down and whispered that the old man should save his strength. But Simeon opened his eyes wider. Speaking as if to everyone about him, he raised his voice. "Those who call upon God in truth are not entirely forsaken," he managed, "even if we are chastised for a short time on account of our sins...."

Michael took Simeon's right hand in his own, and felt an almost imperceptible squeeze. "I will force them to give medical help," he said. "I will force them."

There was a woman at the end of the corridor. She stood in the way of the trolley and held up her arms. Everyone came to a halt just before she was run over. She picked up a page of notes that someone had stuck on the trolley, and glanced at them. "Why can't you speak English" she asked in the same dialect of Greek as the driver had used. She switched into English and gave rapid orders to the men who were pushing the trolley. They all set off along another corridor. Half way along, two of the glass-helmeted police caught up with them. There was an argument between them and the Greek woman. One of them made a grab at her notes, and she shouted until he stood away.

She turned back to Michael. She pointed accusingly at Simeon's swollen arm. "What drug did you give the old man?" she demanded. "Is he your grandfather?" She looked again at the notes. "You share the surname Acominatus." She frowned and looked at Michael's approximation to the machine script that he'd thought was most likely to be understood. "What part of Greece are you from?"

"He's had a seizure because of the needle your people put in him," he answered, trying to keep his temper. "Can't you get him a priest?" he asked, now with a sick feeling in his stomach as Simeon let out a long groan and more bloody froth began bubbling from his lips.

"No priest!" the woman snapped. "Not until you produce your documents—and not until you stop speaking such stupid and affected Greek. Now, go with these men, and leave the old man to us."

"No!" he shouted, laying hold of the trolley. "You're all bloody murderers. I'm going nowhere." The two officers got hold of Michael and pulled him into a darkened room. When he tried to resist, one of them pushed something into the small of his back that sent flashes of pain through his lower body and took away the use of his legs. "Simeon!" he called, no longer worried if these creatures saw him cry. "Simeon!" But the trolley was in fast motion along the corridor.

▶ ▼ ◀

The Greek doctor shrugged and leaned against the bed. "We did everything laid down in our procedures," she explained yet again. She looked at her fingernails. "If he didn't respond to our treatment, it was no fault of our own." She turned accusing. "Why didn't you report his reaction to the testing of blood?"

Michael stared into the still face of his uncle. No one else had bothered, so he reached forward to close the old man's eyes. They'd been left open too long, and they popped open again. For any diplomat, death is an occupational hazard. But it was only by heroic and continuing effort that Michael kept himself from breaking down and crying like a disconsolate child. Perhaps what really saved him was the feeling that death in these surroundings was as beyond regretting as a comrade's death on the field of battle. It was something to be noted and taken into account. When Tarquin finally came into the room, he'd find the strength to make an official complaint. So far as it might count, he'd threaten a report to the Emperor himself.

He went back to trying to understand what the woman was saying, and he gawped stupidly at the sheet of paper she was pushing at him. It was fastened to a stiff board, and there was a short pen dangling from a piece of string. "You must sign here and here," she said, pointing at two small boxes on the closely-written sheet. "It is your legal right to sign in Greek if that is all you can do." Michael shook his head. In Greek or any other language, he'd put his name to nothing until he had a full explanation of what it meant. The woman had made some effort to explain things. But, if he could understand the individual words, their meanings had often changed, and their combination was probably intended to leave him ignorant. She now leaned forward and gave him a rough push on the shoulder. He resisted the urge to strike back and sat down beside his uncle's body. All but one of the police had vanished into another room with unlit white tubes in their mouths. The one who remained had removed his helmet and was gawping at the shrivelled body, and joking with the male assistant who took orders from the doctor.

Michael sat down. His legs were still shaking from more than the shock of the death. "There is a man called Tarquin," he said for about the dozenth time. "He interprets for us, and will explain our situation. Once he is here, you and whoever is in charge of this asylum will answer to the British Government for a degree of negligence amounting to murder." As if she had as much trouble with his Greek as he had with hers, she gave him a funny look before seeming to understand. She spoke again to the police officer. He answered vaguely without bothering to turn away from the body. She pulled an impatient face and said something in a laughed English to the man who was tugging needles out of the body and packing up all the equipment that had, it must be presumed, failed to keep the old man from his final and bloody attack of vomiting.

"Have you at least called for Tarquin?" he asked in his steadiest voice. The doctor looked at him and gave another bored shrug. Some small box that hung about her neck now began flashing. She held it up and read something on its display. She rapped an order to the man that Michael did understand. She wanted the body moved onto the floor so the trolley could be used for some other patient. Not giving Michael a second look, she hurried from the room.

"You could have found him a priest," he shouted before the door closed. Paper tube already in his mouth, the police officer turned and sniggered something at him.

CHAPTER SIXTEEN

How long he'd been sitting in that chair was beyond Michael's ability to guess. At first, he'd expected the Greek doctor to hurry back in. This time, she'd have Tarquin for company, and would be all scared emollience. But it was as if he and his dead uncle had been forgotten. Once or twice, the sound of chaos through the closed door was broken by screams of pain or of horror. The police officer had smoked his paper tube down to the end, and was half way through another.

"There was a man," he said, trying more words of English. *"And his name was Tarquin..."* The officer shouted something fast and menacing, and flicked the still burning remainder of his tube at Michael. The assistant had finished pulling out all the needles and things from Simeon, and looked up from the report he'd been laboriously making. He spoke to the officer in a kind of nervous snivel. Together, they went and stood over the body. The officer grunted out a few words, and laughed at the assistant's reply. He bent low over the body and tugged hard at something. He let out an impatient snort and got up. As the assistant hurried over to a wooden box and picked up various sharp objects, Michael realised that what he'd thought couldn't get any worse just had.

"Not to do such!" he warned in his best English. He pointed at his uncle's hand and at the golden ring the officer had failed to pull from a swollen finger. He shook his head and raised both hands in a gesture of pleading.

"Oh ho!" the officer said gloatingly back. He walked over to where, legs still faintly twitching, Michael had been made to sit. He reached down to his belt and unclipped one of the machines that had been used to immobilise Michael. He held it up and depressed a button on its side. There was a loud clicking, and blue sparks shot across from one metal tip to another. He laughed as

Michael let out an involuntary cry of fear and tried to shrink back. The officer stood over him, glorying in his unchecked power. With every click of the machine, he grated out something in what must have been English, but that Michael couldn't recognise. *"Innit? Na'amin? Innit? Na'amin?"* he seemed to end every sentence. Behind him, the assistant was holding up a set of pincers and whining the English word for gold. The officer paid no attention, but leaned forward and pushed the machine close to Michael's face. Clicking repeatedly, it came closer and closer. *"Na'amin? Na'amin?"* the officer repeated between bursts of sniggering.

When you act in anger—especially when anger is joined by fear—you don't always recall the precise sequence of events. You sometimes even forget what has happened. So it now was with Michael. In a brief flash of clarity as he stood over the fallen officer, he remembered the metal pen he'd brought away from the Prime Minister's office, though couldn't say what it had been doing in the pocket of his orange suit. What for sure he didn't know was how he'd driven it like a nail through the officer's left temple. But that was what he must have done. Eyes wide open, the officer lay before him. In his dying spasm, the man had clenched both fists into tight but ineffective balls.

Now thinking, though not clearly, Michael looked at the assistant, who stared back, as still as if he'd been a locust trapped by a scorpion. Michael stepped over his uncle's body and smashed the palm of his right hand upward against the assistant's nose. The man fell backward, striking his head against the wall. Whether he was alive when he hit the ground, Michael didn't know, and didn't care. He brought his breathing under control and looked about. There was no change in the noise that came from outside. But the door might open at any moment. Bearing in mind the circumstances, the British authorities might overlook an act of justifiable homicide. Then again—and he had just killed one of their colleagues—the police, who would represent the authorities for as long as it mattered, might well take against him.

Stripping the officer was beyond his abilities. Besides, these were clothes that would be noticed at once. The assistant was easier, and, though fat, he was about the same height as Michael. Getting unfamiliar clothes off a man who also turned out to be dead—and doing so with shaking hands—was as hard as he'd expected. But it was manageable. Faster than he'd imagined, Michael was out of his orange suit, and was playing with the fasteners of a pair of trousers that were too large for him. He hitched them up with their belt and turned his attention to the shirt and jacket. It would take more practice than he'd had to pass for normal in clothes so completely alien as these. But Michael stepped out of the room into a corridor that was, if possible, still more chaotic than when his dying uncle had been pushed up and down. No one so much as looked at him as he hurried in his white jacket past the room from where the flickering lights of a picture screen and a cloud of foul smoke advertised that the other police were still relaxing. This building, he knew, was a labyrinth of busy corridors and large hallways. But he guessed right that the Latin word, prominently displayed every few yards, for "he is going out" would get him back to the main entrance. As he walked past the big front desk in the entrance hall, he almost bumped into Tarquin, who looked panicky and shouting into his communication machine. Michael turned his head away and lost himself into a crowd of black people who, with tears and lamentations, were making their way to the revolving door that would take him into the cool night air.

Before leaving the death room, he'd got poor Simeon into a respectable position, and put a sheet over the body. If someone else would steal the ring, that was no longer a matter to be controlled. "Uncle, I promise not to fail you," he'd said, putting a last and reverent kiss on the cold forehead.

▶ ▼ ◀

Michael stepped out of the darkened side street and shivered in the breeze. As he'd hurried along the wide street, where pedestrians carried their own lamps, too many people had turned and looked at his white jacket and the objects that he'd tried to hang from it with an appearance of the natural. Now the jacket and its adornments were stuffed behind a pile of festering rubbish, and no one paid attention to him.

Of course, any sense of being free soon passed off. He'd broken free of captors who meant him and the Empire no good, and who had made their feelings plain by killing Simeon, or providing nothing that a civilised man would regard as medical assistance. But what next? If he'd meekly waited for Tarquin to come in and settle things, he might by now have been heading back to his lodgings. The government here needed someone to convey its bizarre wishes to Constantinople. Why should these people not simply have put him alone on whatever vehicle they'd had in mind for the midnight exit from London?

Too late to worry about this. There were two killings that stood between him and that earlier possibility. And Michael had been sent here with Simeon to get more than yet another threat of conquest for the Empire. The Greek doctor had been about as hostile as anyone could be. But the driver had been half-Greek, and he'd spoken of others who wanted to help. Michael pulled up the collar of his shirt and fumbled with the unfamiliar fastenings that would close it about his neck. His duty was to get to that driver, or to some other Greek, and do whatever he could to arrange for the defence of the Empire. He thought again of what Tarquin had said about a future that was plainly in the past for these people. Sooner or later, the Turks would pour across the frontier and seize the heartland of the Empire—the place where most of its food was grown, the place where most of its fighting men were born. And, somewhere in their unstoppable path, was the family estate of which Michael would, assuming an avoidance of catastrophe, in time become hereditary lord. He would do his duty to country and to family. So far as might be possible, he'd also avenge his uncle's death.

He looked at the thin stream of pedestrians who went about their late business. From overhead came the sound of another flying machine. This one was equipped with a powerful light that cast its shining glow across the road and its pedestrians. Was it there to keep order? Was it there to look for him? He couldn't say. But it reminded him that he was a lone fugitive, in a city he didn't pretend to understand, and with no conceivable plan for making contact with anyone who even might be inclined to give help that could be of use.

As the overhead light moved in his direction, he dodged into another darkened side street. He waited for the loud noise to move away. With a last flash of light on the pavement, it rose higher into the sky and moved towards a main junction far ahead. Uncertain again, Michael leaned against the smooth bricks of a wall. Now it was different authorities he'd be meeting, it was possible for him to walk out into the street. He could stop everyone he met, and say the words "James Duffy." Sooner or later, that would get him back into custody. Since his flurry of bold resolution, his heart had been steadily sinking. If all he had to give the Emperor was an offer of genteel conquest, was that not something he should accept? What on earth was he doing out here but delaying the inevitable?

He swallowed and stood up straight. He would have gone back into the flow of pedestrians, when he heard a single, terrified cry. It came from the impenetrable gloom of the side street. It was impossible to say anything in this darkness. But he had the impression that the cry had come from a narrow turning half way along the side street.

Not bothering to think matters through, he took a step in the direction of the cry.

CHAPTER SEVENTEEN

After a loud splutter, the telescreen in Leicester Square came on with the afternoon electricity. In need of a rest from trying to run away on four inch stilettos, Jennifer put her carrier bags down on the reasonably clean pavement and looked round. It had, the previous afternoon, been easy to get away from Radleigh's men. All she'd had to do was turn on the tears, and then ask the humpy man about transport reform back in the days when there was enough to be worth reforming. It was while he and his friend explained for a second time about the award of unified road and rail franchises that she'd twisted loose from their grip and made a dash for Trafalgar Square. She'd plunged at once into the swarms of the disabled and therefore starving poor, and stepped out on the other side into a rickshaw that had taken her up Charing Cross Road.

It had been so easy that coming out again from the Indian's rooming house and brothel hadn't worried her. She could have sheltered there in the much finer room she'd got by handing over one of her silver pennies. Instead, the smell, and the need to try and think out her next move, had brought her out for an afternoon of recreational shopping. All had gone well until she decided to check out the security surrounding Charing Cross Railway Station. One look at the armoured cars and the tight security barriers, and she'd turned to go back to the streets where everything could be bought without ration coupons. Beside the burned out shell of the National Gallery, she'd come face to face again with the two men Radleigh had set on her the day before. Since then, it had been hard going on these heels to outrun their firm but cautious pursuit. At last, after a detour though a Chinatown where most restaurants and shops had somehow managed to stay in business, she was back in Leicester Square.

Shifting position to try taking pressure off the blisters coming up on her right foot, she watched a woman with an orange face smile down at the gathering crowd and begin today's catalogue of lies. "The authorities took swift and effective action to disperse the protesters," she said with bright assurance. A picture of villainous brown faces spread over the screen. "There was minimal disturbance to local communities, and no casualties were reported." Before the newsreader's face came back into view, there was a shout of approval and some waving of fists from a crowd that had no love of Moslem troublemakers. Her smile broadened to an idiot grin as she moved to a story of how a dog left behind in Surrey had followed the exact path taken by its owners when they were relocated to work in a Wimbledon tin plate factory. No mention how a family pet had survived The Hunger, let alone any kind of journey. Instead, there was a fade to what must have been footage reused from the Olden Days. Jennifer had seen enough. She picked up her bags and continued on her journey towards the Haymarket. She'd covered fifty yards in shoes she should never have tried on, let alone bought, before the yapping of the dog and the cries of its owners had given way to another story about some new hormone that could make sheep grow to the size of cows without a proportionate increase in feeding.

Her heart skipped a beat as two policemen stepped into view. "Got your tickets?" one of them rasped. He cocked his rifle and struck and aggressive pose. But all this was for the shabby workmen who'd been drifting along in front of Jennifer. In her clothes, she was above demands for identification. She walked past the officers. One of them clicked his tongue loudly. The other gave a slow wolf whistle. She tried to keep the sound of her high heels on the pavement to a steady clicking as she walked out of the square and turned left into a road where all the shops were open, and where the armed guards outside every one of the shops had no interest in those who were merely passing by.

There was the boom of another telescreen in Piccadilly Circus. She could hear the androgynous voice of the Government's Chief Scientific Officer. What he was saying she couldn't hear. But it had the soothing quality you associated with a particularly insane falsehood. The last time Jennifer had taken the trouble to listen, he'd been describing some anomaly in the orbit of the moons about Jupiter that might indicate a return to "Normality." That had been two months before. The world since then had stayed obstinately as it was. Perhaps he was now admitting that summer had come a little early, or that this was, at least, the hottest March on record.

Jennifer stood on the kerb and looked over the carpet of liquid filth that stretched twenty yards before her. She stepped back just in time to avoid being splashed by a vehicle that came from nowhere and that left in its wake a cloud of inorganic diesel smoke. Out of her coughing fit, she found herself looking again at Radleigh's men. They stood ankle-deep in the Piccadilly mud. The humpy man was gasping for breath and clutching at his side.

"Jennifer—Jennifer Baldwin!" the other man panted, a look of uncomprehending relief on his face. He took a step forward, but slipped and went face down into the dung. While the humpy man bent to help him up, Jennifer turned and made her best effort to dash along one of the wider streets. But the men were now out of the road, and were trying to catch up with her through the crowd. "For God's sake, Jennifer!" the humpy man shouted at the top of his voice. "If you ever want to see Richard and Catherine again, you've got to come with us."

Jennifer stopped, though didn't turn. These men *did* know her parents. She'd guessed that much the day before, from their Olden Day views and the reference to Madsen Pirie. Before The Break, her father had known many people who worked as lobbyists or hovered on the edge of politics. He'd known many, and there were none he hadn't despised. But she couldn't put names to faces. She'd been too young. Too much had happened for her to try imagining how these men may have looked before the collapse of the world that had enabled demand for their skills. But they were working for Radleigh. It might be that he'd found something.

She turned, but found herself looking at a couple of police officers. "You all right?" one of them asked. Jennifer nodded. She looked past the officers. She could see Radleigh's men trying to squeeze themselves out of sight in a doorway. "You all right?" the officer asked again, now faintly aggressive. She nodded and looked about. If she stayed here, they'd ask for her identity card. She gave them both a sweet smile and hurried off.

Another twenty yards, and she allowed herself to stop and look back again. No sight of Radleigh's men. She quickened her pace along the wide but crowded pavement. There were limits, though, to her speed in these terrible shoes. She thought of stopping to pull them off, and then taking properly to her heels. But there were more officers just ahead. One of them had his rifle cocked and seemed to be looking for someone to stop and bully. Trying to keep her face steady, she walked slowly past the entrance of what seemed a very fine hotel.

"Hello, love," a voice called. "Late for a client, are we?" Frank Wapping opened the door of his carrying chair. He showed the carriers one of his cards and sent them on their way unpaid. "It must be your lucky day!" Before she could kick her shoes off and make for a proper escape, he had Jennifer by the arm and was leading her through the door of the hotel. She nodded her thanks to the uniformed doorman who ushered them in, and was pulled briskly across the polished floor to a group of chairs and low tables at the far end of the lobby. Wapping fell into a leather armchair. Straightaway, his telephone began buzzing. He pulled it out to see what text message he'd been sent.

"Can I help you, Miss?" the waiter asked. Jennifer tried to smile, and wondered how she could get away from this latest horror. She should have stayed inside the old Indian's brothel to think how, if possible, she could get out of London again—and where to. The waiter coughed and repeated his question.

She forced a smile and reached up to see that her hat was still at the proper angle. "I'll have a gin and tonic, if you please," she said in what she was sure would sound a grown up voice.

The waiter looked down at her. "How old are you, Miss?"

"Eighteen," she said firmly.

The waiter stood back to see under the wide brim of her hat. "Can you tell me your date of birth?"

"The 8th January 1998." The waiter looked silently down at her. She reached into her handbag and took out a £100 note. She put it on the glass table.

The waiter frowned. "I won't ask to see your ticket. But you can have a Brit Cola—with ice and with a slice of lemon, if we have any. You can leave when those men outside have been sent about their business."

Jennifer was trying to see past the waiter to the revolving door, when Wapping finished his reply to the text. "The lady said she wanted a G&T," he said loudly. "You just go and get her one, and stick it on my tab." Jennifer did now catch sight of the humpy man. He was hopping from one foot to the other and waving his arms. He seemed to be alone, but couldn't be allowed in wearing such dirty clothes. The doorman was threatening him with a wooden club "Get on with it!" Wapping snarled at the waiter, who hadn't moved. "I'll have a glass of red—make it a big one. And get the lady her drink, and don't skimp on the lemon. If she's my guest, she's a guest of the Home Secretary—don't you forget that!" The waiter allowed himself one disapproving look, before bowing and walking away.

Wapping picked up a laminated menu and fanned himself. "Hot, isn't it?" he beamed. He leaned far back in his chair, not disguising his interest in looking up Jennifer's dress, to see if she was wearing any knickers. Giving up on the door—she was safe in here for the moment—she glanced at the big television set. This had been a ghastly day. She'd been mad to go shopping. Wapping took out his mobile telephone again with all the flurry of privilege, and began reading another text message. The television news was being repeated for the second or third time. She listened vaguely to what the Chief Scientific Adviser was saying. She'd been wrong that the man was promising anything. This time, it was a solemn warning about the dangers of contact with the Outsiders. "Any change in the stream of past time," he intoned, "could change everything about you. It might even cause you to disappear if your intervention led an ancestor not to have children." This was something Jennifer had discussed at length with her parents on their first trip together across the Channel. "We're in a new stream of time," her mother had said, shutting down her father's own convoluted explanation of the obvious. "Whatever happens now has no effect on what happened in our own past."

She couldn't hear the explosion. It came from too far away, and was barely enough to do more than rattle some of the glasses. But it took out the lights and the glow from the television. A few yards away, a woman got up and shouted that she wasn't paying £10,000 a night for power cuts. Someone else joined in with a complaint about the taste of the coffee. The rising babble of discontent at last brought the manager from his office. All emollience, he jollied the hotel orchestra into striking up. To the strains of *All You Need is Love*, he hurried the waiters about, each carrying a tray of baked mice in honey.

"You eat them bones and all, dearie," an aged waitress explained to Jennifer. "They was raised in our own basement—no chance of food poisoning," she went on soothingly.

CHAPTER EIGHTEEN

The lights flickered on and off a while before stabilising. The television was in the last few seconds of an interview with Abigail Hooper. Before Jennifer could decide whether it was safe to make her excuses and run for the exit, the waiter was back with the drinks. "Chin chin!" Wapping smirked, raising his glass to the fading image of his boss and then at Jennifer. He drained it in one long gulp, and made a token effort to hold back on his burp. Jennifer sipped at her own glass of industrial spirit, trying not to show how it burned her mouth and throat. Wapping was back to trying to see up her dress. Jennifer smiled and put her glass down. "It must be very interesting to work for the Home Secretary," she said with a nod at the television. Since she had to sit here, she might as well get him round to the subject of Radleigh.

He smacked his lips. "Interesting isn't the word." He fiddled with his tie. "I sit at the absolute nerve centre of British politics. In a manner of speaking, you can say that Abigail is the British Government. And I advise her." Jennifer tried to think of a question that would avoid revealing any prior knowledge of Radleigh. But he gave up on her knickers and looked at her own unfinished drink. "The new and better life this country enjoys is down to me and her."

New and better life? Jennifer said nothing. How to steer this conversation to something more useful? He laughed. "Oh, but isn't it a better life already? There's work for all—proper work as well. And just look at what else we've achieved. Who'd have though we could keep the whole nation together—black and white, Christian and Moslem, gay and straight and transgendered, all pulling together as one team." Jennifer thought back to the ruthless culling of known or likely dissenters. Her father's escape had been down to his connection with Radleigh. But she put the overweight fixer out of mind, and focussed on Wapping. He'd spread his legs wide, and was showing an area of pinstripe frayed from the continual rubbing of his thighs.

"You don't believe me, do you?" With an abrupt change of mood, Wapping sat forward and pressed his hands together. "One of the men who carried me here used to be a director of fixed asset use management—whatever that was. The other traded bonds. His wife hanged herself when their child died in The Hunger. He stayed alive by eating garden worms and tree bark. One morning, he and all the others like him will wake up and realise this is the utopia they always wanted." He picked his glass up and tried to lick the red smear that had congealed within it. "When Abigail ordered The Pacification, she was only completing a process that began with the Second World War. When you look back at Margaret Thatcher and Tony Blair and all the non-entities who came after them, you can't avoid laughing. They really believed you couldn't build a strong state without also giving prosperity and the pretence of freedom. They were wrong. What most people wanted, even then, was not to have to think for themselves. Give them that, and they'll put up with *anything* else."

He stopped for the rumble of another explosion. This one was closer, but only set the television into a spasm of white noise. Wapping sat back again and smiled. "So not everyone out there is a sheep," he allowed. "But Abigail has a plan for dealing with *them*." His smile shaded into a snarl of hate. "As for the rest, they'll come round sooner or later. Then, we can stop jollying them along with talk about a return to normality. *This* is normality. And it's a better normality. Why—we'll even call an election." He laughed loudly and shouted over at the waiter: "Would you like an election? It'll only be one party this time round—mind you, that's how it always was in the Olden Days, once you looked below the surface!" He shook his head, scattering more dandruff over his lapels. No answer from the waiter.

He stopped and looked over at the television. This had come back on and was showing an item about the Armistice centenary. If there could be no ceremony in France, the BBC was promising endless documentaries about what it called "this glorious victory

105

for British arms." Wapping put his hand up for the waiter, and went pouty when he was ignored. He looked back to Jennifer and smiled. "Don't you ever wonder what happened to everyone else after The Break—I mean, everyone abroad?"

Something in his voice made the hairs stand up on the back of Jennifer's neck. He couldn't possibly be an informer. But this was pushing close to an incitement to Hate Crime. "I don't understand what you mean," she said. To be on the safe side, she added a silly smile and a fluttering of eyelashes. She picked up her glass and pretended to sip at its contents.

"I mean," he went on, the last news we had before the Great Storm was how the Chinese and Russians were threatening a response if the Americans went ahead and nuked Mecca. Isn't it possible that our own world was about to become a ball of rock as sterile as all the others in the Solar System? Wouldn't you like to know? Wouldn't you *really* like to know?"

Jennifer fluttered her eyelashes again. "Since I can't know, I don't see the point of asking. But it may be that, all considered, The Break was for us a very lucky break."

Wapping sniffed and cleared his throat. "Don't tell me you also think this was God's work!" he sneered. "There is no God," he recited. "We are creatures of Nature, and we follow Nature's laws. That's what Abigail says." He fixed his glance on her knees and licked his lips. "Talking of which, are you still seeing Basil tonight?"

"Yes." She'd been hoping he would get round to this. "He's a very important man, and he doesn't have all the time he'd like. But we have our appointment." She leaned slightly towards him, letting the top of her blouse fall open. He swallowed and scratched the top of his thighs, managing to poke a hole in the frayed cloth. "Do you know Basil well?"

"Basil and me, we're like *that*!" he said, lifting his right hand and pressing forefinger and thumb hard together." Jennifer was thinking of a new question, when he spread his legs wider apart. "How much do you charge Basil?"

Difficult question. One of the girls down the corridor had told her the normal price was between £90 and £150. But that couldn't be right. Jennifer had spent more than the upper sum on lunch. "£8,000," she said, thinking of how much she'd paid for her dress.

Wapping's mouth fell open. He sat forward and reached into his pocket for a bundle of notes. "I'll give you £300 for a quickie," he offered. "Abigail's got a suite upstairs on permanent booking. It's even got a bath." He got up. "Don't move," he said. "I'm just going to see if the suite is being used." He hurried off, leaving his cash on the table.

Jennifer could have tried playing Mata Hari. But her idea of getting information out of him hadn't so far come to anything. The thought of going upstairs with him was enough to turn her stomach.

"The men who were following you have been gone some time," the waiter said quietly. "Shall I have a rickshaw stopped for you?" Jennifer nodded, and made sure to give him the £100 he'd earlier refused. The rest of the greasy cash they left where Wapping had let it fall.

▶ ▼ ◀

After the air conditioning of the hotel, the air outside the hotel seemed nastier than ever. It didn't help that, as she got out of the rickshaw in Oxford Street, she was passed by a dozen military trucks. She heard them coming in time to press herself against one of the boarded up shop windows. But she couldn't get far enough away to avoid their clouds of black smoke. It set her coughing and spluttering for nearly a minute. She paid no attention to the old women who stopped and pointed at her. Instead, she looked at the last of the trucks as it hurried towards Portland Place. Its flap was open, and she was able to see the grim-faced men as they clutched at their rifles. All the soldiers she'd seen in Kent had been little more than boys in uniform—barely up to shooting back at the occasional raid by the Outsiders. These were all regular fighting men. Jennifer turned and began walking in the direction of the shattered stump of the Centre Point tower. She got within fifty yards of the ruined junction with Charing Cross Road. It was thick here with police officers. Screaming abuse at anyone who dared watch them, dozens of them were clambering from a couple of black vans. They were soon absorbed in harassing some priests who'd been handing out bread to an army of beggars. But she couldn't afford to be stopped. One touch of her identity card against a reader, and she'd be straight under arrest. She stopped and leaned against one of the few lampposts that had been left in place.

"What to do? What to do?" she groaned softly to herself. There could be no railway journey back to Deal. Radleigh's invitation to his flat for that evening had obviously been just to let his men grab her more easily. She looked quickly round. She needn't have bothered. So many police officers, all shouting and waving their guns, made her safe from Radleigh's men. There was no one else in London she knew—or would have dared approach. She thought of her bicycle. If she gave the Indian a handful of her French silver, he'd probably arrange for a new front tyre. She didn't like the prospect of cycling back to the coast. But she'd been mad to come here. She really should have stayed in Deal. She could have thrown herself on the charity of one of her friends from the days before all the schools were closed. It would have been a few days before the next smuggling boat put in. A few hundred dried out cigarettes to ease her crossing, and she could have made her way to France. What Count Robert might be able to do for her wasn't very clear in her mind. But he was her friend—that much she knew. Perhaps he could use another of his English contacts to find her parents. At the worst, if she had to spend a longish time among the Outsiders, it couldn't be worse than dodging the police here in London. But how to get out of London? Would the patrol points still be unmanned when she got back to the start of the A2?

Oh—"What to do?" she cried louder. "What in the name of God to do?"

"You pray, my daughter," the answer came from behind her. She turned and found herself beside an elderly priest. Except when being polite with the Outsiders, her father had never thought much of the Catholics. "Utterly superstitious God-botherers!" he'd always muttered as one of their priests went by. "Lean too close, and you'll smell the whiskey and potatoes." But they seemed to have taken over all the main welfare functions in London. As for the Anglicans her father had generally found time to praise—why, if not sniffing out and denouncing anyone who dared say he was following the wrong calendar, their main response to The Break had been to say the country was under the Judgement of God for the sins of racism and climate change denial.

The priest was still looking at her. "You must pray, my daughter," he said kindly. "For those who pray with humble and contrite heart, the Lord will surely provide."

Jennifer had been thinking to turn back towards Bond Street. But, as quickly as they'd gathered, the police were being called away. Not looking the priest in the eye, she nodded her thanks and hurried by. There were no shops beyond this point. But she could see if the British Museum was still open to visitors.

CHAPTER NINETEEN

Jennifer pulled up the sleeve of her sweatshirt. She tried to ignore the butterflies in her stomach when she found that only ten minutes had passed since her last time check. 10:40pm, her watch said—over an hour to go before she was supposed to call on Radleigh. She corrected herself for the hundredth time. Radleigh hadn't invited her round at midnight or any other time. He wasn't expecting her. Because she hadn't gone quietly with his men, he'd probably written her off. So she told herself. So, swinging back and forth between hope and panic, she'd been telling herself since the previous afternoon. She was now back to believing that any call on Radleigh would be madness. The priest had been wrong about the Lord's willingness to provide—not that she'd so much as tried to pray. That had left her with nothing else to do but go and change her clothes, and then to drift, almost against her will, in the direction of Radleigh's flat. She'd got to St John's Wood when it was still light, and, when not making herself queasy on acorn coffee in a pub, had been peering round a corner at the block where Radleigh lived. Once darkness had fallen, she'd bullied herself into sitting in the pub. But this was now closed with the shutting down of the power, and she was back to her nervous inspection.

If she went up, it might be all smiles and assurances. Maybe her parents were already up there, drinking real coffee and looking at their own watches. Even as she thought of the hugs, however, and the mock-scolding words about her trip to France, she thought of the alternative—of Radleigh's cruel face when he had her in his power, or of his casual telephone call to the authorities. Though flabby, he was big. On his own territory, he'd have the upper hand. Her heart beat faster. Another moment, and the earlier assurances were running through her mind again. Why get her arrested in his flat when he could have denounced her in the Liberal Club? Why

110

draw attention to his connection with her father? As for attempted rape or murder—she reached down to her belt and touched the knife she'd bought off one of the girls where she was staying. Radleigh might be a big man, but she'd heard any number times that he was a physical coward.

The lack of street lighting made it easy to keep out of sight across the road from the block. She stood awhile, looking at the glow from the fanlight over the main door. No power cuts in there, she could see. Her mother might have commented on the additions to the service charge to keep a generator going—not that Basil Radleigh was a man to worry about the cost of maintaining a normal and even luxurious standard of living. Jennifer leaned back harder against the wall. Thinking of her mother had reminded her of something. She looked about. The street was empty. Every window at the front of the block was brightly lit. Radleigh's flat, though, was at the back. Jennifer crossed the road into the shadows against the wall of the block. Again, she looked about. From her one previous visit, she remembered there was an open gateway to a back yard from where rubbish was still sometimes collected. She dithered. The gateway led in, and was then the only way out. But, unless she managed to think of something that would surprise her, it was this, or hang about till it was time to press the third button from the top beside the front door.

The yard stank of rotting food—now the survivors had learned to stay out of sight above ground, the rats could be missed for their cleaning function. In the light cast by the upper windows, she looked at the mass of twisted steel that began about seven feet up. This had once been the fire escape. During the collapse of order in the early days, the lowest level had been sawn away and the rest bent out of reach. "Not very good security," her mother had sniffed when it was described to her. Her mother always knew what she was talking about when it came to buildings. And Jennifer could see now that anyone able to get onto the structure had an easy way into any flat that wasn't secured by its own alarm or unbreakable glass. It hardly mattered nowadays, of course—the vacuuming up of everyone on the police database had left the better parts of London almost as safe by night as by day. Strange Meaters were for the suburbs.

If not sure what she was about, Jennifer didn't think she was planning a break-in. She had the vague idea of looking to see what Radleigh was doing. Was he alone? How was he dressed? Might there be any indication of what she could expect if she chose to press his bell rather than slink away into a void of uncertainty? She breathed in deep and wiped sweaty hands on her jeans. She jumped up to grab hold of one of the lower struts. Easier planned than done. After three attempts, and only one ineffectual brush of a hand against anything solid, it was a matter of digging into the heaps of stinking refuse for something she could stand on. Again, easier planned than done. This was a world in which rats had been replaced by larger scavengers. The days when you could no sooner look than put a hand on a nice box or broken chair were gone. After a minute of poking a stick into heaps that always turned to slime after the first inch, it had to be a matter of dragging one of the steel bins itself into place—and doing this in a manner that didn't wake the dead. But slime is a good lubricant and damper of sound. Clambering onto the fire escape, Jennifer could see that her mother had been right about security.

The top level creaked with every movement on the steel ladder. Her trainers scraped on its rusted platform. It seemed farther down than looking up had been. But she was sure no one had heard her, and this was Radleigh's flat. She looked through the nearest window. Yes, this *was* the place. She was looking into the main bedroom. Its door was ajar, and she could see the dim shadow of the bed and the shape of the big icon of Saint George left on the wall after the eviction of the flat's previous and suddenly penniless Russian tenant. She held her breath and focussed hard on the bed. No Radleigh—not that he'd be there so early in any event. There was a light on in the next room. To look into that, she'd need to climb onto the left rail of the fire escape and hold herself steady against the sill. She looked down again. If she lost hold, she'd land in or beside the bin. She swallowed and held up hands that were sweaty again, and beginning to shake. But she'd come this far. It was too late even to think of turning back. She took hold of the rail and pushed herself up and made a grab at the sill. So long as she held herself tight, she had a straight view into the sitting room. When she was finished, it ought to be an easy matter of pushing herself to the right and trying not to make any noise when she landed on the unsteady platform.

"My dear Abigail, you really should save all this for the telly. Your viewers might have more patience than I have—or be more desperate to believe." Radleigh spoke with weary contempt, and the sound of a man who knew that he might shut the Home Secretary up, but could never bring her to his own opinion. Looking through the half inch slit between the night blind and the window frame, Jennifer could see him fussing over a cocktail cabinet. Silk dressing gown about his ample form, silk scarf about his throat, he looked as if he'd lived in this degree of luxury since time out of mind. He handed a glass to the seated woman, and, glancing sideways as if at a clock, pushed a cigarette into a long holder.

This was the first time Jennifer had seen Abigail Hooper in the flesh. Nearly facing the window, she looked smaller than she did on television. With rising disquiet, she wondered how important Radleigh was. It had been one thing to learn that he knew the Home Secretary. It was something else to see how close they seemed to be. She pulled herself into a more stable position and waited. Hooper sat up. "You still don't understand, Basil." She took a sip from her glass and swallowed. "These are, no one can deny, unwelcome times. But, day in, day out, some of us have fought to maintain investment in essential public services. The structures of our caring and multicultural society remain intact. Doesn't that record stands for itself?"

"Do go and tell that to the Mozzies!" Radleigh laughed.

Hooper put up a hand to silence him. "Don't blame me for what happened today!" She lowered her voice. "It was that fool Duffy. As usual, he panicked. This time, he turned a simple rescue into a massacre. And, coming back to your own faults, dear Basil— what's all this about the Baldwins' daughter?"

Jennifer went stiff, and she nearly pulled a muscle from tightening her grip on the window sill. "And don't blame me for *that*!" came the delayed and slightly defensive reply. "I assumed she'd been taken off with her parents and killed or whatever. The last place I expected to see her was in the Liberal Club. If your fool of a secretary hadn't tried raping her with his eyes, I'd have nabbed her there and then. As it is, my own people kept partial tabs on her. She was last spotted this afternoon in Piccadilly. She was prancing about like a six year-old who's borrowed her mother's most impractical shoes. The girl knows absolutely nothing, I can assure you. Now, much as I dote on your company, I'm expecting her at any moment—assuming, that is, You-Know-Who doesn't get to her first." He laughed and finally lit his cigarette.

Hooper went into a low nagging about something. But Jennifer heard nothing. *Taken off with her parents and killed*—the words echoed in her mind, registering slowly in their enormity. She felt one of her trainers slide on the pitted rail, and thought for a moment she'd fall. It didn't matter. Nothing mattered. If she did keep in position, that didn't matter either. Her stomach had turned to ice, and her eyes were blurring over. Her parents were dead. The last she'd ever remember of them was her father's biting commentary on the *British Gazette* and her mother's mild reminder not to be out on her bicycle after the electricity was shut off.

She might have let herself fall into the darkness. She might have pushed herself back onto the fire escape and slunk off in despair. But Radleigh's voice cut through the gathering fog within her mind. "Look, Abigail, I didn't expect you to hurry round in person when I called. All I wanted was a one word answer to a three word question." Almost against her will, Jennifer listened to something about a trip to Tenterden. Hadn't he been there the day before? She tried not to make any noise and she twisted left and looked down at the empty yard. All was still in silence. She looked at her watch. If he was expecting her after all, she wasn't due to press the front buzzer for nearly another hour. She looked back in and tried to listen. But the window glass was muffling the sound of whatever the Home Secretary was saying. Suddenly, she got up and came over to the window. Jennifer thought she'd been noticed. Even as she told herself it no longer mattered, she could feel the rising panic. But Hooper turned at the last moment to look at Radleigh.

Abigail, Abigail!" Radleigh was jeering at what had been said. "Why can't you just admit that that the game is up? The whole country's running on empty. How much longer do you think we can get by on cannibalising everything in sight? If that weren't bad enough, do I hear right that the natives have driven us back to the outskirts of Dublin? Talk about armed insurgency—it's turning into Afghanistan and the bloody IRA rolled into one!" He laughed and made an ironic toast. "Shall I remind you who it was said all our neighbours would be in White Man's Magic mode for a century to come? No? Well, let me go back on myself and say how astonished I'll be if we turn out to be months rather than weeks from a new famine. If Duffy is siding with the oil men, they at least have a plan for getting us out of this mess. What have you got to offer?"

Hooper had moved away from the window, but her mocking laughter rang clear through the glass. "I don't think we'll be running too much longer on empty." She dropped her voice. "I can tell you we had a major breakthrough last week," she continued in a tone of quiet triumph. "I think we had another this afternoon. If Duffy hadn't been such a fool, we'd already be putting it to the test."

"Oh, so it *does* work!" Radleigh called satirically. "At least one of your essential investments has paid off. I suppose that will bring the Prime Minister back on side." He laughed. "Have you spoken to yourself yet?" Hooper's answer was to look once more at the window. Radleigh stood upright and waved his cigarette holder as if to assure her they were alone. "Well, if you do, please get some decent ciggies passed over. The supermarkets and bonded warehouses you requisitioned are running distressingly low." He'd lost the tobacco from his cigarette. He clucked with annoyance and took out another. "Any chance you'll relent and let me see this fabulous Gateway of yours? After all, we are supposed to be friends."

The strained silence that resulted was broken by the whine of Hooper's telephone. She looked at the illuminated display. "I told you not to call me from that number," she snapped. She listened. Then: "*What?*" She threw herself into a chair and sat forward. She listened with rising incredulity. "I gave clear orders to keep him in the hotel," she groaned. "Must I do *everything* myself?" She listened again. "I don't care. Just get him back. The boy's a

gawping primitive without a word of English. He can't get far."
She listened again. She got up and went over to a framed map of
Central London that the previous tenant had marked with his
favourite shops and restaurants. She ran a forefinger between two
points. She stood in silence, then finished the drink that Radleigh
had helpfully carried over. "Activate Plan B for the
demonstration," she said, her voice menacingly quiet. "Seal the
streets off. No one's to get out—and no one in! Extreme prejudice
as required." More listening. Then: "I don't care about that!" she
said impatiently. "That danger was over last Wednesday. We only
let it go ahead because it was too much trouble to stop. Now just
stamp it out." She held her telephone between shoulder and chin.
She put her free thumb on the map, and stretched out her little
finger to touch another point. "Withdraw the SSB units and get
them combing everywhere within a one mile radius of the
hospital," She took her hand from the map. "I don't care what it
takes—I want that boy in my office tomorrow morning." She
paused and listened again. She let out an unpleasant laugh. "Yes,
do get me a meeting with Duffy. And I want that ridiculous old
queen there beside him. Professor of Greek?" she snorted. "He'll
be breaking stones in Ireland come Sunday!"

Hooper slid her telephone shut and reached for her black
handbag. "Problems, Abigail dearest?" Radleigh asked, coming
forward with his decanter. "Has Duffy spoiled things again? There
is an answer to that, you know. Margaret Thatcher doesn't need to
have been the only woman to make it to the top!"

Hooper was on her feet and gulping back her second drink. She
turned back at the door, a cold smile on her face. "If the girl turns
nasty, Basil, it's your own affair," she sniffed. "If you're still
breathing tomorrow, call Simkins to have her collected. No one's
too ugly for socially useful work in the Dublin brothels. That, or
she can be put to something equally useful here in London."

She laughed and repeated herself about useful work in London.
Radleigh said something back. But Jennifer was beyond listening
further. She held tight on the stone sill, and tried to keep herself
from falling down in uncontrollable sobs. After a week of fighting
despair, the bottom had dropped out of her world. Perhaps she
should have stayed to listen more, Jennifer told herself as she crept

weakly down the fire escape. Perhaps she should wait till midnight, and then cut Radleigh's throat. Perhaps. Perhaps....

Tired with despair, she sagged forward and leaned against the big rubbish bin. Now it didn't matter if she was caught, she ought to do something. Anyone could have told her that. Anyone could have told her, that is, if he hadn't seen how the sobs were shaking her entire body. She was barely up to creeping back into the street, let alone playing some female James Bond. She needed desperately to think everything through. She'd go back to where she was staying—no, not that: she might have been followed there. She'd go into Regent's Park and sit on the edge of the all night market there. Otherwise, she'd....

That was the limit of her stated options. As she turned a corner into one of the darker side streets, something dark and heavy landed on her head and fell in suffocating folds down to her knees.

CHAPTER TWENTY

"Ooh, but isn't she a right looker?" someone shrilled. "Can't we play with her a bit?"

"Shut up! Let's just get the job over with," Someone else replied.

Strange Meaters! Strange Meaters! The words flashed through Jennifer's mind as if they were a neon sign. She hadn't thought they came into Central London. Free from the heavy blanket, she stumbled forward against a wall and turned to blink in the glare of three torches, one of them slowly moving from her extreme right to the centre. She stepped forward to raise her hands in supplication, but tripped over something soft.

"Come on, you idiot," the second voice said. "Get hold of her while she's still in shock. There's police and the whole sodding army on the streets." It was a body Jennifer had fallen over. Untangling herself from it, her hand made contact with the face of one of Radleigh's men—it was the humpy one, she could see. His head had flopped unnaturally to the left, and there was one golden tooth glinting in the torchlight. She was dragged to her feet, and thrown back against the wall hard enough to knock out all her breath. "Where's Baldwin?" the second voice demanded. "Tell us where your father's gone."

Trying to get her breath back, Jennifer pulled herself upright. Not Strange Meaters, these—but who? And for what? She fumbled with her belt and managed to get out her knife. She squinted into the three intense patches of light, and felt the knife tremble uselessly in her right hand. "Been peeling potatoes, love?" the first voice chuckled. She opened her mouth to scream. But a rough hand reached out from behind the light and slapped her face so hard, it almost knocked her over. Perhaps it was the same hand that plucked the knife out of her hand. She heard it land somewhere to her left. The first voice went into a low and predatory laugh. The other man giggled, and there was a cough from a third man who'd not yet spoken but had been moving about. The torches came closer, and Jennifer made a sudden dash to her left. For a moment, she was out of the pool of unified light. But, as she crashed into another wall, the lights swung round and fixed her again like some animal cornered in a nocturnal hunt.

She did now manage a scream. She put her head down and tried to run forward. But she hadn't thought there would be another body to trip over. This time, she fell into a pair of strong arms. She was thrown forward and taken into another pair of arms.

"Just keep hold of her," the second voice said impatiently. As she struggled to get her arms free, she saw one of the torches go slowly to the ground. At once, there was someone blotting out its light, and she felt two big hands close about her neck. There was a sudden smell of onions and a pleased laugh. Jennifer tried to kick out. But all she managed was a momentary relaxation of the tightening grip. She felt two thumbs press slowly into her windpipe. "Where is he?" the third voice demanded. "No one stitches the Big Man up and gets away with it!"

He loosened his hold on her throat. "Please don't hurt me!" she gasped. Before she could say more, the hold tightened again, and she went limp with fear as she realised she couldn't breathe in. The man squeezed harder, and gibbered with a kind of sexual pleasure when her knees gave way.

He let go again, and bent down to where she'd fallen. "If you don't tell me where to find Richard Baldwin," he rasped, "I'll kill you." She choked air into her lungs and tried to scream again. If all she could bring out was a silly squawk, she heard the man who'd been holding her let out a sudden cry of alarm.

Michael had seen enough. The small man who'd been hanging back made no sound as he was grabbed from behind. His neck broke with only a little twisting. The cosh he'd been carrying fell noiselessly, and Michael picked it up. He swung it at the bigger man who'd been watching the interrogation, and felt the soft and gratifying crunch of a broken skull. That made four English dead in a single evening, he thought with a stab of pleasure more intense than the lights that had guided him over till he could hear the low sounds of the interrogation. He stood away from the pool of light that had led him over and looked at the one man who remained. He'd let go of the boy's throat, and was trying to see past the lights. He held up big, murdering hands and stammered something in a scared voice. At once, he tried to make a dash for freedom. But Michael was expecting that. He caught hold of the man's sleeve and brought him down. He got onto the man's chest and took hold of both ears. He pulled the man's head up, and rammed it hard back onto the slimy cobble stones. It needed two hard knocks before there was another crunch of broken head, and now the splashing of brains.

And that was it. With a bound, Michael was on his feet. He snatched up one of the portable lamps and shone it on the boy, who was curled into a softly weeping ball. He turned and swept the lamp round the enclosed courtyard. For the moment, it was just two of them and three—no, five—bodies. He wondered for a moment if there had been another moment of blurred perception. But, no—he really had killed only three. He looked back at the sobbing figure. Hard to tell with these people, he realised, but his first surmise had been the correct one. Despite the clothes and cropped hair, this was a girl.

He looked round again. Now the killing was over, he was back to dithering. It was madness to stay there and help the girl to her feet. He had no idea why they'd been threatening her, or if there were others in the area. But here he was. There was no stepping back—not for the moment.

Though she was still shaking too hard to stay on her feet without help, the girl was managing to fight back her tears. She tried to speak, but all her bruised throat would let out at first was a croak. She coughed and tried to clear her throat. Eventually, she brought out something in a tone that suggested thanks. Or it might have been a warning. *"You are saved,"* he said, racking his brain for the appropriate Bible verses. *"Come with me,"* he added, trying not to wonder where that might be. The girl steadied herself and let go of his arm. *"Rise in and follow me if you was be saved,"* he improvised. She twisted free of his grip and bent down for another of the lamps, and shone it in his face. She let her arm fall. In the lamp's now gentle glow, he saw a look of confused understanding pass over her face.

"Who are you?" she asked in Latin through chattering teeth. No longer supported, her legs gave way, and she sat down. Letting go of the lamp, she pulled her upper clothing into place. "The secret police are already after you. If they don't get you first, the ordinary police will execute you."

Michael looked down at the girl. Was it worth questioning her? It might have been, had he known what questions to ask. "We need to get away from here," he said in Latin. She stared up as if she hadn't understood. Then she nodded and reached forward to put his own lamp out. She got slowly up and massaged her throat. She took a step forward, and stopped. After a moment of uncertainty, she picked up her lamp and waited for the right words.

"We need to cover ourselves up," she said with a returning croak. She leaned against the wall and squeezed her eyes shut. He thought she'd start crying in earnest. Instead, she pulled herself together. "Help me get these coats off the bodies," she said, her voice more normal than he'd yet heard. It was a more peremptory tone than he might have expected from a girl—especially one he'd just saved. But she spoke Latin, and was fast coming into a mood where she might be more useful than a burden. She bent down again and switched off the one lamp that remained on the ground. She positioned hers to shine over the two smallest of the bodies, and began a feeble effort with one of the coats. It was for Michael to pull off their outer garments.

Nervously, they crept from the courtyard where the girl had been taken. She led Michael into a narrow street without lighting, and, from this into a wider street, also unlit. They were half way to a lit street, when there came the gentle throbbing behind them of a vehicle. Michael saw his shadow and the girl's grow longer and more substantial as it moved towards them. As if by agreement, they both reached up at the time to pull their collars higher. Not changing speed, the vehicle drifted past. "If it's you they're after," she whispered, "they'll not be looking for a couple." They turned into the main street. There were other vehicles here. They bumped and rumbled past, none of them showing obvious interest.

"Where are we going?" the Outsider asked. Jennifer stopped. It was a good question.

"We need to go back to my room," she said when no other answer came to mind. Why not there? She had nowhere else. She pressed the display on her watch. 11:30, it said. Radleigh wouldn't be missing her for a while yet—if, indeed, he'd been seriously expecting her to show. Hooper had said there'd be no police support. Perhaps his own men hadn't been able to find where she was staying. Almost certainly, she felt, they hadn't been up to following her back. She'd have to take that chance. She looked at the Outsider in the dimmed glow of the lamp she'd let him carry. At first, she'd assumed he was the boy Hooper had been so eager to get back. But, if he wasn't very tall—not that Outsiders usually were—he did have a beard. And he had seen off those killers with practised ease. Now he'd finished his work of killing, though, the Outsider gave every sign of being as lost as she felt. His beard looked very thin. It might even have been curled to make it look more substantial. "Come with me," she said. Her mind was beginning to fill with questions. But they were walking along a main road. The steady stream of vehicles passing by didn't count. The pedestrians flitting by were another matter. It wouldn't do even to whisper in Latin.

"So, you have decided to grace my establishment after all!" The old Indian tapped the pause control on his iPad. From a country that no longer existed, and never might exist, women in bright saris were frozen in their dance. "But who would be doing business in the streets on a night like this?" He stared at Jennifer's battered appearance, and at Michael. When another convoy of military lorries rumbled by outside, he thought better of his next question, and contented himself with a demand for the specified rent.

CHAPTER TWENTY ONE

Upstairs, in her partitioned-off area of the boardroom, Jennifer sat on her bed and tried not to cry again. "Who were those men?" the Outsider asked urgently. "Why were they trying to kill you?" Jennifer shook her head. "How safe is this place?" he asked with a glance over at the window blind. "Who knows that you live here?" Still not able to answer, she got up and fumbled with the battery lamp beside her bed until it was fully on. In the harsh light that filled the room, the Outsider went over to a cluttered table and took up a hand mirror. He looked for a while at his bearded face. He breathed slowly out and turned to her. "Can you get me a razor?"

It was an odd request, but it brought Jennifer to her senses. She hurried to the door, and caught the Indian trying to look through the inspection hole. Keeping her voice steady, she brushed aside his grinning whine about concerns for her safety and gave the instructions. Back inside the room, she picked off the blob of Blu-Tac from where it had been moved and pressed it once more over her side of the inspection hole. She pulled off her sweatshirt and adjusted the straps of her bra. In her struggle with the killers, her money belt had also been pulled out of place. Adjusting this, she pointed at Michael to sit on the bed. "He'll be up in a minute with his things," she said in a tone that she hoped would establish her as the senior in this new relationship. "He won't ask any questions, but don't say anything. Let me do the talking." The Outsider nodded and looked away from where she stripped off her dirty jeans. "We haven't time for you to play the gentleman," she said, trying not to show her own embarrassment. Now they were in good light, she gave him a proper look. No longer tearful, she fought off the sudden urge to sit down and laugh. "You've got your trousers on inside out. Everything else is wrong too. Take it all off, and I'll help you dress."

Back in the hospital, Michael hadn't felt confident about undergarments. He was still naked from the waist down, and fiddling with the buttons of his shirt, when the old Indian burst in with his razors and hot water, and a babble of what Michael guessed were ribald comments. Jennifer looked away to hide how red her face was going. It was a lucky moment for the Indian to come in. Things must appear to him as they should be. Probably he'd been asked to help in stranger bedroom antics than playing the barber.

Jennifer watched the Outsider as the last of his little beard was scraped away. Without it, he looked barely older than she was. There could be no reasonable doubt he was the one Hooper wanted. Perhaps she was getting herself into a right mess. But it was too late to worry about that. Once the Indian had finished simpering and muttering, and was out of the room, she threw a sweatshirt at him. "Get this on. It's baggy enough to fit you." She turned the lamp down again and went to the window. The street outside was crowded with pedestrians. So far as she could tell, there was no one in uniform. But that meant nothing. Did Radleigh know where she was staying? She looked again at her watch. It was five past midnight. Odd how time had slowed down—she'd been ready to believe it would soon be dawn. But, if she really was in his mind, Radleigh should still be waiting for her. It would be ten or even twenty minutes before he ran out of patience. How long after that they'd be safe was beyond guessing. She took out clean clothes for herself, and dug through one of her unemptied shopping bags for a pair of trousers that were a better fit than the ones the Outsider had been wearing, without looking too feminine. She found a pair of unisex jeans. They weren't new, but had seemed a bargain too good to pass up.

Michael worked out the correct use of the zip for himself, and sat shirtless on the bed. He picked up the mirror and stared sadly at his face. He'd broken the habit of a lifetime and prayed for that beard. Now it was off, he looked no older than when the first hairs had sprouted. It almost made him want to cry. But he managed a feeble grin at the girl. "What's your plan—supposing you have one?" he asked in Greek, forgetting himself.

Jennifer listened carefully to the words. As it had been at first with Latin, this was nothing like the pronunciation she'd learned from her father. "Can we keep to Latin for the moment?" she asked. He nodded and looked into the mirror again. Jennifer allowed herself a better look at him. He had nice muscles, she couldn't resist admitting. But he wasn't more than an oversized boy. His general freshness, and his good teeth, indicated that he might not even be older than her. She put this out of mind and had another look at her watch. "It's a risk," she explained, "but it's better if we wait here another ten minutes before going back out together. We don't want the old Indian to go to the police." She went to another bag and took out a loaf of moderately good bread. She broke it in half and gave some to the Greek Outsider. Having no plan at all, she hoped he'd not insist on an answer to his question. If only she could sit quietly for a few minutes, she might be able to think out what to do next. But what would that be?...

Michael looked at the girl—and that was clearly all she was. Because he'd saved her life, he'd stick with her—and because she spoke Latin, and because she knew where she was and how to get about, and because it was already unthinkable, even if he'd had any other plan of action, that he could take off without her.

He shivered in the chilly room and ate some of the bread. "You do realise that we may have lost the advantage of going about as a couple?" The girl opened her mouth, then nodded. "So I'll ask again—what next, and where?" The girl looked away. He gave up on questioning her. On the floor beside his old clothes, he saw the lead cosh he'd carried away from the dead men. He got up and balanced it in his right hand. He was lost in London without apparent hope. He really should have given himself in to Tarquin. For the moment, however, things were bordering on similarity with the time in Baghdad when the Grand Vizier had sent assassins into his room one night when he was supposed to be asleep. Luckily, the slave girl he was bedding had tipped him off at the last moment, and it was a matter of carving them up with a sword and making himself scarce till morning, when he and Simeon had their audience with the Caliph. There would be no meeting here with anyone in authority—not the following morning, nor perhaps ever—nor any bowstrings for Tarquin or that chief minister. But any similarity was worth pulling out and holding onto. He looked at the girl while she was fishing into her bags. Here was one similarity that probably wouldn't be, he told himself. Was it a shame?

Jennifer opened a plastic water bottle and drank from it. She handed it to Michael and now did give way to laughter as he squeezed too hard and sent most of its fizzy contents onto the floor. He scowled and managed to hold it to his lips. "My name is Michael," he said stiffly. I don't recall hearing yours."

"Jennifer," she said. She watched his lips move as they repeated the unfamiliar syllables. Alone, she'd have been sobbing on her bed, unable to care about the men Radleigh might eventually send out to take her. But, setting aside how he'd saved her life, there was something about Michael that steadied her nerve. She put out her right hand. "I am very pleased to make your acquaintance," she said calmly.

There was no point in commenting aloud or to himself on this decidedly unfeminine girl's manner. He got up and took her hand in his. He picked up his overcoat from where he'd let it fall. This time, he was able to do the buttons up. They were a clever idea, he allowed. Of course, many things these people had were clever. The real question was how the degenerate brutes with whom he'd had to deal could have developed any of this for themselves. "Since I rather doubt you have any plan at all," he said, "can I ask you to help me get to the Church of All the Saints?" What he'd do there was another matter. But, since she was likely to dither about all night in a place she'd already admitted was unsafe, someone had to take the lead.

"The *what?*" Jennifer asked. She tried to think what the boy could want with a church. Was it to confess himself for the killings?

"It's a Greek church," he said patiently. "My guess is that it's somewhere in London, and that it's the only church with that name." He picked up Jennifer's coat and waited for her to get into it. She put various things into her pockets, and gave him the torch he'd carried away from the bodies.

She thought. She looked once more at her watch. The time had jumped suddenly to half past. She felt a stab of panic. "Come on," she said with a slight catch in her voice. "We're getting horribly short of time." The Outsider was already on his feet. With the coat buttoned up to his chin, he looked as if he's just said goodbye to his mother for a school outing.

CHAPTER TWENTY TWO

Jennifer's idea had been to keep to the side streets before turning into Tottenham Court Road. But she found that every one of the streets was blocked by metal barriers, and most had groups of policemen in front of them, all heavily armed and talking back and forth on their radios. After perhaps half an hour of getting nowhere, she gave up on that plan, and led Michael into Oxford Street. Though it was pushing two in the morning, the whole road, from Bond Street towards Centre Point, was crowded with chattering, joyous pilgrims. Every one of them carried a torch, and there was something in the air that reminded her of late night shopping at Christmas in the Olden Days.

"We'll get into the main street going south," she whispered to Michael. "Once we've passed the big square with a column in its centre, we can try going north again." He tightened his grip on her arm. This vast and murmuring crowd was terrifying even with a girl who seemed to know where she was going. He didn't want to be separated.

But the junction with Regent Street was impassable. All holding up their torches, many arms locked, there must have been ten thousand people crowded together in expectation of something big. "What is happening?" Jennifer finally asked a man whose back was turned, but who wasn't joining for the moment in the cacophony of prayers and hymns.

A bad choice, she realised the moment he was facing her. Giving her the look of someone far advanced into lunacy, he raised a megaphone and took a breath just long enough to let her get out of completely ear splitting reach. "It's the Second Coming!" he bellowed at a volume that silenced every other utterance within a dozen yards. He pointed up at the low clouds, and began a slight but ecstatic dance in the space available.

"The Second Coming?" Jennifer hoped she'd misheard.

No chance of that. "He will descend among us at midnight," the man took up again at full volume. "Every mystery will then be revealed." At midnight? Jennifer thought. She looked at her watch—1:49am, it said. Her heart skipped a beat. These people were going on Outsider time. How had they been allowed to assemble for this? She looked about, her stomach turning to ice as she remembered Hooper's mention of extreme prejudice

The man was continuing his dance of joy, and still pointing upward. "It is written that He will descend from Heaven to Oxford Circus. The graves shall give up their dead, and all who were lost in The Break shall be restored." He did say more. But, from deep inside the crowd, there came a sound of ragged cheering. After a moment when it might have died away again, it strengthened and was taken up closer and closer to where Jennifer was beginning to panic. While it was still possible to hear anything at all unless shouted though a megaphone, a woman behind her took up the cry. "Christ is risen!" she cried. "And those of us now alive shall never die."

There was a sudden roar of excitement and then a slow but irresistible movement of the crowd. The man and his megaphone were carried in one direction. Jennifer and Michael were carried in the other, past a Belisha beacon. "We must get out of here now," she shouted, no longer worried if anyone heard the Latin. Michael tightened his grip on her arm and pulled her over to the doorway of what had once been a McDonald's restaurant. If they pushed together through a thinner eddy in the crowd, they could get into a side street she hadn't noticed: Harewood Place, the sign said. She tried to remember where this led. Except it must go south, she couldn't place it on a map that had turned hazy in her memory.

They were stopped a few yards into the side street. A big man dressed all over in white stood before them. He held up the wooden crucifix that hung about his neck. "You cannot approach the Apostle," he boomed in a voice that reminded Jennifer of the old Underground instruction to mind the gap. He raised both arms and stepped forward to usher them away. Without seeming to move, Michael leaned over to the man and gave him a gentle tap with his cosh. Eyes still open, the man went down like a stricken beast. He took Jennifer forward over the sprawled figure into a narrow street that, if not empty, was passable.

Michael kept the girl close beside and stepped forward. About twenty yards down the side street there were more people dressed in white. Two of them carried a large banner that had on it an image of the Latin Patriarch. Though the cheering from behind was now overpoweringly loud, he could hear the joyous singing of the white figures and they came slowly forward in procession. The girl stopped and tugged at his arm. A scared look on her face, she pointed ahead at the banner. He ignored her and looked to where a platform had risen out of nothing. On this, a short and very fat man was beginning a sermon for anyone inclined to listen. Correction— there was a loud screech as the man held up something that looked like a cosh but that amplified his heavy breathing to a roar that it was impossible not to hear.

Pushed forward by the crowd that had followed them into Harewood Place, Jennifer looked between the dangerously illegal image and the American insurance agent. Since the M25 flyover, he'd cleaned himself up, and now looked decidedly like a televangelist—and what he was about to say, she had no doubt, would never get past the Religious Advisory Council. He waited for someone to reach forward and play with his microphone. The feedback under control, he raised his free hand to heaven and took a deep breath that was blasted from the two huge and battered speakers blocking the way round him. "Brothers and Sisters in Christ," his voice blasted, a pleased look on his face, "I am come to declare that the Tribulation that began with The Break has now reached its middle point, and the Rapture is upon us." There was more feedback, and the man with the megaphone came out of Oxford street to insist that the Rapture was supposed to *follow* the Tribulation. He ended with a massive squawk of "Heresy! Heresy!" and drew a cheer of agreement from his own followers.

The American scowled and pointed. "O ye of little faith," he thundered, "listen not to the votaries of Satan. They are sent only to confuse. It is written that all the saints and Elect of God shall be gathered, prior to the Tribulation that is to come, and shall taken to the Lord lest they see the confusion that is to overwhelm the world because of our sins." There was a louder and more collected cry of disagreement. The American was no longer paying attention. He patted his lacquered hair into place, and waited for six women to climb up beside them. Jennifer recognised the black woman she'd spoken to at the M25 flyover, and someone else who'd lost her husband when he was buying water pipes in Poland. "Know ye not that worse is yet to come?" he continued when they were in place. "I tell you that Christ, this night, shall not come to earth. He will only appear above John Lewis. Then shall He pull up beside Him those who are pure of heart, to wait with Him the moment of His Second Coming." There was a deafening crash of guitar music, and the women began to sing:

> *O Gentle Jesus,*
> *In all we do He sees us,*
> *And from the Tribulation*
> *Shall save His Christian Nation....*

Behind, a fight had broken out between those who held different opinions about End Times. Michael understood nothing of this. Fascinated against his will, he watched the women spin joyously round and round, showing their legs as they kicked up their white robes. The man who'd been speaking was wiggling his enormous hips to their singing, and his hair glowed blue, and never moved an inch out of place, in the lights that shone on him.

Now, he heard a vast grating sound, beyond the fat man in white, as another metal barricade unfolded itself at the end of the road. Armoured police officers were fanning out in front of it. Even as he thought of the Islamic demonstration he'd seen that afternoon, he heard the overhead clatter of one of the armed flying machines. It appeared over the man in white and swooped low towards them. He looked away just in time to avoid being dazzled by the light it shone over the crowd. The man in white was dancing with frantic excitement and pointing up at the machine. The two women beside him were spinning about faster on the platform, their arms held out. The fighting had given way to cries of fear and wonder.

"There must be another way out of here," he shouted in Jennifer's ear once they were back in Oxford Street. "That, or we have to get under cover." He looked at the buildings that loomed all about. Every one of them seemed to be closed off with metal shutters. But there had to be somewhere to shelter before those machines began their stuttering rain of death upon the crowd.

Jennifer heard him, but her main attention was taken by the loud and repeated announcement from overhead: "This is an unlawful assembly," it roared through the noise on the ground. "You will proceed to Marble Arch, where you will be led to safety." Already dazzled by the glare of the helicopter's searchlight, she tried to think of an escape. Before she could think of anything, Michael had led her back into the main crowd, which was now shouting defiance up at the helicopter.

"Not that way!" she warned as he took her left along Oxford Street. "That's what they want." If Michael had heard, he wasn't paying attention. He led her quickly away from the crowd. Though hundreds of yards away, she could see the glare of headlamps by the Marble Arch end of the street. Though too late to be avoided, it all made sense. This was an immense sting operation. Every Christian troublemaker in Southern England had been got here on a promise that Christ would come down from Heaven, or meet the Elect half way. Now, they'd all be rounded up to swell the chain gangs in Ireland. There'd be no Rapture—only more of Hooper's "normalisation." And this time, she'd be completely in charge. Jennifer had heard this in Radleigh's flat. And she'd got herself and Michael right into the trap.

But Michael pulled her forward. He also had seen the lights, and, if he knew less than Jennifer, and hadn't understood the instructions, he could see how danger lay on every side. He'd seen the crowd outside the massive shop. Shutters of steel mesh don't stand up long to a hundred desperate men. Even as one of the flying machines swooped low above the thin, scampering crowd in this part of the street, the shutter went up with a scrape and a smashing of glass. There could be no escape though that building, but concealment was better than running about like frightened bugs when their stone is lifted.

Then, as Jennifer pulled at Michael, and tried to find words that would make him turn round, she saw a flash of bright orange. It came from ahead on their left. She saw the front of Waterstone's explode outward, and a great ball of ignited coal gas rise slowly into the sky. She didn't hear the explosion. Instead, she was knocked backward as if struck by a giant but invisible hand. She fell against the plastic advertising space of a bus shelter, and came to rest, seemingly uninjured, sat against it.

Unable to get up for the moment, she looked stupidly at what had been Waterstone's. The orange ball had risen hundreds of feet into the air, and its glow was fading. In its place, the whole front of the shop was ablaze with the firing of a hundred thousand books. Screaming with terror, a man ran past her. She was sure she could see bodies in the street amid the burning wreckage of the shops. She looked harder—yes, one of the dark heaps was making with slow movements for the far side of the road. Above the roar of flames that were suddenly coming from shop after shop, Jennifer heard a babble of amplified instructions from overhead.

Where was Michael?

CHAPTER TWENTY THREE

Jennifer had known the Greek Outsider for barely three hours. He'd made himself known with a burst of violence so sudden and extreme, it would have scared her witless if she hadn't been scared already. Since then, she'd exchanged a few introductions and gone for a walk with him through Central London. A sheet of paper put in front of her, she'd probably have been able to write more about the sweepers whose bodies were by now being consumed by the few uneaten rats in London. Now he was gone, what had so far still bordered on adventure turned straight to nightmare. She got up and looked at the nearest of the crawling shapes. "Michael?" she asked. It gave no answer. She looked harder. Wasn't it the wrong size? *Don't let it be Michael*, she prayed internally. The shape fell down and moved no more.

Heart going at *prestissimo*, a dull sound in her ears, she turned right, where a hat shop she'd visited that afternoon was belching flames ten foot across the pavement. She got up, not bothering to check if she had been injured. She pushed fingers that were set like claws through her hair and looked about for where she could run. She had to get away. It didn't seem to matter where. She *had* to get away. She swallowed and looked at another of the crawling figures. She took a step forward. "Michael?" she asked again, now louder. To her left, there was a woman howling at the sky. Jennifer blinked and took a moment to focus. The woman didn't look as if she'd been injured in the explosion. Instead, she'd looted a whole side of ham from one of the department stores, and was trying to keep two men from taking it away. Unable to move, she watched them rave and claw at each other, fighting over what might be their only taste of natural protein since The Break.

"Thank God you're safe!" a voice cried from behind her in Latin. "I thought I'd lost you." Michael's face was white and scared.

Before he could speak again, Jennifer clutched hold of him and got him into the crowded doorway of an old Vodaphone shop. They were just in time. As if struck by a rocket, House of Fraser now exploded. The metal shutters of the Vodaphone shop rattled, and the glass it protected shattered inward. She and Michael were swallowed up for a long moment in a blast of scorching smoke.

Dazed and choking, she looked out into the street. The smoke had cleared enough for her to see debris and fallen bodies in the lurid glow of a dozen fires. Michael shouted something in a voice that dripped panic and pulled her into the street. He pointed towards Marble Arch. No longer patiently waiting, the lights of the trap were moving forward. Jennifer ran with him towards the main crowd. Michael stopped beside the junction with Harewood Place, and seemed to be dithering about another attempt to go down it. But he thought better, and hurried them deeper into the main crowd.

The helicopters came directly overhead. They barked warning after warning. Jennifer could hear nothing above the surrounding roar. One arm locked in hers, Michael pressed forward through the crowd. Now weaving, now pushing, he was making for the great separation of building uppers that marked the junction with Regent Street. From the corner of her eye, Jennifer saw someone stand upright on top of a bus shelter. She saw him put a megaphone to his bearded mouth, and heard the ecstatic cry of "*Allah al-Akbar!*" He dropped his megaphone and reached inside his overcoat. He threw both arms up and launched himself forward into the crowd. The force of the bomb he let off was absorbed by at least a dozen bodies, and the force as these were thrown outward was spent against a crash barrier before it could reach her and Michael.

"We must keep moving," he shouted above the roar of helicopters and the screams of the injured and dying. Jennifer wanted to ask where they were moving. She had no doubt Regent Street was as blocked as all the other ways out. She had no time to ask. From somewhere else within the crowd, there was another scream and another explosion. She had a sudden glimpse, far off, of a body turned into a blur of glowing mist. Another second, and something wet and very forceful splashed against her forehead. A few more seconds, and there was a megaphoned cry behind her of

"*Allah al-Akbar!*", and an explosion big enough to shatter the upper windows of the shop on her left.

At last, a scared but still orderly crowd disintegrated about her into a mass of panicked individuals, all willing to tear each other apart if it meant getting to safety. Hitting out right and left with his cosh, Michael pressed on with her through the suddenly looser, though less predictable, mass of humanity. There was another explosion far behind them, and more screams of pain and horror, and then another explosion, and another. Then, just as it had emerged, chaos turned back to order. People who'd been running in no particular direction turned as one and began to hurry away from the junction. No longer able to push forward, Michael got with Jennifer behind another crash barrier. She saw how he gripped it with his free hand, his knuckles white in the glow from the spreading fires.

Motorbike engines roared from the direction of Portland Place. "*Allah al-Akbar!*" the first of the leather-clad maniacs called into his megaphone. He screeched to a halt in the middle of the junction and unzipped his jacket. "Get down!" Jennifer yelled at Michael, pulling him to the ground. The blast went far above where they crouched. The close rungs of the barrier protected them from the detached wheel that was blown across the road.

"What *is* going on?" Michael groaned in her ear. Jennifer didn't answer. She didn't know how to answer. More to the point, she no longer knew *what* to answer. She pulled him harder against the pavement as she heard another biker surge forward along Oxford Street. He went off with a bang muffled by the crowd about him and by the shrieking of the crowd. One of the others got off right in the middle of the junction, and began a frothing speech in one of the Eastern languages. She heard another "*Allah al-Akbar!*" from Regent Street, and another explosion.

It was now that one of the helicopters swooped low into the wide street and let fire with its machine gun. There were more explosions and screams—preceded by more cries in Arabic. But the helicopter also seemed to be firing indiscriminately. Just beside her, Jennifer saw a man throw up his arms and fall against someone else. The helicopter changed direction, now making north along Regent Street. Everywhere it passed, it left a trail of explosions. Taking charge, Jennifer pulled Michael up from where they'd been crouching. She looked at the helicopter's swift progress towards Portland Place. Directly beneath it, people were going down, one after the other, as if they'd been dominoes. She turned and looked back along Oxford Street. Though the lights on the military vehicles were dazzling, there was enough other light from the burning shops to see the row after row of armed and uniformed men, coming on in formation. They were already past Harewood Place. She saw the glitter of flames on fixed bayonets. If there was danger from the overhead gunfire and from the suicide bombers, it didn't seem to worry those grim veterans of the Iranian War.

There were at least three helicopters overhead as Jennifer and Michael pushed south along Regent Street. All were shouting different instructions, and she got nothing from their echoing, staccato rage beyond a sense that everything had gone totally out of control. After a hundred yards, the crowd suddenly thinned, and it was possible to break into a run. She wondered if it might be worth trying for Charing Cross Road. She hardly needed to see the lights, though, far down the street, of the patrol that blocked the way into Piccadilly Circus. She got Michael to a stop and turned to look at the junction with Oxford Street. Another wave of suicide bombings was under way. She heard the gathering wail of terror from a crowd that accepts it has nowhere to go.

From somewhere in or close by the junction, a single shot rang out. Still noisy, the crowd there stopped moving. She heard another shot, and then another. Was it the police? She wondered. Was it another helicopter? Was it the Moslems—this time with guns? Or was it more soldiers, coming from the other end of Oxford Street? Were the jaws of the trap also about to close at each end of Regent Street? Michael pulled her closer and tried to shout in her ear. If she couldn't make out what he said, she could feel, with an icy chill that began in her chest, that he was giving way to outright panic.

They hadn't moved, but were somehow in the middle of a crowd that hit them from behind and was surging back towards the death trap of the junction. Someone pushed her in the back, and she went down. Straightaway, someone tripped over her, and someone else stepped on her left wrist. She was sure she'd be killed. Before the words could form in her mind, Michael had her up by the scruff of her neck, and was hurrying her to yet another crash barrier. The web of streets that led east from here included Carnaby Street, she thought—death instantly forgotten. She thought again. These also must be sealed. Perhaps the best option was to get into another doorway, and hope the soldiers wouldn't go as completely mad as the police probably would.

She heard more gunfire. It came this time from a few yards to her right, though she couldn't see who was firing. Three careful shots sounded. Was that the gunman on top of a pillar box? Was he taking aim with a rifle? Some in the crowd were cheering. Others were trying to get away. Jennifer put both arms about Michael. Keeping on their feet, they moved with the crowd. Directly above them, one of the helicopters was making a different noise. Its engines were roaring and coughing as it reared upward, until its searchlight shone from far above the rooftops. There was one more shot, and the searchlight went out. Jennifer briefly saw the reflection of burning shops on the bubble of glass and steel as the machine fell stuttering towards the middle of the junction of Oxford Street and Regent Street. Because it landed on the thickest part of the crowd, there was no crash as it came to earth. She might have heard the rising and extinguishing of horror, and might have felt the shockwave of human panic that spread out from the point of impact. But she and Michael had, in some manner she couldn't recall, got themselves half way along Regent Street, and the road was almost clear. Ignoring them, another helicopter flew overhead towards the junction.

Jennifer made her mind up. Or perhaps it was made up for her by the circumstances. She began pulling Michael in the only direction she could now think represented any safety. Because this involved going back towards the chaos of the junction, he stopped her and shouted something she didn't hear.

"The Underground!" she shouted back in English. She could think of no Latin equivalent, but shouted the word again. She pulled harder and pointed at the junction. They ran until they were deep again within the surging mass of humanity. Jennifer was already thinking, with rising despair, that they'd simply crash into locked security gates.

Now they were in the pool of light from another helicopter. "Do not go into the Underground!" someone raged maniacally down at them. "The Underground is a forbidden zone!" As Jennifer realised they'd managed to join a stampede, the machine gun above began a stuttering fire. She heard a bullet whizz past her left ear and ricochet from a kerbstone. A whole row of people who'd been running just feet in front of her went down without a sound, and she and Michael were stumbling over their bodies and piles of other bodies. They stumbled. They climbed. They ran. She found herself looking once into the face of a woman who'd gone down but wasn't yet dead. She looked away and pressed over more of the fallen. All the time, the helicopter above screamed its warnings and wheeled round and about, raining death with every renewed burst of machine gun fire.

They had to squeeze sideways through a mound of the dead before they came in sight of the blue and white sign above Oxford Circus Underground Station. They were pushed at once into the doorway by the pressure of those others lucky enough to make it through the hail of death. The gates had been pulled into strands of twisted steel, and there was a blast of damp air from the labyrinth of tunnels that the authorities might not yet have blocked.

Christ had not descended in glory from Heaven. Perhaps their own descent might not be into Hell.

CHAPTER TWENTY FOUR

There must have been a hundred people in the ticket hall. The gathered glow of their lamps gave the place the look of rush hour in the Olden Days. But, if there was no railway train to catch, there was a desperation to reach the platforms that reminded Jennifer of a much older time she'd read about, when the Underground had also been a place of safety—a place of safety from the attacks of a government other than the British.

"Take the Central Line," a young priest quavered repeatedly from just beyond one of the smashed ticket gates. "Beware of possible flooding." He clutched a rosary, and gave a worried look at the stairs up to the street. As yet, the only people coming down were those trying to escape. Would he stay there to direct others to probable safety right to the final moment? Would he look firmly to the last at the boots that would tramp down the stairs? Jennifer took a deep breath and squeezed through the gap. She waited for Michael to make his own way through. She took his hand and ran for the stairs marked in red. Hand in hand, they hurried down until the sound of their own and all the other footsteps had blotted out the sound of the priest in the booking hall.

According to her father, who'd been many times to London for his meetings with Radleigh, the whole Underground had been flushed out with poison gas at the end of the Food Riots and then sealed. The still clothed skeletons that covered the Central Line platform told Jennifer that he'd been right. For just a moment, they looked as if they were all trying to get up to greet this latest wave of refugees from the massacre above. But it was only the rats, squealing and scampering in their escape from one of their only places of safety. The light of a hundred lamps showed the fresh advertisements for holidays to places that no longer existed, and for goods and services that she'd almost forgotten. Jennifer turned to Michael and pointed wordlessly at the dark mouth of the tunnel that led past Bond Street to Marble Arch. There must already have been fifty people hurrying into its depths. She realised that this would take them straight to where the authorities had set up the mouth of their trap. She pulled back from the edge of the platform and pointed in the other direction. Tottenham Court Road might still be clear. Or it might not. She put both hands against the wall and leaned. She needed time to think. She'd been trying to think straight since leaving Radleigh's fire escape. If, somehow, she'd got, without proper thought, through everything since then, she now needed to think what to do next.

Michael reached up and took her right hand. "Come on," he said in a flat and weary voice. "We can't stay here." He looked briefly down at the rat-gnawed skeletons, and helped her to the edge of the platform. They jumped down and pushed their way into the crowd of those who were already picking their way along the rails into the mysteries of the tunnel. She looked again at the western tunnel. Perhaps the least obvious way out was the better escape after all. But there was now the echoing crash of gunfire from the ticket hall, and a noise of pleading cut off in mid-voice. Michael gave her hand a squeeze that might have reassured her if his own hadn't trembled so. "Come on," he said again. "They'll be down here at any moment."

For a dozen yards into the tunnel, Jennifer could tell herself they'd got away. Then, with a flash of light from all about, and a chorus of shrieks that stopped barely sooner than they began, the nightmare was back on at full pelt. "Don't touch the rails!" she cried in English. Her Latin was gone, and she might have struggled at the best of times to explain the idea of electrical conduction. It was hard enough, in the glow from the now bright platform, to make sense of it for herself. She could see ceramic insulators under the rail that hugged the left wall of the tunnel, and under the central rail. Did this mean the others were safe? She remembered her father's joke about drunken youths, fried when they urinated from the platform. "Don't touch *anything* metal," she breathed. Not moving in the central trench of the tunnel, they stood with barely inches either side between them and the dull rails. Jennifer looked back at the platform. Another volley of shots, and a brief silence, and she saw the first of the soldiers filing out of the approach tunnel. One of them raised his gun and picked off a woman as she tried to push her child behind the safety of a refreshment machine. Behind her, there was another flash that lit up the tunnel, and another truncated scream. They were trapped. It was a choice between fried and shot. One look from any of the soldiers, and the choice would be made for them.

She thought the next volley of shots had taken out the platform lights. But she could hear the scampering of people deeper inside the tunnel. By accident or design, the power was back off and it was safe to press deeper into the tunnel. Then, even as she turned her face into the chilly draught and reached back for Michael's hand, she could hear a rhythmical squeaking deep within the tunnel. It came closer, and was joined by a shout of fear that was silenced by a single shot. There were more shots, and Jennifer could hear the terrified cries of people who'd turned back and were hurrying towards her and Michael. There was a long plea for mercy and more shots, and she could now see the beam of an approaching light.

"It's a handcar!" a man shouted. "Get back!" He pushed by her and made for the platform. He was taken down before he could reach it. She heard one of the soldiers laugh and cock his rifle. More people pushed by. More shots. More death. More laughter. But now there was a snarled command, and, with a dimming of the torchlight, she saw soldiers leaving the platform. Two remained. They threw themselves on one of the benches, and reached for their cigarettes. Jennifer looked at the approaching handcar and at the platform. They were caught in another trap.

She turned to whisper in Michael's ear. If they were quiet, and if they kept low enough, they might be able to go past the platform into the far tunnel. Perhaps the handcar would stop here. Perhaps. Marble Arch was the best escape after all. Michael shook his head. He got both hands into the small of her back and he pushed his face close to hers. "On the ground," he hissed. "Just get down, and don't move till I tell you." She tried to fight him off. But he was using the full directed force that had let him kill three men. Before she could get a word out, she was lying face up on the damp, stinking ground of the tunnel, and he was sprawled on top of her.

They lay for what seemed an age as the handcar approached and more shots were fired. Jennifer did try once to get her face from the cover of Michael's chest. He reached quickly over and gave her side a cruel pinch that got her still again and counting the rapid beating of his heart. As they both lay there in full view, she heard a grating of the rails above her, and was aware of voices, and then of bright torches. The handcar passed above them. Then it stopped. There was a smell of tobacco substitute mixed in with cannabis. "Don't waste bullets, Frankie," someone giggled in a drugged voice. "Look at the blood all over them—they're both goners." She felt a jolt against Michael's body that was enough to move his chest so that the glare of a torch could play over her closed eyes. She fought to keep her face absolutely still, and was already imagining the shrill gloat of triumph and the crash of the last thing she'd ever hear, when there was another order from the platform, and an obscenity from the handcar. "I told you they was dead, innit?" The drugged voice said again. Then the pink glow faded from the other side of her eyelids, and there was the renewed squeal as the handcar continued towards the platform.

"Fancy a drink?" Someone called from the platform.

"Nah," came the reply. It was the drugged man speaking again. "This train terminates at Marble Arch." He sniggered at his joke and repeated it. "Don't you know mission's been aborted? I guess that mean we just kill everyone who's seen down here."

On the platform, someone else gave a nasty laugh. "We don't need no police to tell us it's all gone tits up," he said. "If we was in charge, there wouldn't have been no Mozzie attack up there." The argument grew cheerfully obscene, before turning to speculations of where the bikers had got their petrol. It was ended by a loud order from somewhere along the platform. Eyes shut, Jennifer lay still as the squeaking began again and vanished into the far tunnel. There was a distant crying of children, followed by three shots. After that, it was a matter of relaxed laughter from the soldiers on the platform, and the slow retreat—this time final—of their voices.

They lay in silence for what seemed another age. Then, long after the beating of his heart had slowed to something like normal, Michael twisted his face close to hers. "Get up," he whispered. "How far do these tunnels go?"

"Miles and miles," she said, her own voice sounding uncontrollably loud in the darkness. "They reach under the whole of London, and far outside." He helped her up. She looked about for the source of the one light that had survived the mopping up. It was a torch that lay on the platform where the woman had been trying to save her now dead child.

"I don't know," she said again when he asked if it was safe to touch the rails. "They may be off. But I don't know how the—the motivating force works down here." A week before, in France with Count Robert, Jennifer had been telling herself on how well she was doing in Latin. It was something she'd been planning to urge as mitigation to her parents. But that was in a country where just about everything she needed to discuss had words that her father had taught her, or were in *Lewis and Short*, or that she'd been able to guess from their context. She'd never supposed she would need her Latin here in a London of technical miracles—certainly not at a time when she was still numb with fright.

"Stay there," Michael said in a tired voice. Keeping his distance from the raised central rail he moved slowly to the platform. Once level with the abandoned torch, he stepped carefully over the rails until he could climb up. He got the torch and shone it along the platform. Except for the obvious scurrying of rats, all was now silent. Probably, every armed man was needed above for the work of killing and pacification. If she held her ragged breath and listened hard, Jennifer might have heard the faint crash of weaponry. Instead, she looked at Michael. He'd got clumsily onto the platform. Now he was down on his knees and trying not to drop forward onto the skeletons and the fresh bodies of the mother and child.

"Michael!" Not worrying if the power was on or off to the live rails, she stumbled forward. She got to him just as he fell onto his side and showed no sign of being able to get up.

Michael was aware of the hysterical girl who pulled at him. But he was most aware of how the glazed bricks along this tunnel were beginning to ripple like a canopy above the Hippodrome caught in a sudden wind. He knew there wasn't enough light to see anything. He saw it, all the same, in a kind of grey flickering that must have been for him alone. And, keeping time with the rippling of the bricks, a dull roar surged and ebbed in his ears. He lay rigid on the paved floor and put all his fading will into not biting off his tongue. But, even as he accepted that this was the full seizure he'd been dreading for days, every muscle relaxed, and he felt the girl roll him onto his back, and saw her shine the light onto bloody hands where she'd clutched his left arm.

"Michael! Michael!" He tried to put up a hand to slap her face. But it was too early for that degree of control. It took all his concentration not to choke and splutter on the fizzy water she poured into his mouth. He managed to sit up. Though he could still see individual bricks seeming to project forward in every place where he wasn't directly looking, the grey light was gone. He touched his left shoulder, and winced. He let the pain bring him fully back to his senses.

"It's just a flesh wound," he managed to say. "The soldier's spear point missed the bone." But the girl had him down again, and was peeling off his coat. He barely felt the bandaging of his arm. He thought of poor dead Simeon. "At all times," the old man had repeatedly said, "an envoy of the Great Augustus shows no emotion but what is required to get his way." The memory of that advice sent him into quiet laughter that was a welcome alternative to breaking down in tears at the thought of his uncle's death. By the time he'd suffered the indignity of having his own face slapped, he was calm enough to sit up beside an elaborately twisted skeleton and play with the switch of the lamp. It had two light settings, he found, one of them bright, one rather dim. After shining it over the clean-picked skeleton beside him, and noting that the top of its head was missing, he chose the dimmer setting.

"Can you stand up?" the girl asked. He wasn't sure that he could, but nodded. From deep inside the far tunnel, there was another faint crash of weaponry.

"Let's get moving," he said in a voice that still had no force.

"And do keep your voice down," he added in an effort to re-establish his own primacy. His voice failed. He clenched and unclenched the fist of his injured arm. The blade had gone right through, but it really was only a flesh wound. "I'm not so very good after all," he said, his eyes filling with tears of shame. What would his father have said about this? Simeon would have understood. Tears, now of sadness, rolled down his cheek. "What use am I?" he asked between sobs. The girl's answer was to get his good arm over her shoulders and pull him to his feet.

CHAPTER TWENTY FIVE

"Unlace your shoes," Michael advised. "If you take them off, you'll never get them on again." He leaned back on a metal bench and shone his torch at the sign that stretched along the far wall of the tunnel. He stared again at a picture of what looked like an Ephesus more completely ruined than he'd known it, and that did say Ephesus in Roman script. It was the only thing that had made sense at first in the jumble of images pasted opposite. He realised he was looking with too much interest at the almost naked woman who cavorted with a man in front of the ruins, and looked again at the sign. This deeper tunnel was flooded to their knees, and their splashing along it had left them soaked above their waists. The girl pushed her cloth shoes back on and helped him with the pronunciation of *Mornington Crescent*. She was quite a good teacher, he admitted. He'd begun his questions about her language to hide his continuing shame, and because even their low whispering was better than the solitude of these tunnels. They'd soon got into their subject, though, and he'd learned a great deal more about the language.

She leaned against him for warmth and perhaps for a sense of life to contrast with the mass of human decay that hadn't been fully devoured by the rats. If she now fell asleep, he'd not be surprised. But there was more he had to know. He cleared his throat and thought of a question that wouldn't lead her back to the matter of her probably dead parents. "You say it happened a year ago," he prompted. "But can I ask you for a more sequential account of what happened? Of course, take your time. I appreciate Latin isn't your first language, and that there are problems of terminology. But please do stay awake and tell me what really happened."

Jennifer snuggled harder against Michael, then realised she was pressing on his bandaged arm. He laughed and put his arm about her so she could lean against his chest. She tried to ignore the steady beat of his heart and looked over at the people in bathing costumes who were advertising holidays in Turkey. "Though it never came more than three hundred yards from the shore," she started again, "it was the biggest storm ever recorded. It took down communications with the rest of the world. All ships that could came back into port. Every flying machine that wasn't already lost had to land. It went on for two days. When the sun came up on the third morning, everything outside was gone." Jennifer fell silent and thought back. When all electronic contact remained dead, and the Web still didn't reach beyond the mainland, aeroplanes had been sent out to see how damaged the storm had left France. Back then, the media was still no more censored than usual, and she'd heard the recordings of astonished airmen as they described how roads and airfields were all covered in dense forest, and how every town had either vanished or shrivelled to microscopic settlements within the forests. The jets had been able to get only so far, before having to turn round for lack of fuel. But further efforts over the next few days established beyond any doubt that modern civilisation across Western Europe had simply vanished. Though every satellite was gone, and it took months to get news back from what had been the United States and the Far East, it was soon apparent that something beyond comprehension had happened. The entire island of Great Britain was exactly as before the storm. Everywhere else—including islands like Lindisfarne and Anglesey and the Isle of Wight—had "reverted" to an earlier age. Exactly three hundred yards in every direction from the mainland shore, tunnels and cables and oil and gas pipelines gave way to silt or water or solid rock. Beyond that, modernity came to an absolute stop. "1064" was what the astronomers had gone on television to mutter through clenched teeth. This had been confirmed by the first boatload of pilgrims who thought they were returning to Richborough, and who had to be rescued from the mud in which their boat stuck.

"Not just the year," she went on after trying her best to put this in Latin, "but a different month of the year, and a different day of the week." She smiled. "Even the time of day was different. Your midnight in this part of the world is one hour and fifty three minutes and thirty seven and a bit seconds behind ours."

"Your country had an extensive trade with the outside world?" Michael suggested. How this had happened was as much beyond the girl's understanding as it was beyond his. Probably none of these people was up to giving a proper explanation of The Break. But, thinking of the whole island as a city unexpectedly besieged, it was easy enough to understand the huge dislocations and the way in which the authorities had panicked. He sat up and looked at the girl. She was drifting off. He shone the torch briefly into her face. He apologised and asked how many people there were on the island. She had to repeat the number in halting Greek as well as in Latin before he'd believe her. "So why seal the country off from contact with the outside world?" he wondered aloud. "I spoke yesterday with your King's chief minister. He really didn't need to spell out the power of the forces available to you. Why not resume trade with the rest of the world on different terms? From what I heard, your government has only just got round to deciding that it wants any contact at all."

Jennifer shrugged and tried to put an increasingly exhausted brain into gear. The answer, her father had explained more than once, was that any relaxation of border control would lead to an uncontrollable emigration and mixing with the Outsiders, and a collapse of every governing structure. "Even if millions starve, and millions more survive on industrial pap," he'd sneered, "they'll never give up control. They've finally got the police state they always wanted, and they'll restrain any urges to world conquest until they've broken us to unthinking obedience." Now, as all faded about her, she felt as if she was vanishing into the warmth of the Outsider's body. In the normal course of things, he'd have been dead century upon century before she was born. How strange, she faintly thought, to feel the warmth that radiated from him.

Michael gave up on questioning the girl. She was going to sleep even as he watched her in the dim setting of the torch. "You can rest for an hour of your portable clock," he said. "But then we need to be on our way." He didn't alarm her with his own fears about lights and shouting voices, and perhaps dogs, in one of the tunnels. He gently shifted position. "Jennifer," he asked, "let me see the book of maps you got from the Indian. I may not be able to understand any of them. But I'd like to see what I can make of maps and of the words while you're asleep."

She reached wearily into her left pocket and pulled out the book. "Michael," she suddenly asked, "do you believe in God and miracles."

He took his arm away. "Do you also think I'm just a primitive fool? You people are certainly full of yourselves—as if a few machines for enslaving each other make you any better than the lowest savages." Hadn't Count Robert said much the same? she thought.

Michael leafed in silence through the atlas. "What do you think has happened?" he asked, looking up again.

Now she was fully awake again, and they were sitting apart, Jennifer shivered in what felt a growing chill. "My father told me it was most likely a slip in the normal course of time," she said slowly, looking for words that would make sense. "He said it was brought on by the destruction of the world in a big war. Or, he said, there might have been no slip in time. Perhaps everyone was dead, and this was his own dying hallucination." She laughed, wondering how much Michael was following. The more she thought about it, the less she herself could follow. Having the right words, even in English, didn't always bring understanding. "Then he suggested it was my own hallucination," she added. "But that was a year ago. If I am dreaming, it shows a more creative imagination than I think I have. Whatever seems to have happened must really have happened. No one else has managed to explain it." She laughed again. "All I can say is that Jesus Christ *didn't* put in an appearance above John Lewis!" She reached out for the thought that had seemed about to trouble her. But it was gone.

Michael watched her trail into a descending ramble about her father's first meeting with a Count Robert of the Normans, and how this had solved their immediate problems. She may have been asleep half a sentence before she did fall silent. There were only a few skeletons in this stopping place, though a mass of discarded possessions that indicated arrests here rather than the massacres farther back along the tunnel. He cleared some of these possessions away from beside the bench and lay the girl on reasonably clean ground, and pulled her overcoat over her. He tried to look at the maps. But they made little sense without someone to explain them—and, now the girl was asleep, the slow dripping of water somewhere scared him with its reminder of how far underground they must be. He looked awhile at the picture of Ephesus—had the Old Faith been re-established? The woman's whole appearance suggested a dancing prostitute. Thoughtfully, he glanced down at the sleeping girl. He sighed and decided not to look again at the picture. He thought instead of his dead uncle, and of his duty. He knew vaguely what that was—but how to do it? Indeed, what to do next? Michael had once seen a man fall into a swollen river and be carried towards a cataract. The man's movements until he was carried over seemed a good model of his own situation. From the moment of Simeon's death, he'd got by with minimal thought. The need for proper thinking had been further put off by the girl's scream for help. Since then, he'd gone with the flow. It had been a matter of responding to immediate circumstances simply to stay alive. Now, they both seemed out of danger. Whatever he did next would require some plan of action. If only he could think of one....

Michael's arm was beginning to throb with a dull pain. The bandage had been put on with more enthusiasm than skill, and was now too tight. He took off his overcoat and shirt and loosened the bandage. The wound was already caking over, and it didn't look as bad as the girl had thought it. He glanced up at what he thought was a noise from within the tunnel. He realised it was inside his own head. He waited for the dim reality about him to start rippling again. But this was the merest aftershock. He looked over at the sleeping girl and began to cry. Since there was no one to see him and despise him, he rocked back and forth until the chill of the dank, still air got to him, and he put his upper clothes back on. The flexible metal teeth securing an internal pocket, he thought again, were a remarkable invention. They alone were evidence that, if now far into decay, the English had once been a race of giants.

He took a mouthful of water from the girl's bottle, and stretched out close by her. After a longish time of looking at nothing, and trying to think nothing, Michael fell into a sleep total enough for him to dream of the shimmering marbles and cool fountains of his uncle's palace in Constantinople—a palace that had somehow been moved far south to the middle of the family estates. From the corner of his eye, in whichever direction he looked, solid walls wavered and crumbled and fell into heaps that reminded him of the broken pediment of that Athenian church. Hovering around the threshold of the audible, there were sharp cries and a sound of burning. As often as he looked up, he could see the letters, in Roman script, for the English word Turkey. He'd seen the word on that picture of Ephesus. It now loomed above the whole Empire. It might as well have loomed above the whole world.

CHAPTER TWENTY SIX

Cold and stiff, Jennifer sat up and looked into impenetrable blackness. She pressed the button on her wrist watch. 4:45pm, it said. Hadn't the Greek boy mentioned an hour's rest? She brought her knees up under her chin, and thought with a flash of cold fear that she'd been abandoned. Even after she heard the soft breathing beside her, she didn't relax. She reached past him and felt about for the lamp. She turned it full on and cupped her hand about it to reflect light onto the battery gauge. It was half discharged. They had only one station to go, and the light should more than hold out for that. She put the torch down and tried not to shudder. If there was nothing she could call a smell of death, the air down here was as foul as it was chilly.

She prodded at Michael. He let out a snore and muttered something she couldn't understand. She dimmed the lamp and shone it onto his face. She looked at the faint redness left by the Indian's razor and calmly accepted that she'd fallen in with a teenage boy. How he'd lain over her in the tunnel, and hadn't cried out even when a bayonet was thrust into his arm was the bravest thing she'd ever seen. She'd nodded at his lie about how pain had sent him into shock. If it kept him from what he thought the shame of admitting to epilepsy, she'd have nodded at anything else.

"Michael." She prodded him again. "Wake up, Michael. We've been asleep for ages." She poked into his overcoat where she'd remembered bandaging his left arm. He let out a sudden cry of fear and curled into a ball. "Michael," she said, now firmly, "it's only me, and we've slept through most of the day. She illuminated her watch again and pushed it close to his face. Of course, the display might have been Chinese characters for all the sense it could have made. How long had it taken even Count Robert to tell the time properly on his analogue watch?

"No chance of breakfast, I suppose?" he mumbled in plain embarrassment. He rubbed his eyes, then groaned and let his left arm fall back beside him. He tensed his face and sat up.

Jennifer got to her feet. "I'll see what can be arranged," she said lightly. She bent down and picked up a walking stick that had a brass top. She carried it over to one of the big refreshment machines. She'd hoped for a nonchalant smashing of glass, and then an almost patronising distribution of Mars Bars and crisps and Coca Cola. It took a lot of loud bashing, and a repeated levering apart of panels, before they could both get at the still edible goodies within. But breakfast it was.

Jennifer flicked through her London atlas to the right page, and pointed at one of the symbols on the map. "If the church you told me is the right one, it isn't far from Camden Town Station." There was no getting away from another hour of splashing through claustrophobic gloom. Worse than that that, now they were approaching the end of their journey, there was the question of what next? Would Michael dump her when he made contact with his own network of agents? She waited for her stomach to go tight. For some reason, it didn't. How, then, to get out of the Underground station? Getting in at Oxford Circus had been made easy. Surely every access would be locked this far out. If there was still no evidence that these tunnels had been left untouched since the last cloud of poison gas had cleared away, how could she suppose that Camden Town would be other than sealed tight?

Michael looked for a moment into her face. He leaned forward again and pointed the torch away from them both. Jennifer followed its beam until she saw how it ended in a desiccated snarl of death. She looked back at Michael and hoped he couldn't see how she was blinking tears out of her eyes. He touched her gently on the shoulder. "Listen, Jennifer," he said, with the very slightest hesitation over her name. "I want to thank you for everything you did last night." He stopped the protest she was forming and continued: "If I did my bit, you did yours." He stopped and thought. "It wasn't bad for just a girl," he said, now lamely. He looked down and thought. "Can I suggest that we stick together once we're out of here?"

Unable to speak, she nodded and got unsteadily to her feet. Far along the platform, there was a faint splashing. She looked straight down at Michael. "I think it's a rat swimming about," he said in a voice that may have been meant to reassure. He jumped up and put both hands on her shoulders. He leaned forward and kissed her shyly on the cheek. "Thank you, Jennifer," he said.

Jennifer looked into the dark and sewery waters. She waited for Michael to climb down into them. "How old are you?" she asked.

"Nineteen," he said at once. Jennifer took his upstretched arms and stepped in beside him. She waited till he was splashing ahead of her before smiling. In any language, she could tell when someone was lying to her.

▶ ▼ ◀

As expected, Camden Town Underground Station was locked shut. This didn't mean they were sealed in. Just beside the ticket barriers, Jennifer found a door that she and Michael could smash through with an improvised battering ram, and that led into a part of the Underground few passengers had ever thought about in the Olden Days. Checking that they were still alone, and still unobserved, they passed through silent offices and rest rooms and rooms filled with dead monitors. Jennifer didn't know the details of how the system had been shut down. But it looked as if the staff had been called suddenly away and never let back again. In one of the rest rooms, she even found three coffee mugs, each with a rancid pool in the bottom. The easiest way out would be from one of the first floor windows. It would be a matter of opening one of the stiff metal casements and throwing down a fire hose. But the street outside was crowded with building workers, and men dragging pieces of industrial machinery that might have been requisitioned from a museum. Lounging against the wall on the other side of the street—he might have seen them had he glanced up while they were looking out—a policeman was selling drugs.

"Best wait till after dark," Michael agreed, trying to make it sound as if that had been his idea. Jennifer nodded and looked carefully out again. Everything there seemed normal. She went back to rummaging through a desk drawer. Though deficient in most of its listed contents, the medical box she eventually found had bandages and antiseptic enough to keep up their pretence that Michael needed medical attention for his arm. Once he'd gone through the motions of wincing—perhaps more than motions—he was back to a lordly pretence of reading the Health and Safety at Work notice, every so often crunching another Extra Strong Mint.

It was as the light was beginning to fade, and the local factories were changing shift, that the electricity came on, and the telescreen bolted to the station wall crackled into life. "The dead from last night's terrorist attack have now reached fifty seven," the newsreader woman said gravely. Jennifer couldn't see the picture, but the crowd of tired shift workers outside raised a few growls of outrage as the woman fell silent, and the BBC began showing one of the "No Commentary" pieces it favoured whenever there were too many lies to be made up in too short a time.

But the pattern of lights on the assembled faces became gradually less chaotic, and the sound started again for interviews with alleged eye-witnesses. Except they had to be lying their heads off about the selfless courage of the authorities, they sounded tear-jerkingly truthful. These were followed by an interview with the Archbishop of Canterbury, who gushed on for ten minutes about the essential oneness of every religion that agreed with the promotion of gay lifestyles. Once she was done, there were word-for-word endorsements read out by spokesmen for the Chief Rabbi and the Cardinal Archbishop of Westminster. There was even a thirty second slot for someone with an accent who spoke in the name of Allah, the "Mother and Father of all," and who denounced the suicide bombers as "Enemies of God." Next came the stern voice of Abigail Hooper, promising tough new laws against the "enemy within." She spoke on, to a murmur of approval from the crowd, about a set of decrees, to be announced within days, that would finally bring peace to a troubled land. She finished to the sound of the National Anthem, and this gave way to a speech from the King himself. He relayed a promise from the Scientific Committee, that there would be a return to normality "within the year." Then, he went on in a tone of utter conviction, all those outside the country at the time of The Break would be restored to their loved ones— and what a story those who had seen it through would have to tell of how they'd had pulled together in "the Spirit of the Blitz!" With further repetitions and variation, he droned on for another twenty minutes, until he was cut off by a repeat of the National Anthem. Finally, to a ragged cheer from the crowd, someone announced a repeat of the Christmas Special of *Eastenders* from 2013—this in honour of the fallen.

Too depressed to ask for a translation, Michael had listened without understanding. Now, as loud, twanging music was followed by a screamed argument at deafening volume, and then by the smashing of crockery, he watched Jennifer stand up in the gathering darkness and walk from the room. "Come on," she urged. "We can risk a light through here if we pull the blind down."

He sniffed at the contents of the metal container that Jennifer had cut open. It was fish of some kind in oil—possibly sardine. He was glad of the hot shower she'd got working. He was gladder still of the cleanish clothes she'd found that nearly fitted him if he pulled the belt tight.

It was time, Jennifer, decided, to ask her question. "Will your agents be expecting you so late at night?"

Michael put his fork down and looked at a waxed paper box of orange juice. As he opened his mouth to speak, there was a noise in the street. He saw the scared look on Jennifer's face, and was on his feet. He looked about and picked up a small knife. It had a flexible blade, and the handle was made of a red substance best described as somewhere between horn and wood. Whether it would be any good for defence was another matter. He waited for the girl to turn out the light, and led the way back into the front room.

Still twitchy from the night before, Michael had been expecting a few dozen police officers with their glass visors pulled down. Instead, the crowd watching the performance on the big picture machine had been joined by a man with an illuminated cart. He'd got a picture machine of his own going. This played a jingly music not loud enough to compete with the main performance, and showed a swift succession of very clean and very happy people of every age and sex and colour. Every so often, the word RTProt would flash above a table laid with a banquet that he supposed was exactly to the English taste.

"It's a kind of artificial meat," Jennifer explained. She looked behind her, to see if any light could be seen through the kitchen door. She looked again through the window glass, and pointed at the queue. "The Mayor of London has given money to the men who own these wagons. In honour of the dead, they are selling their food at half price." In silence, they watched as, dressed in the ragged finery that had marked their positions in life before The Break, the industrial proles of London tucked in to their sausages and patties. Unless queuing for their ration, everyone was still absorbed in the performance. Whenever the lights flashing from the screen managed to remain still, and in the right combination of colours, it was possible to see the grease splashed over lean and dirty faces—and even to see it dribbling off chins, to vanish into dark clothing.

Jennifer stood back from the window. "It's horrible!" she breathed.

Michael shrugged. *"For ye have the poor always with you,"* he quoted in Greek. "And, so long as their bodies remain fit for work, the poor must be fed," he said in Latin. He stretched. "Now, unless you can find some coffee next door—and, yes, we do know about coffee in the Empire—have you any more of that sweet bubbling drink? I think it's called Coca Cola, if you'll forgive the pronunciation. It has, I find, a subtly invigorating effect on the senses."

CHAPTER TWENTY SEVEN

Michael stabbed again at a piece of disintegrating fish. This time, he managed to get it into his mouth. It had been preserved in spiced olive oil, and was a change from the sweet things he'd eaten. He took another sip of the disgusting coffee Jennifer had made from stirring powder into boiled water, and stared at the bright lamp that hung overhead. "Jennifer," he asked in a conversational tone he'd been rehearsing to himself, "because you speak Latin so well, I suppose your History is also very good. I know that, in your world, the Empire has long since disappeared. I know that its terminal decline begins not far into the future of my world. But can you set me right on events and dates? The current Emperor, by the way, is Constantine Ducas."

"Oh, I really don't know that much about the Byzantine Emperors," she said, giving more attention to the white powder she was dithering about adding to her coffee. "There were so many of them, and they follow each other in a blur of centuries." She stopped and looked harder at the numbers printed small on the powder tin. Michael waited. He let her change the subject and run on about something else. Gradually, he moved her back to the main subject. She spoke for a while about a writer called Gibbon, and another called Finlay. "Well, if this is 1065," she said at last, "there will be a battle in six years at a place called Manzikert." She stopped again and smiled. "But does any of this matter? Because of The Break, your world's future is now different from my world's past." Michael smiled back and waited. "Well, if you must know," she went on, "your army was obliterated, and you lost Asia Minor."

Manzikert? Michael thought. That was near the eastern frontier. It probably meant a two or even three pronged attack—the Turks had sufficient forces for that. Whatever the case, the loss of Asia Minor really did mean the gutting of the Empire. Tarquin hadn't been lying. It also meant loss of the family estates.

He waited for the girl to go on again. She spoke of the appeal to the West that Tarquin had mentioned, and of the uncountable flood of heavily-armed knights that had poured past Constantinople, to humble the Turks and seize Jerusalem and all the Holy Places—to seize them, that is, for independent Latin kingdoms. He listened with a rising horror, checked only by the continual need to convert the dates she gave from the birth of Christ, as she spoke of a fourth Western assault that, this time, would be on Constantinople itself, and of the burning libraries and smashed or melted down statuary, and the shattering of a civilisation that had continued, wave upon wave, from the first emergence of city states after the death of Homer. He heard how the City would be ruled by Latin barbarians, every remaining province snatched by a Latin strongman, or left to the Turks—how the City would finally be recaptured, and how a much reduced Empire would be re-established, only to fall gradually into dependence on the Turks. And he heard how even the City would in time be captured by the Turks and remain theirs forever after. At the longest, the Empire had another four hundred years of life—though only another century and a half before the City was sacked, and only another six years before the irrecoverable loss of its heartland in Asia Minor.

"But, really, none of this matters," she said, having brought him into the present with talk about a corrupt parody of Greece, ruled from Athens. Michael thought of the Greek's he'd met the previous day. Even the doctor had been a stranger in language and manners. "Your uncle's network of agents must already have changed that particular future."

Michael put down his coffee cup and smiled "Agents?" he asked—"What do you mean?"

"Well, you told me you were on a mission from the Empire," she said slowly. "I assumed you'd got separated from your colleagues, who are now waiting for you in the Church of All the Saints." Her voice trailed off uncertainly.

"I really don't know where you got that idea," he said with an attempt at mild surprise. Confusion giving way to fear on the girl's face, he gave his first consecutive account of what had happened since Dover. "So, you see," he ended, "I don't actually know *anyone* in this country. I want to see what help I can find in the church. That will let me decide what to do next."

The girl let out a nervous laugh, then burst suddenly into tears. He reached forward and put a hand on her shoulder. "Jennifer—please," he said. What the "please" referred to he couldn't quite say, though it sounded comforting. He looked round for something clean, and remembered the roll of paper towels she'd got from a cupboard.

Still crying, she mopped at her eyes. She swallowed and made an effort, "You're mad!" was all she managed at first. She pushed herself forward across the table and tried to stare into his eyes. "Listen, Michael," she said, now with intense conviction, "if your people haven't been organising them already, there is nothing you'll get from the Greeks who live here. Because they used to be so deep into things like hospitality and finance, most of them sank straight to the bottom after The Break. They wouldn't know where to begin with getting armed help for the Empire. Besides," she added quickly, "you don't need to do anything. The British Government will intervene in your world. It needs oil and other things, and it needs stability. It will prop the Empire up for its own reasons."

"That may all be so," Michael allowed—the girl wasn't stupid. "Even so, The Break may reverse itself before any intervention can be made. Your Government may decide to continue its policy of non-intervention. I didn't trust your Prime Minister's offer of a deal. I don't imagine Abigail Hooper wanted me for my diplomatic skills. I have to do what I can, while I can, to ensure that, when they do move against us, the Turks get a bloody nose."

"Yes, think about Abigail Hooper!" Jennifer said straight back. "Last night's massacre was about keeping you from vanishing into the crowd. If she lays hands on you now, the only person you'll help is her." She sat back and blew her nose. "Hooper must think by now that you did get lost in the crowd, and that you may be dead. That means that we—I mean, you—can go anywhere if only you can get out of the country. My suggestion is that we sneak across to France. Count Robert there will think of something. All you'll get from going off to that church is Hooper on your back again."

Count Robert again! Always Count Robert, he thought with sudden bitterness. For the blind trust she put in him, he might have been her father. He might have been.... Michael felt a twinge of pain in his left shoulder. It brought him back to the matter in hand. All else aside, the man was a Norman—why should he help save an Empire his own people were already doing their best to push out of Italy? "My duty is plain," he said. "I have to find the means in this country of keeping the Turks from winning at Manzikert."

"You'll be throwing your life away," she pleaded. He watched her dissolve into more tears, and pressed her face against arms that were spread out on the table. There, she sobbed for what might be without end at the madness of his plan, or his lack of plan.

He got up and looked at the weeping girl. "Perhaps I am throwing my life away," he said gently. "But men have died for less than their country, and thought it fair exchange." He stopped and tried to think of a reason that might appeal to a woman. He failed. "Did you ever hear that story about the Spartan who survived the attack on Thermopylae? There is worse than death. If I heard you right about him, wouldn't your father have agreed? Let me take you somewhere from where you can get back to your home town. You can...."

But the girl was no longer crying. "If you won't come with me," she said, sitting up to stare at him with swollen eyes, "I'm not leaving you. Hooper said you'd get nowhere by yourself. She was right. *You need me.*"

He could have laughed into her face. But her voice alone told him that he'd never shake her off. Besides, he *did* need her. If that weren't enough, what would she do if he shook her off? She had no family in England, no friends. Her Count Robert friend— assuming he was such a good friend—was at least twenty five miles across a closely-guarded strait. She took up a piece of broken mirror and stared at her tear-ravaged face. "I'll think about what you've said," he conceded, trying to sound as if he were doing her a favour. She didn't answer. Michael looked up again at the light.

"Jennifer, can you get out your book of maps? We need to be aware of all the streets about the church. We need to get there without using the main roads, and we need to know where to run if—if things don't go as one might hope." She put down her mirror and went over to where she'd hung up their coats to dry. The book had fallen though a hole in the pocket, and was right at the bottom where lining was sewn to the main cloth. He watched as, frowning slightly, she pulled out a mass of wet and swollen paper. She dropped this onto a chair, and reached in again to fish about in the lining. Michael watched as, eventually, she stood back, a small leather bag in the palm of her hand. "One of yours?" he asked, thinking of her French silver. Even as he spoke, he remembered she still had all that about her waist. He sat forward. "Do open it," he urged.

In the good light from overhead, she looked without speaking at the small and slightly irregular golden disc. He took it into his own hand. He pulled the purse fully open and let the other coins fall onto the table. "Where did you get these?" he asked, barely trusting his voice.

"They must have belonged to one of the men you killed," she answered in a voice as nervous as he felt. "We never did check their pockets. Do you recognise them?" Not answering, he turned all the coins over so they were upright. Poking with his right forefinger, he moved them into a rectangle of five by four.

"Can you tell me anything about those men who were trying to kill you?" As he'd expected, Jennifer shook her head. She'd never seen them before, she repeated. All she could say was that they weren't connected with the authorities, or probably with Radleigh—and he could have said that himself. He waited for her to fall silent and look again at the elaborate, flowing script on each of the coins. "Just one of them, and it might mean nothing," he said. "Gold coins circulate into all manner of places, and I doubt your father ran the only contraband network with France. But look at the number of them, and they're all fresh-minted." With a hand that trembled, he picked one up again and looked at the imperfection on one of the characters. He looked at the others.

"They were struck from the same die." Not speaking, Jennifer looked down at the pattern of gold on the table. "These are golden dinars," he explained, "of Arp Arslan, who hasn't been Caliph for a year yet. My uncle and I set out as soon as the first reports of your appearance came to us. It seems that the Turks got here first."

A new thought came to mind. "Those men who were killing themselves at the big demonstration—I don't think I've told you, they were speaking the Arabic that's now spoken in Baghdad. It's something I passively accepted at the time. But, it doesn't now strike me as realistic that Arabic should have remained unchanged for nearly a thousand years. What do you suppose they were doing there? And can you think of any reason why the Caliph's agents should be trying to kill you?"

Michael listened to the wild screaming of a woman on the screen outside. It was followed by shouts of approval from the crowd that still hadn't moved away. Then there was a beating of drums and a repetition of the twanging music. He put the noise out of mind. If only it could have been replaced by a clear understanding of what role a God who might actually exist had set for him in this genuine performance.

CHAPTER TWENTY EIGHT

The priest opened the door a little wider. "Don't you know what time it is?" He squinted and tried to look past her into the gloom of the vicarage front garden. Jennifer stood back a little, to let him see that she was alone. "Stay here," she'd told Michael after much quiet but angry argument out in the street. She'd looked at the darkened and very unexpected Church of All the Saints—it looked more Greek Revival than Greek Orthodox. She'd turned her attention to what might, when it was built, have been a semi-rural home for the priest given that particular living. "No!" she'd finally insisted after more arguing. "If there is anyone lying in wait, he'll be after you, not me. Let me go and check things out. The worst anyone there will do is send me away." Michael had looked as if he might strike her, he was so angry. But every argument he'd made about his "duty" was now magnified by thoughts of what the Turks might be about in England. That, plus the fact that they were standing outside the church, had shut him up long enough for her to get her way.

So, here she was by herself, outside the door of the vicarage not long before midnight. "I am in search of spiritual comfort," she said, putting into her voice the sort of tone she'd heard the night before in Oxford Street. She gave a puzzled look at the priest, then at the building. "But I was given to understand this would be an Anglican church."

The door opened wider, and Jennifer blinked in the light of a dozen candles from the hall table. "And an Anglican church it formerly was," the priest said with a contortion of his bearded mouth that might have been an attempted smile. "The first Orthodox prayers were said here in 1948. It was raised to the status of a cathedral in 1991. That was by Archbishop Gregorios of Thyateira and Great Britain. I am Father Athanasios, and have been Archimandrite here since 2016." He stopped and looked into her face. He sighed and took a step backward. "Do come in, my daughter," he said in the tone of one who gives way to the inevitable.

Jennifer was wondering yet again if this had been entirely the best plan of action. But it was too late to pull back now. She tried for a weak smile at Father Athanasios. Though he looked like all the other scowling, black-robed clerics she'd seen in Greece, his foreign lilt was overlain by a North London accent. She got out her smile and thought of the cosh that she'd been bullied into carrying. It was in the breast pocket of her dry but still smelly overcoat. All she had to do was reach inside. What she'd manage to do with it if the priest turned nasty was another matter.

"But come in, my daughter," he muttered with a reluctant show of duty. "The March nights are very chill."

"But are these the March nights, or the *June*?" she asked, looking closely into the bearded face. He blinked and seemed ready to block her entry. But she was already stepping forward. He sighed again and stood back so she could walk past him into the entrance hall.

"And who are you?" a man asked from behind the glow of the candles. He came forward. Tall, bald, about fifty, he gave her a keen glance, before hurrying forward to look into the darkness outside the vicarage.

Jennifer smiled nervously back at him once he'd shut the door and was looking again in her direction. "What I have is for a man of God alone," she said with simple piety. She staggered and seemed about to collapse. One look at the man's face, and she barely needed to act. Who was he? she thought with rising panic. The priest got a chair under her just in time. She put her hand up to her eyes and managed with an ease that surprised her to bring out a few tears. She hadn't even needed to think of her parents.

► ▼ ◄

"And, so, my child, the young man has declined to stand by you in your moment of need?" Father Athanasios looked as if he'd believed her story. And why not? There was nothing inherently unlikely about it. Jennifer took a sip of herbal tea and played for time with another fit of the sobs. She knew the bald man was standing outside the door—the priest's own surreptitious glances leftward had made that much clear. Who he was she couldn't say, but his mere presence confirmed her belief that there could be no help for Michael from the Greek community. Her best bet was to let the priest explain the Orthodox view of abortion and send her on her way. She waited for him to go over to a bookshelf and take down a big volume. She allowed herself a glance at the clock. She'd been here an hour already. If she didn't make her excuses soon, who could say what Michael would do?

She got up and remembered to sway slightly. "The hour is late, Father. My parents will be worried if I don't get home." Keeping her movements slow and tired, she reached for the coat she'd thrown over a chair.

The door swung open. "Not so fast, little girl!" The bald man walked into the room. He pinched the candle out and hurried across to the window. He looked silently out before turning back to her and the priest. "I think we've heard quite enough of your little sob story." Time to make a run for it—only Jennifer was no more capable of running away than of going for her cosh. With what seemed an iron hand closing about her chest, she missed what the bald man said next. But his grinning face was lit up by the glow of a mobile telephone. He held it menacingly aloft and pressed a series of buttons. It was answered almost at once. "I'm pretty sure I've got him, Prime Minister," he said. He listened. "The driver said he'd already been got at by Hooper's people. But I didn't see any of them on the way here." Another pause, and then a slight gritting of teeth. "I did write the address down for you. However, it's the...." He swore and looked at the display. "Have you a working landline in this place?" he asked the priest.

"No," came the impatient reply. "And I do think we should let her go home to her parents. She isn't the one you're looking for." The bald man laughed nastily and went into a Greek too rapid and in too unclassical an accent for her to catch more than a few words. But it was obvious she'd got herself into yet another trap. It didn't help that she'd already guessed that before taking her leave of Michael. The priest argued back in Greek, insisting, she could more or less follow, that the bald man should let her go, and threatening him with the Archbishop if he didn't keep to his side of whatever bargain had been made. The man paced about, holding up his telephone in search of a stray signal.

Father Athanasios now lost his temper. "Do I take it," he said, again in English, "that the girl is under suspicion? Have you nothing better to do than torment an already troubled soul?" He brought the flat of his hand onto the table.

"She was under suspicion when she opened the garden gate to this building," the bald man answered in a slow Greek that she could understand. "She became an accessory to harbouring an Outsider the moment she knocked on the door." He fell silent as a single green bar showed on the display of his telephone. It vanished before he could make his call. He breathed out in barely suppressed rage. Then, in a very normal voice, he said in Greek: "Who is that man at the window?"

He pointed in silent triumph as, just too late, Jennifer stopped herself from looking round. He crossed the room in a single bound and slapped her face. She fell off the chair, unable even to cry out in the idiocy of what she'd revealed. The man reached down and dragged her to her feet. "Where is our boy from Byzantium?" he snarled. "Tell me now—or, I swear, I'll carve that pretty face straight off your skull!" Somehow, he'd got a knife out of his pocket. If it was beyond him to open it with one hand, there could be no doubt from his voice of what he was longing to do.

Michael had been stupid to let the girl have her way. He'd known that even as she walked away from him and disappeared behind the hedge of the little front garden. He'd not understood the words of Tarquin's threat in English. But he'd guessed enough from the tone. "Put the girl down, or I'll kill you on the spot," he said from the open doorway. With what he hoped was an easy gesture, he clicked on the glass fire lighting machine he'd found earlier and set it to the candle. He stood back and showed the long kitchen knife he'd picked up after creeping through an unlocked window at the rear of the building.

"Michael, my dear fellow!" Tarquin cried, now in proper Greek. He let go of the girl and spread his arms wide. "I'm so relieved to find you again. We were all beginning to fear the worst. Now, do put that silly knife down and see the logic of your position." He reached slowly into his pocket and got out his paper box of tubes. He held them up in a gesture of peace. He sat down. "The Prime Minister's offer stands of help for the Empire. All it needs is for you to come back with me, and we'll arrange for you to fly directly to Constantinople in the morning." He smiled and reached forward to put a hand for Jennifer. She rolled away from him and got up to stand beside Michael. He pushed her behind him and raised the knife threateningly.

"And what about the girl?" He waved his knife again and hoped it would give him time to think this one through. Jennifer had said these people were badly in need of things that could only be had within his own world. Reason of state could usually compel governments to overlook any degree of attendant irregularity. Would the British Government assume the Emperor would overlook Simeon's death? Would it care what the Emperor might think? More to the point, would it risk letting Michael carry back news of this country's actual weakness? For some reason, his knife was beginning to shake.

"Oh, but you can keep the girl," Tarquin said with careless charm. "I don't know who she is, and I don't think anyone else will care." He lit his tube. He sucked on it for a while in silence, Then: "Of course, it was being kept in reserve that we should offer help to take Jerusalem from the Turks. It would be a decided feather in your cap to go back with that promise. Just think of our aerial might on the field of battle—and think how grateful Constantine Ducas would be for turning all the tables for him at the last moment." He set his face into an oily grin and puffed a cloud of smoke at the priest, who muttered something in English and shrank away from him.

Michael stepped back and pushed Jennifer through the door, "You'll need to take his—his talking machine," she stammered in Latin. "We've got to get out of here," she said with recovering purpose. "Hooper's people are already on their way. They'll be here at any moment." Tarquin's eyes narrowed.

"Well, well," he sneered, also in Latin. "Our little tart's belly

169

may not be full of some stranger's trash. But her tongue is skilled in the language of the Romans." He took another puff on his drug and pointed at the girl. "Who are you?" he demanded "What have you done to ensnare the Emperor's ambassador?" He laughed and brought out lewd quotation from Martial. His face twisted into a mask of implacable hate, before relaxing into another shifty smile.

"Stand away from that machine," Michael said quietly. Before he could reach forward and lift it from the table, it lit up with a faint purring." He and Tarquin watched it move with each of its regular vibrations. Michael grabbed it and tossed it over to Jennifer. She looked at its illuminated panel and pressed a button that made it go silent.

"I think it's Hooper," she said. "We must get out of here."

"You're a bloody fool, Michael!" Tarquin shouted in Greek. "If you don't come back with me, it *will* be Hooper's people who pick you up. Wherever you try to hide in this city, they'll pluck you out like a louse from white skin."

"Shut up!" was all Michael said. He tightened his grip on the knife, and steeled himself to step forward. It should now have been just a moment more of unpleasantness. But, while he looked thoughtfully at the priest—how far could he be trusted?—he felt a slight but warning tingle in his chest. Almost at once, this was joined by an area of utter blackness that, with each beat of his heart, spread farther out from the central point of his vision.

"But Michael, you look so very unwell again," Tarquin cried, his voice now steady. He flashed a look at Jennifer and bared his teeth. "Now, why don't we all sit down and discuss the matter."

Michael heard his knife drop onto the carpet, but was unable to look down to see where it lay. He willed himself to keep control, and realised that the sound he'd thought he alone could hear was his own ragged breathing. Another moment, and his legs would give way. But Jennifer had his arm. "Stay where you are!" she hissed at Tarquin. She jabbed with the knife she'd picked up, and got Michael through the door. His vision blurred in time with the sounds that were undoubtedly only in his head, and he just managed to keep himself from falling down when Jennifer let go of him to lock the door with a key she'd grabbed from inside the room.

Even before she could get hold of Michael again, Tarquin was across the room and rattling the handle. "Walk out of this building," he raged, "and all offers are withdrawn. The Empire won't last a dozen years without our help. You won't last a day at liberty in this country. Come back in here and let me save you and the Empire." He rattled the door again and shouted in English at the priest. "Michael!" he roared. "You can and will be killed on sight if Hooper's people don't get to you first—and that won't be good for you either. If she survives, the girl will curse the day she met you. Come back here—please, Michael, come back..." His voice turned to pleading, before fading away as Jennifer led Michael through the front door into the darkness and silence of the street outside.

CHAPTER TWENTY NINE

"It began last August—August in my world, that is," Michael said, his voice trembling with the mortal shame of a confession he'd been left with no choice about making. "Everyone thought it was the one incident. We made the three thousand miles between Constantinople and London without any sign of its return. It can't come back now— not now!" He looked up at the brown, faintly glowing, canopy of the sky. He looked down to where he imagined the slow and oily waters of the Thames must be flowing past the beach. Because they sat in the darkness of an embankment, he didn't need to worry if his tears could be seen. Jennifer took her arm from about his shoulder. He felt her press another of the paper towels into his hand. He blew his nose, and wondered if he could get away with a comment about the effect of coal smoke. But she had her arm about him again just as he gave way to a little sob.

Suddenly, she sat up. "Oh, Jesus!" she cried. She got out Tarquin's communication machine. Obviously, she'd forgotten all about it in the panic of nearly carrying Michael away from the house, and then explaining to him that any return to the tunnels was out of the question—"They'll be watching every single exit before dawn," she'd breathed in his ear. Now, as they sat on the northern shore of the Thames, the machine had lit up and was buzzing like a box filled with summer insects.

"Can't you send it to sleep again?" he asked, his voice reasonably back in order.

"The police can find us anyway," she answered, stabbing repeatedly at one of the buttons. When this failed to darken the display, she ripped the machine from its leather case and pulled its back off. The machine was now in three pieces. She stood up, and the little stones of the beach moved under her feet as she threw the pieces away with all her strength. He heard two splashes as they landed in the River. She reached down for Michael's hand. "We can't stay here."

"Where next?" Michael got up without help. Beyond the flight of steps that had brought them down here, the street lighting came on. Still in the shadow of the embankment, he looked up at the reflection of light from the now orange clouds. He'd been wondering about the tall metal structures that lined many of the roads. He could see he'd been right about their function, though hadn't expected the brightness of their collective glow. He looked about and came to a decision. "Keep against the wall, and try not to make a noise on the shingle."

They hurried downstream, passing under the forbidding spans of two of the bridges. Above them, on the left, perhaps the whole of London was lit up with a wondrous glow he dearly wanted to go up and behold. At irregular intervals, Michael stopped and listened. Once or twice, he might have heard someone walking along the embankment. But he had no sense of being followed. At last, the girl got a stone in her shoe. He helped her under the arch of another bridge and sat down.

"It was a stupid plan," he said, voicing his own thoughts, and, he had no doubt, hers too. "I should have guessed the driver would be questioned." He stopped himself in time from regretting that he hadn't cut Tarquin's throat and trusted the priest not to let on there were two of them. He heard a scrape of feet on shingle. He strained to see in the darkness. "Who are those men over there?" he asked sharply. He got noiselessly up and reached for Jennifer.

She listened, then relaxed. "They're speaking French," she said. "I think there's a big refugee settlement behind us. Perhaps they've come down to catch fish." Still not sitting down, Michael tried harder to see through the gloom separating them from the shoreline. With an uncertain glimmer, the men got a fire alight. They raised a subdued cheer and jabbered away again in a language that wasn't English. He hadn't seen them come down from the embankment. Nor, though, had he been aware of anyone keeping pace on their right while he'd hurried her along the beach. Perhaps they'd been down there all along. There was a gentle glow as the fire took hold of the driftwood, and then a cheerful cry in their language. Jennifer wasn't moving. Unless they wanted to continue along that beach until—for all he knew, late the next morning—they passed right out of London, there was nowhere left to go. He sat down again and stared suspiciously at the fire. Now it was properly alight, he could see there were three men about it. They were bigger than any vagrants he'd ever seen. Then again, until about the time he was first visited by the epilepsy, they might have been men of some importance. The Break, he knew, had caught out multitudes of travellers in each direction.

He put his arm about Jennifer. "It wasn't a complete waste," he said, trying to raise two sets of spirits. "At least we can be sure that I am the one you heard Abigail Hooper discussing last night. We can also be sure that I'd never have been with Tarquin on that flying machine to Constantinople."

Or could he? Like a bubble, pushing its way through a dense medium, he could feel a further thought working its way from the depths of his mind. He looked over to where the southern shore might be. "But, Jennifer," he asked, "didn't Tarquin imply that he was not working for Hooper?" He frowned and thought back to just before his latest moment of disgrace. "*If you don't come back with me, it will be Hooper's people who pick you up*"—that was what Tarquin had said. It might be worth asking about the conversation he'd heard Tarquin having through his machine. If it really had been with Hooper, or her people, why so long for any evidence that he was being chased? Why had they been able to run for miles through London before anyone thought to put on the street lighting? The answer was obvious, and, if he'd only been a proper man, there wouldn't now be any question. All that remained was to ask if he should raise his voice to the girl.

"Michael, I've been thinking," Jennifer said rapidly. "I don't know if you'll believe me, or even understand. But I think I've worked some of this out. Plainly trying for the right words in Latin, she took a deep breath. "Hooper's been running something called the Gateway Project. Her people have found a way to open a crossing back into the world we left behind last year. She's got in touch with representatives of the big power of which Britain was a province—or a *satrapy*, I think, is a better word. Perhaps her idea was to escape through this gateway in time. But she's had someone come into our world to look about, and she hasn't gone back with him." He listened as she drifted from this crisp statement of the outrageous into a circular and increasingly depressed mumble about how, if Hooper were in touch with her own world some time before The Break, she hadn't already been aware of The Break and been better prepared for it.

Michael gave up on thoughts of harshness. If she'd opened with the assumption that all this was too deep for a poor Greek to follow, the girl couldn't have read any Plato—nor heard him explained by Michael Psellus in a classroom of sceptical boys. And Psellus hadn't been anything like the first to talk about multiple universes. Look at those wordy neo-Platonists Michael had been forced to read before he was let into the Diplomatic Service. "I understand you perfectly well," he said, "and, considering what has already happened, I'll take it as a good working hypothesis." He put his thought bubble out of mind. Its contents might not be so important.

"Where time is concerned," he said, returning to the main subject—and still watchful of the vagrants by the shore: they'd now joined hands, to caper in silent joy about the flames of whatever they were burning. "Where time is concerned, we are probably riding as if on some invisible arrow. There's no going back to what has been passed, or hurrying faster to what is yet to come. But there may be an infinity of other universes. Some of these are radically different from our own, and can't be conceived, let alone described. Some are very similar. Some are exactly the same, and some of these are at different stages of their unfolding. If travel through time is impossible, it may be possible to punch a hole through the wall that separates one universe from another." He stopped and smiled. He thought again of Plato. "It's like being in a prison cell, and thinking you're the only person in the world. Then you pull a stone out of the wall, and find yourself talking to someone in another cell, who's been there for a longer or shorter time. From what you say, everyone here seems to think The Break itself was an autonomous breach in the wall between different worlds of appearance. Perhaps it was. Or it may have been an accident brought on by the careless use of the machine that has now been employed to make a more directed breach."

He waited for the girl to speak. She said nothing. Michael smiled again. "If you'll pardon the observation—and I think you will—you share the self-regarding error of almost everyone else in this country. You correctly believe that technical mastery is impossible without an understanding of natural laws. You then falsely believe that, when there is no technical mastery, there can be no abstract understanding." He looked over at the fire again. No one seemed interested in him or the girl. "But let's go back to the matter of what Abigail Hooper wants with me. Do I fit into your hypothesis? If so, how? Or does she only want me to frustrate a separate desire by the Prime Minister to establish a relationship with the Empire along the lines described by Tarquin? Oh, and where, if at all, does your father fit?"

Jennifer leaned hear head on her knees. "I haven't got that far. But perhaps my father was in a conspiracy to shut that Gateway Project down." Her tone indicated hope rather than belief.

Michael decided to change the subject. "Have you any idea what happened with all the people who were on this island in 1064? Any idea what happened to the whole island as it was before The Break? A further question is why, if you people really were about to destroy your own world, would Hooper want to go back there? Or has she found another world in where there is no final war? How would she know she'd found it?"

"I don't know about all these questions," Jennifer said in the voice of someone ready to give way to exhaustion. "But one theory about the England of 1064 is that it just ceased to exist. Another is that the island is now being studied by some very bemused American and German philosophers in 2018. The shock of this may even have stopped the big war that was starting."

Still paying no attention to him and the girl, the vagrants struck up a lilting song. "Well," Michael said, keeping his voice light, "since I can expect nothing from your Government, and nothing from the local Greeks, what have you in mind for tomorrow? Does it involve a visit to the castle of Count Robert?"

There was a sudden barking of dogs, and a beam of light shone down from the Embankment. "We're looking for a man and a woman," Jennifer heard one of the officers shout. One of the vagrants shouted something obscene in French, and they continued their slow dance about the fire. The officer laughed, and the light of many torches shone down to the shore. "You can remember what you said when I tell you that there's a reward of £100,000," the officer added—"no questions asked—for any information leading to their arrest. If you do see them, keep your distance. One of them's an Outsider, and he may be carrying a contagious disease."

Jennifer bit her lip and waited for the denunciation. All that came back from the bonfire was another obscenity and a shout of laughter. She put a hand on Michael's arm. They were in deep shadow of the embankment wall. The officer said something she couldn't hear, then: "You know the penalties for harbouring an Outsider," he said sternly. "If you think life here is bad, you haven't seen Ireland. One hint of anti-social behaviour, and I'll have you straight off that beach."

"Go away, my British chum," someone called in a strong accent from beside the fire. "The only Outsiders down 'ere is us!" More laughter.

Now silent, the officer swept his torch over every part of the beach he could see. He spoke softly with one of his colleagues about the river mud. He stopped as, with a loud crackle, a radio jumped to life. "Red Delta Six Five Zero calling," it said. "Have just seen two figures—possible male and female—hurrying upstream from last fix on mobile telephone. Need armed support for investigation of drainage tunnel ..."

With a satisfied cry, one of the officer's colleagues turned the radio down. "O'Sullivan's got sharp eyes tonight," the officer said with quiet satisfaction. He leaned over the wall of the embankment again. "You've missed your reward," he sneered. "We've got them ourselves." Jennifer heard footsteps that seemed to go away from rather than along the embankment.

She put a hand on Michael's knee. "Don't say anything," she whispered. Not moving, she watched as one of the vagrants walked briskly towards them. He stopped a few yards away, framed in the light of the bonfire, and looked into the shadows where they'd now huddled closer together.

"You may call me Pierre," he said in French. "I do have other names, but this one is sufficient. I am, of course, delighted to make your acquaintance."

"If you knew we were here," Jennifer asked, "why didn't you tell on us?" She realised she'd spoken back in Latin, and tried to put her mind into the right gear for French. She failed, and repeated herself in English.

"Ah, but 'ow could I snitch on my own countrymen?" he asked in English, with a wave of his arms. "It is only a year to go till ze Battle of ze 'Astings. Whatever I can do to 'asten ze defeat of zese English peegs—why, Pierre is your man." He came closer and put out a hand to pull Michael to his feet. He kissed him on both cheeks, and spoke his greeting in the dialect of Old French used nearest to the Channel Ports. Michael's response was a polite clearing of the throat and a little bow.

Jennifer took a chance. "He's Greek." She wondered if they could run away fast enough across the shingle. "He's the Byzantine Ambassador. Abigail Hooper wants him dead."

Pierre stroked his chin. "An 'undred thousand pounds, ze good lady is offering," he said in his unrealistically French accent. "So much to pass up for a little Greek boy." Jennifer got out her purse of Turkish gold and gave it to Pierre. He opened it. He looked at its contents in the light of a small torch he produced from his pocket. He bit one of the coins and laughed. "*Eh bien*—what fine investment I 'ave made! I spit on ze English pound, and wipe my bottom with its 'igh denomination notes."

He weighed the coins in the palm of his hand. "You may have half an hour before the police start tearing London apart again," he said in a voice that, if still French, had suddenly lost all its comic tinge. "Come with me if you want to stay alive."

CHAPTER THIRTY

"Well wouldn't that be interesting?" Father O'Flynn asked, dropping into English from a Latin that he could understand, but had never yet spoken as a language of conversation. "They've built themselves a time machine, have they?" Jennifer nodded—though she might have got the same reaction if she'd claimed the Archbishop of Canterbury was the King in drag. The Irish priest took another swig of distilled beer, before letting out a happy burp.

"Did your people follow us?" Jennifer asked in English. She looked over at Pierre, who was standing guard at the doorway of the railway arch warehouse. He noticed she was looking, and twirled his moustache and blew a kiss back at her. O'Flynn had put his pint mug down and was poking ineffectually at the little coal brazier. It seemed for a moment he'd put it out, and Pierre took a step into the room. But O'Flynn pushed his red face close to the charcoal, and managed, by much huffing and puffing, to get it glowing again. As the smoke dispersed, he motioned to Pierre to shut the door. He sat back with a grunt and reached for his mug.

Beside her, on the stained settee. Michael sat back and stretched his legs. Jennifer thought she'd have to repeat her question. But O'Flynn sat up again and gave a bleary smile. "I suppose, in a manner of speaking, they did follow you," he said. "You see, it's always now that they make a run for it—when the leccie's gone off for the night, and the grand people go up to their beds. The pair of you was spotted doing all the right things. You ran like bats out of hell from a big house. You ran with no apparent place to go. You ended up down at the River—and they always end up down there. It's like moths to a candle. It's as if they know they have to get across that wide Styx of a river to get back to the field of the blessed from whence they came." He smiled, coming to his point.

179

"So it's down by the River that Pierre catches his fish. None of us was supposing we'd go and catch a real live ambassador from the Byzantine Empire. Now, would you ever go believing that?"

There was a noise out in the approach road. Pierre narrowed his eyes and went out with an iron sword that he pulled out from behind a filing cabinet. O'Flynn poured himself another pint of moonshine and looked fondly at Michael. "Can you be interpreting for this young fellow here?" She nodded. "To be sure, we might have guessed you weren't just runaways. They don't go and get the police buzzing about like blue-arsed flies. Nor do they get all the street lighting put on for the first time this year."

He stopped and waited for Jennifer to interpret—as if there were anything so far worth the effort. He took another swig and grinned at the abbreviated version of what he'd said. "Now it's not that I've ever been thinking, mind you, of the correct protocol for a Byzantine ambassador. I mean, can you remind me, young Jennifer, of that church council where Pope and Emperor had thrones at equal height, and were supposed to sort out the Great Schism as equals? No? Well, I can't remember either—if I ever did know. To be sure, it was long after this young man was supposed to have closed his eyes. But we're just a decade after the Great Schism—not that I can remember what that was all about—and the question is whether I should get up and bow to the representative of the Pope's former overlord, or curse him as a schismatic Greek." He paused again. "But wasn't it one of the Gregories," he asked with his brightest smile yet, "who threw off the Emperor hundreds of years before this lad opened his eyes? Oh, but I was never a one for the history. All I ever wanted was to be a humble priest." He burped again, and looked at Pierre, who'd slithered back inside the little warehouse, and was stroking the blade of his sword.

"Can I ask the Reverend Father," Michael broke in, a slight impatience in his voice, "What view the Western Church takes of this whole position? Is it able or willing to give assistance of any kind?" She could have asked what assistance he had in mind— Jennifer couldn't fill in that blank for him. But O'Flynn had managed to catch his drift, and was clucking away over a second refill of his cup.

"Now, isn't that a question we'd all like to see answered?" he sniffed. "It's sure as anything, there's been a Miracle of God. You don't get a whole big island sucked out of the twenty first century, and dumped in the middle of the eleventh—not without a fair bit of the miraculous. The pity is that God has left it to man to try to understand the miracle." He sat back and looked at the door that Pierre had pushed shut. "Even if we aren't always right, you can generally expect uniformity from Holy Mother Church. But we're as divided over this as everyone else." He laughed. "There's no doubt, we look to Rome—but to which Rome no one can agree. Are we to conform ourselves to a Church that still hasn't known Anselm and Aquinas, or a Renaissance and Reformation and Counter-Reformation? What about the Enlightenment and our response to that? Are we to set aside a thousand years of unfolding understanding in response to movements of the secular mind, and adopt the simple piety of the middle ages? Or are we here to bring our Brothers in Christ to our own state of illumination?"

He stopped and creased his face into a look of extreme concentration. But the drink was against him—that or the inherent difficulties for him of giving a straight answer to any question. Or was it? "I only ever wanted to be a humble priest," he said again, though with a edge this time in his voice that almost took away the impression he'd created of rambling sottishness. "Our mission is to save runaways, not try saving the world." His eyes narrowed. "Wouldn't you be the daughter of Richard Baldwin, the novelist and hatcher of more plots that many today get hot dinners?"

Jennifer kept her voice steady. "Did you know my father?"

"Not," came the reply—"which may be, perhaps, why I'm still here on this mortal coil, when our Bishop, who might have known him well, hasn't come back from trying to persuade those poor souls to disperse from Oxford Street." He gave Jennifer a strangely dead look, and ignored her further question. "What did he do, but come and speak to the poor Bishop about his plan to overthrow the State? Do that, he was telling us, and let there be open commerce with the Outsiders—let our own people flood out into Europe, and spread our knowledge, and create a new kind of free civilisation—and His Majesty and all his ministers could be stuck up against a wall and shot, and we could try to set things up to avoid everything that went wrong after about 1914." He took a deep breath and scowled. "Some of us thought it was a fine, musical sound—not least for what the authorities have been doing across the water in Ireland." He stopped for a bleak laugh. "Is there nothing happens to the English, but they find an excuse to do ill in Ireland?"

"Do you know what happened to my father?" Jennifer asked. She tried to keep her mind free of hope, and waited for anything she might learn about them. "Can you say who killed him and my mother?"

"Now, shouldn't you be asking that of the man that betrayed him?" came the answer. "Wasn't he supposed to be your father's oldest friend—all the way back to university days?"

"Do you—do you mean a man called Basil Radleigh?" she asked with a catching of breath. She tried to think of another question that would pin the man down.

O'Flynn laughed again. "What I heard was they were both in with Anglo Oil," he growled. "Your father said the oil men had the same objective interests as he and his so-called friend. The Bishop didn't trust your father. Nor did I," he ended quietly. He saw the look that came over Jennifer's face, and shrugged. "You can ask me anything more you like, so long as you don't mind not getting an answer. But, if you ever see your father again, in this world or the next, you can ask him for me which lunatic it was who went about, lying the simple-minded into gathering in Oxford Street, so to draw armed men away from the Channel ports. Now, wasn't your father close with the Outsiders? Might he have been thinking that a riot in London would be enough to let a few horsemen with carbines get a foothold in Kent? Was he really working with a man anyone with his head screwed on could smell as a traitor—a traitor who eventually got him finished off?"

Jennifer thought about her last conversation with Count Robert. He'd seemed pretty sure that he was in for a chunk of England when the Norman Conquest did go ahead. But her father couldn't have been that stupid—could he? She thought of some of the comments he'd made shortly before she crept off to France. She thought of her mother's perpetual scolding about Radleigh's intentions—and the heated arguments this had caused. She sat back in her chair and bullied herself into thinking about the present and future.

She looked at Michael, whose politeness was wearing thin after the priest's apparently drunken rambling. "What will you do with us?" she asked.

"Now, that's the question, isn't it, my dear? You're just not the standard runaway we set ourselves up to help."

"Who are these runaways?" Jennifer asked impatiently. And she was impatient, though the question saved her from obvious thoughts about her father. Without being noticed, Pierre had gone out again. Now, he came back through the door and spoke in French about what may have been an approaching search of the district. O'Flynn looked at Jennifer and smiled blearily into her long face.

"Talking of miracles, just be looking at young Pierre. What was he in Rouen but cantor at one of the synagogues? Well, a slip in time saves nine, or so they tell. For sure, it brought Pierre over to the True Faith of the Cross. But wouldn't he be wanting to know, just like the rest of us, who the real Pope was?" He looked at Jennifer's tense face, and smiled more warmly.

"But you was asking who the runaways might be," he said with an expansive wave of a cup that he'd managed to refill in just the moment she'd spent looking at Pierre, "Well, before The Break, it was Filipinos and the like that people of quality smuggled in to skivvy for them in their fine houses. Since then, it's been Outsiders. They learn enough English to do as they're told, though not to ask for pay. If they turn uppity, or pine too hard for their fields and forests, it's straight out of a rickshaw they get pushed, to be shot on sight by the police, or dragged away by the Strange Meaters. But those who run off in the right direction—why, we've got our underground railway going deeper into France than your father ever went with his fags and rubber johnnies and oath of fealty to William the Bastard." He stared at Michael. "But, if it's help your young man's wanting for his Empire, he's come to the wrong place," he said with clear finality. As if he'd understood, Michael nodded. "That leaves us the question of what's to be done with the pair of you." O'Flynn turned to Pierre and began a conversation in French too fast and with too strong an Irish accent for Jennifer to follow. But she waited until Pierre had gone out, and O'Flynn was smiling again over his cup.

"For sure, we can get you out of London," he said. "We're thinking the emergency's over down on the Kent coast. Until we can put our things back in order, you'll have to get yourselves down there. Pierre can tell you where and when the little boat will be coming in. Try not to write it down." He coughed from a finger of brazier smoke, and slitted his eyes. "Best way there goes through a place called Tenterden." Jennifer tried not to gasp, but failed and tried to cover this with a cough, as if she also had breathed in smoke from the brazier. *Tenterden!* That was where Radleigh had been going for Hooper. She realised that O'Flynn was watching her. She pulled out a soiled handkerchief and dabbed at both eyes. "I'm told the Managing Director of Anglo Oil has a big house close by," he explained with an appearance of the artless. "Before he got himself lost in Oxford Street the other night, the Bishop was looking for someone to go and have a look down there. What he was thinking to find there he never did tell me. But it's a good town for passing through without being stopped."

Blinking back real tears, Jennifer got up and stared at Michael. O'Flynn still wasn't finished, though. "But isn't the Divine Economy just curious?" he asked, cheerful again. Jennifer stared at him. He gave a drunken burp and giggled. "Of all the people, in all the world, He could have brought together—and He joined two people who were already nearly connected."

▶ ▼ ◀

It might have been Blackfriars—though one Thames bridge is very like another from its underside, and in darkness. Jennifer tried her best on the web of rope ladders hung beneath it, but slipped every dozen rungs or so, to lie with her face parallel to a river she could hear and smell, but not see, as it flowed fifty feet below. It was then that she could hear the peremptory shouting, and the rumbling of traffic, on the upper side of the bridge. After one of the rungs snapped as she fell hard against it, she was finally picked up and carried by someone who had bad breath, and who muttered in an incomprehensible French.

Creeping through one of the bombsites on the South Bank, Jennifer tried to explain "her" plan to Michael. "We get right out of this country," she said. "If my father knew something about the Gateway Project, I think that was part of his involvement in France. Count Robert may know something that will tell us exactly what is going on." Just in front of her, Michael stiffened at the name and tripped against the lower part of a wall. Since discovering he had no rational plan, she'd been trying to get Michael to agree on getting out of England. Now he'd given way to the inevitable, she was simply relieved.

Pierre led them into one of the streets that had survived the flattening all about. He knocked an elaborate code on the door of a building about half way along, and stood back at the muffled scraping of bolts. He looked at her in the light of his dimmed torch and laughed. "Do not ze stars shine so brightly zis evening?" he asked with a blast of his winey breath. Jennifer looked up at the clouds that still glowed orange in the lighting from across the River, and shook her head. "But 'ow can you not see zem? You are young. You are in love. Ze stars, zey always shine on such!"

"What is he saying?" Michael whispered in her other ear.

"He's asking if we believe in God," she lied. There was a light from within the now open doorway. But she stood in the shadow of the wall, and, if her voice shook, no one could see how red her face had turned.

CHAPTER THIRTY ONE

Michael's bottom was sore from the motion of his legs on this still unfamiliar riding machine. The thin cotton shorts he was wearing didn't help. A few yards ahead of him. Jennifer raised her left arm to stop. He squeezed a little too hard on the brakes, and the wheels skidded on the smooth road. He came to a halt beside her, and wiped his face on the already stained sleeveless shirt.

"I think there's another patrol just round the corner," she said wearily. He followed her pointed finger, and looked at the queue of human traffic that was forming at the junction. Her own similar clothing, and the bandages he'd helped her bind tight about her chest, made her look like another boy. All that could betray her was the softness of her face. If the authorities were looking this far out of London, it was a young man and woman they were after— not two boys from the higher classes out for a ride in the sun. So far, the police they'd encountered at the main junctions had barely glanced at their grubby identification documents. But Jennifer had warned him of patrols that had machinery able to tell forgeries. Perhaps this was one of them.

He looked along the fifty yards of country road. The hedges on each side prevented him from seeing what might be past the junction with the wider road. But he trusted her judgement. It had got them this far into the country. He wheeled his vehicle forward another few yards and looked through a gap in the hedge. "If we go along this dirt track," he suggested, "those trees over there should keep us from being seen." She nodded. He reached down for his water bottle and drank enough to set his back into another sweat. He pushed his own machine through, and held the sharp branches back so Jennifer could follow.

"Let me go first this time," he said. He was growing attached to this clever machine, and enjoyed how fast it could go downhill. He got back on and coasted down the bumpy track towards a low building at the end of the field. He felt his hair lift slightly in the welcome breeze, and a chill as the shirt flapped against his sweaty back. For as long as it lasted, he had another of those little impressions that he was actually heading somewhere with a purpose. After a long and pretty blistering day, the sun was going down in the south west—which was the direction in which they were now riding. Still, this turning off their proper direction had got them past the patrol.

Some way beyond the low building, the path turned sharp right—still further away from their proper direction. Before then, it was blocked by a closed gate. Just on the other side, there were more farm labourers, resting with various kinds of food before going back to their last work of the day. He heard their low and tired chatter as he got off his riding machine. He hung back and let Jennifer go forward to the gate. She called out a greeting to one of the older men, who got up and pulled the front lock of his thinning hair. Michael smiled knowingly at the greeting one of the younger men made to him, and nodded as he wheeled the machine past them. He gave a brief but hungry look at the food they were eating. Neither had eaten since morning, when Jennifer had bought something pale and disgusting from a stall within the outer limits of London. With a quick glance back along the dirt road, Jennifer's thoughts had moved in the same course. She stopped and spoke awhile with another of the men. She then reached into her saddlebag and pulled about a couple of paper money strips. The man laughed and waved a big piece of bread under her nose. She went into a friendly negotiation with him, and eventually pulled out two more of the strips. The man took these and folded them inside the loose and once fine jacket he was wearing, and gave over the bread and a lump of what looked like real cheese.

Michael felt someone tap his shoulder. It was a young man, probably not much older than himself. Also wearing one of those faintly striped jackets, he offered a drink from a flexible bottle. Michael took a mouthful of beer and smiled back at the young man. "Ta!" he said in the noncommittal accent he'd been rehearsing. The young man said something else and laughed.

Michael nodded again. Might this have been a reference to the weather? He took and chance and looked up at the sky, which, so far outside London, was almost blue. But the young man frowned and repeated himself.

Michael was about to point at his left ear and give an idiot laugh. But he felt a sudden faint rippling in the pit of his stomach. He forced himself to smile and clutched the handles of his riding machine. He relaxed. It was another attack, and he felt it would continue. At the same time, it was very faint—he could best describe it to himself as a distant sound of thunder. He blinked and looked again at the young man. At once, he let his eyes go out of focus. The young man's mouth was hanging open, and he was swaying gently back and forth. For the instant their eyes had met, it was as if they were forming a complete understanding of each other. Even now, there were jagged flashbacks of a life that wasn't his own.

Jennifer broke in, speaking in her approximation to a manly voice. The young man swallowed and began a sentence that had no context but might have been in Greek. He shook his head and walked stiffly away. Alone with Jennifer, Michael stared down at the clicking of cogs and the circular chain that joined them. Most of the clever things in this world were beyond easy understanding. Some were so brilliantly simple, their working could be guessed by looking at them. This machine fell into the latter class. Thinking about it took him away from the vision, still fresh in his mind, of a room filled with flickering screens and with men shouting into communication machines that had stopped working. It had no easy beginning, but would end, he knew, in a falling back into convulsions similar to his own.

Jennifer stopped again and looked at the faded direction sign. Michael stood beside her. "Does it say another forty miles to Dover?" he asked. She looked surprised, but nodded. "Oh, I think I've got the secret of your numbers well enough," he said with quiet pride. "You do realise, I suppose, that we've been using positional notation for a long time now? The only oddity about your own numerals is their shape. But, given that they are absolutely regular in every public appearance, they were the first thing I really understood in this country. *"But how long, how long, to the great port of Dover, and to the town in where you lives?"* he asked in English. *"Or go we swiftlike to the Tenterden city?"* He put his head back and laughed at the shocked look she gave him.

"How much English do you understand?"

He brushed sweat from his forehead. "More than I can speak. It needs to be simple and spoken slowly—rather like Greek for you." He smiled and wondered if it would be appropriate to reach over and stroke her shoulder. He decided with a strange feeling in his chest that it wouldn't. "One of my duties is to learn the language of whichever people I'm trying to butter up. Compared with Arabic, your language has few difficulties. Another month here, and I'd be able to carry on a normal conversation, and read anything that didn't refer to unknown machines or concepts. Six months, and I could pass as a native." He looked again at the sign. "It's almost a pity we'll soon be out of here." Perhaps it would, he thought. The words Count Robert came once more into his mind. He put them out again, and stared up and the darkening sky.

"We might be able to sleep in some hay," she suggested in an oddly neutral voice.

Michael stopped himself from laughing again. "Hay is normally laid up later than June," he said gravely. "Besides, isn't it still March in England?" Her face turned down, and she stopped looking anything like a boy. But he could feel the advancing chill of a northern evening. "Whatever the case," he admitted, "we can't sleep in the open—not out in the country." He looked about. This was a narrow and twisting lane, lined with big trees that, if he didn't know better, he might have taken for a forest. The farm labourers must by now have gone home for the night. This meant that no one would challenge them if they crept into some farm building.

"But we do seem to be skirting Tenterden," he said. "The Frenchman told us to go straight through." He watched Jennifer go into a disjointed repetition of what she'd insisted after taking leave of Pierre—that Count Robert could certainly tell them something about Hooper's scheme. They might even be able to come back with armed assistance. He'd agreed, and her plan did make sense, even if meeting Count Robert wasn't high on his list of the desirable. Undeniably, though, since getting off that main road, the direction boards had suggested they were going round rather than through Tenterden.

The breeze that had been so welcome earlier turned abruptly cold. Shivering, he reached into his saddlebag for the woollen thing he'd been given that came down to his waist. He stiffened. At the same time, Jennifer clutched at him. He pushed her back and held his breath. He listened. There was the faintest noise of throbbing. He knew the sound of road vehicles. Jennifer was already looking up. She didn't need to point at the dim shape far over in the gathering darkness of the east. "If it comes this way, we'll get under the trees," he said. He looked harder at the bag of floating air. It was miles away.

Jennifer swallowed and continued looking. "They'll have special glasses that can see the heat of our bodies through any amount of foliage. We'd need to get under a solid barrier." Michael looked about. They might be coming to the top of a hill. Because the road twisted yet again before them, it was impossible to say what might be round the corner. Looking back over the darkening patchwork of the field system, there were buildings that they'd taken care to avoid. But, if going back in the direction of London, the floating machine was moving at a deceptive speed. One slight change of course, and it could be over them in barely any time at all. He looked up the hill again, and told himself to stop worrying. The floating machine was moving steadily out of view. But the panic had brought further thoughts to the front of his mind. Whatever the girl had said about getting help in France, he was running away. There was no doubt she'd do everything to keep him in France. Even if he got away from her and her Norman friends, how could he come back without her as a guide? On the other hand, what was there left for him to try in this country? He looked up again at the floating machine and felt the lump that had come into this throat. His duty was to stay, and, whatever risk might be involved, find some way of averting the tidal wave that was about to sweep over his country. Instead, he was running for the coast. He'd been set on that path by a pack of Latin schismatics. He was being led along it by a silly girl, who was easing every bump in the path with Norman silver. The best word to describe all that was failure. There was worse to life than being a worthless epileptic. Though pitiable, that wasn't a defect anyone could blame. He thought again of the man who'd got out alive from Thermopylae. Aristodemos he'd been born—Aristodemos the Coward was what he'd been called back in Sparta.

He climbed onto his machine, wincing as the strain in his leg muscles from the pedalling was transferred to his bottom. "Come on, then," he said wearily. "We can at least see what's ahead before it gets dark." He stopped again and reached back for a half-eaten block of chocolate. This was another of those foods that gave a boost to weary muscles. He broke off a couple of squares and gave half to Jennifer. Still not sure about the gears she'd explained more than once, he pushed hard on his pedals and set off in a wavering line that steadied after a few yards of continued effort.

He'd nearly reached the top of the hill, and was waiting for Jennifer to catch up, when he heard the unmistakeable sound of hooves. They came from just over the hill, and he could hear five—maybe six—riders. He looked anxiously back at Jennifer, who seemed more concerned about the floating machine, still visible in the east. Before he could suggest getting off the road, they were both in sight of the riders.

Michael had been wrong. In his own world, wheels on cobblestones could be heard from half a mile. Black padded wheels on English roads were a different matter. The open carriage was pulled by two horses and accompanied by an escort of two riders dressed in black leather. Everyone was looking so intently into the east that no one saw how Michael had to jump off the road with his machine. The passenger snapped an order at Jennifer, who seemed rooted to the middle of the road and had raised both arms to cover her face. He reached forward for a riding crop and looked as if he might set about her. Michael got forward in time to get her and her machine out of the way. Still looking east, the escort riders chatted and laughed as they passed by.

"Well, well!" said Michael. He wanted to listen for anything else he might catch. But Jennifer was still curled into a ball by the side of the road. He hurried over. He could swear the fat man hadn't touched her with his crop. Gently, he pulled her arms down. "What is it, Jennifer?" he asked. "Did you hear what they were saying?"

She shook her head and stared up at him, her face pale in the fading light. "That was Basil Radleigh," she was able to gasp. She looked about to cry, but steadied herself. "Were those dark men with him talking Arabic?"

Michael nodded. "Arabic, it was," he said. "One of them, if I'm not mistaken, was speaking it with a Turkish accent."

CHAPTER THIRTY TWO

"If it's working, that box up there can see us," Jennifer explained. She pointed at the wires that, hung on ceramic insulators, topped the high wall. "Those will hurt us if we touch them, and will also give warning of our presence." She pulled herself back into the shadow of the nearest tree to the cleared and brilliantly-lit zone that surrounded the wall about the house. This much she could easily have expected. But the thrill of hurrying along with Michael in pursuit of Radleigh had kept these obvious facts out of mind until she had no choice but to face them.

Michael didn't argue. He didn't ask for explanations. Instead, he sat down and crossed his bare legs. "Since we've reached what may be our first moment of free choice," he opened calmly, "I think we need to talk." There was something in his voice that Jennifer found disturbing. But, if he felt his choice was free, she sat down beside him and waited for him to speak what was in his mind.

"I don't like your idea of France," he said with a firmness that ruled it straight off the agenda. "I don't like it for any number of reasons, though I accept you've been pressing it on me with the best of motives. I also don't question your motives in getting me away from Tarquin. There's no doubt he was working for the Prime Minister, and what they both had in mind was to send me home with an offer of military support." Jennifer wondered if she could change the subject. But, if in darkness, she could feel the look on Michael's face. "There was too long a delay for us to get down to the River before Hooper's people went into action." Jennifer's heart skipped a beat. If only Michael could have seen her, she'd have tried for a smile.

"This being said," he went on with quiet force, "I also accept that Hooper is the most energetic mover in the British Government, and that she'd never have let me out of the country. If I could see he wasn't lying, I also agree that Tarquin was making worthless promises. Your stratagem to get me away was, in the event, a favour when I was in no position to decide for myself. So, if we aren't going to France, and if I can't give myself in to the Prime Minister, we don't have that many choices. I could suggest a return to Constantinople. Even if your people do nothing at all, I may have enough foreknowledge to change my own world's future. I can certainly make sure we get a more effective Emperor than the one we have. But you want to see what your friend Radleigh had to do with your parents' death, and my duty is to see what those Turks are doing here."

He laughed and stretched out his legs. "As for getting into that house, I'm not at all sure. How do we get in? How do we get out again? What do we do while inside? You were lucky with your last spying mission. You managed to overhear something important. For all we know, everyone in here is fast asleep, and we'd have to look through several dozen rooms to find your man. Then, of course, since I'm the best person to ask the questions—and then finish him off—there would be the problem of interpreting."

Michael put his head up and laughed, now bitterly. "Have we a moment of free choice? Will you put a case for hurrying off to your Count Robert? Or was our last moment of free choice when I decided to go calling on Tarquin? Or was it the night before, when I heard you scream?" No longer bitter, he laughed again.

Jennifer tried to think. "Do you—do you think my parents were brought here and killed?" In the darkness, he might have shrugged. She bit her lip. "Do you know where in France the priest's men would put us down?" Michael still said nothing. She tried harder for a sensible thought. "What do you think we should do?" she asked in the tone she'd always before used when she couldn't get one of her father's tougher Latin exercises.

"The priest was right that our paths have converged. Your father was up to something that Hooper didn't want to succeed. I don't want her to succeed in whatever she is doing. Move her out of the way, and your Government might be worth trusting. And I'd really like to know more about the Turkish presence. If it was Turkish agents trying to kill you, why was your father working with a group of people who are in with the Turks? Above all, what are the Caliph's men up to in England?"

He got to his feet, and Jennifer heard him brush soil from the back of his shorts. Now outlined against the reflected glow of the security lights, he stood over her. He bent down and stared into her face. "Come on, then," he said, for some reason amused. "Since you must be right that there's no way in over the wall, the only way left is through the main gate." He tapped her on the chest and snorted at the wince of pain he drew. "I told you to get out of those bandages," he said grimly. "It doesn't matter now what sex you appear to be. Even if you won't be bruised for days, I need you able to move freely. Get that shirt over your head, and I'll untie you."

► ▼ ◄

At his third and obviously clumsy attempt, the guard made a dull clicking noise with his weapon, and stepped from the flood of light that fell all about the open gateway. His eyes still not adjusted, he tried to look forward into the undergrowth. "Who is out there?" he cried uncertainly in Arabic.

"I am sick, O brother," Michael called back. "The Infidel beer has surely killed me." He let out one of the high pitched giggles of the Eastern races, and reached over to shake a bush that was a few feet to his right. The guard had taken out his communication machine, and was dithering between it and his weapon. Michael could feel that Jennifer was beginning to panic. "Surely, I shall die out here in this cold northern darkness," he sobbed in a voice that dribbled out the self-pity of the badly hung-over. Still looking from weapon to communication machine and back again, the guard took a step deeper into the shadow beneath the wall.

"Who are you?" he asked. "I don't recognise your voice." It looked as if he might put his weapon down. But he checked himself and tried once more to see who was calling at him from the undergrowth.

Michael forced out a convincing burp, and gave another groan of pain. "Help me to safety, my brother—or, let the Prophet be my witness—you shall answer to the Commander of the Faithful in person. I have messages for the one called Basil, and cannot appear before him in a raiment covered in vomit." The guard stepped back against the wall. He looked about as if for advice. He looked again at his communication machine, now for a long time. As he took a step towards the light and raised the machine to his ear, Michael got him just below the turban with the large stone he'd been holding in reserve. He shook himself free of Jennifer's hold on his arm and rushed forward. He got himself within the shadow of the wall and reached for the guard. But controlling a man who must have been twice his own weight, and who was only stunned, was easier said than done. Michael hadn't got him by the legs before he was raising himself on both arms and opening his mouth for a cry of alarm. Giving up on his first plan, Michael threw himself forward and snapped the man's neck before he could finish drawing breath.

"Come and help me," he called softly to Jennifer. "I can't lift him by myself."

"But you've killed him!" She didn't move from where he'd left her.

"Were you expecting me to try bribing him?" he laughed. He pulled again at the dead body, this time rolling it over. "Now, come and help me. Since no one's running out from the house, I'll guess we haven't been observed."

▶ ▼ ◀

"You're mad!" Jennifer said again as he finished arranging the turban. Michael shook with quiet laughter and set about pulling the stripped body deeper into the shadow of the wall. Not helping, she sat down. "Couldn't you at least have questioned him first?"

He stood up and shrugged. "Things don't always work out as you wanted." He gave the body a kick that rolled most of it under a bush. The bits that showed might not be seen till morning. "The key to success in all these matter, though, is to keep moving." Jennifer gave him a worried look as he played with the three foot projectile weapon. He'd seen these used many times on the entertainments on the picture machines back in his lodgings. But he tested its weight. It was heavier and more complex than he'd expected. He put it down. He kicked the still dormant communication machine fully under the bush.

"Very well," he said, now brisk and commanding, "we'll go in together, and make it look as if I've caught an intruder. Don't struggle. Depending on what happens next, we may need to change that story."

"But you're the wrong colour!" Jennifer groaned. "We'll not get a dozen paces in there."

"Oh, I don't know about that. As for the colour, this is a funny light." He pulled her close. "Do remember that speed is of the essence. Shall we go in?"

Their feet crunched loud on the gravel as they covered the hundred or so feet that lay between the gate and the main door of the house. Take away the elaborate machinery that secured it, and Michael failed to see how anyone, of whatever quality, could bear to sleep in a house like this. Even its ground floor was studded with glazed windows. His own family's manor house had windows only to its inner courtyard. The outer walls were of rendered brick, and his father had always been fussing over the depth of the surrounding moat. This house, so far as he could see, was a single block, with glazed windows on every side. England must long have been a very safe country if the rich could trust themselves in the like.

The front door opened inward as he set foot on the steps leading to the porch. Michael had three stories ready in Arabic that should cover all the possibilities. He hadn't expected the red and bleary face of a native. Swaying slightly, he began a nagging lecture in an English that he spoke slowly and expected to be understood. Before Michael could step on her foot, Jennifer answered for him. At once, the man was sober. A close look at Michael, and he was stepping backwards, and pulling out what might be a communication machine, or something else.

Not moving from the rectangle of light that stretched a dozen feet beyond the open door, Jennifer looked down at the man's flickering eyes. She wanted to cry out at the enormity of what she'd seen. But her mouth was too dry.

Michael looked at her and sniffed. He pulled her into the shadows. "First rule of intruding is that you kill everyone you can't avoid or trick. I don't suppose you've ever killed anyone yourself. But haven't you seen enough death in the past few days?" Not answering, she looked at the body. "Now, if you don't want me to kill too many more of these people, you'll keep your mouth shut, and stay out of sight!" He thought she would be sick. He put both hands on her shoulders and shook her. "Jennifer, did you suppose diplomacy was all a matter of giving presents and general buttering up?" He shook her again and stared into her moist and wide open eyes. "I can't remember how many men I've killed in the past two years. Nearly every one of them would have killed me, if I'd given him the chance." He let go of her and smiled. "What did the man say?"

Still unable to speak, Jennifer pointed at the door to a room just to the left of the main entrance. It was ajar, and Michael stepped into the glow of a dozen picture machines, all showing colourless images of the house and its surrounds. He looked at each of them, trying to get some kind of bearings. The view he had over the gateway couldn't have shown the Arab guard's death, but showed clearly where he and the girl had rushed forward into the illuminated clearing. Tough on the old native he hadn't raised the alarm while he could.

So long as no one turned on a light, the space underneath the bank of picture machines was in deep shadow. Not bothering to ask for help, he dragged the body in and put it out of sight.

He pulled the door back ajar and wiped his hands on the long robe he'd put on. "I take it we haven't been seen by anyone now alive?" When the girl said nothing, he led her across the floor of polished wood and pushed her gently beside a bronze statue of Saint George that mimicked the ancient style. "Where do you suppose we can find Basil Radleigh?" He poked her sharply in the breast and waited for the pain to bring her back to her senses. "Jennifer," he said urgently, "I did explain before we started that this wasn't a game. If we're caught, we can expect to be killed— eventually if not at once. Either we make a run for it—and that means two completely pointless deaths—or you can pull yourself together and try to work out where that man is sleeping."

Jennifer looked about in blank despair. It was only once he began to lead her out of the house that she stopped choking back the sobs and twisted free of his grip. "In there," she said, pointing at the room where he'd left the dead man. She swallowed and threw off the shudders he could see coming over her. "There might be a list of names."

Michael leaned against the place where he'd pushed the body and watched the movement of the hands on the clock. He still wasn't entirely sure how time was measured in England. But the girl was taking a lot of it to pull out every drawer and rustle every sheet of paper she could find. The little hand was pointing at the second mark down on the right, and he watched the big hand move steadily three marks up till it was hovering past the three quarters point. "I can't find anything," she whispered after she'd finished making a noise that ought to have woken everyone in the house who wasn't already stone dead. "Can't we just go up and look into all the rooms?"

Michael took a deep breath. "No. If you think I'm touched in the head, you should try listening to yourself." He pulled the door open a few inches and looked into the continuing silence of the hall. "Come on. We've tried our luck as far as it will stretch. We're getting out of here while we can. We'll think of something else when we're a couple of miles down the road towards Dover." He controlled his temper. This was his own fault. He should never have let them in for this stupid mission. How they'd get across the Channel remained as big a mystery to him as it had been all day. But there was nothing to be done here.

He stood back from the main door just in time to avoid being caught in the glare of the vehicle that swept with a gentle purr through the gate, to crunch to a halt on the gravel. He muttered one of the English obscenities he'd learned and pushed the girl back into the little room. The vehicle was barely a dozen feet beyond the main door, and he could hear low voices and the soft thudding of metal doors into metal bodywork. Another moment, and a man was walking about the hall and speaking in a raised and impatient voice. A light now went on, and the man spoke again, now apologetically. Michael leaned noiselessly forward and looked out into the dim light of the hall.

The main spoke again. Another voice took up in Latin: "Your driver apologises, My Lord, for the lack of any reception. But the hour is late, and we were unable, for security reasons, to send ahead with a definite time of arrival."

"Not the end of the world, you can say for me," came the answer in the rough Latin of a barbarian. There was a low but wolfish laugh. "Unless you'd laid on something carnal, forget the greetings and get me a drink." This was followed by a sound of tinny music and the double grunting of a pig.

Michael looked round to where Jennifer had fallen silently to her knees and was trying not to cry out. He wondered if she too had recognised the voice of Gordon Jessup. Its quiet yet fussy Latin had made him almost nostalgic for those interviews in Dover.

CHAPTER THIRTY THREE

Now he'd let go of her, Jennifer had to twist like a landed fish to avoid hitting her already aching breasts on the floor. "If you don't get up and pull yourself together," he murmured into her ear with a silky calm that nearly finished the work of scaring her witless, "I'll have to go after them alone."

"No!" she gasped in a voice that she'd meant to be a whisper, but that sounded like a shout in the little room. She shut up, then tried again. But Michael was already through the door and padding towards the staircase. She could hear Count Robert laughing with a failed attempt at the discreet. His voice came, she told herself, from one of the corridors that must reach out from the first landing of the staircase. She looked round. In the light that came through the open door, she could see the sagging face of the porter Michael had finished off in cold blood. In its own way, this was as nightmarish as Oxford Street had been. She took hold of a chair back and pulled herself up. At first, she thought her legs had turned to jelly. But the sight of Michael creeping on all fours up the wide stairs was a shock that got her moving again.

By the time they reached the landing, everything was quiet again. Jennifer swallowed and looked nervously along the right hand corridor. From behind, she heard the sound of a distant light switch. Or it might have been a closing door. She turned and followed where Michael was already moving swiftly. At every closed door, he stopped and pressed himself against the wall, listening for any hint of movement. He looked back once and glared at her as she traipsed along the middle of the long carpet. She would have copied him, only she knew she'd only have knocked the ornaments off one of the tables placed every few yards along the lavishly decorated walls. They reached the end of the corridor and passed into an oblong room that had neither carpet nor oil paintings. From this an open door showed a flight of narrow and uncarpeted steps. Here, the dim electric lamps gave out, and it would mean creeping on in darkness. Michael pressed a foot onto the first of the steps, and jumped back as it gave a gentle squeak.

"Follow me up slowly," he whispered. Put your feet where I put mine." This meant going up wide-legged, each foot pressed on the extreme edge of the steps. Jennifer had read novels that involved breaking at night into big houses. They'd always thrilled her, and her father had sometimes urged her to try writing a novel of her own in the style of Ian Fleming or Sapper. Now she was living the fantasy, it was more like the dreams she'd often had as a child about being where she had no business to be. There was the same oppressive dread—the same slight remove from outright hysteria. She nearly stumbled on the top stair, and had to be caught by Michael before she could fall with a crash onto the rough boards. She pressed the button on her wrist watch and tried to look round in its feeble glow. So far as she could tell, they'd reached the top floor of the house. This was where the servants had once been lodged. Servants there must still be somewhere—especially in a house of this kind, and now that labour was once again cheaper than dirt. Perhaps they were all Outsiders—or perhaps all Arabs or Turks.

But, even as they were steadying, her thoughts were scrambled again by the sudden rattling of a door handle. Half way along the narrow corridor, just where Michael was trying to press his ear, a door opened a few inches, and a narrow slit of very dim light streamed across the floor. *Oh no!* she thought—there was nowhere to run. They'd both surely be caught.

Michael pulled his ear back from the door the moment he knew it would open. He reached inside his robe for a knife that wasn't there. As he looked back at Jennifer, the door steadied, and he heard low voices speaking English. There was no point hoping that Jennifer would get down on the floor and press herself against the wall. She stood twelve feet along the corridor, waiting to come into full view of anyone who looked out to the right. There was nothing else for it. He jumped noiselessly forward to the far side of the door and coughed politely as it eventually swung open.

"Who are you?" an old man called out in English. He peered into the gloom at Michael, his back to Jennifer. Michael bowed, so that he hoped his face was in the shadow of his turban. "Oh—isn't that you, Ibrahim?" the man continued in Arabic. He laughed. "Well, you may be exactly what I need. Come in, my boy of manifold beauty, and peace be upon you."

"And peace be upon you, My Lord," Michael answered. This wasn't what he'd wanted, but was pretty much what he should have expected. He bowed again and followed the old man into the room. Except for a table and more chairs than were needed, it was bare of furniture. Its only light came from a candle that had been placed on the table, and was already burned half down.

Count Robert gave Michael a single look, and, with a slight jingling of chain mail, was on his feet. "And what, in the name of God, is this?" he growled. "I thought I was brought here to deal with Englishmen, not Saracen unbelievers." He threw the tube he'd been smoking onto the boards and crushed it under foot.

"Peace, peace," the old man said in Latin. He spoke in English to Jessup, who interpreted that everyone was a friend in this room, and that much benefit would be had from keeping it that way. Robert had his sword half out of its sheath. He let it fall back in with a loud rasp. He looked suspiciously at Michael, who got himself against the far wall from the door and folded his arms in a gesture of passive respect. He laughed and put a tube into his mouth. He lit this from the candle, and now puffed happily on it. Concentrating on his own tube, Radleigh sat beside the old man at the small table. Both looked across at Robert, and all three sat at right angles to Michael. When he thought everyone had gone back to drinking wine from cups big enough to serve as flower pots, he turned up his eyes and found himself looking at Jessup. Beardless and turbaned, he had hoped that Jessup also wouldn't pay attention. He'd been wrong. From the other side of the candle, face immobile, Jessup stared back. Michael darted his eyes quickly about the room. The other three men were hard at work with their wine cups. Ready to jump into whatever action he might achieve before Robert could get his sword out again, Michael gave a single wink. Jessup's face tightened for a moment. Then, he closed his eyes and turned away. Michael bowed his head lower and waited.

"I must thank you, My Lord Robert, Count of Crèvecœur, for having come at once on such very short notice," Jessup interpreted for the old man once the wine cups had been put down. *Robert?* Michael kept himself from leaning forward for a closer look. It explained the girl's loss of nerve—though, considering what she'd learned about her father's business, she shouldn't have been *that* surprised. Not moving his head, he looked at the Norman. Big, powerful, a glutton for wine—except he'd acquired the English taste for smoking, he was standard to his kind. He must also be in his late thirties. More of a second father than anything else, he thought.

Jessup was speaking again. Without waiting for any response, he followed with a question of his own. He seemed deliberately not to be looking at Michael. The old man pursed his lips and thought. Then he nodded. "Since this is our first meeting, all three of us together," Jessup interpreted, "I think it would be useful if we were all to be clear about where we stand. Though the British Government continues, for the moment, to insist on no contact with the outer world, I represent an interest in this country that does not share this determination." The old man stopped and frowned, as if wondering what to say next, or how to say it. He spoke rapidly with Jessup, who nodded.

"You will be aware that, since our sudden appearance among you," Jessup said to Robert, now speaking largely in his own right, "England has been in continual difficulties. These can only be settled by connecting ourselves with the outside world. We need access to certain mineral and other supplies. In due course, we shall need markets for the textiles and other goods that we are learning to make again. Before then, however, we must have access to those supplies. One of the most vital is a dark liquid that has many uses. We know that this can be found, in unlimited quantity, and of the highest quality, beneath the sands of the Arabian Desert. We have maps to show us where it can be extracted nearest to the surface or nearest to the sea. We need at most two years of heroic effort. Apart from that, we need the consent—and perhaps the assistance—of those who rule the territories where the liquid must be extracted, or over which it must be transported."

Robert flicked ash into a ceramic bowl. "Is that why you have called an embassy of the Greeks to England?" he asked sharply. "Duke William was inclined to have them killed in a tavern brawl. Sadly, one of the bishops threatened him with an interdict."

"The Greek Empire is of no active importance," the old man explained through Jessup. "You may see it as the oldest and greatest power in the world. It can do nothing to us. The deal we have offered the Caliph is that, in exchange for giving us all that we want in and about Arabia, we shall give him the means to take Constantinople and every non-European territory of the Empire. We made this agreement six months ago. Your task in the plan is to assist us in overthrowing the current British Government. Your reward cannot, of course, be rule over England. But you are to be given the means to conquer Germany and Italy."

The answer was a contemptuous grunt. Well it might be, Michael told himself. Anyone who made a bargain with the Normans quickly found himself on the losing side of it. For all their knowledge and weaponry, the English were fools if they thought it would be different for them. Sure enough, Robert thought little of them. "We've had twenty thousand men in arms for a month now," he sneered—"every one of them with a hundred rounds of ammunition. All we needed was the signal for us to get them into their boats. We waited and we waited. We saw men withdrawn for a day from your coast. They were back the following morning. Do I now hear right that the distraction you'd planned *did* go ahead?" He laughed. "If you want another go at using us as mercenaries, you'll need to give us some of those flying machines as well. Don't try telling me there's any element left of surprise."

Radleigh cleared his throat. "This was due to a most unfortunate break in the line of communications," he said smoothly through Jessup. He explained how the London demonstration had gone according to plan, and that an army larger than—and almost as well-armed as—anything the British authorities could assemble might easily have landed. Robert muttered angrily in his own language, and looked about to get up and walk from the room.

But the old man was leaning forward with more wine. "My Lord Robert," he said through Jessup, "we had no idea until it was too late that our link man had gone missing. Even then, we did everything possible to turn a feeble demonstration into a riot bordering on civil war. We did then try to get an emergency message across the channel." He smiled sadly. "I sent more than a dozen of my best men into action. All of them sworn to die at my command, every one of them suffered martyrdom with willing heart. There is no point in asking how our message never reached you. We must simply conclude that a plan that had been months in preparation ended in failure."

"So these are suicide fighters?" Robert asked with a change of tone. Plainly, he still thought little of the English. But he turned and gave Michael an appreciative look. "I know a man who spent time in Cairo. He told me there are private clubs where...."

"Indeed, there are such!" the old man cut in with evident relief at the change of subject. "I was last in Baghdad just before our own Christmas—and the new Caliph, I can assure you, is a man of very broad vision. For a modest outlay, one can behold acts of the most varied, and always willing, self-immolation." Before Jessup had finished, Radleigh was speaking in a bored voice. He finished with a sour look and lit another tube. "Oh, don't worry about Basil!" the old man said. "I will tell him later of our new plan, to take direct action against the Government. But, dearest Robert, can I tempt you—as a mark of my personal esteem, and as a token of what can be done when a man places no value of his own life—to a private demonstration of the loyalty that I command?"

What the old man went on to say Michael didn't hear in Latin. Jessup had abruptly stopped interpreting, and was into some plainly contrived coughing fit. It didn't matter. Robert already had his sword out, and was holding it up, hilt pressed into his waist. "Ibrahim, my glorious young flower," the old man said, back into his rather modern, but still comprehensible, Arabic. "Ibrahim, the time has come for you to do as you promised in your freely-given oath to the Caliph."

Michael kept his face turned down. "What would My Lord have of me?" he asked, trying not to let his voice shake.

"Do you see that western barbarian's sword?" the old man answered in a mild and slightly sorrowful voice that didn't fit with the anticipatory gloat on his face. Michael said nothing, but tried to think what to do next. "Well, Ibrahim, it is to propagate the Faith that I command you to impale yourself upon it. Do it slowly, and with a joyous smile. Perhaps you could recite that lovely poem about blue stones in the desert."

CHAPTER THIRTY FOUR

Whether or not he knew Arabic, Jessup had got the burden of the old man's command. He said something low but sharp to Radleigh, who tried to frown him into silence. He spoke again. Outraged, the old man seemed to tell him to mind his own business. Radleigh was beginning to look confused. Jessup may have said he'd be no party to murder. The old man laughed. Michael fought against the panic rising from his stomach. While three pairs of eyes focussed on him, he wondered if he could reach the door without being cut down by Robert.

"Oh, but Ibrahim!" the old man suddenly cried, tapping his forehead in an admission of how thoughtless he'd been. "How can I possibly ask you to spoil such fine, ceremonial clothes as you are wearing tonight?" For a moment, Michael thought he'd be sent away to change into something that wouldn't soak up the blood. But the old man spoke a few words to Radleigh, whose own face still showed something between boredom and distaste. The old man turned back. "Take off all your clothes, O beauteous vision of boyhood. You must die as naked as you were born." He called something over to Radleigh, but his voice was hoarse with excitement, and he seemed to trail off without coming to any main point. Radleigh looked at the clock on his wrist and lit another tube.

There was a curtained window to Michael's right. Since it must be sixty feet up from the ground, there could be no getting though that. His face shining with the joy of an approaching death, Robert twisted in his chair and held his drawn sword at the ready. The old man called something that was supposed to be encouraging, about the seventy two virgins who must be growing impatient. Michael slowly undid his turban and wondered if he could throw his main robe over Robert before making his dash from the room.

"Not very dark for a Saracen—is he?" Robert observed once Michael's face could be clearly seen. "Decidedly pale, I'd say."

Jessup had given up on interpreting, and was looking at the wine jug—Michael had already given up on this as a weapon. But the old man got up to help with the robe. "You are young Ibrahim?" he asked uncertainly. Before Michael could grab hold of it, he took the robe and hurried over to the other side of the room, to place it carefully over the back of an unoccupied chair. "You *are* very light for one of the Faith," he said from behind the chair.

"I have turned pale in the bathing water of the Infidels," Michael said with a sinking heart.

"And why are you wearing the ridiculous underclothes of an Infidel boy?" the old man asked. Michael's answer was something vague about the northern weather. "Oh, never mind that!" the old man laughed. "Just take everything off, and come into the light, so we can all see the last moments of such pride and beauty. Do this, young Ibrhaim—then press yourself slowly into the barbarian's sword. Let it go in just above your navel." He repressed the more obvious signs of excitement, and came forward again to stand beside Robert, who was sucking hard on the last inch of his tube and filling the room with more acrid smoke.

Michael took his shirt off. Whatever doubts the colour of his skin might have raised, he'd never be taken as a Moslem once his shorts were off. Perhaps he could leave them on and try for one of the dances he'd seen those boys perform in Baghdad. Yes—these men wanted a show. He'd stretch this one out until he could get close by the door. But, as he raised his arms over his head, and went into a squatting move, Robert barked out a laugh and got up. He stepped towards Michael, his sword arm pulled back for a stabbing motion.

With a sudden flickering of the candle, the door flew open. "Get over here, Michael!" Jennifer shouted. Whatever was going on, she could see she'd got here just in time. She looked about to see if anyone had more than a sword. If Robert had brought his pistol with him, it must still be buttoned into its holster.

"But Little Bear!" Robert cried, his face twisting into one of his charming smiles. "What a delightful surprise!" Still keeping his sword ready, he turned and bowed to her. The nasty old man in the tweed jacket shouted something at Michael in what she guessed was Arabic. Not moving, Radleigh sat in his chair. He was breathing out a lungful of smoke and looking at Michael with dawning realisation.

"Get over here!" she shouted again at Michael. Robert was within eighteen inches of her, when she let off the fire extinguisher into his face. She'd found this at the top of the staircase. Getting it free from its housing had taken her the whole time that had passed after the explaining of the plot. Now, she fired off a jet of compressed and nearly freezing foam. It knocked Robert straight over onto his back. His sword landed with a clatter on the boards. Ignoring him, she turned on the old man, who hadn't yet thought to switch his squeals from Arabic into English. Unlike Robert, he didn't go over, but did get an inch of foam into his eyes and mouth.

"Not him!" Michael said as she turned the red cylinder towards the other old man in the room. He darted over to get his big robe. But this was wet through from a stray jet of foam. He gave up on it and went for the sword. Robert was getting up with a roar of outrage. With one hand, he rubbed at his eyes. The other was already feeling inside his tunic. Jennifer gave him another blast of foam that also put the candle out.

Somehow, Michael had got behind her, and was pulling her from the room. With another loud hiss, she sent more foam into the room, this time at random. As Michael pulled harder on her arm, she swung the cylinder in her right hand, and threw it at where Robert had last been standing. How it landed she wasn't able to tell. Within seconds, she and Michael were stumbling downstairs into the lighted areas of the house.

At first, this was as still and silent as they'd found it. But the noise made far above had been noticed, and, as they hurried down the main staircase, they came face to face with a bearded Arab. He lunged up at them, sword in hand. Michael swung his own sword, and, with a crunching of bone, got him across the face. The Arab fell back with a scream, and they stepped over his writhing body. By the time they'd reached the foot of the stairs, though, the main hall was filled with men, all shouting in a cacophony of Arabic and

English. One of the Arabs lifted a rifle to his shoulder and took careful aim. Crying out in two languages, Jennifer tried to pull Michael down. But the gun jumped up as it was fired, and whatever came out of it missed by a mile.

Michael took hold of her, and, shouting in Greek, got her back to the main landing. This time, they took the right turn and hurried into a now brightly lit corridor that might have been the mirror image of the one they'd just passed through. There was another loud crash of gunshot behind them, and an exultant scream. Except a vase far ahead of them burst into a mist of fragments, the shooter might have saved his bullets. Jennifer thought for a moment she could hear someone shouting over and over in English—it might have been Radleigh. But Michael now pushed down on one of the door handles and got the pair of them into a grand bedroom. Jennifer pushed him away from the door once he'd closed it and turned the lock. She felt a momentary tremor of fear, then got a chair propped under the door handle.

Michael looked about the room. "Can you get the window open?" he asked with surprising calm. Jennifer nodded and tried not to make any noise as she raised the bottom sash.

He stripped the bed, and, paying no attention to the loud shouting outside in the corridor, used his sword to start ripping each of the sheets in two. Someone rattled the door handle. There was a loud thump as someone tried to knock in one of the heavy wood panels. Then Radleigh was there. "No shooting!" he roared. "I want neither of them harmed." Regardless of what he said in English, someone outside let off a bullet that smashed a two inch hole through the topmost door panel. But the old man who spoke Arabic was now outside, and was passing on the instruction.

Jennifer looked at the sheets that Michael had quickly twisted about and tied together. She hurried over to the window and looked into the bright stillness far below. "We can't go down that!" she whispered. There was a loud crash of men against the door, and shouting in many languages.

Michael put his head out and came back in, a scared look on his face. He thought for a moment, and picked up the end of his strip of twisted sheeting. "I suppose not," he said with a return to the decisive. "But we can make it look as if we have. Tie this round that ring there that holds the curtains." He hurried over to the bed and came back with some pillows that he threw down. He looked about. "Can you make that light go out for good?" She grabbed a bolster from the bed and swung at the light fitting. With a dull pop, its bulb went out at her second attempt. Before she could draw breath, Michael was pushing her under the bed. He was hardly beside her when there was an immense splintering of wood, and, in the light from the corridor, she could see the feet of a man who was shouting in Arabic.

Radleigh was second or third into the room. "No shooting!" he demanded. "One more shot, and it's Ireland for all of you!" Just as urgently, someone repeated him in Latin, and what may have been the old man spoke in Arabic. Jennifer saw five pairs of feet gather by the window. Someone spoke in Arabic and laughed. The old man gave an order, and two pairs of feet hurried back to the door. She could just hear them padding along the corridor. There was more distant shouting.

"They can't get far," the old man quavered. "But who is the boy? What is he doing here?" In the silence that followed, Jennifer forced what control she could on her ragged breathing. This was lunacy, she could have told herself. But she knew that already—and it was suddenly as if she were reading about herself in one of those novels. It was a strange feeling, but came with a growing feeling of serenity that did now get her breathing under control.

She heard the click of a cigarette lighter. Two polished shoes moved slowly toward the door. She saw what was left of it pushed into the frame. "If you ask me, they haven't gone far at all," Radleigh laughed. There was the unmistakable smell of Lambert & Butler. "I knew that all those American films I used to enjoy would come in handy." He turned towards someone who was wearing dirty trainers. "Tell that French oaf to give me his revolver," he ordered.

Robert's first answer was an obscenity. Then, after a whispered argument through the interpreter: "One hair of her head, and any deal you've made with us is off." More whispering. Whatever Radleigh's answer, she heard the rasp of gun metal on chain mail.

"But wasn't my Little Bear ferocious tonight?" Robert staggered slightly, and laughed. "That stuff she sprayed was like quicklime."

"Go and open that wardrobe properly," Radleigh muttered. The old man said something she couldn't hear. "Must I always be surrounded by fools?" Radleigh snapped. She watched his feet move softly to the big wardrobe. She heard the whoosh of air as its door was pulled wide open. "So, if they aren't in there," Radleigh said with a quiet laugh, "There's only one other place they could be." He lowered his voice. "Tell the oaf to go and stand on the other side of the bed. Tell him to bend down when I raise my hand."

For some reason, the interpreter put this as a command for Robert to take his gun back and leave the room. But Michael seemed to have understood. While Robert went for Radleigh, and he swore back, Michael swung quickly from under the bed and pulled Radleigh down. "No one moves, or I kill him," he said in English.

Jennifer scrambled out, to see Michael with his sword at Radleigh's throat. "Come, Jennifer!" he said evenly, hands stretched out before him. "Be a love and tell our nude young god to stop this silliness. There must be two dozen suicide bombers in this house. You'll not get more than a few yards whichever way out you care to try." Cigarette still between his lips, he allowed Michael to pull him to his feet. "I know who the boy is," he said after a quick drag. He lifted his right hand slowly to take out the cigarette, and blew out a long stream of smoke. He smiled. "Do tell him that neither of you will be harmed if he puts the sword down. You can add my assurance to the oaf's demand. You don't know the half of what's going on. Your father didn't know." Jennifer's tongue stuck to the roof of her mouth. Radleigh laughed. "Look, do get him to use his common sense and put the sword down. We can then have a civilised discussion over a late supper."

Jennifer's answer was to make for the revolver that had fallen unregarded to the floor in the struggle between him and Robert. Even as she moved, though, she could see Radleigh reach quickly down and stub out his cigarette in Michael's side. Michael gave a sudden yelp, and let his right arm go limp for a moment. She didn't see how on earth Radleigh managed to get free without a scratch.

But he did nearly beat her to the gun.

Nearly! That wasn't good enough. With a shout of rage, Michael pulled him back by the collar, and Jennifer had the gun between two shaking hands. "Get back against that wall!" she shouted—"all of you!" She repeated herself in Latin, and pointed the gun at Robert when he didn't stop his increasingly ludicrous cries of endearment.

Now might be her one chance of killing Radleigh. All she had to do was point this heavy gun and try to keep it steady as she squeezed the trigger. But could she keep it straight? Wouldn't she need all the bullets to get out of here? From all over the house, she could hear distant shouting and a clattering of boots. Far beneath the window, she could hear more tramping on gravel. Could she spare even one bullet? Still keeping the gun on Robert, she glanced at Radleigh, who was lighting another cigarette beside him. She couldn't doubt he'd betrayed her parents—just as he was engaged here in some act of betrayal—but she still hadn't questioned him. Could she kill Radleigh? She might have killed once before—but that wasn't in cold blood.

Radleigh caught her uncertain glance, and smiled through a cloud of smoke, "It's time to grow up, Jennifer," he said in his sternest voice. "This isn't a game. So give me that gun before someone gets hurt. Hooper wants the boy, and won't stop until she gets him." The old man began a confused protest. "Oh, shut up!" Radleigh told him. "You'll get your oil concessions—but it will be Hooper's way, not yours." He turned once more to Jennifer. "My dear girl," he said, as smoothly as if he were already sitting down to his late supper, "that boy is the key to a better world. One way or the other, he's going back to London. You can make that easy for us or hard for the pair of you."

Jennifer forced herself to make a decision. "Cover them with your sword," she said to Michael. His face was dark with anger and with shame, and he waved his sword menacingly. She went over to the window. After the comparative darkness of this room, the outside floodlighting was like the day at noon. She stared down at a dozen bearded and waiting faces. She pulled back the hammer and held the gun hard between both hands and aimed it down. The

214

crash was deafening as she pulled the trigger. Even before she was really aware of that, she'd come close to knocking her head on the upper sash from the recoil. This was like nothing she'd ever fired. She was lucky she hadn't dropped it out of the window. She looked over the dark outline of the gun for something that might resemble a safety catch. Finding nothing that looked obvious. She stuffed it into the back waistband of her shorts, and tried not to think how far down the ground was as she climbed backwards out of the window.

"Go down alone," Michael said. "I'll follow." Unable to speak, she shook her head and tried not to slide uncontrollably down the smooth fabric of the sheet. She was half way before she could get a proper hold. By then, Michael was also inching down from above her. She could feel rather than hear the ripping of cotton as it slowly gave up on supporting what must be a combined weight of sixteen or seventeen stone.

"Tell them I want no violence," she heard Radleigh say with hard finality. "Hooper knows all about your dealings with the towel heads, and doesn't care. Harm that boy, and it'll be Ireland if you're lucky." She looked up, but saw only the off-white bottom of Michael's shorts. The old man was above her, shouting in Arabic, as, with a stab of relief, she felt the gravel beneath her feet.

CHAPTER THIRTY FIVE

Dark shapes fanned out all round them while Jennifer hurried a bare-footed Michael round to the front of the house. "Make for the trees," he hissed. He pointed with his sword at the fifty yard distance to the open gateway and the darkness beyond. "I'll try to hold them off." He yelped as he stepped on one of the large stones that marked off a flower bed before one of the ground floor windows. Ignoring him, Jennifer took his right arm over her shoulders and helped him across what seemed the impossibly wide expanse. She was just in time with her free hand to stop the gun from working its way out of her shorts. She held it in one hand and waved it theatrically at a man who'd come within a few feet of them. He fell back with a shrill cry of alarm in Arabic.

It really was bright as day out there. Mindful of the continuing overhead cry in Arabic from the old man, no one pointed his own gun. But there were perhaps a dozen men about them, all dressed in Eastern robes, and all in a circle that was tightening by the second. They'd never make it to the gate. If they did, they'd never find where the bicycles had been propped out of sight. If, by some continuing miracle, they got this far, it was almost a joke to wonder how far they'd get on bicycles.

"The—the vehicle," she cried wildly. But Michael had already seen the dark and shining car, and was pulling her in its direction. He slashed out with his sword at a man who'd come too close, and nearly got him. Over by the gate, two big Arabs stood in their way. Their own curved swords glittered wickedly in the floodlighting. Behind her, in the house, there was a crash of many feet, and angry shouts. There would soon be dozens of men out here.

The gun shook with a life of its own as she pointed it at the driver. "The keys—give me the keys!" she screamed in Latin at him. Somehow, he understood, and pointed inside the car before getting his hands up. "Get in!" she shouted at Michael, now in English. He shouted something back in Greek and waved his sword to cover her as she got in. Putting the gun into her left hand, she pulled her door open and fell into the seat.

"Oh, Jesus, Jesus—no!" she sobbed with a thrill of horror. She'd noted the odd lettering on the number plate, and seen the ring of yellow barbed wire above the D for Germany. It still hadn't got to the front of her mind that this wasn't an English car. She was sitting in the passenger's seat, staring at the glove compartment. They'd got so far. They'd got so far—and she was sitting in the passenger seat, with a boy right out of the middle ages sitting in the driver's seat. Her heart thudding away like a tribal drum, she squeezed her eyes shut and tried to blot out the sound of shouting that was soon all about the car. Michael had spoken earlier of a "moment of free choice." She could have laughed at the use they'd made of this—only there were now men banging on the roof and doors.

She opened her eyes to a universal clicking of locks, and looked left in time to see Michael turn his attention from the controls on the door to the mass of dials and levers before him. "I have seen these things driven," he said calmly. "This one's all the wrong way round," he added with a turn to fierce concentration. "But I think you still need to turn the key to the right of the steering wheel." She heard him patting about until he found the ignition key. He turned it so the internal lights came on. He frowned and pushed one after another on the pedals. Before Jennifer could find any Latin that might describe the next step, he rubbed his nose and grinned. "Silly me!" he said brightly. He twisted the key fully and shouted something as the engine roared into life. He let his left foot slip off the clutch pedal, and the car lurched an inch forward, before falling back to where it had been parked. Someone was hammering on the rear window. A sword blow left a bright crack near the top of the windscreen. Jennifer shrank into her seat and pressed her eyes shut.

"Oh!" he cried. He laughed and pointed at the handbrake. "I should have moved this lever down." She closed her eyes again in time to another sword blow, opening them to see how her own side of the windscreen was become a mass of shining cracks. Still calm, still concentrating, Michael was pushing his feet up and down on the pedals. He found how to turn the key fully back and then all the way forward to get the car started again and put it into second gear. He poked a bare foot at the accelerator, remembering just in time about the clutch. There was a loud crash of shattered glass as one of the rear passenger windows caved in, and a series of what sounded like hammer blows on the roof. There was a sword already stabbing through the broken window when he got the car moving slowly forward and turned the wheel sharp right.

As he accelerated towards the gate, Jennifer kept just enough presence of mind to stretch past Michael and look for the light switches. She might have told herself that she should have got into the driver's seat—only she'd forgotten how to say anything so complex. And, even if there had been the time to waste, she wasn't sure she could have driven the car to better effect than Michael was achieving. She got the lights on in time to see a man dressed in English clothes outside the gate. He moved directly before them, pointing a rifle. Either Michael had forgotten about the brakes, or he wasn't bothered. The man's body crashed forward onto the bonnet, and slid off somewhere to the right.

Michael turned the car left into the narrow road that Jennifer thought must, after a few miles, lead to the dual carriageway. After a spell of continuing uncertainty with the pedals, he pushed hard on the accelerator and laughed maniacally at how the car shot forward. "Isn't this wonderful?" he cried. She looked at his profile. In the glow from the dashboard lights, his whole upper body gleamed with a light sweat. His eyes were open wide, and his lips were drawn back over his teeth. He was going into another cry of triumph, when he took a bend at full speed and almost tipped the car over. She thought they'd crash into a signpost. But he spun the wheel again, leaning briefly into her lap, and got the car steady. Now he'd pulled off the bandage she'd managed to get on with so much fuss and effort, she could see that his stab wound was turning to a faint depression on his upper arm.

Jennifer remembered the seatbelt, and pulled it into place with a reassuring click. "Should we not slow down a little?" she found the strength to ask. Her answer was the glow of headlights far behind.

"They're coming after us!" If Michael heard this, he didn't think to look into his mirrors. Considering their speed, and his erratic steering, this may not have been so bad an oversight. He drove on in silence, the lights coming ever closer. She twisted round to look back, and was just in time to see the two lights she'd thought part of a car move wider apart. They were being chased by motorbikes—and almost certainly by the same kind of men who'd blown themselves up in Oxford Circus. Would they remember the orders the old man had been relaying to the end? Too scared to tell Michael to push his foot right down, she watched the motorbikes close the distance between them.

Another minute, and she could hear the roar of powerful engines. A few seconds later came the crash of something heavy against the rear window. There was a second crash, and now a third. The concentrated beam from the motorbike that hadn't yet caught up became a diffracted glow across the whole window. Another blow, and cubes of shattered glass splashed over the back seats, and the roar of the motorbike engine became louder still and more urgent.

Were they trying to get ahead of the car? If they did that, what next? Jennifer had seen police riders on the television, able to stop a car in a few minutes. But had the riders enough experience to do more than catch up and hack away with their swords? Michael took another bend without slowing, and the motorbike that had caught up with them fell back beside the other. She looked forward. The road was straight for as far ahead as she could see. "Michael, go faster," she said. He nodded and pushed his foot all the way down to the floor. It was a couple of seconds before this had any effect on the speed. But the dark hedges lining the road were soon flashing past at terrifying speed. Surely, she told herself, no motorbike could keep up with this speed.

She was wrong. Now they too were through the bend, both motorbikes put on speed of their own. It may not have been half a minute before they hacking away again at the car. One of the men even managed to twist low enough to push his sword deep into the car and prod the back of her seat. She clearly heard his squealed exclamation. There was now a series of slight bumps in the road, and the motorbikes fell back again. She turned to Michael. He didn't seem aware of anything but the pool of light in front of him.

On the dashboard, an orange light was on that she hadn't seen before. She thought back to the Olden Days. Her father's car had gone for miles and miles before he got twitchy about the fuel warning light. But it was a question of speed and fuel quality. How far would she and Michael get before the engine cut out?

There was another approaching roar. Jennifer put hands each side of her face and squeezed as she tried for a useful or even a connected thought. In a flash, she remembered the gun. She'd put it on the dashboard as a failed warning to everyone back inside the gate. Michael's wild driving since then had knocked it to the floor. She undid her seatbelt and reached down. The gun had somehow wedged itself under her seat. Remembering she hadn't managed to find the safety catch, she got it carefully into her right hand. "Try to keep in a straight line," she shouted at Michael. Still looking forward, he nodded and licked his upper lip. She took hold of her seat and pulled herself into the rear of the car. She felt but ignored the pricking of little glass cubes and knelt on the back seat. Holding the gun in both hands, she tried to aim at one of the approaching lights. Before trying to aim, the light had seemed so steady. It was now jumping all over the place. She waited until the sights of the gun were framed for a moment in the round light, and squeezed the trigger. If Michael had lost control of the car in the terrible crash that followed, she wasn't aware of it. The next she knew for certain, she was trying to pull herself up from the floor. The gun had flown out of her hands in the recoil, and both lights were still approaching. She lay on the back seat and pressed clammy hands together. Where had the gun fallen? She got up and looked through the unglazed rear window. The motorbikes were coming on fast again, but were still about fifty yards behind. She turned round to Michael. "Stop the car!" He wasn't listening. As if in a trance, he was clutching tight on the steering wheel. She pushed her upper body to the front of the car and repeated herself. His mouth moved slowly in a Greek she couldn't understand. They were increasing their speed as the car flew down a gentle hill. In the up and down bouncing of the headlamps, she could see how, a mile ahead, the road twisted left. At this speed, they'd go straight off the road. "Put your foot on the brake," she shouted He looked in her direction, and said something she still didn't understand. But taking his eyes off the road had set the car into a slight wobble. She looked round. The motorbikes were closing fast. She could keep screaming at Michael until, doing ninety, he hit a tree. Or she could try something of her own that, however wild, had worked once before.

Jennifer shouted in English for Michael to brace himself. She got behind the front passenger seat and reached forward with her left hand, to take hold of the handbrake. She breathed in and shut her eyes, and pulled the brake up as far as she could. At once, her already bruised chest was pushed against the back of the seat, and there was a squeal of tyres and a smell of burning rubber, as the car spun left out of control. Then, as the engine went off, her window smashed inward and something big and heavy landed on top of her. She thought at first they'd hit a tree. "*Death—that would be a fine adventure!*" she heard herself inwardly quote

A fine adventure it might be—though not yet. After a long silence, Michael unclamped his hands from the steering wheel and stopped pushing at the accelerator. "What did you do?" he asked in a dreamy voice. Jennifer pushed ineffectually at the dead man who was pinning her to the floor of the car. She managed to get her head up to look about for anyone else who might still be alive. But she was stuck in her place. All she could say was that the only lights on were their own.

"Are you hurt?" she gasped. She moved her own arms and legs. She was all right. She repeated her question.

"I don't think so," he answered in a more normal voice. He raised trembling hands and looked at them. He let them fall into his lap. "I had the strongest impression," he said, now wearily, "that I and this vehicle had merged into a single creature. I'm told cavalrymen have this experience on the field of battle. It also happens now and again with...." He stopped himself and tried for a smile. "But I never thought such speed was possible." He stopped again and seemed likely to drift off into a reverie of his own. But he sat up straight and looked round. He leaned back and tried to push the dead man back out through the window. He was too heavy. Michael got his door open and went round to pull him from behind. With much shoving from Jennifer, the body finally slid backwards and landed with a kind of splash on the road. He got back into the car and looked at the controls. "I feel very cold," he said. Shivering, he leaned back and closed his eyes. Jennifer put a hand onto his chest. He was bathed in sweat, and was beginning to shake uncontrollably.

"You'll catch a cold if we don't find you some clothes," she said with a firmness she was beginning—don't ask how—to feel. He nodded, but did nothing. Jennifer reached for the door handle. The dead man had hit the car at speed, and his impact had bashed the door out of shape. Forcing it open needed all her strength. She got out into the darkness, and had a moment of fear when her legs gave way. It was only a mild shock. She'd stumbled rather than fallen down. She stood upright, and noted how dark it was outside the light still thrown forward from the car. Her idea had been to try stripping the dead man. He'd been dressed in leather. But it seemed that his entire body had turned to jelly inside his clothes, and it was as much as she could make herself do to raise one of his arms. She stood up again and looked round for the other man. His motorbike had bounced back from the car, and its dim shadow could be seen a few yards away. The man himself was gone. If he'd flown over one of the hedges, he might be anywhere. She went and opened the boot. Here, she found a picnic rug. She could get that round Michael. She looked back along the road. No one else was following. They were alone.

She got back into the car. "If we reverse," she explained, "you can turn the wheel right. If that isn't enough, you can reverse again. But I don't know how long we have before this thing runs out of fuel." She left aside the question of where they'd go. As sure as anything, though, the one possibility she'd had in mind throughout, and that had always been in reserve to comfort her, was dead. She'd not be visiting Count Robert again in his castle.

CHAPTER THIRTY SIX

Jennifer got back from the village to find Michael bathing in a pool formed by the cold stream. He sat up to his waist in the clear water, splashing it over his head in time to a strange song in Greek. She put her carrier bag down and watched him from behind a tree. They'd dumped the car a hundred yards away, under cover of some bushes. It would still drive in an emergency, but must have too little fuel in its tank to go more than another few miles. Michael stopped singing, and, with a laugh, slid under the water. He came up almost at once and began rubbing at his hair.

O let me be awake, my God!
Or let me sleep alway

she found herself reciting. Michael stopped rubbing his hair and looked about. "Is that you, Jennifer?" he called. He stood up and reached for his sword. Not caring how wet she got, Jennifer hurried over for his embrace. He kissed her, before standing back and pointing at the dark patches he'd left on her shirt. Smiling, she took her clothes off and climbed into the freezing water beside him.

Afterwards, they ate some of the bread she'd managed to buy without ration coupons, and sat together on the grass for a long time in silence. The sun was rising steadily in the blue sky. Whatever the official clocks might say, this was mid-morning. Over behind a hedge, the farm workers were resting from their first four hours of labour, and were being directed about their next shift by a man with a rough voice. Michael was first to speak. He stretched back and put his arms behind his head. "I've changed my mind about France," he opened. "I'll confess that I wasn't keen on meeting your Norman friend. But, since he's here in England, we can forget that danger. My suggestion is that we get ourselves somehow across the Channel, and make for the people that Simeon and I had to leave behind. We have horses and money and a few guards. If we get a move on, we can retrace our steps to Bari— which is a port on the south eastern coast of Italy. This is still in Imperial hands. From there, it's an easy matter of taking ship to Constantinople. Whether anyone will believe a word of my report is something we can worry about once we get there."

"Yes." If he'd suggested walking to the Scottish Highlands, or setting up home on the Northern Line, she'd not have said otherwise. But there was a punishment beating somewhere beyond the hedge, and a woman's loud screaming brought Jennifer to her senses. This was an idyll that couldn't last. "We can't run away, Michael," she said flatly.

He sighed and sat up. "But what else is there? Nothing we can do will bring your parents back. I'd like to have met them. But there it is. As for me, those people your father was working with want their mineral oil, and will dangle the Empire as a bribe to the Caliph. The Prime Minister might be able to impose on them his own idea of a protectorate over the Empire. He might then use us as a weapon to control the Arabs. Otherwise, Hooper might go through with her own plan, whatever that is. In any event, there's nothing the pair of us can reasonably do to change how things work out in this country. Show me what to do, and I'll take any risk to get it done. But all I can think at present is how to get back to my own world. We can survive there. We might even flourish. I see nothing for us in England but to hide out until we're finally discovered." He stood up and reached for his picnic rug. He looked about and shrugged. He looked down at her with a smile of infinite sadness. "In the normal course of things, the Empire would have lost. According to your history lesson, the collapse would have begun six years from now. Perhaps I'd have died at Manzikert. Thanks to The Break, some things will now be different. The essentials will be the same. But come back with me and see the Empire while it lasts." He reached down for her hand. "It is worth seeing. Every scholar I've met here is longing for a sight of unplundered Constantinople."

Hand in hand, they walked back to the car. Jennifer turned on the radio for the 8am news. It was still mostly about the Oxford Street "tragedy." It seemed the scale of killing had been too great for the initial cover up, and the Government had been forced to bring out claims of a plot by dissident religious leaders. "It was," she caught Hooper saying, "an affront to the basic tenets of our society, which are multiculturalism, tolerance and peaceful co-existence." She went on to explain a new set of Hate Crime laws, these to involve the closure of the last public libraries, and the shutting down of what little Internet remained. She then paused, and went on in softer terms. It had to be accepted, she said, that there were many Outsiders in the country, and that it was no longer possible to regard them all as spies or carriers of infection. This being so, they were not from now on to be killed wherever found, but were to be arrested and turned over to the authorities for peaceful repatriation. She mentioned in particular a young Greek male, who was to be valued for his knowledge of ancient literature. She announced a reward of £7 million in gold for anyone who could hand him over alive.

As the National Anthem began to play, Jennifer turned off the radio. "Perhaps if Hooper wants you so badly," she said, "the least we can do is get out of England."

Michael hadn't understood the bulletin. But he nodded. "In France," he said, "we can regard ourselves properly as man and wife."

Man and wife! Jennifer had often wondered about marriage. But a proposal after barely four days of a courtship that had mostly been spent running away! She reached for Michael's hand. It all seemed right and proper to her. Everything seemed right and proper in ways it never had before.

CHAPTER THIRTY SEVEN

Once the engine was off, there was nothing to hear but the calling of the birds high above. Jennifer thanked the young pilot of the speedboat. He smiled and pointed at the tall priest who, standing up to his knees in the surf, had watched the boat on its approach to the shore of France. "I'll go first," Michael said. As he jumped from the boat, the sailcloth cape he'd put on against the cold of the crossing fell off, and he reached the priest looking almost as if he'd just swum the Channel. There was a brief conversation, and Michael pointed back at Jennifer. The priest, though, pointed at a small tent placed where the beach gave way to main undergrowth of the shore. Michael looked at her. But the priest spoke again, and Michael waved reassuringly, before darting straight for the tent. Jennifer watched him run. It was as if he were chasing the ball in some beach game.

She was still watching him when the priest transferred his wooden crucifix to his left hand and reached out to help her down. "Thank you for everything, Father," she said in Latin.

"Think nothing of it, my child," he said in an English more clipped than she'd heard outside old films on the television. His clothing had said Outsider. But he might have flown Spitfires before taking holy orders. He grinned and gave a little bow. "The Church protects all those it takes under its wing." She turned and looked nervously back over the wide sea to the low darkness on the horizon that was England. She looked up into the blue sky, clear of everything except the wheeling birds. "And don't worry about that," he said cheerfully. "The health and safety officer in Dover has announced a fault in the airship that ought to keep it grounded till Monday."

He looked closely into her face. "You are Jennifer Baldwin, if I'm not mistaken." She nodded. "Well, you can call me Father

Lawrence. I am, among much else, Vicar Apostolic *in partibus infidelium*. But that's neither here nor there between us." He led her beyond the line of the waves, to where the sand became white and powdery

Jennifer looked again at Michael. He'd stopped outside the tent, and was embracing what seemed to be old friends. One of them was trying to get a blue robe over his head. "Who are those men in funny clothes?"

"Those are His Excellency's companions," Lawrence answered. "The elderly one is Alexius, his late uncle's under-secretary. The younger ones are the embassy guards." He laughed and took her hand again. "Dearest child, Holy Mother Church overlooks nothing. We got a coded message from London the night before last. We had plenty of time to get everything ready." He led her towards where, one after the other, Michael was embracing everyone again. They stopped in a place where the sand was held down by scrubby grass. "Every priest between here and the borders of Orthodoxy will soon be ready to do whatever it takes to get these people safely back to Constantinople. Urban II won't become Pope for some while to come. Indeed, things may already have changed in ways that will get someone else crowned. So far as we're concerned, though, the Crusades have already started. *Deus vult!*" he cried softly and almost self-mockingly. "*Deus vult!*"

Michael looked up at Jennifer's approach. He quickly wiped his eyes and hurried forward. "Alexius," he said in Latin, "here is the Lady Jennifer. Though we shan't be officially married till we can stand before the Patriarch in the Great Church, she is already to be treated as my wife."

The secretary bowed gravely, and silently tried the unfamiliar syllables of her name. "I greet you as My Lord's Lady," he said. Lawrence frowned slightly.

Leaving Jennifer with Alexius, the priest took Michael aside. "I have to warn you," he said in Greek, "that the Church is not all-powerful on this side of the water. We have influence, but this can be ignored almost at random by the secular power. Neither Duke William nor the Count of Flanders can be regarded as allies. And, for all he dislikes them, His Majesty of France dare not stand against the Normans. With this in mind, my advice is not to retrace your steps along the short route into Italy. You'll have to strike out east, towards Germany. The authorities there will be more understanding, and will do nothing to slow your journey towards the Empire's Bulgarian provinces."

They were at the point where beach merged with the land. Lawrence sat on a clump of grass and took out a wad of paper from his robe. He unfolded this into a map of many colours in the English style, and secured it against the breeze with heaps of sand at each corner. Michael sat down beside him and looked at the map. Bearing in mind the uncertainty of the scholarship that, after so long, had gone into its drawing, some of the colours might be conjectural. The Empire's northern borders were a matter of uncertainty even for him. But he knew he could implicitly trust this map's objective features, and the distances it measured between places. As usual with maps of this kind, nearly everything was marked in Latin.

Lawrence traced a long curve through what had to be mostly dense forest. "I'm afraid we can't manage better than this. It is absolutely necessary for you to be out of hostile territory, and too far inland for anyone to try finding you from the sky. There is also the obvious benefit of taking a more or less unexpected route."

"Thank you, Father." Michael looked about for the right words. "I know there have been differences between your church and mine. But I hope we shall be able, once I'm back home, to put these all away."

The priest laughed quietly. "My dear boy, I still live half in a world where the mutual anathemas of eleven years ago were jointly withdrawn fifty two years ago."

He stopped, as if waiting for a look of confusion to come over Michael's face. But Michael smiled steadily back. "Reverend Father, bearing in mind what's going on in London and in Baghdad, can we not forget the past few centuries, and try to avoid the next nine? If you want the word *filioque* in the Latin Creed, please be my guest. There are matters of secular authority that require much compromise on both sides. But, unless I'm locked up for mad when I've made my report, I don't think anyone in

Constantinople will be inclined to dig his heels in over the theological issues. Our joint interest lies in settling everything in almost the same time as might be needed to draw up the right form of document."

Lawrence beamed at him and began folding his map away. "I can tell you that the spirit of reconciliation is mutual. I was in Rome a few weeks ago. His Holiness regrets the impetuosity of Cardinal Humbert, who seems, in any event, to have exceeded his brief." He paused and looked over at the sea. Now they were farther up the shore, the dark shadow of England was clearly visible. "Yes, Humbert was a fool," he sighed. "His orders were to go to Constantinople and find out what your Patriarch was up to. He had no instructions to drop a bull of excommunication on the altar of the Great Church. I might add that your man Cerularius was also a fool. He was lucky to die before he could stand trial for treason. You simply don't want to know the centuries of evil that followed those anathemas."

He would have said more, but another priest hurried over and coughed politely. "My Lord," he said in English. He looked at Michael and bowed. "We've just had a response from London to your message," he continued in Latin. Lawrence took the sheet of paper covered over in small machine writing. He read it, his face going tight. He looked again across the water, and again at the message. He got up. "Michael," he said, "you must forgive me for taking your young lady aside, and for speaking with her in English. But there is a matter of great urgency."

►▼◄

Cardinal Lawrence stood just beyond the highest point of the Channel tide. Jennifer sat before him on the thin grass. "Are you completely sure," he asked, "that it was General Rockville you saw by Vauxhall Bridge?" Jennifer nodded. The old man she'd spoken with had been emphatic. Aside from that, she had seen the American Secretary of State on television. His increasingly wild threats weren't things anyone could overlook. Lawrence pursed his lips, and asked her to repeat other details of what she'd seen and heard.

"Then we really must conclude that these people have adapted their Doomsday Project." He shaded his eyes and looked again towards the English coast. He looked for a long time, a faint longing on his face. Jennifer began to think the interview was over. But Lawrence pulled his eyes away from England.

"It's something the British and American Governments had been working on since the 1980s," he explained. "It was always ultra-secret, and all we ever got was rumours at second or third hand. Some of us even wrote it off in the early days as propaganda to scare the Russians. But the outlines were clear enough. Its idea was the teleportation of matter—just like in those episodes of *Star Trek*. The twist was that the same human soul—these people never spoke in such unscientific terms, but it didn't work for inanimate matter, or animals—couldn't exist in two places at the same time: whatever soul was interjected would itself by annihilated, and would annihilate several million times the mass of the body in which it was contained. It was hoped that one teleportation machine could be put together in Moscow, and a human being pushed through it from another machine in the Pentagon. This unfortunate would arrive several seconds earlier in time, and make the Kremlin vanish in a puff of smoke."

"Is this what caused The Break?" Jennifer asked.

Lawrence shook his head. "So far as we can tell, they never got it to move anyone back in time for more than a few millionths of a second. It was just long enough to indicate that the weapon could work, but not enough to bring on a mutual annihilation. But is seems that, after The Break, the British side of the Project was able to reach through all the infinite dimensions of space and time to re-establish contact with the Americans. What you tell me implies that they have made contact some while before The Break. Americans can step through into our world, so long as none of them already exists here. His Majesty's ministers cannot go across, because they already exist on the other side. But this is conjectural. Our interest before The Break was moral and intermittent, rather than practical. Since then, we have not been able to find an able or a trustworthy spy to tell us what is happening."

"So what are they planning to do?" Jennifer asked. "And why do they want Michael?"

Lawrence shook his head. "Too many questions, my dear, and too few answers. You will already have seen how rudimentary our English network is. We're eleven months from The Break. Most of the higher reaches of the Church remain committed to the established order. Like everyone else, we dissenters were too busy at first with staying alive, and then with trying to puzzle out where our duty lay. I was appointed just a few weeks ago. It will be weeks more until I can start my mission in England. In the meantime, all I can do is keep one step ahead of Abigail Hooper and her *de facto* allies on this side of the water, and try to piece the facts together of what is going on in London. Until a few minutes ago, I knew less than you did. Perhaps I still know less."

He stopped and looked once more across the Channel. "When I was a boy, I used to enjoy the novels of John Wyndham. Do you remember him?—*The Day of the Triffids, The Midwich Cuckoos,* and so on?" Jennifer nodded. "Well, if this were a John Wyndham novel, you could imagine a less dark working out of the plot than we've seen. In his imagination, square-jawed ministers would clench firmly on their pipes, and bring in a fair rationing of food and petrol. Scholars would be sent out to study the Outsiders. Little by little, another and equally benevolent *Pax Britannica* would be established over this new world, and everything would work out for the best."

He smiled. "Sadly, if you were to derive a motto from the actions of those who have ruled England since the 1980s, it would be something like *Better to serve in hell than reign in heav'n.* They lost their European Union and their New World Order. They lost their membership of the global ruling class. And so, at their first opportunity, they shone the lights of their perverted science into the void, and were able to whore themselves back into America's good books. Whatever they have in mind is evil. We can take it as read that they have no good intentions towards His Excellency the Byzantine Ambassador. Your duty is to get that young man safely back to Constantinople. There, he must do what he can to ready the Empire to play its part in a defence that Holy Mother Church will lead. I say that the Crusades have started. But our crusade is not, this time, against the Moslem. It is against this hideous parody of

231

England."

He stopped to watched Michael walk across the sand towards them. Dressed now in the clothes of his proper station in life, he seemed taller and immensely more commanding. Lawrence smiled. "I see you are preparing to leave at once," he said in Latin. "Before then, however, we have business to transact that you will surely agree is of the highest importance." He hardened his face. "Since our churches should be already regarded as in full communion, you will not object if I insist upon an immediate ceremony of marriage. Whatever age we care to call now—whoever may be the Patriarch to whom we look—the Church does not and never will regard fornication as an acceptable mode of conduct." He pointed at a low building a few hundred feet beyond the line of sand. "I suggest we get our business out of the way over there."

He turned to Jennifer. "Are you a Catholic?" Confused, she shook her head. Wasn't marriage, in this age, a matter of mutual promises? What claim was being made here for church authority? But Lawrence continued: "Then I see that I shall need to baptise you first. Since your heresy doesn't yet exist on this side of the water," he went on with another smile, "I will dispense you from any formalities of recantation from the Errors of Canterbury—which, I regret, have proliferated beyond the ability of an ecumenical council to number, let alone condemn. But do you consent to be married?" Still dazed, Jennifer nodded again. "Then let us proceed with all due haste."

Michael stood back and bowed to Alexius, who took Jennifer by the arm. Everyone bowed to Lawrence, who was putting on what may have been a deeply anachronistic Cardinal's hat.

And so, on the northern shore of mediaeval France, according to a rite that no one present saw fit to question, Jennifer and Michael were pronounced man and wife.

CHAPTER THIRTY EIGHT

Jennifer reached down to scratch a fleabite behind her left knee. The movement made her all the more aware of how her lower body ached from day after day on horseback. "So Michael's family is really important?" she asked again in Latin. Alexius gave his standard answer in Greek—the three Emperors in the maternal line, the estates in Asia Minor and the Peloponnese, the palace in Constantinople, the silk spinning workshops in Athens, and so on and so forth. Limited though her knowledge was of Byzantine history, she had read somewhere of the Acominatus family. She tried to smile as Alexius repeated himself with slow patience. If what he said only set her nerves on edge again, it was useful to make sense of the Greek that he'd been appointed to teach her.

"If I might be so bold, My Lady," he said after a further question, this time in Greek, "the basics that your father taught you are sound in grammar and syntax. But they are enough only to let you read the pure tongue of the ancients, and your pronunciation is systematically vicious. The Lord Michael is insistent that, before we pass into Imperial territory, you should be fluent in the language of the higher classes. Some accent will be inevitable. Nevertheless, his mother and his aunts will judge you primarily on how you speak. So long as they find that acceptable, they can be trusted to welcome you as a suitable bride for the Lord Michael, and to train you in such female graces as you may currently lack."

Jennifer looked forward at the endless and dusty path they'd been following through the forest. They'd left Flanders far behind, and were travelling through territories that owed a vague loyalty to the German Emperor. This political fact was important, but had no impact on the scenery. The Cardinal had taken leave of them at the edge of the forest. Since then, it had been a mostly silent desert of green. With interruptions for rivers and mountain ranges, so it might continue all the way to the Bering Strait. But the agreed plan was that they'd make for the Danube. They had neither gold enough nor time for the longer route through Hungary. By water, it couldn't be long before they reached Belgrade or Nicopolis, and continued into the Black Sea. This assumed no danger from the air....

A dozen yards ahead, Michael was chatting happily with one of the guards in a rapid and colloquial form of Greek she couldn't yet understand. If, every half hour or so, he turned his horse back to whisper endearments, it did nothing to raise her spirits.

A stranger might have looked through her eyes, and seen nothing very different from the visits she had made with her father, or even her lone visit with Count Robert. Then, however, for all she might imagine herself a grand lady of the Outsiders, she'd always felt as if she were swimming underwater. Always, the game would end, and she could go home to the house in Deal. All she could think now was that she'd never see England again, and that she was passing, day by day, towards a world where she had to be seen as a barbarian. The beautiful and charming fugitive, who'd needed her as much as she had him, was now the Lord Michael, treated by all about him with awed respect. He was leading her towards what could only strike her a prison with a mother-in-law for head gaoler. What favour had Lawrence done her with that ceremony? How long would Michael put up with her in Constantinople? And, if it seemed she'd not be allowed to show herself in public, was that so much better than being a laughing stock?

Michael had gone a long way ahead. Now, he stopped and raised his right arm. Without turning, he called out something she couldn't understand. "We shall stop here for the night," Alexius explained, pointing at what must have been the outskirts of a settlement. Jennifer looked at her watch. The green covering overhead told her nothing about where the sun might be. But it was pushing 8pm Outsider time—perhaps they were already in a later time zone. At last, she could fall off her horse. That would have pleased her, but for the thought of another stinking, vermin-ridden bag of straw on which she'd pass the night. She smiled and resolved to keep her temper. It was only because of her that

Michael was following any path at all. Alone with his men, he'd have been deep inside the forest, sleeping on damp ground.

"Could that be thunder, My Lady?" Alexius asked. Jennifer shook her head. The aeroplane must have been a mile overhead, and going at several hundred miles an hour. It could take dozens of high resolution pictures every second, and these could be enlarged and inspected for any sign of a travelling party. But she was sure the cameras couldn't see through leaves and branches. It would be another matter, she thought with redoubled misery, once they were on the water.

► ▼ ◄

The man shook his head, and spoke again in colloquial Greek. He noticed the intense look on Jennifer's face. "I found nothing untoward," he said, speaking Latin with a northern accent. "No flying ship has ever put in there. They know England only from stories and from the goods that sometimes find their way to market."

"Surely, we've outrun them," Alexius said. Cross-legged on the ground, Michael said nothing. Jennifer certainly knew better. From the Channel to Cologne on horseback, it seemed they'd been travelling half across the world. In terms of the European motorway network, they were four hours east of the Brussels ring road, which itself was four hours from the coast. Call that forty minutes by aeroplane. On the other hand, they hadn't heard anything overhead in days. There was no reason for Hooper to suppose they'd got out of England—Lawrence had said his people would report sightings of them all over the Midlands. Even otherwise, how do you look for people in an area as vast as Western Europe? It had been hard enough before The Break, when the authorities could rely on a dense network of security cameras, and a banking system able to flag up card payments within seconds. They might as well be half across the world.

As if he'd read her mind, Michael had the obvious reply. "These people aren't completely stupid. They'll turn England upside down to get us. But they can also spare the resources to look outside." He pointed at the map. "There are just two likely routes we can take.

Both involve choke points here and here." He drew a finger along the route they were taking. "If I were directing a search from London, I'd have men watching every crossing point across the Rhine. I'd focus on Cologne."

The man interrupted. "My Lord, the old woman I questioned was emphatic—no one from England, she said. Nor anyone new from Normandy or Flanders."

Michael shrugged. "Don't ask why they aren't here. What matters is that they *can* be here. The next worst thing to being stopped in Cologne is any record of our passing through Cologne. Show them that, and they'll turn a vague poking about into a dragnet overseen from the air." He smiled at Jennifer. "As a mutual friend told us in London, we'll be picked off like lice on white skin."

"What *shall* we do, then?" Jennifer asked. Michael stood up and led her from the cover they'd taken beneath some trees to the top of the hill. Together, they looked over mediaeval Cologne. It was a small but a beautiful sight—of high churches and stone buildings within high defensive walls. Beyond it, the bright waters of the Rhine flowed towards the sea. The arched Roman bridge ran from within the city, and continued where the arches had fallen down on planks supported by small boats. Running straight, the road on the other side ran into the unbroken green of the forest. He passed her his binoculars. She could now see workmen on top of the biggest church, and a stream of people crossing the bridge in both directions. Even without the sight she had of the toll booth on the city side of the bridge, she could see the problem. To get in, they'd have to state their business at one of the gates. Once inside, thirty thousand pairs of eyes would be fixed on them. Even so, it would be a glorious thing to go inside those walls. This was like an illuminated manuscript come to life.

Michael still seemed to be reading her thoughts. "We're told that travel broadens the mind. Even before reaching England, I could see how the West was growing in wealth and numbers. Some of the Italian cities are magnificent with new buildings. Cologne is impressive, though you might find it disappointing if you went inside." He stopped for a private thought. Jennifer tried to imagine the size of the modern city and what she'd once seen of the greatest mass of industrial capacity in Europe. More telepathy. "You are, I suppose, looking at the birth of your own civilisation," he said. "It has a thousand years to run before collapsing—not bad for a civilisation."

He looked upstream. "We do need to go across. It will halve our journey to the Danube. It will give us an impenetrable hinterland for taking refuge if we need one. Since we can't walk across or swim, we need a boat." He pointed at the small monastery a mile upstream. "All contact involves risk. But the monks won't ask questions or turn us in. I doubt any foreign interpreters your people bring along will assist in torturing them. We'll see how far and wide Lawrence has spread the word about us."

Jennifer looked at the sky. Michael squeezed her hand. "It's only a crossing. We might be able to get everyone in a single boat." He stopped again. The question she hadn't yet dared ask came out as the single word *Danube*. He understood and nodded. "Sooner or later, we'll have to break cover. But the Danube is busier than the Rhine, and may be more out of area for your people."

Jennifer looked again at the busy walled town. "I don't like this Michael. Don't you think it's been too easy?"

He smiled. "I do. Then again, some things just *are* easy." They stared awhile in silence into the western sky. For as long as they'd stood here together, it had been almost like a return to their early days in England. Then he took her by the arm. "Shall we go back to the others?"

CHAPTER THIRTY NINE

Michael looked at the watch he'd borrowed from Jennifer—it said just after midnight. Once across the river, they'd pretended a dash north, before turning south east off the road. It had been a hard day's travel. But for Jennifer, they'd have continued deeper through the night. But she'd been worn out, and the abandoned and derelict hunting lodge had been too good a find to pass up. Now, while she slept, it was time for everyone else to sit together and look over generalities they'd so far avoided. Trying not to make any noise, he put the heavy weapon he'd taken from Count Robert on the table. Alexius and three of their guards looked at it in silence.

"It fires projectiles at great speed and force," he said, picking it up again and swinging out the chamber that held the projectiles. He let them fall one at a time into the palm of his hand. "You can see that these have a brass body and a pointed lead top. My understanding is that they are filled with some explosive mixture that causes the lead to fly out when ignited. Here is what I take to be the igniting force." He pushed the empty chamber into place and pulled back the sprung hammer. He held the weapon in his right hand and pulled on a lever beneath the main body. The hammer made a loud click as it hit the main body of the weapon. "You aim and discharge. When the chamber is exhausted, you refill with other projectiles. I have seen weapons similar to these in action. They can be deadly at a great distance. I strongly doubt if there is any armour that will protect against them."

"And the Turks are being equipped with thousands of these?" Alexius asked.

"There are differences of opinion among the English on this point," Michael said. "Indeed, given time, we may be able to take advantage in the usual way of their internal disagreements. For the

238

moment, however, we must assume that the Caliph's army will be given many thousands of similar weapons, and trained in their use."

"Then, surely, My Lord," one of the guards broke in, "they will ride straight through us." Alexius looked down and began muttering a prayer.

Michael focussed on putting the projectiles back into the weapon. "There is a story of how, in ancient times, the Romans made themselves supreme at sea as well as on land. They captured a warship from the Carthaginians, and made copies that were adapted to land fighting tactics. The next time there was a battle, the Carthaginians lost. We must do the same. I'll grant that many things I saw in England worked on principles we don't begin to understand. This weapon, however, looks rather simple. It may have taken ages to develop—beginning with very simple and almost useless stages. But I'll be surprised if we aren't up to copying this in a couple of months, and turning them out by the hundred. If we can manage that, it's a fair assumption that the Caliph's men won't know more about how to use them than we shall. The English, I do know, are short of fighting men. Those they have will need to be kept at home to protect against the Normans they have, most short-sightedly, armed."

He paused and looked about the room. Everyone here could be trusted. "The further question is what to do about the Emperor. He was put in because of his alleged military virtues. He's turned out no better than the idiot he replaced. We need to find someone who can get the Empire into fighting shape. That means someone who can face down families like mine—to restore land to the peasants, and turn the peasants back into soldiers, and pay off all the mercenaries we've let ourselves think will save us from the dirty work of fighting. We need a revolution against the current ruling order, as well as a revolution in military tactics."

Alexius looked doubtful. "There are the Comnenus brothers," he suggested. "One of them might have some fire in his belly." He went on to say more, but stopped in mid-sentence. "Did you hear that noise?" he whispered.

Michael had heard it. He also recognised the sound that

Jennifer's feet made on the beaten earth. He was still trying to stuff the weapon back inside its leather sheath, when she walked into the room.

He'd hoped she would only be annoyed that he'd left her alone. But it was plain, the moment she came close enough to the rush light for her face to be seen, that she'd followed the drift of their conversation. "You told me nothing about going home to fight in a war," she said accusingly. "In England, you were all talk of giving in to the inevitable and trying to survive. You're now full of talk about war—war preceded by revolution." The guards knew no Latin. Alexius sat back and stared at the table. But her voice had said it all. Michael had married an exotic barbarian—and she was turning, one day at a time, into a nag.

"Go back to bed, Jennifer," he said firmly. "This is men's talk. I'll be with you soon." She looked at one of the guards until he stood up to make room on the bench across the table from Michael. She sat down and stared at him. He thought at first she'd start crying. He didn't want her to do that—not cry, not in front of everyone else. Shrill nagging he could put up with: that was a matter of waiting till she ran out of breath, and a few sideways looks at faces resigned to his ordeal by their own experience of women. Tears were different.

But Jennifer was neither shrill nor weepy. "The English cardinal spoke of war," she said in halting Greek. "But this is a war that must be won or lost in England. If we lose there, suicide campaigns against the Turks will change nothing." On second thoughts, Michael would have preferred tears. Still calm, she picked up the weapon and reopened its projectile chamber. "If you think anyone in your world is able to copy this thing, you weren't long enough in England. You don't have the tools to make one of these. You don't have the tools to make the tools to make one. You can't make steel of the right hardness and consistency. As for the powder, that is a work of art in itself. You can no more copy this than you can copy one of the moving picture machines, or the horseless vehicles."

Alexius brought out another long sigh. The other men were silent. Michael swallowed and took the weapon back from

Jennifer. "Then there must be something *else* we can do," he said defiantly. "There must be some way of adapting this device to our own abilities. I've told you many times that we aren't painted savages."

She waited, a grim smile on her face, till it was clear that Michael had nothing more to say. "Oh, but I think I can help you with something," she said, now in Latin. "I'd give up on trying to copy this. But, in the days before The Break, my father obtained a great deal of information about weapons from a web of knowledge that covered the whole world. After The Break, this allowed us to survive the looting of houses. Even then, we used water pipes of more solid metal than you can easily make. But, if size doesn't matter, I'm sure I can explain how to make tubes of iron and brass that can shoot stone balls or lengths of chain. On a battlefield, or on city walls, these can smash up any attack that doesn't involve flying machines." She continued with a discussion of ignition powders that her Latin wasn't good enough to explain clearly.

"Then we're in business!" Michael said quickly in Latin. This was a double relief. The matters raised by Jennifer had been continually at the back of his own mind. Also, he had seen the looks on her face when she thought he wasn't watching, and heard the inflections in her voice when they spoke of their future life together. He smiled and sat back. He switched into slow and simple Greek. "In view of what assistance she can give the Empire in its defence, my wife is dispensed from the usual formalities of her sex and of her station in society." One of the men opened his mouth in shock. Alexius allowed himself to look doubtful. But the Lord Michael had spoken. And the Lord Michael's father would somehow be cajoled into standing behind his words.

"Jennifer," he said, back in Latin, "do go to bed. We have a long ride tomorrow, and, whatever you may be in my own heart, you are now the most important subject in the Empire." He looked at his wooden beer cup. "Yes, go to bed," he repeated. "We have an early start. In the meantime, we do have further talk of politics that is for men alone."

Michael looked out again from the arched gateway of the fort. "Keep the horses under cover," he ordered. He put a hand on Jennifer's arm. "Are you sure they can't see us here?" She nodded. She said they might be safe even under the dense covering of trees. But she was convinced no one in the floating machine could detect motion or body heat through courses of Roman brick. "Then we are safe," he answered. He laughed easily and patted one of the nervous guards. "Don't worry," he said. "My Lady knows their machinery and their ways. They will hover a while overhead, then be off to look somewhere else."

Jennifer tried to believe him. It was weeks since they'd crossed the Rhine. Except when puzzling out names everyone else might understand for things like potassium nitrate, and trying to describe the extraction of phosphor from urine, she'd been thinking as much in Greek as in English. Constantinople was still far away. But England and the evil it represented seemed farther still. And now England had reached out with its airships and thermal imaging equipment, and was hovering not a hundred feet above them.

Michael took her by the shoulder and moved towards the other side of the gateway, where they wouldn't be speaking in front of everyone else. "How far from home can these things get?" he asked in Latin. Before she could confirm that she didn't know, he went on, more for himself than for her. "How many of these things are there? Do they always float singly? Or do they operate in fleets?" He watched her shrug. "Can I take it that everyone up there is in immediate contact with England?" Jennifer did nod yes to that question. Michael pursed his lips. By comparison, the other questions bordered on the unimportant.

"We'll have to see what it represents," he said. "Depending on how long that propelling screw can be kept turning without fresh supplies of its fuel, it might be no more dangerous than a fish that has poked its head out of water." He looked carefully out again. The floating machine had moved a few degrees to the west. It was now on the other side of the ruined wall. Still keeping under cover of what brickwork remained, he drew Jennifer behind him and tried to see if anyone was looking down from the gigantic bag of air that held steady in the breeze.

Alone with his wife, he could try to pull himself together. If the English were up to extended operations all the way along the Danube, his plan was madness after all. Still worse, if the English were willing to show themselves so far from home, would Constantinople itself be safe from an armed raid?

He led Jennifer back within the undoubted safety of the gateway. He sat on a stone lintel that had fallen down and pretended to mop his brow. He looked at a broken inscription that must have been a thousand years old. It recorded how the fort had been built by an unnamed military governor, for a Legion whose number was missing, and was part of the fortifications in depth for the two hundred mile gap between Rhine and Danube that was the weakest point in the Empire's northern frontier.

He noticed that everyone was silently watching him. He sat up and smiled. Time to show some leadership. The men would follow him to their death—so long, that is, as he led them there. He took out and unfolded the now tattered map. It showed how any movement away from the river course would take them straight into mountains. The numbers printed beside their contour lines showed that many of these were thousands of feet high. The map was too general to indicate the kind of passes they would need through the mountains. How long would their gold last on a wider circuit? More important, how long would their luck hold? The few bandits they'd so far come across had taken one look at their horses and armed men, before going off in search of easier throats to cut. Trying to feel their way through narrow passes without tree cover would expose them to more than one danger from above.

He'd take it as read that anyone looking down from the machine would be able to see in the dark. It was an added complication. He pointed at the map. If his navigation had been correct—and he had no idea if it had been—they were close by a town called Ulm. "This looks fairly substantial," he said, squinting at the round dot beside the name. He moved his finger north and south and east and west, and noted the contours and the line of the river. "I'd say it was a trading centre. You'll have cut timbers floated downstream from here, and perhaps a little spinning and weaving." Michael stared again at the broken inscription. "We need reasonable numbers of people," he thought aloud. "If we can lose ourselves in a crowd, we're in with a chance. That thing can't be carrying more than a dozen armed men—perhaps not half that. If Hooper is behind the chase, they'll have orders not to risk harming me. Unlike in London, they won't be able to use their weapons indiscriminately. They might even be under orders not to make themselves too obvious." He looked down again at the map. Everything said Ulm. It was all a question of what the directors of that floating machine had in mind.

He fell silent, racking his brains for a scheme that would keep them heading towards the Empire. Ulm was a diversion. Two days it might take to get there—longer if they had to travel under cover. He looked up. The gentle throbbing of the machine had became louder and more insistent, and it began to move west. Jennifer gave him a trusting smile, as if he knew more than she did. "Perhaps it does need to go back," she said. "It might be running short of fuel to let it move about."

Michael hoped she was right. Everything worked better without that thing overhead. Keeping out of sight, they all watched the floating machine pick up speed. It continued west until its throbbing had faded into the distance. They waited under shelter of the gateway until Jennifer's watch had shown the passing of half an hour. Michael got up and stepped cautiously inside the ruined fort. He forced his way through the bushes that covered the old parade ground, until he had an unbroken view to the west. The floating machine had gone completely out of sight.

He laughed and turned back to the rest of his group. "We continue south along the old military road. If the town is big enough for a bishop, we can see how effective the Latin Church really is on our behalf."

CHAPTER FORTY

The silk merchant fiddled with the electronic calculator hung round his neck. "I have heard stories of them," he said in slow Greek. "One of my apprentices met someone in Basel who claimed to have seen one—a ship floating in the sky, able to carry armed men, who run continually up and down ladders to the ground." He touched his calculator again. "I can have no reasonable doubt such things are sent out by the wonder-working race that has appeared in England. But have I seen one? No!"

He said something in German. A woman who was selling chickens laughed back at him. "If you've been speaking with old Heinrich," he added in Greek, "do be aware that he's a poet and an habitual drunk." He laughed again. "Don't ask which is worse."

Jennifer stood aside for men with brooms to set about cleaning away some animal dung that had been left in the square. The main church in Ulm was a low building, built mostly from wood. The other buildings were generally thatched. The only tiled roofs she'd seen were on a large monastery beside the church, and on a building that served some mercantile function. The walled city was larger than Cologne had seemed, though had an appearance less quaintly mediaeval than of an extended settlement. Despite this, it was cleaner than she'd expected of a city without piped water, and no one had suggested that she and Michael should be burned as witches for having brought flying demons with them. In most respects, the Outsiders took a calmer view of The Break than those immediately affected by it.

Dinner was at 4pm in the silk merchant's house, and was the first enjoyable food she'd had since leaving the Channel coast and striking out into the forest. Dressed in a robe that looked feminine, but allowed movement, Jennifer had been taken by the merchant's wife on a tour of what amounted to an agglomeration of rooms on one floor about a central courtyard. She could see that the merchant and his wife had done well in Germany. But the furnishings were plain to the point of minimalism, and every room smelled with a pungent mix of lavender and beeswax. The woman knew only enough Latin to say her prayers, and communication was mostly by hugs and tones of voice.

The meal was in a long room close to the main entrance, and she and Michael were seated beside the merchant and his wife at the top table. As well as the first enjoyable food in weeks, this was also Jennifer's first appearance in polite company since Alexius had taken her in hand. She could see how he watched from his own seat, half way down the secondary table, at the manner in which she broke her bread, and her patience in letting Michael drink first from the cup that was placed between them.

There was much singing, between the courses, by some apprentice boys, and a long series of jokes, throughout a beer course, from a man with a red face. Taking a rest from jokes that his hand gestures indicated were of a kind never allowed nowadays on television, the man belted out a couple of songs Jennifer couldn't understand, but that were filled with complex rhymes.

"Do rich merchants eat like this every day?" Jennifer asked while all the cups were being refilled. In Normandy, hospitality had been a matter for the nobility, and had varied from place to place. Since she and her father had avoided the main commercial centres, her only experience of merchants was of very low hawkers.

"I don't know about Germany," Michael said. "But, except in times of siege or really bad harvest, this is part of daily life in Constantinople. You show your position by keeping reasonably open house." He dropped his voice. "By the way, you shouldn't be pinching little bits from your platter." She looked down at the wide circle of bread on which every piece of meat he'd broken off for her had been placed. "It's for the poor," he reminded her. "If you're still hungry, you should wait for the honey cake." She'd known that, but had forgotten. She flushed red as she followed the slight turn of his head, and realised that the meal had been silently watched throughout. Perhaps everything she'd carried to her mouth had been watched closely by several dozen small people dressed in shabby grey. A couple of serving men were already collecting some of the juicier and more disintegrated platters, and were carrying them over to the hungry poor. Without standing, without seeming actually to notice, the merchant acknowledged the gestures of respect and blessing. "For ye have the poor always with you," Michael recited again. "And there's a lot of truth in Scripture. Whatever else, the poor must somehow be fed." He reached over and took a couple of wedges of what looked and tasted like bread pudding.

"There will be a few dozen barges leaving on Thursday morning," he continued in brisker tone. "They'll be carrying cut timber for a dam that's being built downstream. There will also be a group of pilgrims going east. If we mix ourselves in with those people, we ought to be safe. My impression is that your people's floating machines can't go far. The ones that fly very quickly, high in the sky, may not be any danger to us."

There was a loud cheer from about the tables. The comedian was back on his feet, and began dancing about the room with a broom handle topped by a pumpkin and some sacking that did duty as a wig.

▶▼◀

Jennifer dreamed that Michael was driving very fast with her on the wrong side of the M2. It must have been before The Break, as the headlamps of the oncoming traffic were dazzling. She could hear the frantic sounding of horns, and possibly the overhead clatter of a police helicopter. She tried in three languages to get Michael to stop. But he paid no attention. His eyes shining, his mouth slightly open, he drove straight on as if the road had been empty.

Still dazzled by the oncoming lights of something huge, she sat up in the darkness. She could hear only the soft snoring that indicated that Michael had rolled over on his back. She put a hand on his warm chest. He groaned and muttered something that may have been in Greek. She was in Ulm, she told herself. She was in bed with her husband about a hundred miles south of a Würzburg, where she and her parents had always stopped to sleep for a few hours on their annual drive to Slovakia. Michael had only the haziest understanding of refuelling needs, but may have been right about how far airships could go. They might need only another hundred miles before they were in the clear.

She lay back and wondered if it was a flea or a mosquito that had brought up a lump on her right forearm. She'd have that answer when it began to itch. They were lying together on a mattress that had been put directly on the floor. She reached left and patted the boards for her wristwatch. She pressed the display button— 2:47am, it said. What the local time might really be she neither knew nor cared. It was enough that she'd been asleep for five hours. Back in Deal, she might only just have nodded off. Her parents might still be sitting together downstairs with a single candle to let them see each other speak. But the Outsiders mostly went to bed when it was dark, and were up with the dawn. She had another couple of hours to go before the old woman who'd put them to bed came in with washing water, and Michael could set properly about travel arrangements for the next day. Or was Thursday the day after next? The change in day between England and the Outside had always confused her in practice. Add to this now that she couldn't tell any more how long they'd been travelling. It might be Wednesday. It might be Tuesday. The old woman spoke no language she'd ever heard. But the merchant would know.

Yes, the silk merchant would know what day of the week it really was, and he'd know more about the departure of those barges that would allow their escape downstream along a Danube that, in the afternoon sun, had been a most beautiful blue. She wondered again how, so far from the Empire, he could have known Greek. But he was a silk merchant, she thought. It seemed that trade networks in this age were more extended than she'd supposed. She closed her eyes and waited for sleep to reclaim her. Drifting back into soft oblivion, she thought she could hear the distant approach of another lorry on the M2. Was that a dog barking? She opened her eyes again and sat up. If it was a dog, it had stopped. There was a draught in the room she couldn't recall from earlier. Trying not to cover Michael's face, she pulled the blanket up a little.

"Did you think you'd got away from us?" someone spat softly in what she took a second to realise was neither Latin nor Greek. "Did it never cross your stupid little mind that you were tracked every inch of the way?"

"Oh, do shut up, Tarquin!" Radleigh drawled. "Don't move, Jennifer," he said. "You can't see us. But we can see you as clear as day." Jennifer opened her mouth to scream. Someone took hold of her from behind and put a hand over her mouth. "Wake the boy," Radleigh said again. "Tell him that, if he cries out, we'll gas everyone in Ulm. Tell him also that, if he tries to resist, we'll shoot his bit of fluff in the stomach."

Before anyone could reach forward to shake him, Michael was awake and trying to shield Jennifer with his own body. As Tarquin finished his whispered but triumphant threat, the room filled with an intense light. By now everyone had pulled off his night glasses. Radleigh looked up from inspecting the clothes she and Michael had left scattered on the floor. Unable to move, Jennifer blinked until she could see clearly. A cold smile on his face, Radleigh stood up and straightened his jacket. For just a moment, she had sight of a glass pendant that seemed to reflect the LED lamp in a riot of strange colours. Then Radleigh buttoned his jacket, and the pendant was covered up. Three men stood over the bed, rifles ready to point at her the moment Michael could be pulled out of the firing line.

"Have you explained things to the boy?" Radleigh asked. Tarquin nodded and went into a long and sibilant gloat. Radleigh silenced him again. "One slip, and I promise that Hooper won't give you another last chance." He laughed and lit a cigarette from which the tobacco showed no inclination to drop out. He stood over the bed. "You really are a couple of stupid children," he said pityingly. "It's only down to me this honeymoon went on as long as it did."

Outside in the darkness, Jennifer heard the Peppa Pig theme tune and a double grunt.

CHAPTER FORTY ONE

It was early afternoon when the airship reached the centre of London. Regardless of who might hear them, the engines had been set at full speed above Ulm, and had been kept going ever since. Between long bouts of trying to see and think nothing at all, Jennifer had watched the forests and clearings of Western Europe give way to the bright silver of the Channel, and then to the varying greens of an England that, from the air, looked much the same as before The Break. The great difference, of course, was London. She'd been paying attention to its ravaged, if still magnificent, expanse ever since they'd passed within its covering of smog. You could look down on Canterbury, and think nothing had changed. One look at London from the air, and it was plain that something—perhaps everything—had gone fatally wrong.

Something still was going wrong. Before the airship turned left to follow the line of the River, she'd noticed smoke over much of the East End—smoke and more than a single tongue of yellow flame. Another Pacification?...

Tarquin noticed that she was looking out of the window. "Glad to be home?" he crowed. "Look well at England, then—it's the last you'll see of it." He leaned back in his seat for a better view of her face.

"If you can't keep a civil tongue in your head," Radleigh grated from behind Jennifer, "we do have another interpreter." He sniffed and took out his cigarette case. "Now, please go outside and make yourself useful. For some reason, best known to herself, Abigail wants that Norman thug kept alive. You might, therefore, persuade him to come inside for the landing."

She looked out of the window again, this time at Count Robert. Hardly any time after carrying her on board, he'd been reeling drunk. Much of the time since then, he'd spent snoring in a bunk, all damp chain mail and bad smells. Since coming back to life, he'd gone out to lean on the rail, moving only to light another cigarette, or to stare disconsolately in at Jennifer. She watched Tarquin get himself on to the viewing deck and lean beside Robert. If the idea had been to jolly him back inside, it was a failure. Robert let out a stream of what anyone could have told was foul invective, before moving to the far end of the rail.

Radleigh smiled to himself and lit his cigarette. "Am I right in thinking you broke into that oilman's house to kill me?" he asked with no indication of holding it against her. Jennifer nodded. He grunted and looked up to avoid breathing smoke at her. "Well, you can be glad you made your usual rotten job of the attempt," he said. "If you had killed me, you'd both have been dead long before I decided it was time to reel you in."

Jennifer held up her cuffed wrists. "Why can't I be with my husband?"

"Because Hooper's orders were that you should be kept apart," came the flat reply.

She looked past Radleigh, to the screen that had been put up to keep her and Michael from seeing each other. Behind that, also cuffed, he was sitting with the armed guards. Claiming that she needed to go to the toilet, she'd managed once to see the back of his head. Apart from that, she'd been alone. Her eyes filled with tears, and she struggled not to show weakness in front of the man who'd helped kill her parents.

"Don't suppose, Jennifer, this is giving me any pleasure," he said. He narrowed his eyes and looked at her. "Like your father, you have the ability to get yourself into the deepest and most avoidable trouble. Of all the boys in England, why did you have to fall in with Michael Acominatus?"

"What does Hooper want with him?" she asked.

Radleigh held up his cigarette and stared at its glowing end. "The price of my being able to answer that question will be paid when I give him to her." He looked down at her cuffed wrists. "You know, Jennifer, all I've wanted for the past year was the chance of getting back to normality. I really am sorry if it's thanks to that scowling but ineffectual young man of yours that I'll soon have my chance."

"And I hope you blow Washington sky high when you step across!" she replied.

He frowned, as if not sure of what she'd said. Then he smiled and took a long drag on his cigarette. "You're not as stupid as your father's genes might have made you—that, or my old friend Lawrence has been his usual garrulous self." He smiled again. He even smiled at the co-pilot, who'd come over again to point at the No Smoking sign.

"Talking of Lawrence, by the way, I trust you don't believe he expected you to make it to Constantinople, or cared if you did." He waited for Jennifer's face to tighten. "His plan was to keep the boy out of reach while he directed a better uprising than your father ever managed." He glanced out of the window. "But I spoke with Abigail yesterday. Michael's her Get-Out-of-Jail-Free card. It's only in expectation of his arrival that she's held off dropping a few atom bombs." He lit another cigarette. "Yes, the boy is the key to a better world."

Jennifer looked miserably out of the window. She'd been aware for several minutes that they were approaching Big Ben. Now, as the airship seemed to be readying to land in Parliament Square, the radio burst into life with a string of panic-ridden gibberish, and they drifted up again with a more insistent throbbing of engines. Jennifer had a momentary view of what may have been a sea of banners filling the Square, and the airship came to rest above the roof a couple of hundred yards from Westminster Abbey. This had no landing tower for airships, but did have a flat expanse marked out for helicopters. She stared out with a dull feeling in her stomach as the engine was switched off, and men below hurried about with the holding ropes.

"What have you been doing for the past six weeks?" Frank Wapping shouted up from the rooftop. "I'm told you watched them get half way to Vienna."

"Wapping, Wapping, charming as ever!" Radleigh sneered. He climbed hesitantly down the rope ladder, and stretched out an arm for Jennifer. "Come on, my dear. No one wants you to trip and break your neck. We'll soon have those cuffs off you."

"Abigail isn't pleased," Wapping pressed on. "We've got trouble—big trouble all over." He looked at Jennifer and twisted his face into a faintly welcoming smile.

Radleigh straightened his tie and went over to where he could see the protest that covered Parliament Square. He looked back and smiled. "My dear Francis," he said, "I just wanted to know if our young lovebirds would be joined again by that Cardinal who's been causing so much trouble. He would have been a bag worth waiting for, don't you think? In any event, where's the fun in a chase where the prey don't think till the end they've got clean away?"

"The Pope's man is already here," Wapping nearly shouted. "If we don't get help soon, we'll lose control *everywhere*." Though in the wrong position to see anything, he nodded towards Parliament Square.

"Oh dear!" Radleigh beamed at him. "Have all our helicopter gun ships been called away on other business?" he pursed his lips at the scowl his words got. "Well, it's Basil to the rescue, if I'm not mistaken. But I'd have hoped Abigail would be here with a welcoming kiss." Wapping swallowed nervously as a shift in the breeze carried up a faint sound of singing from the Square. He pulled out a handkerchief and wiped some of the dandruff from his collar. He looked at the stained and greasy cotton. He wiped sweat from his face. With savage impatience, he stuffed the handkerchief back into his breast pocket.

There was another shift in the breeze, and they all watched in renewed silence while Michael came down the ladder. "Try anything at all," Jennifer heard Tarquin say in Greek, "and your slut's chest will be smashed in as if by a giant hammer. She might live long enough to die choking in your arms." He looked up with a cruel smile. Michael ignored his offer of help and jumped down beside Jennifer.

He lifted his wrists and took her hands in his. "We'll get out of this," he breathed in Greek. "Trust me." Jennifer nodded. She saw no point in arguing the obvious. She leaned forward to kiss him.

Before their lips could meet, Wapping pushed between them.

"No contact—it's Abigail's orders. No contact of whatever kind."
He stood back for two armed guards dressed in black to come
forward to take hold of Michael. He looked at the Greek boy. "He
is an Outsider?" he asked, uncertain. "I thought they all had
pockmarks and rotten teeth." He mopped his brow again, plainly
worried that he might be handing over the wrong person to
Hooper. He turned to Jennifer, his jacket flapping open to show a
lining held together with safety pins. "What a waste!" He said.
"What a stupid waste!" He put up a hand to stroke her face.

"You leave my Little Bear alone!" Robert snarled in his own
language. He'd been struggling with the rope ladder, and was at
just the proper height for getting one of his booted feet into
Wapping's chest. Wapping let out a burp and flew backwards. He
landed heavily, and, with a ripping of trouser cloth, continued for
another foot. Robert managed to jump down the last few rungs. He
laughed and went for his sword.

"Stop this at once!" Radleigh shouted. One of the guards had
already let go of Michael and was cocking his rifle. Radleigh
shook his head. He pointed at Tarquin. "Tell him to hand his sword
over. He can have it back when Hooper's done with us all."

The guards helped Wapping back to his feet. While they
discussed how to get everyone off the roof, and to where, Robert
tried, even without his sword, to look fierce. "My dear young
children," he said in Latin, "this was none of my doing—or, if it
was, I am bound by oath to My Lord of Normandy." He spread his
arms wide. "O, Little Bear," he cried dolefully, "how and why did
you get yourself mixed up in this terrible business? I should never
have let you back into England." He stopped and looked about for
what else to say, but didn't find anything. He clutched his head
again and muttered something about English boiled wine.

▶▼◀

Radleigh close behind her, Jennifer stepped through the door
from the ministry basement into Westminster Underground
Station. It was clear of decayed bodies, and was clean and brightly
lit. All the moving stairs were in operation. Except there were only
six people to see it all, plus the two guards, it might have been the

Olden Days come again. She wondered if Michael, who had no background memory of the Underground, was thinking of the horrors they'd been through in Oxford Circus. She didn't suppose there was any railway service, but still found herself looking at one of the big Underground maps.

All injured dignity and torn out crotch, Wapping said nothing. He waited for everyone to catch up with him in the booking hall, then made for the moving stairs that led down into the cavernous depths of the Jubilee Line. Here, Count Robert stopped. He looked at the continuous forming of grooved metal into steps. "I'm not going on that thing," he said firmly. "It doesn't look right to me." He watched Michael get onto it, flanked by the two guards. He moved aside for Tarquin to push by him. Still, he refused to take the necessary step forward.

Radleigh sighed and took out his cigarette case. He looked at its contents and put it away. "You know, my dear," he said to Jennifer, "in the time I've known him, this oaf has been exposed to motor cars, electric light, any number of guns, and an airship. He's left it rather late for a white man's magic moment. If I'm not mistaken, there's far worse to come. Now, do get him on to this staircase. Young Francis is already down there and waiting. We really wouldn't want him to have a stroke."

"Please take my arm, Robert," she said. "I'm worried I'll fall in these cuffs." He swallowed and nodded. He put an arm about her shoulder and made himself step forward.

By the time they arrived at the bottom of the stairs, Wapping had crossed over to a metal door that had no handle and was flush with the wall. It might have been the entrance to a broom cupboard or some forgotten office of the London Underground. Jennifer could imagine how none of the commuters—and probably none of the guards and ticket inspectors—had given it so much as a first look, let alone a second.

"Ah, the Prime Minister's own entrance to the Underground!" Radleigh said with an enthusiasm that seemed to be his alone. "Would it not have been easier to cross the road and then walk to Downing Street? Or is Whitehall also crowded with feral hymn-singers?"

Wapping scowled and took out a white plastic card. He held it against a raised panel beside the door. With a gentle click, the door swung outwards.

Michael and the guards went in first behind Wapping. After that, it was Jennifer, followed by everyone else. She found herself in a corridor that smelled partly of damp and much of electricity. There was a desk here for guards, and a body scanner. The desk was empty, the scanner unplugged. Wapping led the way round a corner, and along a wider corridor carpeted in red. It ended in another metal door. Here, Wapping had to stand before a camera and wait for a manual inspection. It needed three mentions of Hooper, and a cautious showing of his left forearm, before the door opened. Inside, a lone guard sat at a desk. He didn't blink, or move his right hand from a button on a control panel. He took the creased letter that Wapping produced from a pocket, his eyes flickering cautiously between the sheet and the six people before him. He barely relaxed when the other guards came in behind Radleigh. He had them line everyone up for photographs and eye scans, and give out the plasticized badges that were made from these. Meanwhile—hand still close by his control panel—he spoke softly into a telephone. He read out the names he'd been given. He listened. He spoke again, evidently troubled by an order not to have everyone disrobe and walk through his body scanner.

He finished his conversation. "Don't lose your ID tickets," he warned Michael. "Once through that door, you're in the high security zone. Orders are to shoot suspected intruders on sight." Wapping pushed in front of Michael. His effort at nonchalance didn't impress.

From here, they were directed into another corridor, lined with cameras, that widened insensibly into a long room. It was here that Wapping seemed more sure of himself. He stopped at a door where the linoleum was dirtiest and most worn. He swiped his plastic card, and rocked the door backwards and forward to free its securing bars.

Jennifer had to shut her eyes in the unexpected and dazzling glare of daylight. She'd had no feeling that they were going uphill. But they were in a courtyard enclosed by buildings that had no windows. In the middle of this was a low brick building topped by a dome of glass bricks. Making sure the everyone was close behind him, Wapping stepped over to its entrance. This time, he pulled up his left sleeve and showed the silver spot on his forearm. There was no doubt this time of its function. It shone brighter than the sun, and he moved his bare arm over a glass panel "Wapping, Francis," he rapped in a voice that invited wonder in all who beheld his importance—"CT76482."

If he'd wanted to impress, he failed. For all the door of brushed and unstained metal moved, he might have shouted "open sesame" at a brick wall. He coughed and stepped back. He tried again, and nothing happened. "You could try wiping that panel," Radleigh suggested. "Some of us wouldn't wish to be out here all afternoon." Wapping glared back, but took out his handkerchief again. He rubbed at the panel and repeated his code with a pause between each character. With a clicking of unseen bolts, the door slid open.

They were now on a landing at the top of a spiral staircase that hugged the edge of a wide central column and went down perhaps a hundred feet. The wall panels might have glowed softly, or might have reflected the cold light that was filtered through the dome. His dignity returning, Wapping stopped after one turn of the spiral. He waved dramatically about. "Do you remember those atom bomb shelters from the Olden Days?" He looked at Radleigh, as if challenging him to try for a deflating comment. He took another step down and leaned against the wall. "Well, here is what used to be the biggest one of all. It was meant to keep all the necessary people safe if the Russians ever turned nasty. It was two years in the building, and has been extended and changed almost every year since the 1960s."

Jennifer looked up at the glass dome. What little she'd thought about blast and fallout shelters didn't correspond to any of this. Nor had anything she'd seen since landing prepared her for its newness and cool elegance. Had this entrance been built since The Break? But she was in no mood to ask questions, and didn't suppose Wapping would be inclined or able to give straight answers. She waited for him to tire of showing off, before letting Radleigh keep her steady for the rest of the winding descent. The deeper she went, the stronger became the smell of electricity and of new rubber flooring.

From the bottom of the stairs, they passed along an arched corridor. After a dozen yards, this inclined left, and they faced a door of glass that might have been three inches thick. "We're on Red Alert security," Wapping explained. "We've five seconds to get through. Then the door slides shut and can't be opened again for another half hour." He looked at Robert. "Get him through last," he said to one of the guards. "Tough titty if he gets cut in half." He bared his forearm and repeated his code. They stepped through into a blast of air conditioned heat. The door closed behind them, and they were sealed within a world for which nothing that happened outside might have direct significance.

Jennifer looked at Michael. Though he'd made his face a careful blank, she could see that he was as scared and overawed as she was—as scared and overawed, and as worried about what might be waiting.

CHAPTER FORTY TWO

The main room of this underground complex was more cavernous than the entrance to the Jubilee Line. It was, so far as Jennifer could tell, a high and broad circle with an inner hub. Wherever she looked, there was equipment of a sort she'd never seen outside of elderly science fiction films, though all was modern in its details. This was looked after by a small army of men in white coats, who darted from place to place, looking at bright displays and comparing readings with each other. Beyond their activity, and just by the inner hub of the complex, there was a railed off oval gap in the floor, from which it seemed possible to look down to a lower floor. There was a now overpowering smell of electricity and a low purring that seemed to come from all directions.

Radleigh looked about. "So here, I take it," he called with a slight evidence of joy in the lack of echo made by his voice, "is the place where the Gateway is kept guarded but ever open—the place from where an entire world shall soon be governed with many rods of iron."

Wapping was still busy with the door security. "You've got your orders," he said impatiently. He waved at the card readers and body wands held at the ready. "Abigail's in a hurry. Yes, the Norman is in chain mail. But, if you think he's got a bomb under that lot, I can get you moved to checking railway permits." He laughed and turned to Radleigh. "Basil, you haven't seen the half of this!" He led the way to the railed gap in the floor. Jennifer had been right about a lower floor. Lit brightly, this was filled with more mainframe computer equipment. More men in white paid no attention to the watching strangers above, but hurried about work that they found of compelling interest.

Radleigh grunted and took a bunch of keys from his pocket. He sorted through them and unlocked Michael and Jennifer. He stepped back from where they were embracing. He seemed to have forgotten the orders about no contact. Wapping was hurrying about with other thoughts on his mind. Radleigh was still taking no chances. "There is nowhere for you to run." He motioned at the guards who'd come in with them, and who were keeping close to Michael. "But I would remind you, dearest Jennifer, of your need to keep every movement you make slow and predictable. These men have orders to wound in the first instance. Please don't require them to act."

He stopped at a sound of footsteps on the left. "Oh, darling Abigail!" he gushed. "This place is more than I ever expected. It was well worth waiting for." Hooper glanced at him before going back into conversation with a couple of men in white. One of them was holding up a long strip of perforated listing paper. The other looked worried. Hooper jabbed a finger at one of the sheets and stared both men into silence.

Once she was finished with giving orders, she came over. Ignoring Radleigh's repeat of his greeting, she stopped a few yards in front of Jennifer. There was something of the 1980s about her padded shoulders and the tight fitting of her skirt. But there could be no doubt of the power she radiated. "Why didn't you pick them up outside Cambrai?" she asked coldly without looking at Radleigh, who fiddled with his cigarette case. "Didn't I make my instructions clear enough? Thanks to your delay, we're in big trouble." Jennifer stared into what resembled the eyes of a calm but predatory insect.

"Where is the Greek boy?" she asked, still looking at Jennifer. A man in a dark suit came over and softly touched her arm. She looked at a sheet of paper covered in print. She pushed it back at him. "Glasgow doesn't matter!" She looked at Michael and smiled. "No, Glasgow doesn't matter at all. Keep the bombers waiting, but ready to go at my order." She patted a lock of hair into place and walked past Jennifer. "Hello again, Michael!" she said. She put out a hand.

"I stand before you in captivity," he said, speaking an English he might have been rehearsing all day. "My wife please release, and with me as you will may do."

Hooper dropped her hand and stood back. "No one told me he could speak English," she said accusingly.

"It's not an accomplishment I'd ever noticed," Radleigh answered from within a cloud of tobacco smoke. "However, I think he should be told the deal in his own language." He stared at Tarquin, who swallowed and looked nervously round at things he didn't begin to understand. He was barely up to explaining that Michael would be needed to play his allotted part with full internal willingness. That was the limit of his cowed explanation. Then Hooper broke in to emphasise that, if he did exactly as required, Jennifer would be turned loose into the street. Michael stared back, saying nothing.

Jennifer put her arms about Michael again. "What are you going to do with him?" she demanded. Some of the toiling men in white stopped and looked in her direction. Hooper's response was to snap her fingers at the guards and turn again to the man in the dark suit. As she was pulled away from Michael, Jennifer managed to add: "Whatever you do to my husband, you'll do to me as well." She had intended it to be a ringing declaration of love. Instead, her last few words trailed off into sobbing. Hooper didn't bother looking at her.

"Do whatever they ask," Michael called to her. "I will see to it that they let you go." He struggled with the guards, but was pulled farther away from her. "Trust me—I *am* a diplomat."

Jennifer sat down on the floor and put her face in her hands. She heard Tarquin mutter something in Greek too low for her to catch. Then she could smell Radleigh's smoky breath as he pulled her to her feet. "I told you, dear girl, I'd save you for your mother's sake," he whispered with quiet urgency. "Don't cross me, and the offer still holds. Hooper needs the boy. She doesn't care who'll take charge of you afterwards." He let go of her, and, when she didn't fall down again, stood away. He took out his cigarette case again and looked about for Hooper. For the moment, she was nowhere in sight. He held his case out to Robert, and leaned forward to share a match. He blew smoke at Tarquin, whose hands fluttered over a pocket, before his nerve failed and he let his arms drop to his side.

A man coughed politely behind Jennifer. "We haven't exactly been introduced," the interpreter she'd seen in Tenterden said. "But my name is Gordon Jessup. I know this isn't at all the time and place. Even so, please accept my congratulations on your marriage. Michael is a fine young man." He continued in whispered Latin: "If it kills me, I'll do what I can to see that you are happy together." Back in English, he raised his voice and looked over the rail at the masses of flashing computer equipment that spread out below them. "I really never thought this sort of place existed."

"And, Siree, it doesn't officially exist," a man with a broad American accent called cheerfully up at them. Jennifer looked at down at General Rockville. He was leaning against the back of a chair and had been staring at a long print out. "To my certain knowledge, it hasn't existed since Margaret Thatcher and Ronald Reagan signed the first cheques back in 1983." He laughed. "You know, I was right beside President Reagan. This place was just a dripping bunker in those days, filled with asbestos and tins of your bully beef. It took true vision to see what it could become—yes, Sir, *true vision!*" He caught Jennifer's eye and laughed again. He looked at the other faces that peered down at him. Still smiling, he turned once more to his print out.

Jennifer continued staring at Rockville. The business suit he'd been wearing for his tour of London had been replaced by his military uniform. His whole manner suggested ownership of all about him. She looked a few yards to his right. There, hunched over each side of a small table, two men were playing cards in silence. One of them, she realised after a few seconds, was the old man she'd seen in Tenterden. The other one—she looked again....

"Yes, it *is* the Prime Minister," Jessup said quietly in Latin. "I was picked up with my client and the Lord Robert a few hours after you had made your rather dramatic exit. My understanding is that the man now smoking with Count Robert had betrayed everyone to Hooper. Mr Duffy was brought here about a fortnight ago. I haven't heard any news, but there seem to have been many changes in the past few weeks." He looked over to where Hooper had reappeared. "I'd better get back to them," he said, holding up the teapot he was carrying.

Hooper leaned over the rail. "Oh, there you are, Madison." He waved back, a boyish smile on his face, and, almost knocking Jessup out of the way, bounded up a small metal staircase to take her hand. "I must apologise for a delay that was longer than I'd expected," she said. "But Sweeting tells me that we're back up to full power." She motioned at a short man with thinning hair and a very wide mouth who stood beside her. His face took on a look of dreamy eagerness, and he nodded in agreement.

"Aw, shucks, Abigail!" Rockville cried. "You know I've been having the time of my life here in little old London town. You just take your time. We'll soon be on the offensive against these fundamentalist terror attacks." He looked at his watch. "I reckon the e-mail I sent earlier should have got you everything necessary to retake control. We just need to get the Gateway open for physical traffic." He stopped and sniffed. He looked at Radleigh and Count Robert, who, leaning against one of the larger blocks of equipment, were trying for a basic and unspoken conversation. Rockville frowned. "Say, Abigail, isn't all this supposed to be no smoking?"

CHAPTER FORTY THREE

Jennifer was beyond guessing how far deeper into the earth they'd gone. The inner hub of the complex had contained a single lift. After the first dozen, she'd given up counting the levels passed in this renewed descent. They'd finally stepped out into what the echo of their voices suggested was a high chamber dozens of yards across. No one had met them here. It had been necessary for Professor Sweeting himself to turn on the intense and buzzing arc lights bolted at close intervals onto walls of smooth black rock. Now, following a short walk along one of the wide galleries that radiated out from this central point, they were in a room about thirty feet by twenty. One entire wall of this was a sheet of darkened glass. Though just a few faint outlines could be seen through the glass, it seemed reasonable to think the next room was smaller.

It was cold down here—very cold—and she was glad of the travelling clothes she'd been made to put on when dragged from her bed in Ulm. She stood beside Hooper with her back to the glass wall. On her other side, Radleigh, still smoking in defiance of anyone who dared frown at him, was staring into a dull mirror that almost covered the opposite wall. This looked decidedly makeshift in construction, and had been set up as if by afterthought. It was the smaller though still substantial mirror elsewhere in the room on which every piece of computer and other equipment seemed to have been focussed. It was beside this other mirror that Michael and Count Robert were listening as Tarquin did his best to put Sweeting's lecture into Latin. If she'd already worked its basics out for herself, the mathematical digressions were almost as obscure in English as in Tarquin's Latin.

"Because it was already switched on," Sweeting said in answer to a question from Radleigh, "it was left on." He was standing beside a grey steel box that looked, on first inspection, like part of an old telephone exchange. He tapped it gently and smiled. "When orders were finally given to shut everything down, I gave it one last spin. I don't need explain how surprised we all were when, almost at once, we detected a burst of energy as big as a supernova, and found we'd locked onto the Pentagon six months before our own date—our date before The Break, that is." He went into a rambling explanation of how, once the connection had been made across a void that no one had known to exist, every nuclear power station in the country had been set working at full burn to keep the connection open—even if, for the most part, only plaintext messages could be exchanged.

He fell silent at another impatient sigh from Hooper. She'd been looking through a sheaf of reports. Jennifer could, from the corner of her eye, see words and sentences that suggested a gathering loss of control in the north of England. Sweeting bowed and went to sit at a computer terminal. He typed for a long time, answering a scrolling text that was white on a blue background. At last, he sat back and reached for a microphone. "Come in, Washington," he called. "This is London. Are you receiving us?"

"Coming across loud and clear, London!" an American voice replied with minor distortion through a loudspeaker beside the terminal. "We thought we'd lost you after voice contact went down." Sweeting spoke briefly about an interruption from the northern sector of the National Grid. Was Lawrence trying to close the Gateway by cutting its power supply?

The American voice faded for a moment before stabilising. "We have the President here beside us, and your own Home Secretary, come over from our London." Jennifer saw a flash of wonder on Hooper's face. It was followed by a look of alarm.

But Rockville had taken the microphone. He carried it as far as its wire would reach and stood before the smaller mirror. "Are you there, Bill?" he asked urgently. "You've read my report on the problems we're facing on this side?"

There was a long silence, during which Sweeting muttered anxiously to himself while typing and retyping numbers at the terminal. Rockville put the microphone down and looked about. He took it up again. "Are you there, Mr President?" he shouted, a nervous edge to his voice.

Another pause, and then: "Thank God you're there, Madison," a man said in a voice as sharp as any razor. "I've got the Congressional Chiefs with me. I think a few words from you would be most helpful." Though she'd paid little enough attention to the news before The Break, Jennifer knew the voice of Bill Hagen, forty sixth President of the United States. The last Jennifer had seen of him was just before the Great Storm, when he'd made a televised appeal to the Russian and Chinese peoples. His plea for calm might have been more effective if the missiles shot down over Mecca hadn't been launched on his orders, and if his face hadn't looked as sharp and cruel as his voice.

Rockville closed his eyes and swallowed. "Mr President," he said dramatically, "now that voice contact is renewed, I can confirm that everything you've been told is the truth. We are in possession of the ultimate power in the universe." He put the microphone down and grinned at Sweeting. "Isn't that so, Professor?"

"Oh, yes," he said airily—"the ultimate power in this or any other universe, I have no doubt. The difficulties we're facing in the streets are nothing by comparison."

There was a murmur of American voices on the other side. Hagen laughed gloatingly. "Then you'd better get the Gateway open again. Seeing is believing." He laughed again. "Yes, my friends," he added in a faintly triumphant voice that seemed more distant from the microphone, "seeing is believing." Rockville looked at Sweeting, who nodded. He looked at his watch, and drank from the paper cup of coffee he'd brought down with him.

Hooper pushed herself close to the microphone. "Hello, Abigail," she said in a strained voice. "This is Abigail! Can you hear me?"

There was a strangled cry, then—"Have you kept your weight off," the other Hooper asked. "You must remember the sweat I've been raising on that treadmill!" They let out a simultaneous and strained giggle.

Michael coughed for Tarquin's attention. "Can you ask Hooper if she remembers having had this conversation with herself?" Tarquin's mouth fell open, and he stammered slightly before

266

relaying the question. Hooper's answer was a look of confusion and fear. But Sweeting laughed and slapped Michael on the back.

"*Bravo, bravo*—not bad for an Outsider!" he said with another of his disconcerting smiles. "You're the first who's ever asked that question of me. The answer is that the Home Secretary *doesn't* recall this conversation with herself, because the universe on the other side of the Gateway isn't the one we left. We have no idea how many universes there are. The best I can say is that, while time is an absolute constant, and cannot be traversed, there's an indefinite number of universes running parallel with our own, all at slightly different times."

Since he'd already got this much by himself, Michael began his next question before his first had been properly answered. "This being so, do you suppose The Break will happen on the other side of your gateway?"

Sweeting shrugged. "Who knows? There are structural anomalies in this present universe, compared with the one we left." He stared at the microphone and then at the speaker. "There are different anomalies over there. They are all at the sub-atomic level, and don't seem to make any practical difference to our calculations. But, if there is a Break in the universe beyond the Gateway, I assume that everyone on this island on the day in question will vanish into another eleventh century. If so, this will allow us to step across without violating the rules."

Radleigh interrupted. "If that isn't our own universe over there," he asked while Tarquin was wobbling between Latin and Greek, "why can't I go across now? The Basil Radleigh on the other side isn't me. It can't matter if two similar people share the same universe."

Sweeting's face tightened. Not welcoming the drift of these questions, he pushed his hands into the pockets of his white coat. "It's early days yet," he said quickly. "We don't fully understand the rules. But we have experimental evidence that, in whatever universe there was another version of you, your own presence there would be a fatal breach of the rules."

"Many bodies, one soul," Michael said in Latin once Tarquin had interpreted.

Sweeting got the meaning without help, and muttered something about the avoidance of metaphysical theories. *"Hypotheses non fingo,"* he added, quoting Newton.

He was rescued by Hooper. "We aren't here to discuss philosophy. Your job is to open the Gateway." Sweeting nodded. He went over to the glass wall. For the first time, Jennifer noticed it had a glass door. He touched a darker area of the darkened glass, and lights came on to show what lay beyond. For the most part, it was an empty space. The only equipment visible was a glass tube, perhaps eight feet high and three across. It stood on a black platform, and had a spaghetti of wires connecting its top to the ceiling. But Jennifer didn't see this at first. What she did see the American insurance agent. She'd last seen him ranting away in Harewood Place. She hadn't thought about him since. If she had, it would have been to assume he was dead or slaving away somewhere in Ireland. There was almost a moment of doubt as she looked at the still, orange-clad figure who, at one end of a small metal bench, must have been there since before Sweeting had brought everyone in. But, if his face had the vacant stare of one who's been stunned by some dreadful shock, or drugged, and if there was a semi-healed gash to his forehead, there was no mistaking his general appearance. It was the American—the one who'd been full of his conversations with God at the time of The Break.

Sweeting went in and helped him to his feet, and led him out into the main room. The American stared at Rockville. Still not speaking, he managed a stiff salute and stood to attention. Sweeting stepped behind the American and stroked his shoulder. Still looking at Rockville, he seemed not to notice. "The immediate problem we faced," Sweeting explained, "was how to make physical contact across the Gateway. Movement between two terminals in one universe requires only a great deal of electromagnetic energy. Between universes, as I've said, it took about half the power available to the National Grid to maintain voice contact. Just keeping this lot turned on needs its own power station."

"So that explains all the power cuts," Radleigh laughed. "Might it also be connected with the sudden fuel shortages last year?"

Sweeting ignored him. "You might call our solution a stroke of genius," he said proudly. "Never let it be said British science isn't the best in the world." He looked at Rockville and nodded.

"Private Ezra Q. Jones," the General said in a rough, military voice, "I hereby call you back into the Army, and promote you to the rank of Lieutenant. Are you ready to do your duty to America, and to Jesus?" The reply was a further straightening up and another stiff salute. Unable to say why, Jennifer felt a sweat breaking out all down her back. She looked at Jones the lunatic insurance agent. She looked at Hooper, who was staring at Michael, delight openly on her face.

Robert ended the silence. "I don't know what I'm supposed to be doing here. I don't understand a word of what's been said to me." He walked over to stand close by Jennifer. "If I'm not to walk out of this place, I want to know what relevance these proceedings have to the agreement made with Duke William." He pulled a sour face and reached up to tug at the brooch securing his cloak.

Tarquin put this to Hooper. She looked at the two guards, who'd been brought along to keep order. She smiled reassuringly at Robert. "Do tell him," she said to Tarquin, "that he will have a privileged role as ambassador to the Normans."

"And don't tell him there's to be nothing for his stupid lord!" Wapping added. He came forward from where he'd been skulking, and grinned knowingly at Jennifer. "Now we've got the Greek Outsider, every other deal is off—especially deals not made by us. He's lucky not to be a prisoner."

Radleigh looked up from where he was sitting. "If I were you, Francis, I'd not go into one of your long speeches. You've seen that the Greek boy understands a little English. Don't assume less of our Norman friend." He reached into his jacket and took out a fresh pack of Marlboro. He stripped off the cellophane and opened it. He cupped it in his hand breathed in the smell of new tobacco with a long and appreciative groan. He offered one to Robert, who'd walked back to him. Radleigh smiled at Jennifer. "For the avoidance of all doubt," he said in the voice of someone who's telling a joke, "that oilman outside gets his low-hanging fruit in Arabia. State and big business, after all, still need each other like the two sides of an arch. It will just be on different terms. Our backing for a certain people to conquer Western Europe, however, is quite off the menu. Now, Jennifer, breathe a word of this to our friend, and he'll never get out of here alive." He lit his cigarette and paused. "Leave everything to Abigail. This really is her show."

CHAPTER FORTY FOUR

Rockville cleared his throat for attention. When everyone was looking at him, he stared ostentatiously at his watch. He nodded to Sweeting, who played with the volume knob on the speaker. On the other side, Hagen was explaining a point of physics to someone else. "I think we'd better get on with testing and recalibrating the physical connection," Rockville said. The President fell silent, only speaking again to shut up a man called O'Halloran, who was asking what all this meant for the "folks back home" in Milwaukee. Rockville looked at the American insurance agent, who was still standing to attention, and who gave a third salute. "Lieutenant Jones," he said in his military voice, "once you do as we ask—and do it of your own free will—the President of the U.S of A. will step into this room. And Jesus will be standing right beside him. Are you prepared to smooth the Coming of the Lord?"

"That's right, Lieutenant Jones," Hagen called soothingly across the Gateway. "I've got the Lord Jesus sitting here on my right hand side. You're doing all this for God's own Son and God's own country. Are you ready to do your duty?"

"Yes, Mr President, Sir!" Lieutenant Jones barked, going into an almost permanent salute.

Jennifer watched Sweeting and Rockville lead the man back through the glass door, and open a door into the glass tube. With much encouragement and talk of "Jesus" and "America," they got him inside. What looked like a wreath attached by many wires was put about his head and tied in place with leather straps. He was shut in, and Sweeting and Rockville came back inside the main room and closed the door. Before the entrance to the tube was sealed, Jennifer was sure she'd heard Jones singing the American

National Anthem.

"There is some as yet unlocated quality about certain human bodies," Sweeting said, speaking fast again, "that can be made to resonate at a certain frequency, and that will—though briefly—produce an energy great enough to punch holes between different universes. This particular specimen was arrested a month or so back, and spared transportation when he was found to possess the right qualities." He stopped and caressed a lever in a glass box that he'd unlocked. "When I depress this, I think everyone here—excepting, of course, General Rockville, who's already seen it in action—will be astonished." He raised his voice. "Are you ready, Washington, to proceed?" When he got his answer, he and someone on the other side counted slowly down from ten. Sweeting took the lever in both hands and pressed it down. There was a momentary flickering of all the lights, and a loud sputtering of arc lights that could be heard from far off through the open door, as the mirror coating on the panel began to glow softly.

Jennifer dodged past the guards and caught Michael before he could hit the floor. Though her body had been going weak from the horror dawning in her mind, she'd seen how, as the background hum and chatter of electrical circuits swelled to a roar, his face had drained of colour. Now, while the noise was falling back to normal, she tried to keep him from striking his head on the floor. Eyes turned up and flickering, he'd stopped breathing in. His back was arching further and further. His lips were beginning to move in what may have been words from one of the Far Eastern languages. Robert had thrown his cigarette down, and was trying to help keep the boy steady in Jennifer's arms. The two guards were backing quietly away.

"Don't touch him!" Sweeting shouted. "Leave him where he is." He would have pulled Jennifer away, but looked at Robert's face and jumped quickly out of reach. He hurried back to his lever and, with a shouted warning across the void, stopped whatever process he'd started. Michael's body went limp, and no one stopped Jennifer from taking him into her arms. He was still conscious, but was struggling to breathe properly from the shock of whatever had been put through him.

"You were right!" Sweeting cried at Hooper, his voice loud and exultant. "I've never seen a reaction so immediate or powerful." He watched Jennifer and Robert get Michael to a chair. "Not there." He looked through the glass wall to where Lieutenant Jones was holding up his arms in his tube and praying ecstatically. "Get him in there. No—just do it. The closer he is to its source, the better he'll be shielded from the polarised emanation." He turned to Jennifer and tried for a friendly smile. "Can you tell me about any strange behaviour he may have shown at the time of The Break?" he asked. "I mean anything like what we've just seen?" Bobbing and grinning, he stooped forward over her.

"You're not putting him in that thing," she said in a dull voice. She looked again at the still ecstatic American. Without warning, and with a strength she'd never noticed was hers, she clutched harder at Michael and made a rush for the door. She'd got it fully open, before the guards could grab her. They pulled Michael from her and forced her into a chair. "Keep yer hair on, love!" one of them grunted.

"Yes, you silly little girl," Hooper laughed, "he *will* go in there." She stood before Jennifer, breathing hard with excitement. She held up her glass pendant. Deep within, its colours writhed and twisted as if demented. Hooper deepened her voice. "The Force is strong within this one," she intoned in a black American voice. She spoiled the effect by going directly into a giggle. But Wapping and Rockville made sure to laugh politely at the joke.

Speechless, Jennifer felt as if she'd known this was coming since the moment she'd perched listening outside the window of Radleigh's flat. Or perhaps it was all a dream, and she'd wake in Ulm with Michael snoring contentedly beside her. She pressed her eyes shut. She opened them. Everything was as it had been. She looked about the room. No one moved.

"I think we can proceed with the demonstration," Sweeting said. Together with his counterpart in Washington, he counted down again and pushed the lever. This time, the smaller mirror glowed brighter and brighter, until faint outlines could be seen. It was like looking at something through the jet from a boiling kettle, or perhaps at an almost familiar landscape through heavy fog. There was another flickering of lights, and Jennifer looked through the glass wall at Michael. Tarquin had been sent in to sit beside him. One hand on his shoulder, he was speaking to the boy. Still shaking, Michael stared back in silence. Behind them in his tube, the American had fallen to his knees, and seemed to be babbling incoherently with his eyes turned up. When she looked back to the panel, Jennifer was in time to see its bright blur resolve into a view of the President at his desk in the Oval Office, and a somewhat thinner Abigail Hooper leaning forward almost close enough to reach through into this universe.

"I believe we'll have to call each other Sister!" one of the Hoopers cried girlishly. They both went into a shrill laugh, and they both stretched forward until their noses almost touched the barrier of the Gateway from each side. But it wasn't a barrier in the sense that it could stop anything from passing through. A couple of men now came into view on the other side and laboriously moved a wooden crate closer and closer. Watching it come through was like seeing something jump from a television screen. No—the whole surface rippled like water as, making sure not to let their hands go though, Sweeting and Rockville pulled it into the room. Jennifer heard it scrape heavily on the floor and they pulled it out of the way. The whole screen now rippled until nothing but a glow of colours could be seen on the other side. Then, as if recovering from the effort of allowing a physical passage, the screen stabilised again.

"A case of Johnnie Walker, one can hope," Radleigh said with a dry chuckle. While most attention was on the box, Wapping crept forward and put his face close to the Gateway. Jennifer wondered if he'd poke a finger through. But he thought better. He fumbled inside his jacket and took out one of the safety pins, and threw it across to the other side. Interested against her will, Jennifer watched as it passed through with no more deflection than if it had been thrown within the room. A fat man in a suit had stepped away from the group behind Hagen, and stood just on the other side. He turned and picked up the safety pin. Awe on his reddened, bleary face, he threw it back across, still without visible deflection. Wapping stared for a moment at the two inches of steel wire that had just passed and repassed a distance that had no physical reality and that might not be conceivable. Then he bent and picked it up. Holding it aloft like some holy relic, he carried it over to the far side of the room and showed it to Radleigh, who put his cigarette between his lips while be bent the pin back and forth, as if to see whether it had suffered from the journey.

"Come across, Mr President," Rockville called. "This universe is wonderful. You can do *anything* you like over here." He looked shyly at Hooper, and repeated the word *"anything."*

"I'll take your word, Madison," Hagen said drily. "But you'll sure forgive me if duty keeps me right here in Washington." He twisted in his chair to face the men behind him. "Do I get full approval in the closed session?" he asked. "I don't think we need concern ourselves with those notes from Moscow and Peking." There was a subdued nodding of heads. He turned back, a thin, anticipatory smile beneath eyes that didn't blink.

"Prevention's sure better than cure!" Rockville laughed. "I've been told I'll do all I can in the coming crisis to talk sense into our enemies. It still won't be enough—not, that is, without the help of our good British friends here!"

Before he could finish his last sentence, there was a splutter from all about, and, without actually losing its translucency, the brightness went out of the colours on the other side of the Gateway. Rockville swore and turned to Sweeting. "Say, what's going on?" he demanded. "It was longer than this the first time. Even that nigra woman lasted longer. The President or I might have been passing across."

Sweeting lifted his eyebrows. "Oh, it's purely down the quality of the specimen." He played with his lever. "It's enough to show, however, that everything is still working after the power loss."

Jennifer looked at Lieutenant Jones in his glass tube. It was like watching a piece of fruit that, unobserved, had been rotting from within. One moment, Jones was still on his knees, resting against the wall of the tube. The next, he'd imploded into a shrivelled thing that no longer looked remotely human. There was a further crumbling into dust as his clothes fell in upon themselves.

She screamed and tried to get up. But she was held fast by the guards, and made to look in the direction of the Gateway. She tried to close her eyes and scream again, but Sweeting slapped her face twice and very hard. With a cocking of rifles, Robert was forced to stay where he was. Silent, she watched Rockville step forward and push his military cap at what had, a few minutes before, been permeable enough to let a safety pin fly through. For the first half dozen passes, the cap moved easily. Then as the colours on the other side began to blur and fade, the cap moved back and forth through a membrane with the quality of fast-setting toffee. Rockville let go of it for a few seconds, and it was held firmly in place. As he pulled it back, Jennifer could see her own face looking back at her.

"One minute, twelve seconds," Sweeting said, looking up from his watch. "The overall time varies with the quality of the specimen. The fade out time, though, is always the same." He smiled so that the edges of his mouth disappeared into the sides of his face.

Jennifer was now free to look again at the tube. Sweeting was already there, and raking out the remains of what had been Ezra Q. Jones. "Don't make him go into that thing—please." Hooper stood over her and tried for a sisterly look. "You won't get him in there!" Jennifer sobbed. "I won't let him go in."

"I don't think, dearest girl," Radleigh said beside her, "you have any choice in the matter. I believe the idea is that he steps willingly into that bottle, or you take a large calibre bullet in your stomach while he's made to watch." He looked up at Hooper. "That is the idea, Abigail, isn't it?"

Not looking away from Jennifer, Hooper smiled. "Jennifer's your name, isn't it? Well, let me give you some very sound advice: All men are bastards! You think you're in love now? But we've all thought that at some point. One of these days, you'll thank me for this."

"That's right, Jennifer," the other Hooper called through the loudspeaker. "You listen to Abigail. She really does know what she's talking about. If it starts with your sinking into his arms, it always ends with your arms in his sink." Again in unison, the two Hoopers laughed. Then the Hooper who stood before her turned to Sweeting and the smile dropped from her face.

"How soon can we get the boy in there?" she asked.

CHAPTER FORTY FIVE

Michael closed his eyes and tried to gather his thoughts. It was rather like being drunk, but without any recollection of pleasure. He took a deep breath and opened his eyes again. "If I step into that machine," he said to Tarquin, "I want some reasonable assurance that my wife will be released." He brushed Sweeting's arm away and stepped into the main room. He leaned against the back of a chair and willed the clouds to withdraw from the front of his mind. "Give me the assurances I want, and I'll do whatever you tell me. Otherwise, you might as well kill us both now." Rockville growled menacingly at Tarquin once this was put into English. He started a low and worried conversation with Hooper.

Telling himself how the sun can still peep through the heaviest cloud, Michael willed himself to think. He was a diplomat. Even when it couldn't be avoided, catastrophe didn't need to be total. There was always *something* that could be negotiated. He switched from Greek into Latin. "My Lord Robert, I have a favour to beg of you." Robert shoved past the guards. "Our peoples are at war," Michael said, his voice beginning to fail again. "The last time we met, you tried to kill me. But I give my wife into your hands, and charge you with her safety."

Robert came closer and brushed ash from the front of his tunic. "As one man of honour to another," he said, speaking loud, "and with God as my witness, I swear that I will die before I allow any harm to come to Jennifer. I will take her from this accursed country, and swear that I will treat her as if she were my own daughter." He held out his right hand. Michael took it. For the first time since they'd been lifted out of Ulm, he felt as if he were back on firm land. Robert leaned forward to embrace and kiss Michael. "If I could think of anything that didn't put Jennifer's life at risk," he breathed, "I'd rip these animals apart and spit into their blood."

Michael stood back and nodded. "Explain in English what has been agreed," he said to Tarquin. He listened carefully as his words were relayed. Hooper shrugged and looked at Robert. She looked at Radleigh. He nodded and spoke firmly in English. She smiled and gave a casual nod. She pointed through the glass wall at the now empty tube, and spoke several sentences with a careful absence of any tone that might help him to understand them.

"She agrees to the arrangement," Tarquin said in a voice that faltered with sudden excitement. "She only reminds you of the need to give full cooperation once the tube is sealed. Whatever thoughts and fancies fill your mind, you must resist nothing." He paused and had to steady himself by biting hard on the sleeve of his jacket. "Hooper says that, once you've gone into that tube, Jennifer will be of no value to her, and the Norman pig is welcome to her." He stopped again and tried to bring his voice under a semblance of control. "She also says that you are strong enough to survive inside the tube. She says that the one who died was of much lower quality."

Michael swallowed. He took a step towards Jennifer, but was immediately pulled back by the guards. Tarquin and Hooper took hold of Jennifer and pressed her into a chair. Robert came forward again and stamped his foot. "This is an outrage!" he bellowed. "The two are man and wife. They must be allowed to say goodbye." As if she'd understood the Latin, Hooper smiled slimily and shook her head.

"Take him away," Michael heard her say to the guards.

Michael resisted the pull of the guards. He reached out a hand for Jennifer. *"If avoiding this meant that I'd never have met you,"* he said quietly in English, *"I'd do it all over again, and be happy."* As if by accident, the guards relaxed their hold, and he was able to reach a few inches further. For one moment, his fingers made contact with Jennifer's.

And that was it. She was forced harder into the chair, and Michael was allowed to walk by himself through the door and over to the glass tube. He turned away from Jennifer as the wired wreath was tied about his head. The door closed, and he felt a buzzing in his head that began slowly to pass through his entire body. If it was of the same nature as the seizures, it left him strangely calm. He hadn't believed a word of Hooper's assurance about his own safety. He knew that he'd soon be dead. He tried not to think about the other man, and wondered if it might be worth the effort of praying for his soul. He did try, but found himself only praying that Jennifer wouldn't see him in obvious pain.

In the next room, Tarquin pressed his face close against the glass wall. "I want to see this!" he snarled. He pulled himself back and looked triumphantly at Jennifer, who was still weeping out of control. "If I can't have him, *no one* can!" Beside Radleigh, Robert lit another cigarette.

Radleigh sucked hard on his own cigarette. "Isn't this all rather close to cannibalism, Abigail?"

Hooper giggled and picked up and caressed the microphone. "Too late now, Basil, to call us cannibals. In the past year, we've arrested twelve million people. How many of those do you imagine we really need in Ireland?" She cleared her throat and sang:

> ...*Healthy and lean,*
> *Clean and green,*
> *Eat it while it's steaming hot!*

She stopped and clutched at her side with helpless laughter. "You've never been stupid enough to eat the filthy stuff?" she gasped. The guards went into a low giggle, and one nudged the other. Radleigh stared back, his mouth open in speechless shock. Even Jennifer was dimly aware of what had just been revealed.

Sweeting looked angrily round from another conversation across the void. "Is any of this relevant? We need as clear a mental state in the specimen as can be arranged." He walked over and jabbed at Tarquin, whose breath was steaming an area of the glass wall. "We've no more need of Greek," he said impatiently. "Your presence is disturbing the boy. Go back to the main level. Look for a man with red hair called Barlow. Show him your badge and tell him you're to help with preparing the goods lift to carry stuff to the surface."

Tarquin looked defiantly round at him. "But what about the Norman? You still need me for that."

"The girl can interpret for him," Hooper said. "If he makes any trouble, he can be shot." She bared her teeth at Jennifer. "Now we've got everything we want, his usefulness is at an end."

Sweeting waited for Tarquin to shuffle reluctantly from the room, and then for the clatter of far off lift gates and the whine of electric motors, before hurrying back to his terminal. "I think I can now show you how this thing really works," he cried. Trembling with excitement, he finished his countdown and pushed a second lever. At once, both mirrored panels began to glow.

With a visible effort, Radleigh pulled himself together. "Something you haven't got round to telling me," he asked Hooper, "is why you need the Greek boy for this. Can't you make do with an endless succession of local specimens?" He flicked more ash onto the rubber floor.

Another happy smile spread over Hooper's face. "Dearest Basil," she said, "I can answer that." She walked over to the panel and poked at her makeup in the reflection. She stared at herself until she was replaced in the panel by gradually solidifying shapes beyond. She turned back and spread her arms. "We need a long and stable connection, so we can bring masses of equipment through. We need materials from America, and from Germany and Japan. We need things that couldn't be made on this side in a hundred years. We haven't found anyone else to guarantee the continuity that we need. We think the boy will last for two weeks. By then, we should have everything we need to stabilise the connection on other principles. Long before then, we'll have the means to end the extremist attacks that your own negligent sloth has allowed to run out of control. Oh, just a few days, I think, and we'll be set up on both sides to do everything that needs to be done."

Radleigh looked at the glowing tip of his cigarette, and waved it in the direction of General Rockville, who grimaced and fanned away any stray wisp of smoke that might drift in his direction. "I

suppose we can all rejoice that, with a bound, you'll soon be free
of Cardinal Lawrence," he said. "However, you still haven't fully
explained what it is you have in mind."

"Full spectrum domination of two worlds," Rockville broke in
fiercely—"that's the name of the game!" He went and stood beside
Hooper and glanced suspiciously at the smoke from Count
Robert's cigarette. "Look," he said to Radleigh, suddenly more
reasonable, "we've got ourselves an absolutely virgin planet here.
Our corporations know exactly where to drill or dig for everything
we could ever need. We can use this to bring peace to a suffering
world on the other side. Just imagine—we can perform full
geological surveys here, and use the data to cause devastating and
apparently natural earthquakes in Moscow, in Peking, and
anywhere else where democracy is under threat. We can develop
weapons here, safe from any spies. We can test them without threat
to the lives of our own people. Think how the discovery of
America allowed Europe to fight off the threat of Islam. This is our
new and bigger America. It means permanent victory for peace and
human rights throughout the world."

He stopped and turned to look at the restored view of the Oval
Office. "Mr President," he cried thrillingly, "we have lift off!" The
President opened his mouth in a silent howl of joy, and got up from
his desk and came forward. Keeping just on his own side gave him
an oblique view of the larger Gateway. Flickering, and just
sufficiently misted to close off any sense that the room had opened
out, this showed a vast warehouse heaped up with crates, and an
army of men at the ready to start moving them across. The men
stared back. At a command from someone out of sight, they went
into a round of cheered applause in the American fashion.

The President waited for the applause to finish, then returned to
his desk. "And I can promise, on behalf of the Government of the
United States," he said with silky insincerity, "that our Special
Relationship with Great Britain has moved to the forefront of our
foreign and domestic policies. He turned to the man with the red
face. "I don't think we can see any objections to that, can we,
O'Halloran?" He turned back and smiled. "We can take it as read
that this is the final End of History," he took up again. "On both
sides of the void that separates us, this is our moment of triumph—

a triumph that will never end." Hooper gulped loudly, and looked about to start jumping up and down. She was stopped by the sight of the flag that the President had produced. It showed a Union Jack and the Stars and Stripes, held apart and joined by a bolt of lightning. "Mighty fine, don't you think?" Hagen asked with a flash of expensive dentistry. "Vice-President Candyburg designed this himself." He turned again to his Congressmen and stared their protests into silence. Somewhere else in America, the men who were to carry out his instructions began another round of applause.

Jennifer had been let out of her chair. Ignored by people who were more interested in the goodies about to be handed across the void, she stood looking at Michael. Eyes pressed shut, he was still on his feet. Two weeks, it had been said he'd last in there. She looked at the crumbled remnants of the American "specimen."

She felt someone touch her sleeve. "Little Bear," Robert whispered, "let's get out of here. Michael wouldn't want you to watch to the end." He leaned closer. "Give the boy his dignity. I don't know how we'll get out of here. But we can at least leave this room of devilish magic."

Jennifer looked again at Michael. There was a brightening halo about his head and upper body, and she could see his hands stretched out and trembling from the strain of the energy that, little by little, was stealing his soul. She could have given way again to helpless tears. She could have thought of many things. Instead, she recalled how he hadn't so much as twitched when he took that bayonet through his arm at Oxford Circus. Suddenly, her mind was clear. "You go," she said. "I'm getting him out of that thing."

CHAPTER FORTY SIX

Robert put his big hands on her shoulders. "My oath to that boy is absolute." He looked carefully into her face. "This isn't like France, Jennifer. It isn't a game. If I don't get you out of here now, they'll kill you."

"Then I'll die where I belong," she said. She looked about. Still, no one was paying attention. The guards were watching the President hold up the new compound flag for everyone to salute. She stepped quickly across the room. She pushed the glass door open. It was only as she turned to close it that she realised Robert had followed her. He gave one of his black smiles and closed the door. All was suddenly quiet. Even by comparison with what she'd just left, the room was cold. There was a faint but omnipresent hum of something powerful. Michael had turned again, and, eyes still shut, was facing in her direction. She looked through the glass wall. The President had begun a speech, and was waving a handgun to emphasise his points. Rockville was in conversation with someone across the bigger Gateway. She reached for the metal handle on the door of the tube.

Her impact on the floor knocked all the breath out of her lungs. For a moment, she lay shaking as if she'd just laid hands on a live mains cable. She got up dazed and made again for the tube. She'd been noticed. Hooper was rapping frantically on the wall. The impact of her rings on the glass made a dull and repeated click. Jennifer looked left to see both guards beating their hands on the door. Behind them, Sweeting was shouting with a passion she couldn't hear. In the second that she gave to looking at it, the bigger Gateway dissolved into a patchwork of interference. Hagen had put his head through his Gateway, and was looking at her with cold fury. But Robert had shoved his dagger across the inner handle of the door. For the time being, it was locked shut. Jennifer looked again at Michael, unmoving in the tube, and nerved herself for another attempt. She noticed the faint shimmering of a field she hadn't before seen about the tube.

She was shoved roughly aside. "Don't touch it, you fool!" Robert cried in a voice that was choked with fear. "The door is filled with electricity." He pulled her away with enough force to knock her down again. She was up almost at once. By then, he was already standing before the tube. He looked at it for a moment. Then he stepped back. "God give me strength and preserve me!" he said calmly in Old French. He picked up the metal bench with both hands, and swung it and let go. As it struck against the lower part of the tube, he gave a wild and agonised bellow and flew backwards, blue sparks playing over the exposed area of his chainmail. There was a simultaneous loud smashing of glass, and a louder flash of burned out circuitry.

No longer caring if the door would hold, Jennifer ran forward and pulled at Michael. His heavy jerkin saved him from the shards of glass that lay round him. She pulled him harder, and he came properly free just as the upper part of the tube gave way and, with a flash of circuitry that hadn't gone in the general burn out, fell like a jagged guillotine. The room was filled with smoke and the smell of unextinquished electrical fires.

There was a single and very loud smack of something against the glass wall. It was easy to guess what this might be. But Jennifer was pulling madly at the straps that held smoking, fizzing wires to Michael's head. Careless of the guns that would surely soon be jammed into her body, she got Michael onto his back and patted his face. "Michael! Michael!" she wept. "Come back to me."

He opened his eyes and blinked. He tried to sit up, but failed. He moved his lips in what might have been Greek, and smiled. "I saw things," he whispered, "that I remembered from the dreams I had last year. They made no sense the first time, but a little more now."

Jennifer put her arms about Michael and pulled him over beside Robert, who was sitting up and looking at hands that wouldn't stop trembling. "Did I really see God?" he asked, still in Old French. "Or was it the Virgin who saved us?" He stroked Michael's hair. "Someone told me the boy would live." There was another and much louder smack on the glass, after which angry shouting could be heard from the main room. Somehow, Michael was getting to his feet. She got up with him and took his arm, and looked over at what had been a glass wall, but that was now a cobweb of cracks with a small hole in its middle. She helped Michael across the floor to see through a hole that, with a continual popping and jumping away of glass cubes, widened by the second. If they were both to die, they might as well see how the end would come.

How to take in the changes of the previous two minutes? She'd already seen that the bigger Gateway was dead. Her first clear sight was of the two guards. They both lay face down on the floor, one of them still moving his legs, the other in a pool of blood. Clutching at a darker patch on the right shoulder of his uniform, Rockville twisted like an agonised worm a few yards beyond them. Still beyond connected thought, Jennifer felt that the shrill cries of pain and fear must be his. Her main sight, though, was of *two* Abigail Hoopers. As if thrown far away from the one Gateway still in operation, they were getting to their feet beside the door from the room. Not speaking, they stared at each other.

"Take your friends back against the far wall," a voice warned. "You're in the firing line, and I don't know how precious General Rockville is to his President." A cigarette dangling between his lips, Radleigh had squeezed himself into a corner of the room where he couldn't be seen from the other side of the Gateway. In both hands he held Robert's gun—the big revolver she'd grabbed in Tenterden, and that Michael had carried in so much hope all the way to Ulm. She'd have recognised its shape anywhere. How Radleigh had guessed he'd not be put through the body scanners here was only one mystery to add to the others.

It was Rockville who brought her to her senses. "In God's name, Bill," he gasped—"get me out of here. It's all a Goddam Limey double cross." He tried to crawl towards a Gateway that was already turning dull. He got eighteen inches, before the movement of his wounded shoulder sent him into a screaming, curled up ball of pain.

Radleigh took out his cigarette. "I'd stand away from that lever, dear boy," he said to Sweeting. "Or would you like to feel your bladder shot away?"

The Hooper Jennifer had known was on her feet. "Have you gone mad, Basil?" She stood away from her counterpart, who, opening and closing her mouth, remained crouching. She walked into the centre of the room. She pulled her jacket and skirt into order, and tried for the voice she used on television. "Get her back through while you can. Do you want to get us all killed?"

"She's right," Sweeting added. Ignoring Radleigh's gun, he hurried across to the Gateway, and pushed his hand through. It was beginning to set. Gun still in his hand, the President backed away with a shouted warning. Sweeting turned to Radleigh. "Get her through while you still can," he urged. "Don't you understand what you've done?"

He spoke again, about timings and repairs. But his words were covered by a savage roar. Perhaps thirty seconds had passed since he'd sat, shocked as a child who's survived pushing a fork into an electrical socket. Now, Robert pushed Jennifer and Michael aside to leap through the shattered glass wall and lay hold of Mike Wapping.

"Oh, no—please!" Wapping squealed, as he was carried in one hand towards the Gateway. On the other side, the President snarled an obscenity and took aim at Robert. But, like an insect dropped into pond water, Wapping struck against the Gateway just in front of Hagen. Screaming and twisting, he was held there, one arm and his lower body dangling free on the other side. Slowly, his weight carried him downward on both sides of the fast-dulling Gateway. Robert laughed and gave a hard push. Excepting his left forearm, Wapping's whole body went through. Too late, Hagen fired at Robert. The first bullet struck against the Gateway with a dull, plopping sound. It worked its way through, to fall uselessly at Robert's feet. The next shot recoiled, and Jennifer dimly saw O'Halloran jerk backwards, his chest spurting blood. Watching the reflection of Robert's grinning face take shape, she heard a cry of pain and incredulity though the voice contact speaker, and saw Wapping's left arm drop twitching to the floor.

"Rot in hell, bag of stinking filth!" Robert chuckled. He looked down and stamped on the fingers of the severed arm. He turned and bowed to Jennifer. "Call that my wedding gift, O Little Bear," he said with one of his nastier laughs. He stamped again, and sent one of the bullets skipping across the floor.

Radleigh walked over to the speaker and switched it off. The rising chaos of shouts and the sound of sound of more gunfire went off abruptly, and everyone stood in a silence broken only by strange but distant clattering noises from outside the room.

The main Hooper was first to speak. "Why?" she asked. She tried to say more, but her voice was shaking too much. "Why?" she whispered.

Radleigh sat down, and flicked the ash that had accumulated on his cigarette. "Oh," he said easily, "I've been working towards this moment ever since Brother Lawrence told me about the Gateway." He pointed at Robert, who was still breathing like a steam engine. "I don't imagine this oaf understood what he was doing. But he took things a stage further than I'd thought possible." He smiled at Hooper and tightened his grip on the gun. "Did you ever trouble yourself during PPE at Oxford with a reading of *Paradise Lost*?" He laughed at the dead look on her face. "Probably not," he sneered. "I've only ever heard you quote from John Rawls." Bending his arm to keep the gun trained from an easier position, he quoted:

> ....*a broad and beat'n way*
> *Over the dark Abyss, whose boiling Gulf*
> *Tamely endur'd a Bridge of wondrous length*
> *From Hell continu'd reaching th' utmost Orbe*
> *Of this frail World; by which the Spirits perverse*
> *With easie intercourse pass to and fro....*

He laughed again. "I think that sums up your plan very nicely, Abigail dearest. I don't think I need explain my own little plan to break down your bridge, and close the Gates of Hell forever. As with every successful plan, much was thought out in advance, and much left to fortune. But I do think it's turned out rather well."

He glanced at Jennifer and Michael, who, with Count Robert, were edging slowly towards the door. "My dear and stupid children!" he beamed. "You couldn't have done better if I'd coached you for a month of Sundays."

He stopped at a sudden noise, as if of breaking wind. Everyone turned and looked at the other Hooper, who'd turned pale and was trembling. "What have you done to me?" she cried. As she spoke, there was another noise—now of tearing fabric—and the middle buttons of her blouse burst to reveal areas of grey flesh that seemed to expand by the moment. She reached up to wipe sweat from her brow. She tried to scream, but her voice died when she looked at her hands. Where she'd pressed hard, both eyebrows were now stuck to her palms. She opened her mouth to try harder for a scream. Instead of sound, light as if of a thousand LED bulbs streamed from the back of her throat. She collapsed slowly to the floor, and the hands she'd clasped together as if in prayer began insensibly to merge into one translucent mass.

"Help, help, I'm melting!" she found the strength at last to cry in a voice that was barely human. She tried to speak again. But some kind of seizure took hold of her limbs, and she sprawled on her back. More light streamed from her open mouth, and from her eyes, and a bright glow formed about an entire body that seemed to be swelling larger even as it dissolved.

"Kill her!" the main Hooper shouted. She grabbed at a chair and raised it over her head. "It's souls, not bodies, that count. Let's kill her!" She struck at her "sister" with frantic energy. She missed and lifted the chair again. The hit she managed this time reminded Jennifer of a hammer blow into putty.

Sweeting sat down on the floor, and put his head in his hands. "It doesn't matter," he said with quiet despair. "It's at least an hour—maybe more—until death makes a body inert." The main Hooper looked down at the silently writhing body. It was beginning to glow and flicker all over, and, with every shuddering spasm of the limbs, appeared to be spreading across the floor like an ice lolly left out in the sun.

"Help me!" the dissolving creature called again in a low buzzing voice. It tried to sit up, but was stuck where it had begun to dissolve. "I'm so cold!" Hooper dropped the chair and stepped over Rockville. No longer writhing, he was still conscious. He tried to clutch at Hooper's ankle. She kicked his hand away, and looked wildly about the room.

Sweeting put his hands down. "Look, Basil," he said, trying to keep his voice steady, "we've still time to mend things. We can use Hooper instead of the boy. It won't reopen the Gateway. But, once she's burned up, her counterpart's presence here won't matter. Do you understand what will happen if you don't see reason?"

"Of course I know what will happen," Radleigh smiled. "It's mutual but disproportionate annihilation. Things are nicely set up to blow this project, and all knowledge of its working, to smithereens. I'm taking out the lot of you here in London—and now, I suppose, all your friends in Washington. What lucky worlds there will be on both sides of the Gateway! Now, my good man, make yourself useful, and tell me how long we've got."

"May Jesus bring you to reason!" Rockville croaked with an attempt to sit up. His left hand slipped in the blood from his shoulder, and he fell down with a sharp cry of pain. "Use Abigail, for God's sake," he sobbed. "Just get me out of here."

Radleigh glanced at the still chattering though incoherent thing that had been the other Hooper. She was steadily deflating into a pool of her own bright slime. The main Hooper had fallen to the floor, and was looking about like a caged animal. "Well, come on, Sweeting," he prompted. "How long?"

Sweeting stretched his legs out and smiled feebly. "I really don't know. We've never got this far until now. Besides, didn't I say that the laws of physics are slightly different in this universe?" He watched the dissolving Hooper. "It is, of course, fascinating," he added, his voice resigned to the inevitable—"Nobel Prize stuff at its best." He stopped and looked at Radleigh. "Oh, if you can put up with an informed guess, I'd say forty five minutes. She ought to blow when she's formed an undifferentiated pool on the floor. But I'm only extrapolating from her rate of dissolution. You never can tell—she might get a sudden move on." He looked down. "Now, you really should stop talking about mutual annihilation of matter. That's very loose stuff. What actually happens is vaporisation, followed by equidistant permeation...."

He fell silent and looked about. "Let's assume her mass is seventy kilogrammes," he went on thoughtfully. "You can multiply that by 2.17 x 104, and get a sphere with a volume of...." He stopped and grinned. "Give or take a few yards, there'll be nothing left within a mile of here in all directions—nothing at all, and within forty odd minutes." He stopped again, and waited for Hooper's long wail to die away. "Do you know, Radleigh, how many people have had to die to get us to this point? Can you imagine how many will die, now you're letting it all go up? It won't just be the Gateway you're destroying." He looked at the reflection of everyone in the big mirror. "I do suggest you put that gun away, and let me do what I still can to stop the countdown." He looked from one Hooper to the other.

Radleigh pursed his lips. "You've heard it from a good authority, Jennifer. Get yourself and that boy out of here. Get the other side of Westminster Bridge—or get beyond Trafalgar Square. Just run, and don't stop running." He waved his free hand at Robert, who was looking completely lost. "Take the oaf with you. He's earned it. Besides, he'll be a good exit permit if your badges fail." He looked at his watch, and took out another cigarette. "If you can bear to touch it, there's also what may have been the most useful part of young Wapping's anatomy on the floor." He looked again at Jennifer. "Go!" he ordered. "There's much I'd like to say. But the clock's against you."

While she beckoned to Robert to help with Michael, Radleigh spoke again. "Something I can tell you, however, is that you'll find your parents where I had them locked away. Unless your mother has finally murdered someone and broken free, they're in the bridal suite of the Royal Hotel in Deal—not two hundred yards from your house!" Already outside the room, Jennifer stopped and looked back. Radleigh was out of sight, though she could see the smoke from his cigarette. Rockville was twisting about in another spasm of pain and terror. Hooper was on her knees, rocking backward and forward and staring at the big screen. Sweeting had scooped some of the other Hooper's slime on to his ballpoint pen, and was holding it up to the light.

"Fascinating—utterly fascinating!" his rapt face described.

Radleigh laughed. "You're a silly girl," he called. "If you hadn't gone gallivanting off to France with that oaf, you'd have been picked up with your parents. If you'd only stayed put another hour when you got back, my people would have bagged you then." He laughed again, and his voice began to echo strangely now Jennifer was leading the two men into the wide space where the lift had somehow returned and was waiting with open doors. "If you'd shown an ounce more of common sense than your father ever has, none of this would have happened!" His mocking laughter was silenced by the noise of the shutter doors that Jennifer dragged together. She pressed the topmost button on the control panel, and there was the familiar drone of motors. "Do remember me to your mother," was the last she distinctly heard from Radleigh. "Richard doesn't at all deserve her!" he seemed to add. But the main Hooper was letting out a scream that might never end, and the lift was closed and moving upwards. Another second, and there was no chance of hearing anything more.

CHAPTER FORTY SEVEN

Jennifer stepped from the lift into a main area that was just as she'd left it. If she could see a digital countdown in her mind's eye, no one else seemed yet to have noticed the wrecking of the project that had brought this complex together. There was a crowd by one of the mainframe terminals. Two men were reading against each other from sheets of listing paper. A third was trying to make sense of this as he typed in strings of code. One of Hooper's people had taken over an unused desk. He had an old telephone receiver cradled under his left ear, and, nodding every few seconds with evident relief, was taking notes. One of the guards stopped to look at them. They were Outsiders, and without anyone in charge of them. She smiled and spoke English, and pointed at the badge pinned to her tunic. Not replying, he continued about his other business.

Michael was alive and recovering almost by the second. Robert was a hero. Her mother had been flat wrong about Radleigh. *Her parents were alive.* She stilled the rising of her spirits, and thought of Radleigh. She wished he hadn't stayed behind, to make sure nothing changed before the other Hooper turned to a wafer thin pool of slime. Hooper and Rockville deserved all that was coming to them. *Ditto* Sweeting—or perhaps he was a special case: science is science, after all. She checked herself again. Had her mother been genuine in her dislike of Radleigh? Jennifer never had. Or was she already reshaping the past in light of the present?

"This is not the time or place for historical revisionism," she said firmly to another of the guards. He nodded, and the sound of her English drew his hand away from where it had come to rest above his holster. Better to think how to get out of here. That remained as vague in her head as when she'd pressed the top button in the lift.

She took a couple of files from a cardboard box that had been left under a table. This was a trick her father had told her about from his brief spell in the Civil Service: *Bored? Fancy a walk? Carry a stack of files with you. It works every time.* So it might now. "Keep behind me and try not to speak," she said in Latin. Robert nodded and stepped away from Michael, who, so long as it didn't involve running away, seemed able to move by himself. They set off towards the exit. Jennifer looked briefly down as they skirted the railed gap in the floor. Still holding up their cards, still silent, the oilman and the Prime Minister might not have moved since she'd first seen them. Another of Hooper's people caught up with them, and overtook in a self-important bustle. He glanced back at the oddly clothed trio—but the sight of the badges, and of those files, settled any tendency to suspicion.

Sweeting had mentioned a goods lift. That made sense. The way they'd come in didn't allow movement of large objects, or in bulk. The goods lift was being readied for a transfer of material from that American warehouse to the armed forces. Normal routine there might be out of order. It was the obvious place for a getaway. All Jennifer needed was to find where it was.

Teapot in hand again, Jessup stepped from behind one of the computers. He looked at them and raised his eyebrows. "So Basil has done it!" he said softly in Latin. He transferred the teapot to his left hand and gave a concerned look at Michael, who was looking ready again to fall asleep if he stopped moving.

"Come with us," Jennifer whispered. "This whole place will blow up in about half an hour."

He smiled and looked about. "I thought he was more out of his mind than your father," he said in English. He put his teapot on the floor and stood up straight. "But he has closed the Gateway. Who is the double you left downstairs with him?"

"Hooper."

Jessup nodded. "That will have pleased him more than you can know." He raised his voice. "The ending of a work glorifies the work," he said in Latin.

"We need to get to the goods lift," Jennifer said.

Tarquin laughed behind her. "Going somewhere, are we?" he

asked in Greek. Jennifer turned. He stood with three guards, their pistols at the ready. He shifted his weight to one leg. "*Finis opus coronat,* eh?" "We'll see about that!" He spoke to one of the guards: "Any trouble, shoot the girl first, and then the Norman. The boy belongs to Hooper."

"The Gateway is closed," Jennifer said in Latin. She looked for words that would make sense in the language. How, without giving the game away in English, to say that everything for a mile in any direction was about to become a ball of incandescent gas?

Tarquin saved her the trouble. "You're a lying bitch!" he said in English, hate blazing from his face. He switched into Latin. "The boy is going back for use as charcoal in Hooper's furnace. You'll stand there till he's raked out as ash. Then I'll kill you with my own hands." He turned to the biggest of the guards. "Take them in charge," he said, back in English.

Jessup coughed politely. "If you look in my breast pocket," he said to the man, "you'll find a warrant card that proves I'm an officer of the State Security Bureau." A few seconds more, and all three armed men were busy saluting. The big one laid a warning arm on Tarquin's shoulder. "Lock him into one of the offices," Jessup ordered. "I'll seek instructions from the Home Secretary herself over his punishment." He took off his spectacles. He folded them away. He pointed at the big man. "Escort these three agents from the complex. Tell anyone who asks that they're on business for the SSB."

Jennifer stared at a man suddenly taller and more confident than the dreamy scholar Michael had described. If this whole narrative was some kind of incomplete jigsaw puzzle, she'd found another piece. Or she'd found a piece and didn't know where it went. "Aren't you coming with us?" she gabbled in Latin.

He smiled sadly. "You wouldn't have me leave Basil all alone down there? Besides, my running days are long past—in every sense." He stared at the teapot. "Do light a candle for me in the Great Church, Michael."

He looked at Tarquin. "Go quietly, my dear fellow. We've never spoken, but I did much admire your thesis on the cult of Antinous in fourth century Egypt. Such a pity you'll never get any closer to your sources."

Jennifer waited till they were all out of sight. "Come on," she said to Robert. "We're losing time." They set off again, now at a brisk pace, for the only exit they knew. Still, nothing seemed to have changed. She was beyond making sense of the equipment, or of the army of men in white who tended it. But, if incomprehensible, the computers continued radiating assurance, and the men fussed happily with questioning and directing them. Jennifer had put her files down. There was no need now of any cover story. The guard was on a mission for the SSB. Self-importance stamped on his face, he'd not be stopped or questioned.

Within minutes, they were by the glass door. "You'll need to open it for us," Jennifer said to the guard.

He shrugged. "Not *my* job, that," he said with a nod at the unattended security desk. He looked suddenly round. "Here, what's all that noise?" There was a commotion far within the complex. He walked back a few yards, to try for a better view. Jennifer's stomach went cold. Had Jessup's ruse failed? *Had he changed his mind?*

"We could try this." Robert held up Wapping's forearm, and waved it as if it were a magic wand. Jennifer looked round. Lucky for them, the guard still had his back turned. She told herself not to shudder, and took the limb into her own hands. Cold and immobile as a piece of butcher's meat, it was surprisingly heavy. She held the implanted microchip a few inches from the sensor panel. A red light began to flash. But the door remained shut.

The code! Jennifer felt another chill in her stomach. Wapping had used an identification code. What had it been? She'd had so many things on her mind on the way in. She turned to ask the guard to go looking for the desk people. She bit her lip. How long would that take? She looked at her watch. She hadn't checked it on the lower level. The time it now said was meaningless.

She looked up. With a frantic cry of "Michael! Michael!" Tarquin was running forward. He was followed a dozen yards behind by the two guards who'd taken Jessup's order. One of them stopped and lifted his gun. It had a red aiming light, and this played all over the place. But the guards down here seemed to be under instructions not to fire when close by any of the equipment. He lowered his gun and put up a warning hand to his colleagues.

"Take me with you, Michael," Tarquin pleaded in Greek. "I understand everything. Don't leave me behind.

Michael had grabbed Wapping's arm from Jennifer. He lifted it from within his cloak, and held it up as if it were his own. "Take him away!" he cried in unaccented English. He showed the silver disk. "Take him away!" he repeated, now impatient. Ignoring Tarquin's long wail, he turned and pressed the barcode against the panel. "Wapping, Francis," he said slowly and clearly— "CT76482." With a gentle click, the door slid open. Michael waited for Jennifer to go through. "Doesn't it close by itself?" he asked. She nodded. Five seconds seemed an awfully long time. She saw Tarquin pulled to the ground. The big guard stamped heavily on one of his outstretched arms. Laughing, he shouted orders at the others.

"Please, Michael—please!" Tarquin squealed in Greek. "Take me with you to Constantinople. Let me behold its wonders...."

The door slid shut with inexorable force. Too late, Tarquin had wriggled free. He got to it and slapped both hands against the glass. From the other side, the three fugitives watched his silent scream. They watched a red splash erupt from his chest, and heard the *smack* of the bullet. Hands still pressing on the glass, he fell to his knees. His mouth sagged open, and he toppled sideways.

Robert beat the glass with the flat of his hand. "And I thought the Greeks were a shifty race!" Another bullet slammed uselessly into the thick glass, glancing sideways and taking out a sliver. Robert laughed and put up the middle finger of his right hand at the guards, who may have understood that they were shut into their own tomb. He shouted something in Old French that Jennifer couldn't understand, though its meaning was plain. More bullets turned the inner surface of the glass to something with the appearance of a bathroom window. But the door was closed in an airtight seal that, if Wapping had told the truth, couldn't be broken for another half hour.

Half an hour! Jennifer thought. She took Michael's hand. "If I pull you upstairs," she said, "Robert will push. But we must hurry."

▶ ▼ ◀

After the first minute, she and Robert had needed to drag Michael up the long spiral. It was as much as he could do to repeat his trick with Wapping's arm. They stumbled into a courtyard dim beneath the clouds of a late afternoon sky.

Where next? Trying for Westminster Underground Station would be madness. Even if they got past the suspicious guard, Wapping had used a swipe card on some of the doors, and this was somewhere in another universe. Jennifer hurried into the long room. She looked at the other doors, choosing one where the carpet was also worn. This took them into a filing room that led into a corridor, and then up a flight of stairs into what could only be the entrance hall of Ten Downing Street.

A few years earlier—this was in the Olden Days, of course— Jennifer had nearly been entered for a competition at school that would allow the winners to meet the Prime Minister, and nag him into agreeing to some particularly fatuous use of the taxpayers' money. Back then, she'd briefly wondered what it must be like to go through that shiny front door. All she wondered now was which of the many old and new locks on the inside of the door would let them into the street. It was, she discovered, an electronic release button behind a plastic bust of Tony Blair.

"There's an atom bomb about to go off underneath us," Jennifer shouted at the policemen outside the door who'd trained their guns on her. "It will blow any minute now." For a moment, they looked back at her. Then, as one, they dropped their weapons and made for the iron gates that separated Downing Street from Whitehall.

A black drizzle was beginning to fall when Jennifer got Robert and Michael through those wide open gates. She resisted the urge to look again at her watch. It was only worth noting that, while deep underground, they'd heard nothing of the helicopters that had scattered gas bombs over the crowds of praying demonstrators. It may have been that Parliament Square was carpeted as thickly with bodies as Oxford Circus had been. In Whitehall, the still heaps lay every couple of yards. Here and there, policemen—most still wearing masks against the now faint smell of brimstone, though many now uncovered—were turning the bodies over. There was no chance anyone might have survived the gassing. This was a search purely for jewellery and cash.

She turned left. "This way!" she shouted in Latin, nearly going over on paving stones made slimy by the polluted rain. She steadied herself and pointed at the high statue of Nelson. "Come on—we must get over there." Michael's legs gave way after about fifty yards. For another few yards, she and Robert dragged him along. Finally, Robert stopped and threw him over his shoulder. Now faster, they ran through the gathering darkness towards what might or might not be safety.

From the moment Radleigh had doubled the number of Abigail Hoopers in one universe, Jennifer had been asking what effect this might really have. Perhaps it would have none at all. Perhaps Radleigh had been overpowered, and Sweeting was finding some way to stop the countdown. The continued stability of the world about her had settled her into counting down not from Sweeting's estimate, but from the banging shut of the upper door to the complex. If they had to keep moving, it seemed more a question of getting away from the scrum of armed and angry guards who would, whenever the half hour wait was over, burst into the courtyard.

She was wrong. As they passed by the Banqueting House, the ground began to shake. At first, it was the merest rumble—as if the Underground were working again, and they were standing above one of its shallower tunnels. One of the policemen looked up as they came within a few feet of where he'd been bending over. She thought he would get out his gun and call a challenge. But he only transferred his glance to the handful of gold coins he was holding up, and called something in a shrill, triumphant chatter that must have been in English but had no meaning to her.

The rumble became a tremor. The tremor became a continuous and powerful beating from beneath the paving stones. By the time they were level with the statue of Butcher Haig, the tarmac was beginning to ripple as if a stone had been dropped into water. A long fissure opened along the road, and the statue toppled in.

Jennifer watched another policeman try to jump clear of a secondary fissure. He failed, and slid into it. Screeching for help, he managed to hold himself at waist level. A few seconds more, and the fissure opened wider, and he was gone. The paving stones were now lifting and falling as if laid over boiling mud, and they had to slow down to avoid tripping. Robert cried out in fear, pointing at the wide road that went about the Square. The tarmac here was melting by the second. Looking back, Jennifer could see that the tarmac in Whitehall and the ground beneath were already melted, and the huddled dead were sinking out of view as if into mud. The remaining statues were sinking with their plinths, or toppling without any noise. Those officers who'd been fast enough were stumbling forward over the paving stones. The rest were stuck fast in the liquefying tarmac—in their black uniforms and helmets, they reminded her of nothing so much as flies stuck to a gummed strip. A mist was coming off the ground, and that and the fading light were blotting out the creatures who, screaming and waving, realised that they would soon be as one with those they'd helped murder, and had now spent too long plundering.

With a loud crash to their left, one of the High Commission *façades* fell down. Jennifer looked back again. Still in one piece, the whole of the Whitehall Theatre had sunk to its upper windows into the liquefying ground. She took Robert's hand and pulled him into the sticky mass of a road that might still be safe to run across. It was slow going across the road, but they got to the southern side of the Square. The Column was swaying slowly back and forward. She didn't look round at the shuddering crash of its falling. The armed men whose job it was to guard Charing Cross Railway Station had come into the Strand, and, transfixed with wonder, looked at the spreading wave of destruction.

Gasping and clutching at his side, Robert flopped down beyond one of the crash barriers that had, at the entrance to Villiers Street, once separated road from pavement. "Take him, Little Bear," he gasped, pushing Michael towards her. "I can't go on." But, though trembling, the ground here was still solid. The wave that had its epicentre somewhere close by Parliament, seemed to have stabilised half way across the railway station forecourt. Beyond that line, all that hadn't sunk already was falling in on itself with a loud crash of masonry. On this side, the ground buckled and rumbled from the communication of force. Jennifer stood up and looked at the firm shape of the cobble stones across the dozen yards that separated them from what had become a boiling mass.

And now, the mist that had risen from the ground rose higher. Hardly aware of her own exhausted body, she watched it rise higher and higher, and arch over until it disappeared beyond the low covering of the rain clouds. She watched it form a blurred dome, perhaps a mile across and a mile high. "Get down, Jennifer!" she heard Michael cry weakly. A hand took hold of the riding coat she was still wearing, and pulled her behind the cover of a flight of steps. She felt Michael's hand drop over her shoulder and try to pull her completely down. But she struggled free, and continued looking over the top of the steps. The blurred dome had now solidified and taken on the dull shine of the Gateway panels. She looked across the forecourt to the dome at its nearest point. She could see the distorted reflection of the cast iron railings and of the white buildings on the far side of the Strand.

It vanished.

Jennifer's mind told her there should have been a loud crash, and perhaps a still more terrible shaking of the ground. There had been nothing at all. In one instant, the dome had sat upon Central London with all the apparent solidity of the Great Pyramid. Another instant, and it was gone. She tried to get properly to her feet, but was now pulled down with the whole of Count Robert's returning strength. It was just in time. The dome had extended itself without the slightest sound. Equally quiet, it had vanished. One second—perhaps two—later, and she was struck from behind by the full and deafening blast of a hurricane. Robert screamed something, as they were lifted by some invisible but gigantic hand and hurled against the metal barrier. All about them was the crash and skipping of roof tiles and other building debris. Jennifer saw one of the armed station guards carried past into the vacuum that had opened, and another, and then a rickshaw with two passengers waving and calling out.

And then, with a kind of burp, the air that had been sucked from all sides into the vacuum met in the centre, and there was an almost gentle returning wave.

Jennifer shook herself free of the two men and stood up again. She looked up into a clean and almost painfully violet sky. It was already set with unblinking stars. She looked about. All the way back along the Strand, not one building was standing in its entirety. Half of the building above the railway station was cut away. The rest had collapsed and been mostly sucked into the void. Wherever she looked, she could see for miles—and all was as low and ruined as she'd seen in the black and white footage of Berlin or Hamburg after the bombing raids. And, where the centre of London had been, there was now a crater gouged out by the counterpart of the dome that had towered so high. Glistening smooth as glass, the perfect hemisphere stretched from Charing Cross to Vauxhall and towards Piccadilly. It covered the ground where Parliament had been, and Westminster Abbey, and Buckingham Palace, and the ministry buildings. It had swallowed the Liberal Club whole, where afternoon tea might still have been serving. It covered where countless multitudes must have been caught and annihilated. It had cut away a whole reach of the Thames and part of the South Bank. She looked down, and could see the filthy waters boiling and surging into what would soon be a vast and effectively a bottomless lake. She looked away from the wreckage of people and things that were carried here and there by the torrent.

Robert stood beside her. "It is the Judgement of God!" he announced in Latin with a smack of his lips.

Michael looked up from the crash barrier on which he'd been leaning for support. "Why must everyone keep talking about God?" he asked with quiet ill humour. "Can you not see a certain disregard for life in all that's happened since The Break? I think I'd rather assume that it was Sweeting who got everyone here by pulling on the wrong lever."

Robert snorted. "Did God show mercy in the days of old, when He smote the Cities of the Plain?" he asked with evident pleasure. "Or when He visited plague after plague on the people of Egypt?" He found an uncrushed cigarette and put it between his lips. He patted up and down his tunic for a box of matches. "Clear Judgement of God, if you ask me," he ended.

"Oh, have it your way!" Michael sighed. He went back to leaning on the crash barrier. And Robert would, Jennifer told herself, have it his way. He and Duke William of Normandy would have it all their way, just as soon as they could get their men across the Channel.

There was a flight of pigeons overhead, and sounds of returning life along the Strand. Michael stood up and scratched where his beard had started to grow again. He touched Jennifer's hand. "I suppose we should be making a move." Jennifer nodded. She knew she'd never understand what had just happened. But she did wonder how that exact hemisphere had come about from an epicentre so deep underground. She put the question out of mind and took Michael's hand. Together, they began picking their way through the rubbish of a broken city towards Waterloo Bridge.

EPILOGUE

Constantinople, September 1071

Jennifer looked into the mirror and tried not to laugh. She turned her attention to the big television set behind her. Though she'd had the volume turned down, she could still hear the presenter's gushing commentary on the better life that a plumber could enjoy with his family if they relocated to Thessalonica. If she focussed, she'd be able to see the reversed Greek subtitles at the bottom of the picture. "It really doesn't matter," she said in Greek to the weeping handmaid. "Won't I be wearing a veil?"

"But, Your Majesty," came the shocked reply, "it has to be just so!"

A door opened behind her, and her private secretary hurried in with a sheet of paper. "Your Majesty!" he cried after a low bow. He held up the laser printout. "Your father regrets that he and your mother are still detained in Venice by mechanical failure."

Jennifer took a final look at her spoiled makeup and got to her feet. "Well, that doesn't matter either," she said firmly. "Daddy wants to be here for the reading of the Emancipation Decree. Since that won't be for another week, it won't hurt him to hang around for a bit. There must already be something nice to look at in Venice."

Michael now walked in through the open door, followed by the Grand Chamberlain, who was reading out yet again from a stack of stapled sheets half an inch thick. The secretary and all the maids fell to their knees. "What is going on?" he said to Jennifer. "You were supposed to be on your throne twenty minutes ago. The Pope is muttering the most horrible things in English. The television people are in a panic. The Caliph will be very upset. All else aside, the chains I'm supposed to strike off him are heavy."

304

The Chamberlain took that as his prompt. "The Commander of the Faithful will come forward three paces," he recited. "The sultans and kings and other former tributaries will stay back for their prostrations. The Caliph will perform his at the third stroke of the gong. He will then swear allegiance and render up the Holy Places and all his realms. His Holiness of Rome will be followed, after the smallest interval, by His Holiness of Constantinople, as they...."

"Do shut up!" Michael groaned. "Much more of this, and I'll wonder if the Caliph isn't having a better time of the occasion." He sat down beside Jennifer. "I was told your cheeks were still painted different colours," he said accusingly. "You really should have let the makeup girls do the whole job themselves." He looked at her and frowned. "But I can't see any difference of colour." He got up again and reached out a hand. "Come on. There are twenty thousand people waiting outside the Hall of Audience. If we keep them waiting much longer, women will start delivering babies, or whatever happens when these things go on too long."

Jennifer let the maids tie the veil over her face. Someone else rushed in unbidden to place a gold crown on her head. Hand in hand with the Emperor, she crossed the floor, nearly tripping over a dress of silk brocade that felt as heavy and unyielding as a suit of plate armour. She let her husband push her first into the carrying chair that would take them to what everyone would have called the greatest victory ceremony since Heraclius, over four centuries earlier, had celebrated his total defeat of the Persians—or would have called, that is, if Heraclius hadn't almost immediately lost everything again to an enemy that only the present Great Augustus had been able to crush.

"Please don't do that!" she cried in Latin as Michael climbed in beside her.

"Now, why shouldn't a man pinch his own wife's bottom?" he asked grandly.

"Because I still worry that I might wake up!"

They both laughed. They were still laughing as they were carried into the glittering immensity of the Great Hall of Audience.

THE BREAK

END MATTERS

Many thanks for reading my book. If you liked it, please consider taking the time to leave a review at your favourite on-line bookseller.

You may also wish to read some of the other books I have written. There are many of these, both fiction and non-fiction, and as both Sean Gabb and Richard Blake. My novels as Richard Blake are published by Hodder & Stoughton in London, and have been translated into Spanish, Italian, Greek, Slovak, Hungarian and Chinese. My other books are listed and described in the following pages. All are available in both printed and e-book editions via your favourite bookseller.

I am very active on the Internet. You can follow my doings in these places:

As Sean Gabb

http://www.seangabb.co.uk/
https://www.facebook.com/sean.gabb
http://libertarianalliance.wordpress.com/
http://www.lulu.com/spotlight/seangabb
https://www.smashwords.com/profile/view/seangabb

As Richard Blake

http://richardblake.me.uk/
https://www.facebook.com/richard.blake.7773

The Churchill Memorandum
Sean Gabb
Hampden Press, London, 2014
290pp., £12.99
ISBN: 9781311160829

Imagine a world in which Hitler died in 1939. No World War II. No US-Soviet duopoly of the world. No slide into the gutter for England.

Anthony Markham doesn't need to imagine. It is now 1959, and this is the only world he knows. England is still England. The Queen-Empress is on her throne. The pound is worth a pound. Lord Halifax is Prime Minister, and C.S. Lewis is Archbishop of Canterbury. All is right with the world—or with that quarter of it lucky enough to repose under an English heaven.

Not surprisingly, Markham loves England. He *worships* England. Never mind that he's Indian on his mother's side, nor entirely as he'd like to be seen in one other respect: he keeps these little faults hidden—oh, *very* well hidden!

So here we are—twenty years after Hitler died in a car accident, and Markham is taking leave of a nightmarish, totalitarian America. He has a biography to write of a dead and now largely forgotten Winston Churchill, and has had to go to where the old drunk left his papers. Little does Markham realise, as he returns to his safe, orderly England, that he carries, somewhere in his luggage, an object that can be used to destroy England and the whole structure of *bourgeois* civilisation as it has been restored since 1918.

Who is trying to kill Anthony Markham? Who is Major Stanhope? Where did Dr Pakeshi get his bag of money? Is there a connection between Michael Foot, Leader of the British Communist Party, and Foreign Secretary Harold Macmillan? Why is Ayn Rand in an American prison, and Nathaniel Branden living in a South London bedsit? Where does Enoch Powell fit into the story?

Above all, what is the Churchill Memorandum? What terrible secrets does it contain?

All will be revealed—but not till after Markham has gone on the run through an England unbombed, uncentralised, still free, and still mysterious.

The York Deviation
Sean Gabb
Hampden Press, London, 2014
(Forthcoming)

Edward Parker is getting old. He's overweight. His knees are going. So are his teeth. His career as a barrister has been mediocre at best. Family aside, his main outside interest lies in libertarian politics. All this has given him is a ringside seat for watching England's descent into a grotty police state, riddled with political correctness and police brutality.

Oh, but there's also his dream life. This is vivid and spectacular in all the ways that real life isn't. In particular, the dreams he's been having since childhood of a primaeval city, inhabited by reptilian bipeds, are almost a second life.

Then he opens his eyes into his most vivid and spectacular dream of all. He's an undergraduate again at the University of York. It's Monday, the 16th February 1981. In great things and in little, everything seems at first exactly as it had been.

Only it isn't.

As the dream unfolds, and shows no appearance of ending, deviation after deviation from the remembered past accumulate, and settle into the appearance of a coherent narrative. But where is this taking young Edward parker? What is his old "friend" Cruttling up to? Where have all his real friends gone? What secret lurks in the vast Temple of Isis being uncovered behind the main library? Why is Professor Fairburn so desperate to lay hands on that secret? Will Margaret Thatcher get what *she* wants?

Above all, what do other dreams keep bleeding into this one?

Or is this a dream? If it isn't what does it mean for and England not yet in the gutter, but only hovering on the kerb?

In this concluding part of his "England Trilogy," Sean Gabb leaves both alternative history and dystopian fantasy. *The York Deviation* is a novel about second chances—second chances for its narrator, and perhaps for England too.

Cultural Revolution, Culture War: How Conservatives Lost England and How to Get It Back
Sean Gabb
Hampden Press, London, 2007
Second Edition 2014 (Forthcoming)
120pp, £12.99
ISBN: 9780954103224

An Anglican Bishop nearly arrested for stating Church doctrine. Villagers actually arrested for making fun of gypsies. Museums stripped of "imperialist" symbols. This is life in the Britain of today.

"Political correctness gone mad" some will say. Not so, says Sean Gabb. In this short book, he explains how England in particular, and the English-speaking world in general, have been conquered from within.

We face a new ruling class made up of the student radicals of the 1960s and 70s. Now in power, they are creating in their own behaviour all the corruption and bigotry and hypocrisy that they falsely alleged against the liberal democratic rulers they have replaced.

This being so, the leading writers of the "New Left"—Antonio Gramsci, Louis Althusser, and Michel Foucault—become highly relevant for conservatives and libertarians. They are relevant not because their analysis of liberal democracy was correct, but because it explains what their disciples are trying to do.

Before we can change the world, we need to understand it. This book helps towards that understanding. It explains the nature of the enemy and how it has so far carried all before it. And it outlines a set of strategies for the comprehensive defeat of that enemy.

Every battle fought so far for liberal democracy has been lost. Even so, the war remains uncertain.

Smoking, Class and the Legitimation of Power
Sean Gabb
Hampden Press, London, 2011
204pp, £9.99
ISBN: 9781447757726

The "War against Tobacco" is one of the central facts of modern life. In this book, Sean Gabb analyses the nature and progress of the "war". The stated reasons for the war have varied according to time and place.

According to Dr Gabb, however, all reasons have one thing in common—they rest on a base of lies and half truths. But this is not simply a book about the history of tobacco and the scientific debate on its dangers. It also examines why, given the status of the evidence against it, there is a war against tobacco. Dr Gabb shows that this war is part of a much larger project of lifestyle regulation by the ruling class, and that its function is to provide a set of plausible excuses for the extraction of resources from the people and for the exercise of power over them.

This book provides a kind of "unified field" theory to bring within a single explanatory structure some of the most important attacks on free choice and government limitation that we face today.

Literary Essays
Sean Gabb
Hampden Press, London, 2011
183pp, £9.99
ISBN: 9781447817284

Why bother learning Latin? How did the Romans pronounce Greek? Should the Elgin Marbles be handed over to the Modern Greeks? Did the ancients have market economies? Should Epicurus be venerated above Plato and Aristotle? Why is Carol Ann Duffy not even a bad poet? What makes Macaulay a great historian and L. Neil Smith a great science fiction novelist? Why is The Daily Mail—easily the best newspaper in England—not fit for wrapping fish and chips?

Sean Gabb deals with these and other issues in this collection of essays. Lively and provocative, they are written for every lover of ancient or modern literature.

Freedom of Speech in England:
Its Present State and Likely Prospects
Sean Gabb
Hampden Press, London, 2013
200pp, £12.99
ISBN: 9781291545692

We live in a world where *Lady Chatterley's Lover* is an A Level text, and where documentaries about oral sex are shown on television. Even so, the battle for freedom of speech has not been won. More fiercely than ever in England, it rages on other fronts. There are panics over the promotion of terrorism, and the alleged sexualisation of children. The feminists have taken up the demand for sexual puritanism even before the churches can fully lay it aside.

Above all, there is the official war on "hate." In the name of good community relations, or simply to protect minorities from being upset, whole areas of debate that once were free are now policed. Dissidents risk punishments that range between formal imprisonment and unemployability.

In this set of forthright, and often very controversial, essays, Sean Gabb puts the old case for freedom of speech in the changed circumstances of today. His subjects include holocaust denial, the possession of child pornography, the rights of BNP members, and the persecution of Emma West, the South London "Tram Lady."

> "Libertarians can perform no greater service to freedom and humanity than by coming to the defense of the indefensible. The greatest victories for liberty have been won by those who would champion the rights of the outcast and despised rather than the popular or sympathetic.... In past eras, authoritarian rulers and censors who would seek to destroy liberty did so in the name of protecting society from religious heretics. In the modern world, the authoritarians and censors have not gone away. They have simply reinvented themselves as righteous crusaders against pornography or racism. Dr. Gabb's book brilliantly exposes the contemporary Inquisition for what it is." (Keith Preston)

War and the National Interest:
Arguments for a British Foreign Policy
Sean Gabb
Hampden Press, London, 2005
158pp, £11.95
ISBN: 9780954103231

British involvement in the war against Iraq may have been a crime: it was certainly a mistake. It advanced no British interest. It has instead caused thousands of deaths, and destabilised the Middle East, and has brought this country into various degrees throughout the world of hatred and ridicule. To say this, one does not need to be a socialist, or an internationalist, or in any sense disloyal to Queen and country. Opposition to the war is the most natural response of any conservative or libertarian.

So argues Sean Gabb in his latest book. Made up of essays written between September 2001 and May 2004, it can be read as a running commentary on the war with Iraq It may also be read as a sustained argument that the only legitimate foreign policy for the British Government is one that preserves the ability of the people of the United Kingdom to go safely about their everyday business. Such a policy need not be simple or direct, but it must credibly relate to this end. Perhaps the only benefit this war has brought the country is the destruction of Tony Blair as a credible political figure. But great as it may be, can this be justified in terms of the suffering inflicted on others?

Conspiracies of Rome
Richard Blake
Hodder & Stoughton, London
Hardback Edition: February 2008
Paperback Edition: January 2009
368pp, £19.99/£8.99
ISBN: 9780340951125

Rome, 609 AD. Empire is a fading memory. Repeatedly fought over and plundered, the City is falling into ruins. Filth and rubble block the streets. Killers prowl by night. Far off, in Constantinople, the Emperor has other concerns. The Church is the one institution left intact, and is now flexing its own imperial muscle.

Enter Aelric of England: young and beautiful, sexually uninhibited, heroic, if ruthlessly violent—and hungry for the learning of a world that is dying around him. In this first of six novels, he's only here by accident. Without getting that girl pregnant, and the resulting near-miss from King Ethelbert's gelding knife, he might never have left Kent. But here Aelric is, and nothing on earth will send him back.

The question is how long he will stay on earth. A deadly brawl outside Rome sucks him straight into the high politics of Empire. There is fraud. There is pursuit. There is murder after murder. Soon, Aelric is involved in a race against time to find answers. Who is trying to kill him? Where are the letters everyone thinks he has, and what do they contain? Who is the one-eyed man? What significance to all this has the Column of Phocas, the monument just put up in the Forum to celebrate a tyrant's generosity to Holy Mother Church?

Aelric does at last get his answers. What he chooses to do with them will shape the future history of Europe and the world....

"Fascinating to read, very well written, an intriguing plot and I enjoyed it very much." Derek Jacobi, star of *I Claudius* and *Gladiator*

Terror of Constantinople
Richard Blake
Hodder & Stoughton, London
Hardback Edition: February 2009
Paperback Edition: May 2010
420pp, £19.99/£7.99
ISBN: 9780340951149

610AD. Invaded by Persians and barbarians, the Byzantine Empire is also tearing itself apart in civil war. Phocas, the maniacally bloodthirsty Emperor, holds Constantinople by a reign of terror. The uninvaded provinces are turning one at a time to the usurper, Heraclius.

Just as the battle for the Empire approaches its climax, Aelric of England turns up in Constantinople. Blackmailed by the Papacy to leave off his career of lechery and market-rigging in Rome, he thinks his job is to gather texts for a semi-comprehensible dispute over the Nature of Christ. Only gradually does he realise he is a pawn in a much larger game.

What is the eunuch Theophanes up to? Why does the Papal Legate never show himself? How many drugs can the Emperor's son-in-law take before he loses his touch for homicidal torture? Above all, why has wicked old Phocas taken Aelric under his wing?

To answer these questions, Aelric has nothing but beauty, charm, intellectual brilliance and a talent for cold and ruthless violence on his side.

> "[Blake's] plotting can seem off-puttingly anarchic until the penny drops that everyone is simultaneously embroiled in multiple, often conflicting, scams. Aelric's survival among the last knockings of empire in Constantinople depends not on deducing who wants him dead, but who wants him dead at any given moment." *The Daily Telegraph*

Blood of Alexandria
Richard Blake
Hodder & Stoughton, London
Hardback Edition: June 2010
Paperback Edition: February 2011
502pp, £19.99/£6.99
ISBN: 978-0340951163

The tears of Alexander shall flow, giving bread and freedom . . .

612 AD. Egypt, the jewel of the Roman Empire, seethes with unrest, as bread runs short and the Persians plot an invasion. In Alexandria, a city divided between Greeks and Egyptians by language, religion and far too few soldiers, the mummy of the Great Alexander, dead for nine hundred years, still has the power to calm the mob—or inflame it . . .

In this third novel of the series, Aelric of England has become the Lord Senator Alaric and the trusted Legate of the Emperor Heraclius. He's now in Alexandria, to send Egypt's harvest to Constantinople, and to force the unwilling Viceroy to give land to the peasants. But the city—with its factions and conspirators—thwarts him at every turn. And when an old enemy from Constantinople arrives, supposedly on a quest for a religious relic that could turn the course of the Persian war, he will have to use all his cunning, his charm and his talent for violence to survive.

> "As always, Blake writes with immense historical and classical erudition, while displaying an ability to render 1500-year-old conversations in realistically colloquial English." *C4SS*

Sword of Damascus
Richard Blake
Hodder & Stoughton, London
Hardback Edition: June 2011
Paperback Edition: January 2012
432pp, £19.99
ISBN: 978-1444709667

687 AD. Expansive and triumphant, the Caliphate has stripped Egypt and Syria from the Byzantine Empire. Farther and farther back, the formerly hegemonic Empire has been pushed—once to the very walls of its capital, Constantinople.

All that has saved it is the invention of Greek Fire. This has broken the Islamic advance and restored Byzantine control of the seas. Is it a gift from God or the Devil? Who knows? But, without this "miracle weapon," Constantinople would have fallen in the 7th century, rather than the 15th, and the new barbarian kingdoms of Europe would have gone down one by one before the unstoppable cry of *Allah al akbar!*

What is all this to Aelric, now in his nineties, and a refugee from the Empire he's spent his life holding together? No longer the Lord Senator Alaric, Brother Aelric is writing his memoirs in the remote wastes of northern England, and waiting patiently for death.

Then a band of northern barbarians turns up outside the monastery— and then another. Almost before he can draw breath, Aelric is a prisoner and headed straight back into the snake pit of Mediterranean rivalries.

Who has snatched him, and why? What is the nature of young Edward's fascination with a man more than eighty years his senior? How, together, will they handle the confrontation that lies at the end of their journey—a confrontation that will settle the future of mankind?

Will age have robbed Aelric of his charm, his intelligence, his resourcefulness, or of his talent for cold and homicidal duplicity?

> "Blake's plotting is as brilliantly devious as the mind of his sardonic and very earthy hero. This is a story of villainy that reels you in from its prosaic opening through a series of death-defying thrills and spills." *The Lancashire Evening Post*

Ghosts of Athens
Richard Blake
Hodder & Stoughton, London
Paperback Edition: April 2013
448pp, £8.99
ISBN: 9781444709704

612 AD. No longer the glorious cradle of all art and science, Athens is a ruined city in one of the Byzantine Empire's less vital provinces. Why, then, has the Emperor diverted Aelric's ship home from Egypt to send him here? Why include Priscus in the warrant? Isn't Aelric needed to save the Empire's finances, and Priscus to lead its armies against the Persians? Or has the Emperor decided to blame them for the bloodbath they presided over in Egypt?

Or could it be that Aelric's latest job just to manage a council of Eastern and Western Bishops more inclined to kick each other to death than agree to a wildly controversial position on the Nature of Christ?

Hard to say. Impossible to say. When did Heraclius ever explain his reasons—assuming he had any in the first place? The only certainty is that Aelric finds himself in a derelict palace of dark and endless corridors and of rooms that Martin, his cowardly secretary, assures him pulse with an ancient evil.

Add to this a headless corpse, drained of its blood, a bizarre cult of the self-emasculated, embezzlement, a city rabble on the edge of revolution—and the approach of an army rumoured to contain twenty million starving barbarians.

Is Aelric on a high level mission to save the Empire? Or has he been set up to fail? Or is the truth even worse than he can at first imagine?

This fifth novel in the series blends historical fiction with gothic horror. Not surprisingly, Aelric may find even the vile Priscus a welcome ally. Or perhaps he won't....

"It would be hard to over-praise this extraordinary series, a near-perfect blend of historical detail and atmosphere with the plot of a conspiracy thriller, vivid characters, high philosophy and vulgar comedy." *The Morning Star*

Curse of Babylon
Richard Blake
Hodder & Stoughton, London
Paperback Edition: August 2013
496pp, £14.99
ISBN: 9781444709735

615 AD. A vengeful Persian tyrant prepares the final blow that will annihilate the Byzantine Empire.

Aelric of England—now the Lord Senator Alaric—is almost as powerful as the Emperor. Seemingly without opposition, he dominates the vast and morally bankrupt city of Constantinople. If, within his fortified palace, he revels in his books, his mood-altering substances, and the various delights of his serving girls and dancing boys, he alone is able to conceive and to push forward reforms that are the Empire's only hope of survival, and perhaps of restoration to wealth and greatness.

But his domestic enemies are waiting for their moment to strike back. And the world's most terrifying military machine is assembling in secret beyond the mountains of the eastern frontier.

What is the Horn of Babylon? Is it really accursed? Who is Antonia? What is Shahin, the bestial Persian admiral, doing on a ship within sight of the Imperial City? What exactly does Chosroes, the still more bestial Great King of Persia, want from Aelric? Is Rado a failed dancing boy or a military genius? Will Priscus, the vile and disgraced former Commander of the East, get his place in the history books? Must it be written in Aelric's blood?

In this sixth novel in the series, can Aelric rise to his greatest challenge yet—and find a personal happiness that has so far eluded him?

Intrigue, sex, black comedy, spectacular crowd scenes and extreme violence—you will find it all here in luxuriant abundance.

"[Blake] knows how to deliver a fast-paced story and his grasp of the period is impressively detailed" *Mail on Sunday*

Lightning Source UK Ltd.
Milton Keynes UK
UKOW02f0701271114

242264UK00012B/233/P